555 South Third St, RM M-149
Memphis, Tennessee 38101-9421

GONNA LAY DOWN MY BURDENS

GONNA LAY DOWN MY BURDENS

MARY MONROE

Dafina
BOOKS

KENSINGTON BOOKS

DAFINA BOOKS are published by

Kensington Publishing Corp.
850 Third Avenue
New York, NY 10022

Dafina Books and the Dafina logo Reg. U.S. Pat. & TM Off.

ISBN 1-57566-911-0

Printed in the United States of America

With thanks to my super agent, Andrew Stuart;
my wonderful editor, Karen Thomas,
and the rest of the Kensington family.

ACKNOWLEDGMENTS

I am extremely grateful to David Akamine for the lunches and editorial assistance and Maria "Felice" Sanchez for leading me to the best margaritas this side of Mexico. Special thanks to my friends Sheila Sims, Heather King, and Anita "Wuzzle" Sanchez. I am most grateful to Mom and St. Teresa for the pennies and the roses.

CHAPTER 1

January 2001

I had just stepped out of my hot shower when a mysterious gust of ice-cold air blew against the left side of my face and made me shiver.

The small window above my shower, covered in steam, was closed, and it was warmer than normal for Alabama this time of year. There was no explanation for what had just happened to me. Looking back on it now, I think of it as the wind of misfortune that blew into my life that night. But even before that night, I had already lost my way.

Still shivering, I stumbled toward my living room, a large towel in one hand, my pink terry-cloth bathrobe in the other. My wet hair felt like vines against the sides of my face as I wrestled myself into the bathrobe, clutching the towel between my teeth, then wrapping it around my head like a turban.

I had been home from work for two hours and my telephone had not rung once. I couldn't believe that during the ten minutes I had just spent in the shower, my answering machine had recorded six messages.

As I rubbed the spot on my face where the strange wind had assaulted me in my bathroom, my heart started beating a tattoo against the inside of my chest, and my head started aching on both sides. A large framed picture of a Black, woolly-haired Jesus on the wall directly above my big-screen TV offered a little comfort, but not enough to calm my nerves.

The only painkiller in the house was some leftover margarita in the refrigerator. I made my way to the kitchen. In the dark I drank straight from the blender, licking the last few drops as it trickled down the side of my trembling hand.

I returned to the living room. Before I could rewind the tape on the answering machine, the telephone on the end table next to my living room sofa rang again. I lifted the receiver with caution before the answering machine clicked on, knocking a stack of old *Essence* magazines off the end table to the floor.

Before I could say anything, a female voice whispered, "Carmen, he's going to kill me. . . . Come get me." Then the phone went dead. I had cancelled caller ID and I was too afraid to hit *69, but I had a good idea who it was. As soon as I hung up, the phone rang again.

"Carmen, did you get my messages? Where were you? I've been calling and calling!" Just as I had thought, it was Desiree Lucienne, my best friend and the one with the most baggage. That Desiree. She was a beautiful person inside and out. She was intelligent and her heart was in the right place, but she represented the dark side of the African-American dream. She was weak, self-centered, and foolish. Every time her bad choices got her in trouble, I was the broom she used to sweep up her mess.

"Desiree? What's the matter?" I asked in a labored voice. The noisy neighbors in the apartments on both sides of me were both blasting Whitney Houston. I heard a car backfire outside and then the scream of a siren. Peeping out of the window behind my sofa, I saw a dog running around in circles chasing his own tail under the yellow glow of a dim streetlight. A storm that had started right after I left work had intensified. The wind was howling and blowing the branches on the sumac tree outside my living room window against the side of my building so hard, I could barely hear Desiree, even though she was yelling at the top of her lungs.

"Carmen, Chester knows!" Desiree told me between raspy sobs. There was some static on the telephone line that made her voice seem even more irritating.

"Knows what?" The towel that I had wrapped around my wet hair had come undone. I took a deep breath, braced myself, and held the towel in place with both hands. I pressed the telephone between my shoulder and chin as I eased down on the sofa and crossed my legs.

"He knows I am planning to leave him. He knows everything. He even knows that you are the one who hid his gun!"

"Shit! How did he find out?"

Even with all of the windows in my living room cracked open, I started sweating profusely. I untied the belt to my bathrobe to keep it from sticking to my naked body. I let the bathrobe fall open, fanning myself with the tail.

"I don't know how he knows, but he knows." Desiree's voice changed from pleading to demanding. "You have to come get me. I need for you to bring my stuff to the house and get me out of here. *Now.*"

"Where is Chester now?" I asked firmly, still fanning myself. A trickle of sweat slid from my face and dropped into my lap. I licked my lips, trying to savor the margarita I had splashed.

"He just left. He ran out of here when I locked myself in the bedroom. I don't want to be here when he gets back. When I tried to leave, he stretched out on the ground in front of my car. Oh—I've never seen him this mad."

"Listen to me. Calm down," I advised, holding up my hand. "Chester is not crazy. I know him better than you do. He's mostly talk," I added, as I roughly wiped my face with the sleeve of my bathrobe.

"Carmen, he said he was going to kill me. I have to get out of Alabama tonight." Desiree's voice had risen to a howl.

"Tonight? Girl, I'm getting married tomorrow. You're supposed to be my matron of honor," I reminded her. "You guys been drinking?" I leaned over to pick up the magazines that I had knocked over and placed them on the coffee table next to a bowl of brown bananas and bruised apples.

"I haven't had a drop, but he's had a few. He's gone crazy, Carmen. You can even see it in his eyes!"

"Calm down," I insisted, holding the telephone away from my face for a brief moment.

"Calm down? How can I calm down with a crazy man on the loose?" Desiree hollered. "Threatening to kill me!"

I sighed and held the phone closer to my ear. "Let me call you back in a few minutes. I just got out of the shower and I'm still wet. Let me dry my hair and put on some clothes. I promise, I'll be there in half an hour."

"Half an hour? Girl, I don't have that kind of time. I got to get up out of here now," Desiree wailed impatiently.

"Well, I can't fly and it'd take me at least ten minutes to get there anyway." I snatched the towel off my head and hurled it across the room. It landed on top of my TV, covering part of the large screen like a curtain. I had turned off the TV. A news break had interrupted a *Cosby* rerun to report a late-breaking story about some fishermen stumbling across the nude body of a dead young Black woman. I didn't want to have to deal with *anybody's* death on the eve of my wedding. "Listen, catch a cab and come on over here until Chester cools off."

"I don't want to catch a cab. I want you to come get me and take me to the airport in Meridian."

"Airport? In Meridian, *Mississippi*? What's wrong with you, girl?" I had a hard time getting my words out without choking on them. "You're not going to be around for my wedding?"

"I won't be around for your wedding or anything else if I don't get out of this house and out of this state before Chester gets back."

This was not the first time Desiree had disappointed me. Though it didn't surprise me, it saddened me to know that of all things, my wedding was being upstaged by her latest dilemma. But she was my best friend, and though I had never burdened her with my problems, she had been a good friend for seventeen years. And even though it was with hesitation, I accepted part of the blame for her being so quick to turn to me when she needed help. I had allowed our friendship to come to this. I couldn't remember one single time when I hadn't come through for Desiree—and just about everybody else for that matter.

"I *know* I can count on you, Carmen. I always did. Girl, you are so good to me. I hope that one of these days I can do something for you," Desiree added, speaking in a much calmer voice now. But then she broke down and cried like a baby for a full minute. "I . . . I'm sorry, Carmen," she rattled. She sniffed and cleared her throat.

"Just hang on a little while longer. Everything's going to be all right. I'll be there as soon as I can get dressed." I sighed and sucked in my breath before continuing. "Desiree, this is the last time I'm getting involved with you and Chester. I can't keep bailing you out of one mess after another. Shit." My words surprised me as much as they surprised Desiree. I heard her gasp.

"You won't have to after tonight," she said distantly, clearing her throat. "Chester is going to be out of our lives for good. Carmen, I am so sorry I won't be with you tomorrow. I don't know how or when, but I will make this up to you. I know how you must be feeling."

Desiree didn't have a clue about the painful things I hid behind my smile, and I didn't want her to. I was the poster girl for strong young Black women. I kept my tears and my weaknesses to myself. I had carried my burdens alone all my life, twenty-nine years now. I was tired of the way things had been, but not tired enough to say no to Desiree that night.

I bit the side of my bottom lip before responding. "No, you don't, Desiree," I said, talking between quivering lips. I had to blink hard to hold back my own tears.

As soon as I hung up, the telephone rang again. This time it was Regina Witherspoon. Before Desiree had roared into my life, Regina had been my best friend. Desiree, the spoiled daughter of a doctor, and Regina, a proud ghetto princess, didn't care that much for one another. I fell somewhere in between. They tolerated one another just to please me.

"Carmen, you ready?" Regina always sounded like she was in a hurry. I could hear her tapping her telephone impatiently with the tip of one of her four-inch nails. Tupac was rapping in the background on her end.

"Ready for what?" I asked in a tired, worn-out voice, hoping my tone would encourage Regina to limit her phone call to a minute or less. "What are you talking about?" I snapped. The call from Desiree had put me in a mood I was not particularly proud of. I was sorry to be taking out my frustrations on Regina.

"Well, excuse me," Regina hissed. "But I thought you wanted me to come over to braid your hair for tomorrow." She turned down the volume on her music before continuing. "I canceled another appointment for you," she whined.

"Oh—Oh, yeah. I do want you to come over. But . . . uh . . . I'll have to call you back. I have to go out for a little while. Desiree's in trouble and I have to go pick her up."

There was a long moment of uncomfortable silence before Regina responded. "Again? What is it this time? She break one of them ten-dollar nails of hers? Somebody stole her credit card?"

I sighed and rolled my eyes. "Well, no. Chester's acting a fool and she wants to get out of the house until he calms down."

"Hmmm-huh. That heifer knew Chester was out of her league when she hooked up with him," Regina snarled, sucking her teeth. "I'm surprised they lasted this long. Why you let her drag you into her mess?"

"She's my friend, Reggie," I answered levelly. "I promised her I'd come get her." I had also promised myself that I would stay out of Desiree's business after the time she had told me to when I interfered in another one of her relationships. It seemed like I had trouble keeping promises to everybody but myself.

"She's just as grown as you and me, and if she can't handle her business by now, shame on her. Shit."

"I know. I know. But I told her I'd come get her. Desiree is my girl, you know." I was tempted to remind Regina about all the times *she* had leaned on me.

"All right, now," Regina grunted. "That Chester is one big-ass, gun-totin' motherfucker. You better be careful."

"I will," I replied in a low but steady voice. I took a deep, painful breath and looked around my living room. A small mountain of empty gift boxes and wrapping paper sat on the floor at the foot of my TV. I hadn't cleaned up after the bridal shower Desiree had thrown for me three days ago. Regina and Desiree had agreed to clean up my apartment while Burl and I were on the week-long cruise in the Bahamas that we had planned to take after the wedding. And that was only after I told them I'd let them divide everything in my apartment that I didn't want to take with me to the house I had planned to share with Burl.

"Reggie, if I don't call you back in an hour, come over to Desiree's house. And bring your cellular phone in case . . . in case we need to call the cops. I have a funny feeling about going over there getting involved," I muttered, blinking my burning eyes. There was more than worry in my voice. I was scared.

There was a moment of grim silence before Regina responded. Instead of speaking in her usual quick, loud manner, she spoke in a slow, crisp voice that was disturbing to say the least. "Don't go over there, Carmen. I know Desiree is your girl and you told her you was comin' to get her, but this is one time I wish you'd listen to me. *Don't go over there.*"

I sat still for a moment, allowing Regina's words to sink in. In the back of my mind I could still hear Desiree begging me to come pick her up before Chester returned.

"And what if Chester hurts Desiree?" I asked in a low, uncertain voice.

"And what if he hurts *you?!*" Regina screamed. Her shrill voice pierced the air. I had to hold the telephone away from my face and rub my ear. "You my girl, too," she added passionately. "And, you know how I feel about funerals."

"Oh, I am not worried about Chester hurting me," I replied with confidence. "I've known him all my life. He's just a show-off with a big mouth." I paused just long enough to catch my breath. "He doesn't scare me one bit," I lied.

"Carmen, please—"

Regina didn't get a chance to finish her sentence before I cut her off. "Regina, drop by the liquor store and pick up a bottle on your way over. A real big one. I have a feeling you, Desiree, and me are going to need to take a serious trip to Margaritaville before the night is over. Bring some Advil, too. I don't want to be too hungover for my own wedding tomorrow." I looked at the telephone for two minutes, trying to decide whether or not I should take Regina's advice. I jumped when it rang again. I prayed that it was Desiree telling me things had cooled off between her and Chester and that she didn't need me to come rescue her. It was Desiree again, and she was more frantic than ever.

"I was just checking to see if you'd left yet," she wailed.

"I—I'm on my way," I told her. I was so nervous I dropped the telephone on my bare foot. The pain was indescribable, but I ignored it.

Ten minutes later, I left my apartment, hopping, more concerned about helping Desiree than helping myself.

CHAPTER 2

The drive from my apartment to the house on Carlson Street where Desiree lived with Chester Sheffield normally took about ten minutes. But because of the storm, traffic was heavy and there was an accident at the corner of Carlson and Becker. Stopping to get gas had slowed me down, too. The difficult ride took twenty minutes this time.

The rain, hammering down out of the north, thumped on the windows of my dependable old Nissan like little rocks. Not only had my headache returned, but a knot that felt like it was the size of a melon had formed in my stomach. And it seemed like every other muscle in my body was aching, too. By now the foot I had dropped the telephone on was the only part of my body not throbbing.

By the time I reached my destination, Chester had returned to his house and was standing on his front porch. One hand was in his pants pocket, the other was clutching a bottle of Schlitz Malt Liquor. Chester was a complicated, unpredictable man, but I tolerated him because of Desiree. However, I fed him with a long-handled spoon.

Even with the fierce scowl on his face that he greeted me with, and wearing a long unbuttoned plaid shirt and ripped jeans, Chester Sheffield was the most gorgeous Black man I had ever seen. He was over six feet tall, and from years of weight training he had muscles where some of the men I knew didn't even have places. He was a warm, evenly toned dark brown like me, and he had small, slanted black eyes that seemed to look right through me. His thick, shiny black hair was naturally wavy and always neat. A neatly trimmed mustache and goatee framed his full lips.

"Evenin', Miss Taylor," Chester said casually as I trotted across the well-kept lawn in front of the sprawling white house he lived in rent-free, thanks to his generous daddy. This was the kind of neighborhood where I didn't want to get loud and ugly outside and attract an audience. Next door to Chester on one side lived a dentist, and on the other side lived a blabbermouth of a deacon from the church Chester, Desiree, and I attended. I had parked my car in Chester's driveway and left the motor running in case I had to leave in a hurry. Surprisingly, he smiled. This confused me. He was not behaving like a man who was about to kill his girlfriend.

I risked a smile back. I was glad he could not see my legs trembling as I made my way up on the porch, stumbling as if I was drunk. The margarita had done me no good. I was as sober as a trout. Before leaving my apartment, I had slipped on a pair of jeans, a loose T-shirt, and a pair of backless house shoes that had once belonged to Daddy. Even though the storm had been downgraded to a drizzle, I was not concerned about my floppy ponytail getting frizzy. Especially since Regina had agreed to braid my hair later that night. I cleared my throat and said firmly, "Uh . . . Desiree called me." My voice betrayed me and cracked. "I'm here . . . to pick her up." I stopped in front of Chester and gasped. On both sides of his neck were several sets of bloody teethprints. It looked as if a greedy vampire had got ahold of him. "Did Desiree do all *that*?" I whispered.

Instead of answering my question he sighed and lowered his head. He took a loud sip from his bottle and then let out a belch that was so loud and aggressive he flinched. "And whose idea was it for you to come pick up Desiree?" he slurred, wiping his lips with the back of his hand. There was another set of teethprints on the side of his hand, and cruel scratches curled around his wrist like a bracelet. He sighed again.

"Well . . . hers I guess," I replied cautiously, looking toward the door. I wondered what kinds of wounds Desiree had. Nothing disgusted me more than unnecessary violence. I had never known it to solve anybody's problems. However, I felt that self-defense was a whole different story. I was curious to hear who had got up in whose face first: Chester or Desiree.

Chester sniffed and tilted his head, frowning as he slowly slid his fingers across the teethprints on his neck. With tears in his eyes he said, "Desiree get hysterical over the least little thing. You know how emotional them Creoles can be. And when Desiree get like that, she say a lot of shit she don't mean." He tried to laugh but his voice cracked. He cleared his throat and shook his head. "Aw, shuck it! You know that woman don't wanna leave me. She hate bein' alone more than I do. When you love somebody, you wanna be with 'em. Shit." He blinked hard, but it wasn't hard enough to hold back the large tear that slid down the side of his face. I wanted to cry myself. I knew better than Chester and Desiree put together how painful it was to be alone or not to be with the person you loved. . . .

I couldn't let his discomfort distract me, so I looked away and moved toward the door with him following behind me, sniffling and clearing his throat. "Well, I want her to tell me that," I said firmly, blinking nervously.

I made my way into the expensively furnished living room with Chester following so close behind me, he stepped on the backs of my well-worn house shoes with his steel-toed black boots.

"Girl," he continued in a surprisingly gentle tone. "Shouldn't you be at the beauty parlor gettin' yourself ready for your big day tomorrow?"

Him reminding me that I was just hours away from marrying a man I did not love made me stumble, but I ignored the comment and kept walking. The thick, maroon carpet on the floor in the living room looked like a crime scene. I had to hop to avoid stepping on large broken plants, a three-legged frying pan, a baseball bat, and a rolling pin. Two large cream-colored lamps had been knocked to the floor, and there was broken glass everywhere else I looked—even on top of the smoked-glass coffee table next to a large Bible and a five-pound steel weight. The light-blue La-Z-Boy that I had given to Desiree and Chester for Christmas was on its side in the middle of the floor. There was a small fire in the fireplace. From where I stood, I could see the flames licking up what was left of a large poster of Desiree and me sitting on top of a black stallion.

"Chester, I didn't come over here to start any trouble. I just came to pick up my friend," I said, my eyes scanning the room further. There were at least half a dozen empty beer bottles and a half-empty Jack Daniels bottle on one of the two end tables by the black leather sofa.

"Me and Desiree had a little run-in and both of us got loose, see. That's all. Everything is fine now. It's all good. You can go on back home," Chester informed me, following me as I started walking through the house. I found Desiree in the kitchen at the table, holding her head. Her long, thick reddish-brown hair was askew, and her white silk blouse was missing a sleeve. The sleeve, balled up on the table in front of Desiree, had been ripped out of its socket. Even with two black eyes and a busted lip, Desiree was a beautiful woman. Next to my five-feet-eight-inch frame, she almost looked like a dwarf at five-three. She was so petite, she could still fit into preteen dresses. Dark purple bruises dotted her lemon yellow skin. With the exception of her slightly protruding teeth and a nose that was too large for her small, heart-shaped face, she was flawless. She could have had any man she wanted. But she had chosen Chester.

"Desiree, are you ready?" I asked, rushing over to her, forcing myself to remain calm. The last thing I wanted Chester to know was that I was scared. Underneath bangs that almost covered Desiree's eyes were even more bruises. I realized that when I brushed her hair back to kiss her clammy forehead. She flinched as soon as my puckered lips touched her. She looked at Chester before responding, as if seeking his approval.

"Baby, Carmen is taking me to her apartment," Desiree said meekly, offering a half smile. Blood oozed from a crack on her bottom lip. She cleared her throat and licked her lip dry.

"Now listen, y'all," Chester began slowly. His beer bottle slipped from his hand, and more glass ended up on the floor. He hopped over the broken glass and rushed over and stood between Desiree and me. "I—we—Desiree, you don't want to leave me now, do you, sugar?"

Desiree tightened her lips into a thin line and stared hopelessly at me, her eyes shining like new dimes.

"Desiree, what do you want to do?" I asked, getting impatient. Once when I had interfered in an altercation between Desiree and Chester, they had both ended up mad at me! Recalling that, I chose my words carefully. "I really don't want to be up in here in the first place," I admitted, glancing toward the door. I rubbed my neck and took a few deep breaths; then I turned to face Desiree. Her head was swiveling like a barber's chair. She stared from Chester to me and back with her mouth open.

"Carmen, don't you leave here without me," Desiree croaked. With her eyes still on Chester, she rose slowly and started walking toward me, limping all the way. I grabbed her arm and led her into the living room.

"Come on now, y'all," Chester pleaded. "Let's have a drink and straighten out this mess. What the hell." We ignored him. I didn't realize how close he was behind me until he grabbed me by my ponytail and spun me around. "Don't y'all hear me talkin'?" He blinked hard and glared at me, his hot gaze searing my face. Then, a look of complete despair crossed his face, but he still had a grip on my hair.

"Chester Sheffield, you get your hands off me," I ordered, pinching, then slapping his hand. He jumped back and grimaced like I had stuck a burning match to his flesh.

He sucked in his breath and threw up his hands and grinned. It was a desperate move for a desperate man. "Look, y'all. I'm sorry—"

"Desiree is leaving with me," I announced firmly, my words cracking like a whip. I don't remember everything that happened during those next few tense moments. Chester started shaking his head and waving his hands. Then he reached for Desiree. I don't know if he was trying to grab her to hug her or hit her, and I never found out, because Desiree's small fist sucker punched Chester's jaw and chin. He was just as stunned as I was. With wide eyes, he massaged his battered face.

With a look of complete exasperation, he weaved toward Desiree. "I done had enough of this mess," he said, calmly reaching for Desiree again. I don't know why, but I jumped in front of her. I was the one Chester grabbed. I can honestly say that I didn't know what he planned to do to me, but I covered my head with my hands and closed my eyes. I remember Chester and me falling to the floor, knocking over the coffee table. But I don't remember picking up the five-pound steel weight that fell off the table. I just remember bringing it down across Chester's head with all the strength I had. For a few seconds, everything went black, and I stood up. Desiree gasped and dropped to her knees, shaking Chester's shoulder. There was a huge, mean bruise on his forehead where I had hit him. Thick, dark blood squirted out and cascaded down the sides of his sweaty face. For a few moments that felt like an eternity, Desiree and I stood straight and stiff, like we had been frozen in time. Her eyes were stretched open so wide they looked like saucers. Finally, she let out a weak gasp and dropped to her knees to Chester's side again.

"Oh shit . . . oh shit . . . oh shit," Desiree chanted, shaking Chester harder this time. "Chester, baby, are you all right?" He moaned for a few seconds and then he stopped. The house was now as quiet as a tomb, and suddenly it felt like one. My T-shirt was soaking wet with my sweat and plastered to my body like a shroud. I could hear my watch ticking. We were several yards from the kitchen, but I could even hear the water dripping in the sink. Chester's twitching feet were the only things moving. Desiree stood up and staggered over to me, folding, then unfolding her arms. With her bruises, wild hair, and one-sleeved blouse, she looked like she was made up for Halloween.

Chester had pulled my hair so hard, the rubber band that had held my ponytail together had broken. Now my wiry hair looked as unruly as Desiree's.

"Let's go," I said. "Let's get out of here before he comes to."

"He's dead," Desiree said gently, shaking her head and hugging her chest. The whites of her eyes were red. Blue veins that I had never noticed before ran the length of her neck on both sides. "Carmen, you just killed Chester."

I fainted.

When I came to, seconds later, I was lying belly-up on top of Chester. Desiree grabbed my arm and pulled me up.

"What did you say?" I managed. I had to leave my mouth open to keep from choking on my own tongue.

"You . . . killed . . . Chester," Desiree whispered, clutching my arm as I stumbled, to keep me from falling again.

Once I was firmly on my feet, I couldn't move. My entire body had shut down. When I was able to, I moved so close to Desiree, I leaned against her. Somehow, she managed to lead me to the sofa, where she eased me down and propped me up with a pillow like a corpse.

"Girl, you have really fucked us up this time," she told me in a detached voice, standing over me with her arms folded like a guard.

I couldn't even look at her face. I kept my eyes on my trembling hands as I spoke. "Desiree, it's time for you to help me now," I told her.

CHAPTER 3

"Put that telephone down. Who are you calling?" I yelled at Desiree.

"We have to get help for Chester," Desiree hollered, then lowered her voice to a whimper. "I'm calling the police." Her eyes looked like they were about to pop right out of the sockets as she gripped the back of the sofa with one hand. I knocked the telephone out of her hand and it landed on the floor between Chester's feet.

"Get out of the way," I yelled. I pushed Desiree to the side and leaned over Chester. A pool of blood had formed around his head and shoulders. The pool was getting wider by the second, saturating all of his hair in front and seeping into his ears and nose. His lips looked like they had been smeared with the same plum-colored lipstick Desiree had on. "Chester, get up," I managed, wringing my hands so hard they became numb. "Chester, I am not playing with you. Get up, please," I begged, not touching him. I hopped out of the way to keep from getting his blood on my flimsy house shoes. I looked down at the floor, squinting my eyes at the bloody weight that I had used to kill Chester. It was one of those silver steel weights; the kind people use to do a few arm curls as a warm-up before a real workout. The weight was already shiny, but the blood made it shine even more. Then I looked at my hands. Even though my hands were clean and dry, I wiped them roughly on the sides of my jeans. "Chester, this is not funny!" I touched his side with the toe of my shoe and he still did not move.

"We have to call the police," Desiree wailed, looking toward the telephone.

"And tell them what? That we just killed a *policeman?*" I yelled over my shoulder.

"We? You are the one who hit him," Desiree squawked, waving her arms, shaking her head.

I gave her an incredulous look. "I was trying to keep him off of you!" I reminded her. "What was I supposed to do? I didn't want to come over here in the first place. If you hadn't called me, I wouldn't be here."

"Well I didn't tell you to hit him. And in the head? With that piece of steel? You of all people should know better than to hit him on his soft spot."

"It—it was—self-defense," I stuttered. "You saw everything. He'd already hit us both," I replied quickly, in a defensive voice, smoothing back my wild hair. I felt like a rag doll somebody had stuck pins in.

Desiree leaned down to pick up the telephone, but I slapped it out of her hand again. "Didn't I tell you to leave that telephone alone?"

"We have to do something, Carmen. The longer we wait, the worse it's going to look." Her lips quivered and then, with her head bobbing, she blurted, "We'll say he fell." Her eyes blinked frantically. Her mouth was still moving, but no words were coming out.

"And how will we explain your fucked-up face?" I asked, rotating my neck, my arms, and my eyes.

"Nobody has to know he hit me. Nobody has to know you came over here. I swear to God I won't tell," Desiree replied, shaking her head so hard, snot splashed out of her nose onto my chest.

"Regina knows," I said calmly, shaking my head to keep it from ringing.

"What?"

"Will you calm down?" I told her, holding my hand in front of her tear-stained face.

"What all does Regina know?" Desiree asked in a low, hollow voice.

"Nothing. Uh . . . I mean, all I told her was that you and Chester were having a problem and that I was on my way to help you."

"Oh, that's great," Desiree yelled, flapping her arms like something getting ready to fly. "That was a smart thing for you to do. That big-mouth bitch will blow everything. Why did you call her?" Desiree roared, stomping her foot so hard the pictures on the wall rattled.

"I didn't call her. She called me right after I talked to you," I snapped. I shook my head, hoping it would help me organize my thoughts, but there was too much going on up there and it was too late, anyway. Everything seemed to blend together into one big ball of confusion.

"I can't go to jail," Desiree muttered, pacing back and forth. "I'll go crazy in some jail. I'll die."

"I can't go to jail, either." I was surprised at how calm I sounded. Inside, I felt as raggedy as a bowl of sauerkraut.

"If you hadn't been so busy yip-yapping with Regina you could have made it over here before Chester got back and I'd be on my way to California by now." Desiree sighed and blinked, her eyes shifting from side to side. Just trying to follow her eyes made me dizzy.

"You can still go."

Desiree gave me a blank look. "What?"

I leaned toward her and whispered, "Nobody knows what happened here tonight. You can still go to California."

Desiree let out a restrained chuckle and then gave me an incredulous look. "Well, with me gone and Chester stretched out on the floor with a knot the size of a shot glass on his head, it won't take them long to put two and two together!" she blasted. Her voice suddenly softened. "I wouldn't feel right knowing you were in jail."

"Oh, I'm not going to jail either," I said through clenched teeth. I put my arm around her shoulder. I didn't even realize what I was saying. The words slid out of my mouth like a serpent. "I'm going with you."

"Wh—what?"

I sniffed and said firmly, "If you still want to go to California, you can go. But I'm going with you."

Desiree pulled away from me and moved back a few steps. "What about your wedding?"

I shrugged. Marrying Burl Tupper was suddenly the last thing on my mind.

"If you go, I am going with you," I said firmly before I let out a breath that was so deep my chest hurt. Staying out of jail was all I could think about now. It even overshadowed Chester's death. Missing out on my own wedding paled in comparison.

"Do you realize what you're saying, girl? When they find Chester, and if we run, it won't take them but a minute to figure out we had something to do with all this. I told you that already. You're talking crazy, girl," Desiree said, shaking two fingers in my face.

A feeling of extreme anxiety consumed me. I couldn't tell Desiree then, but Chester's murder was not the only crime I wanted to put behind me. Running away from the burdens that I had carried like a yoke around my shoulders for so many years seemed like the best way out for me. The *only* way out for me. A warm feeling crossed my face as my thoughts continued to roam. By running away, I could finally lay all of my burdens to rest at the same time. A wide smile I could not control took over my face.

Puzzled over my odd behavior, Desiree frowned at me. "Carmen, are you having a nervous breakdown?" she asked gently.

I shook the smile off my face and gave her a serious look, my lips forming a tight line.

"I'm all right," I told her, barely moving my lips.

Desiree shrugged and cleared her throat. "You'd be willing to leave Burl? Even if they don't figure out we did this, what about Burl? You're supposed to marry him tomorrow. Don't you love Burl?"

I sighed and bleated like a lamb, "I guess I do. But Burl got along all right before he met me; he'll get along all right without me," I said thoughtfully.

Desiree just stood there staring at me with eyes that had started to swell and darken even more.

"Say something!" I barked, stomping my foot.

"We'd better hurry and get up out of here." Desiree motioned with her hand for me to follow her.

Once we made it back to the kitchen, she snatched a yellow nylon windbreaker off the back of the chair she had been sitting in when I arrived.

"Do you have any money?" I asked. "I have about three hundred I pulled from the ATM on my way home from work."

"I closed out my savings account yesterday. It wasn't much. A little over five hundred. I got that, and about a thousand in emergency money we keep in the house," Desiree announced, buttoning her jacket. "Oh, that nigger was slicker than a politician. I found out he emptied our joint savings account this morning." I followed Desiree back to the living room where she dropped to the floor and started rooting through Chester's pants pockets.

"What are you doing?" I asked, pulling her up.

"He got paid today. He keeps two, three hundred on him all the time. Besides, he must have some of the money he took from our account on him."

"Well, we can't take his money, too. It . . . it wouldn't be right."

Desiree gasped in horror and then gave me a look of extreme bewilderment. "Right? Well, it's a little late for you—us—to be thinking about what's right." Desiree slapped my hand and it stung like a bee. I didn't try to stop her when she squatted over Chester again and removed a wad of bills from his wallet.

"Only a hundred," she mumbled, flipping through the bills before stuffing them into her bra.

With my head bowed I asked, "Other than me, who else knows about your sister Colleen living in San Francisco?"

"Nobody. As far as I know, she didn't keep in touch with anybody after she left here."

"Who else has a key to this house?"

"Chester's mama and daddy, but they don't come around that much. His mama never did like me. That old heifer! Besides, they went to Birmingham for the weekend."

"So nobody would be looking for Chester for a while? What about his boys, Duke and Nick and Perry . . . and . . . that detective Clyde?"

Desiree shrugged her shoulders. She was leaning on the back of the sofa, looking like an old woman. She was only a few months older than me. "Those dogs all went fishing this evening for the whole weekend. Chester stayed behind so he could—go with me to your wedding."

"Shit. When he doesn't show up for work on Monday, his goddamn cop buddies will be snooping around here," I mumbled. My agitation had doubled, and I could not hide it. I couldn't stop wringing my hands and shifting my weight from one foot to the other.

"He had planned to take Monday and Tuesday off to go fishing in Mobile Bay. Nobody will miss him for a while," Desiree said firmly. "Carmen, I am scared as hell," Desiree muttered, wringing her hands, too.

I nodded, again looking at the bloody weight that had slain

Chester. It was hard to believe that such a small item was capable of taking a man's life. Even though it was only a five-pound weight and not a sword or a gun, he was still dead.

"We have to think this thing through. If we call the cops now, they might buy our story and they might not. Do you want to take that chance?" I said sharply.

"What are our options?" Desiree asked, her voice hard and demanding.

"Options? We don't have any options," I snarled, giving her the most incredulous look I could manage.

She dismissed my hot look with a casual wave of her hand, glaring back at me out of the corner of her eye. "Aw, shuck it! If we stay here and call this in and if they don't buy our story . . . that he fell . . . somebody goes to jail."

"Yeah. *Somebody* goes to jail."

"But even if we leave, once they do find him, they will come looking for us anyway."

I nodded. "They will."

I was aching all over. I was tired. All I wanted to do was lie down in my own apartment and take a long nap. And that's just what I would have been doing if Desiree had not called me to come pick her up. If I had not been stupid enough to go.

"When they find us, we'll go to jail anyway," she mumbled, her voice cracking.

"*If* they find us," I said firmly.

The thought of never seeing my family again, or at least not seeing them for a very long time, made my head swim. I couldn't imagine the pain Mama would go through just over my sudden disappearance. She used to cry when I was late getting home from school. Daddy, with the weak heart he was convinced he had, would finally have an excuse to have the heart attack he had been predicting for twenty years. But as much as I loved my family, my freedom seemed more important at the time.

Without warning, Desiree hugged me so hard I couldn't breathe. After a few seconds I pulled away from her and said, "Let's get the hell up out of here."

CHAPTER 4

Times had changed. From watching almost every episode of *America's Most Wanted, Unsolved Mysteries,* and *Cops,* and from reading too many true-crime books, I knew that criminals didn't have a leg to stand on anymore. Something I had supported wholeheartedly.

Until now.

I didn't tell Desiree, and I had a hard time believing it myself, but I didn't think we would make it to California—or even out of the state of Alabama, for that matter. I didn't even think we would make it to my apartment after we left the house Desiree had shared with Chester for the past seven years. But at least we would try. All that mattered to me was staying out of jail no matter what it took, and the longer we remained free the better. Even with my confused state of mind, I believed that there was a slim chance we would get away with murder. There was a chance that people might believe that Chester had fallen or that someone else had attacked him. Being a policeman who had helped put dozens of criminals in jail, he had made a lot of enemies over the years. Even his ex-wife had threatened him a few times all the way from Texas. At the time, another suspect didn't seem that far-fetched, but it seemed too weak and I wasn't willing to rely on it.

The bloody weight was in my purse, where it would remain until I figured out what to do with it. We had passed a lot of Dumpsters and bushes. I had thought about tossing the murder weapon out the window of my car, and it would have been the smart thing to do. But nothing we had done so far could be called smart.

The rain had stopped; traffic was light, but my mind was not on driving. I went down the same street twice and sideswiped an abandoned car in an alley. I finally pulled over to the side of Patterson Street and placed my head on the steering wheel.

"Let me drive," Desiree said, pulling my arm off the steering wheel. I lifted my head and told her, "I'm all right."

"You're not all right. You're in no shape to drive. *You want to kill us, too?*" Desiree didn't wait for me to respond. She flung open the passenger's door and hopped out of the car. Before she even made it around to the driver's side, I slid from under the wheel onto the passenger's seat.

With Desiree driving like somebody being chased by the devil, we arrived at my apartment in less than five minutes, a fraction of the time it normally took from where she had taken over the wheel.

This was one night I didn't like having nosy neighbors.

As soon as we parked the car in front of my building, lights went on in the apartment below mine and a pair of shiny, catlike eyes appeared in the front window. Jimmie Lee Cross, the busybody middle-aged homosexual who lived in the apartment, kept a chair in front of that window. Out of the corner of my eye, I saw that old queen hold up a pair of glasses to his eyes as he boldly watched every move we made. Curtains moved at the window in the house across the street, and a large, beefy red face appeared.

"I thought you said this was a nice neighborhood," Desiree said thoughtfully.

"It is a nice neighborhood full of nice, nosy people. Nothing gets past this hawkeyed bunch. We don't even have to lock our doors around here," I announced proudly.

We took the stairs to my second-floor apartment. Because I had left all of the gifts I had received at my bridal shower on my living room floor, I had locked my front door when I left to go pick up Desiree.

"The police hardly ever have to come out here." As soon as I said that, I lowered my head and started fumbling with my purse, trying to locate my house keys. I was one step away from being delirious. I thought I heard a car alarm go off. I knew that my mind was playing tricks on me, but I still panicked and dropped my purse. The weight inside made a tremendous noise when it hit the concrete landing. Desiree lifted the purse.

"You—you got blood on your shoe," she whispered and pointed to my feet.

I gasped and hopped like I had just stepped on a piece of hot coal. As careful as I had been, I had still stepped in Chester's blood. The rim on my right house shoe looked like somebody had taken a dark-red crayon and outlined it. "Shit!" There was not much light coming from the streetlights or the lights on the outside of my building. I couldn't really tell if I had tracked an incriminating trail of bloody footprints when I turned around and looked down at the steps. It felt like an invisible noose had wound itself around my neck and was getting tighter by the minute.

"It's all right. You probably left the rest of the blood on the lawn at Chester's house," Desiree assured me.

"What about my car? The pedals, the floor mat. What if I left blood in my car?" I wailed, looking toward my car, parked on the street where I planned to leave it. I wiped the soles of my house shoes on the thorny welcome mat in front of my apartment door.

"We don't have time to worry about that now. We need to get inside and figure out what we are going to do." Desiree opened my purse and rooted around in it. She let out a short, muffled scream when she pulled the bloody weight halfway out. She dropped it back into my purse immediately. With her eyes closed, she found my keys at the bottom of my purse. I slid off my house shoe and clutched it, standing on one foot against the building while Desiree fumbled with the key to unlock the door.

Even though I lived in a quiet and crime-free neighborhood, I usually left my lights on when I went out at night. As soon as we got inside, Desiree ran around clicking off lights. The only ones she left on were the lamp on the end table next to the telephone in my living room and a lamp in my bedroom.

"Carmen, did you mean what you said about going with me?" she asked, whirling around to face me as I stood rooted in my spot like a tree.

Finally, and with a great deal of effort, I sat down hard on my sofa and started rubbing the back of my head, unable to face the picture of Jesus on the wall looking down on me. The back of my head was aching more than any other part of my body. Chester had gripped my hair just that hard.

"I would not have said it if I didn't mean it," I told Desiree. I jumped up as fast as I had sat down, and headed toward my kitchen with Desiree behind me still holding my purse. I flipped on the light and fished the murder weapon out of my purse. I wrapped it in a handful of paper towels. Then I returned it to my purse. "We can throw it in some bushes or something. My shoe and that jacket you have on, too."

Desiree stared at my purse, then my face, and then she jerked her head in a nodding motion. There was blood on the cuff of her windbreaker, but I didn't know if it was hers or Chester's.

She nodded again and frowned at the sleeve of her windbreaker as she spoke. "It's not too late, you know. We can still call this in, tell them what really happened and pray they go easy on us. My aunt Nadine scalded my uncle to death when I was nine, and she got off by pleading self-defense," Desiree told me, peeling off the windbreaker, then the one-sleeved blouse that Chester had ripped. Rolling them into a tight ball, she slid both into a plastic grocery bag she'd snatched off the counter.

"Is that the same aunt nobody would hire because of her past and she ended up working the streets turning ten-dollar tricks?"

"Yeah. Aunt Nadine," she replied, staring grimly at the plastic bag dangling in her hand as she leaned her hip against the sink.

"And last year she jumped out of a window in Brooklyn and broke her neck?" I was way too jumpy to relax. I didn't want to sit down, and I knew that if I stretched out on the sofa or on my bed, I might not be able to get back up. I stood in front of my stove, shifting my weight from one foot to the other.

"Well, Aunt Nadine had been depressed for years, you know," Desiree muttered.

"So much for her getting off. Just think how much better her life would have been if nobody ever knew she killed your uncle."

Desiree sighed and nodded. "You better hurry up and get your shit packed before we go on the lam."

Trying to decide what to take with me was something I didn't know how to approach. I'd never been "on the lam" before. Desiree had not taken anything from Chester's house other than what she had on her back and in her purse. She had already packed what was important to her in the two suitcases she had stored in my bedroom closet on the floor below my color-coded designer suits.

"I can't take both my suitcases," she announced, moving toward me. "It'd be too much trouble. Where's that travel bag you won at the church raffle last year?"

"That's what I was planning to use," I wailed.

"You got another small bag?"

"I don't know. My sister left a lot of her stuff here when she got married and moved to Nigeria. I'll look through it and see."

Desiree followed me to my bedroom, where she dragged her two suitcases out of the closet and hauled them into the living room. I pulled the black-leather travel bag that I had won at church from the top shelf of my closet and placed it on the bed. I unzipped it and stood up looking around the room. I slid into the Nikes I had left on the floor by the side of my bed, but I planned to pack a second pair. Without thinking I bounced from drawer to drawer, pulling out jeans, comfortable blouses, sensible underwear. I had enough makeup in my purse, so a half-used container of Arid Extra Dry and a fresh bottle of Lubriderm lotion were the only things I took from the bathroom.

"There's that commuter bus at five in the morning. Thank God we don't know anybody who rides that bus. Not that many people ride it on a Saturday anyway. It'll get us to Mobile, where we can connect with a Greyhound," Desiree said, peeking into my room.

My mouth dropped open so wide, I could feel the night air coming in through my cracked window all the way to the back of my tongue. "Greyhound? How far do you think we'll get on a Greyhound bus?"

"I know you hadn't planned on hopping on a plane." Desiree wailed like a wounded raccoon and looked like one with her blackened eyes and swollen lips.

"I hadn't planned on any of this," I said thoughtfully. Until now I had not even considered what mode of transportation we were going to use to leave the state. "We have enough money for a plane ticket."

"We don't have that much money between us. What we have is not enough for us to pay for two spur-of-the-moment tickets to California and have enough left over to last us until . . . until we get out of this mess. And if we fly we'll be leaving a paper trail. You have to show a

picture ID when you fly these days. Everything will go into their com-
puters—shit. And don't even think about driving your car."

"I don't have that many miles on it. It would make it to California,"
I said.

Desiree shook her head and snapped, "Are you out of your mind?
The highways are full of patrolmen lying in wait. Like spiders. If we
go, we go by bus." I could tell by Desiree's tone of voice she was determined to do things her way, even though the heaviest part of our
crime was on my shoulders. "We're catching a bus," she said with res-
ignation.

"All the way to California from here?"

"We have to get to Mobile first. Didn't I just tell you that? We don't
have a Greyhound station here. After we leave Mobile we'll have to
transfer left and right, and it will still take us three and a half days to
get to California." Desiree sighed and patted her chest before she
fanned her face with her hand. There was so much sweat on her forehead, her hair was plastered to her flesh.

"Well . . . what about the train?"

"What about it?"

"Wouldn't we get to California faster on a train?" I asked, blinking
stupidly.

"It would be about the same as a bus. I know because that's how my
sister went to California." Desiree blinked and managed a weak smile.
"Since we have a little time to kill, we better get some rest because
we're going to need it."

As soon as Desiree left my bedroom, I sat down hard on the bed
and exhaled. A picture on my nightstand caught my attention. I had
to blink hard to hold back my tears. It was a framed eight-by-ten glossy
picture in color that had been taken at Rocco's, our favorite local bar.
In the picture, standing next to me, was Desiree grinning so hard her
eyes looked like slits. Her mouth was stretched open so wide; she
looked like she had twice as many teeth as me. She had on a red
jumpsuit she had made herself. That was the happiest I had seen her
in a long time. Standing behind Desiree was Chester, looking straight
into the camera with a crooked sneer on his face. His long arm was
wrapped around *my* shoulder when it should have been around
Desiree's. That Chester. He was one complicated man. Directly in
front of me was Burl Tupper, another enigma, the man I had agreed
to marry. Burl was almost as light as Desiree, and his curly black hair

framed the top of his plump, round face like a dark cloud. Everybody liked Burl's large gray eyes and the dimples in his cheeks. That's what had initially attracted me to him in the first place.

It brought tears to my eyes when I realized just how much the three people sharing the picture with me had impacted my life. Burl especially.

I focused my attention on Burl's image. Through warm and unexpected tears I stared at the huge, shiny silver wheelchair he occupied. His thick, useless legs were hidden inside a pair of baggy designer jeans.

As expensive, fancy, and comfortable as the wheelchair looked, it was the prison that I had sent him to for life.

CHAPTER 5

"Carmen, where is that bottle I left over here the other night?" Desiree had cracked open my bedroom door just wide enough to lean her head in. She stared at me as I lay on the bed in a near-catatonic state. For the first time in my life, I knew how it felt to be obese and disabled. I felt like four hundred pounds of useless flesh. My long, willowy legs were like logs. I had to move each one with both hands. The rest of my body felt like a side of beef. With great difficulty I managed to lift myself into a sitting position. My shadow on the wall was a fright. My head, my hair reaching up like antlers, resembled the head of a reindeer. I was glad to see that Desiree had covered the bush on her head with a baseball cap that Daddy had left in my apartment. And she had replaced the one-sleeved blouse with a thin blue pullover sweater.

"What bottle?" I asked, clearing my throat and blinking hard.

"The one—" Desiree paused and bowed her head for a brief moment before returning her attention to me. *"You're crying."* She gasped. "In all the years I've known you, the only other things that made you cry were funerals and the IRS. A big old strong, strapping thing like you." I could tell that my tears were giving Desiree something else to be concerned about. Big old strong, strapping women like me didn't let people see us in tears if we could help it. Now here I was mooing like a cow.

"And it won't be the last time you see me cry," I replied stiffly, wiping my eyes. I attempted to smooth down my hair with my hand. All I did was make it point in a different direction.

Desiree sighed and nodded. "Well, you'd better save those tears. You're going to need them and then some before we get out of this mess."

"Did it ever occur to you that I'm just as scared as you?" I sobbed, my chest heaving.

"I never thought otherwise. But you'd better get a grip." Desiree shook her finger in my face before placing her hands on her hips. She had changed from the leather skirt she had worn during our brief but deadly encounter with Chester and slid into a pair of jeans. "How do you expect to make it to California in one piece? We can boo-hoo all we want to once we get there."

Suddenly, I didn't feel half as strong as I thought I was. "I'll be fine." My voice was so thin and shallow, even I didn't believe my own words.

Desiree grunted and shook her head. "We still have a lot of time to kill, and a few margaritas wouldn't hurt. I left half a bottle of tequila over here after your bridal shower the other night. Did you make more margaritas with it?"

"Oh, that bottle," I replied sheepishly. "I finished it off just before you called me to come pick you up."

"Oh." Desiree shrugged and gave me a pitiful look. "Well, you got any weed up in here?"

I rolled my eyes. Everybody knew that alcohol was as far as I went when it came to getting high. I didn't even allow my friends to smoke cigarettes in my apartment, let alone weed.

Desiree nodded. "Sorry."

"That liquor store down the street is open until midnight," I told her. The insides of my nostrils burned when I sniffed, and ached when I took a deep breath.

Desiree snorted and looked around the room. "I don't want to go out again . . . until . . . until it's time for us to leave." She looked around my bedroom again. "You got a lot of nice stuff in here. It's a shame to run off and leave it all behind," she said quietly. "Were you really going to let Regina and me divide up some of the good stuff, too?"

I nodded. "I was." I lowered my eyes first; then I looked up and scanned the room. I did have a lot of nice stuff, and with the exception of my new brass bed, everything was paid for. Daddy had given me the daybed by the window and the brass lamp in the corner. But I had worked overtime two hours a day, five days a week for three weeks to pay for the DVD on top of the portable TV facing my bed.

Desiree shook her head, and a sad smile appeared on her swollen face. "I packed everything that means anything to me. Chester can keep—Chester . . ." Her voice trailed off. She cleared her throat. "His mama can have all that stuff." She sighed tiredly and glanced at her watch. "I'm going to go take a long, hot shower and then I'm going to stretch myself out on the sofa and try and get some rest. I was up most of last night fucking that horny bastard, and I feel like I've been gored by a bull." She rubbed the insides of her thighs, then her stomach. One of the few things I didn't like discussing with Desiree was her sex life with Chester. Not because I was a prude, but because I didn't have a sex life. The gift-wrapped vibrator that Regina had given to me at my bridal shower didn't count.

"You want some milk or something? There's some cold chicken in the refrigerator," I blurted, praying that Desiree would not torture me with more details of her last romp with Chester.

Desiree shook her head. She opened her mouth to speak again, but nothing came out. She grunted, then covered her mouth and bolted. I jumped up and sprinted across the floor and out of the room. I followed Desiree to my bathroom, where she threw up all over my floor and my nice, fluffy, shaggy white throw rugs. By the time she leaned over the commode, everything that was going to come up had already formed slimy puddles on the floor.

"Are you pregnant?" I asked, a new fear forming in my brain.

"Two months," she whispered. "It was the one thing Chester prayed for every night. He wanted a child more than anything in the world."

"You're carrying his baby and he still hit you?" I growled.

Desiree would not look at me, and she was taking too long to answer. More for me to worry about.

"Desiree, talk to me." I hovered over her like a hawk. My threatening shadow on the bathroom floor was even more sinister than it appeared on the wall in my bedroom.

"I wasn't going to tell him until I got away. If he had known, there is no way in hell he would have let me take this baby and leave him."

After I helped Desiree clean up herself and my bathroom floor, she curled up on my sofa. I dragged myself back to my bedroom.

I stretched back out on my bed, facing the window. The wind whistling through the open window made the crisp, ruffled curtains rise and flutter like the leaves on the pecan tree in the fenced-in yard in back of my building. I was going to miss that tree and those pecans. A streetlight flickered off and on like it was running out of juice. I felt the same way.

Stiff, lying on my back with my hands folded across my chest, I felt like I was already dead. With what little life I had left in me, I blinked at that weakening streetlight as I tried to make some sense out of my life and all of the events that had led up to this day.

CHAPTER 6

June 1982

Every girl that I knew over the age of eight developed a crush on Chester Sheffield sooner or later. I was no exception. But mine was more than a crush; it was a mission. I felt I had an advantage over the other girls because he lived three houses down on the same street as me in a cul-de-sac and had to pass my house to go anywhere. I monitored his movements like an ambitious spy. Even peeping at him from around trees and from behind parked cars. I was twelve and it was the deepest summer of my life.

It wasn't just Chester's good looks that had captured my attention and triggered my obsession. The way he interacted with females he cared about had a lot to do with it. "You can tell if a man is worth his salt by the way he treats his mama and his sisters," Mama told my older sister Babette and me on a regular basis. My own daddy treated all of the women in his family like Nubian queens. He showered us with gifts and ran when an argument erupted.

At least once a week, Chester hauled huge bouquets of roses and neatly gift-wrapped packages to his mama and his baby sister, Kitty. Katherine "Kitty" Sheffield was my best friend at the time. She and I were the only girls Chester allowed in the tree house he and his boys had built in his backyard. Chester never gave me roses. And I didn't get too upset that time he slid a frog down my blouse when Kitty and I followed him to Lake Mead, where he went fishing with his boys.

That slimy frog was a small price to pay to retain my position as Chester's sister's best friend. Chester and I were two halves that would eventually come together as one. I knew it right after that time he goosed my butt during a game of hide-and-seek when I was ten and he was fourteen. It didn't matter to me that he had already done the same thing to three other girls that same day. It meant something when he did it to me.

Because of my long, sturdy legs and the fact that I could kick a ball as far as most of the boys and hang upside down from trees, kids had a lot of nicknames for me. Slim, Long Tall Sally, and Stretch were just a few. Chester was the only one who called me Crazy Legs.

Chester's parents owned Sheffield's Market four blocks from our house, and Mama sent me there a few times a week to pick up one thing or another. And whenever I had money, I went there on my own to buy magazines or junk food. The only thing I wouldn't buy when Chester was in the store was tampons. I always knew when Chester was in trouble because his parents punished him by making him work in the store. I spent a lot of time visiting Kitty when Chester was home, so I could keep an eye on him.

I was confused, but I had decided that I was "grown" enough to make my move on Chester. With all the mean tricks Mother Nature played on young bodies, my moods would swing from one extreme to the other. I had been a tomboy all of my life and didn't want to give up grungy clothes and marbles for dresses and makeup. I was willing to make these sacrifices to get Chester's attention and keep it.

That hot Saturday afternoon that June haunts me to this day. I had eagerly volunteered to walk to the Sheffields' store to pick up four cans of corn. Mama needed it for the bowl she was planning to donate to our church dinner the following Sunday. I didn't like church, but watching Chester lead the youth choir at the Second Baptist Church on Third Street kept me from falling asleep before services ended.

I had seen Chester strutting past our house bouncing a basketball on the sidewalk an hour earlier that Saturday, so I knew that he was on his way to the basketball court. The court was three blocks down the street from my house.

"The Piggly Wiggly is cheaper," Mama reminded me, handing me a crumpled five-dollar bill. "And everybody knows Brother Sheffield jacks up his prices."

"I thought you and Daddy said we all need to support Black businesses more," I said proudly, knowing how much Black pride my folks had. I reminded them when it was necessary. It was the one thing that worked every time.

Mama sighed and gave me a slightly exasperated look. Then she smiled weakly and shook her head as she glanced at her watch. "If Sister Sheffield is behind the counter, tell her I said she is putting way too much salt in the headcheese. We Black folks need to be more careful about what we eat." Mama was tall like me, but a lot heavier. With her light-brown skin, light-brown eyes, straight black hair, and sharp nose, people often mistook her for Creole. But she was quick to deny it. She was one of the few Black people I knew who didn't run around talking about how much mixed blood they had. I don't think my mother realized how exotic she was. If she did, she must not have considered it anything to make a fuss over like other women I knew who looked like her. Mama was a serious woman and didn't smile a lot. Sometimes when I caught her staring off into space, I wondered what she was thinking, but I never asked her. I do know that she had a rough life growing up in the South when it was still segregated. She was proud of the fact that as one of the most aggressive Civil Rights marchers, she had helped make the South a better place for me. I was proud of her for doing that. I couldn't imagine being told what to do because of my color.

"We sure do need to watch what we eat, Mama. If the Sheffields got some fresh okra, I'll get some of that, too." Knowing how much I hated most vegetables, Mama gave me a suspicious look before she waved me toward the door.

Chester was not at the basketball court when I went to the store—just some boys from the projects. Dancing around the perimeter of the basketball court trying to impress me, they kicked up a lot of the orange sand Alabama was famous for. But not enough to hide their homely faces and scrawny bodies. I ignored them.

On my way back from the store, Chester was on the court with the same dusty, ugly boys. Seeing me prancing down the sidewalk, Chester tossed his basketball to one of the two other boys and headed out to the sidewalk toward me. His two beastly friends followed close behind him, all three marching like warriors about to fight a battle. Even though my breasts had not made their presence known yet, I had started filling out in other places. My slightly curved hips and bubble butt made up for my flat chest. I was glad I had on my tightest and shortest shorts. As long as it was not something too outrageous, my parents told my sister and me they didn't care what we wore as long as it was clean and didn't stink. I wasn't allowed to wear makeup yet, but I had smeared on some lip gloss to cover a scab on my bottom lip. Even though Chester was sixteen and I was just twelve, I knew that when he got around to asking me out, I'd find a way to go. I knew a lot of girls my age who were already sneaking out of the house to hang out with boys. That's what windows were for. A lot of girls envied me because my bedroom was on the ground floor of our two-story house. If and when the time came, I was confident that I would have no trouble easing out of my window to be with Chester. Since I'd spent so many years climbing trees and running track, unlike my slightly plump, clumsy sister, I was as graceful as an antelope.

Chester stopped in front of me and folded his arms. The sleeves on his shirt were rolled up to his elbows, revealing soft hair on his arms that looked like black corn silk. I couldn't believe how tall and thick his body was. I was already five-feet-six myself, but he was still more than a head taller than me and outweighed me by at least fifty pounds. He was about my shade, pecan brown, maybe a little lighter then. But from spending so much time outside fiddling around with balls and fishing in the hot sun, he would get darker as he got older. His wavy black hair was in cornrows, a style I didn't particularly care for on boys. But his small, slanted black eyes, full lips, and high cheekbones made up for his natty hairdo. He didn't smile that often when he was around me, but when he did, he showed off some of the whitest, straightest teeth I'd ever seen.

I was facing the sun, but I didn't need its blinding rays to give me a reason to start batting my long black eyelashes. I thought I was being cute. I thought my heart was going to leap right out of my chest and bust through my new Bob Marley T-shirt. I had to start breathing through my mouth. It was time for action. Besides, I was getting impatient. Still batting my lashes, I started grinning, hoping Chester wouldn't make too much of a fuss over how cute I was and embarrass me in front of his friends. I wondered why Chester had such a scowl on his face. I had so much work to do on this boy.

"Where my five dollars, Crazy Legs?" he growled, stabbing me once in the chest with his long, hard-knuckled finger. I didn't mind him getting sand on my clean T-shirt.

Stunned, I stopped grinning and batting my lashes right away.

"What five dollars?" I asked nicely. That was the first time I'd been close enough to him to see that his left ear was pierced. I was glad he didn't have an earring in it. That was another thing I didn't like on boys.

"My sister Kitty told me you the one what knocked over my bike in front of Ray's Poolroom. The side of my back rim is all scratched up and I got to get it painted. Shit!"

"You better tell your sister to get her some eyeglasses. She didn't see me knock over your bike or nobody else's bike. I am not even allowed in the same block as that poolroom with all those nasty boys and men slopping all over the place like alligators." Chester's friends laughed at my comment, but he didn't.

"You callin' my sister a liar?" he hollered, stabbing me in my chest again. This time the sand he left on my top bothered me and I wiped it off.

"Well, she must be if she told you I knocked over your bike," I said, attempting to leave. I figured he was just trying to show off in front of his friends. But as much as I liked him, I was not willing to let him do that at my expense.

Chester blocked my way and then grabbed my shoulder. "Look, I ain't playin' with you, girl! I want my goddamn money!"

I gasped as Chester's two friends stood on either side of him with anxious looks on their faces. All three of these boys were sweating like hogs, but I was as cool as a cucumber.

"I don't have no five dollars no-how," I said, walking around Chester.

"Crazy Legs, don't you be walkin' off while I'm still talkin' to you. Shit." He kicked some sand on my leg. The oily lotion I had waxed my legs with made the sand stick to me. Then Chester took a long step toward me. He grabbed the back of my arm and spun me around so hard I fell. I landed on my side on top of the four cans of corn in the plastic bag. As much as it hurt, I didn't do anything to let Chester and his friends know I was in pain. While I was on the ground, Chester hawked a wad of spit the size of a walnut onto the sidewalk, missing my leg by a few inches. I jumped up, brushed off my scratched-up thigh, and started walking away again.

"Where you think you goin'?" With a sinister laugh he added, "Don't you know I'll break them crazy legs of yours in two? I ain't through with you yet, girl." His friends laughed so hard they had to squat down on the ground.

"Well I'm through with you." I slapped his hand, an indication that I was about to lose my cool, but he didn't know that. Before I realized what was happening, he lunged at me. But I moved so fast that he missed me and fell face first to the ground. His friends stood back up but kept laughing as I stepped over Chester's long body. With sand covering his face like a cheap mask, he jumped up with his hand poised to slap me. Before he could touch me, I closed my eyes and I started swinging the plastic grocery bag in his direction. At the same time, I saw what seemed like a flash of light, even with my eyes closed.

To this day, I never heard another human being howl the way Chester did that afternoon when I hit him. When I opened my eyes, he was wallowing on the ground. Blood was pouring from a wound on the right side of his face about two inches above his eye. The plastic grocery bag had broken, and one of the cans of corn was on the ground next to Chester's head. The top of the can was covered in his blood.

I never ate corn again after that day, and it had been one of the few vegetables I tolerated. I didn't know at the time that I would not hit another person again, until seventeen years later when history repeated itself.

CHAPTER 7

Belle Helene, Alabama, an hour's drive north of Mobile, had about forty thousand residents when I was growing up. Meridian, Mississippi, was closer, which was where a lot of Belle Helene's six thousand Blacks worked. Most of the Black men in Belle Helene worked for the turpentine or logging companies. There was a garment factory near Lake Mead, between Mobile and us, and several downtown department stores and a mall where a lot of the Black women I knew worked.

Our house was in Belle Helene on Heggy Street in what we all considered a middle-class Black neighborhood. Our houses looked a lot alike, just different colors. We all had nice, neat front and backyards complete with barbecue pits and surrounded by fruit and pecan trees. Every house had a two-car garage and at least two vehicles. A lawyer and his wife lived on one side of us. A retired airline pilot lived on the other side.

My daddy, Charles, was a mechanic and owned a garage in Mobile. My uncle Redmond and four other men worked for my daddy, so Daddy didn't have to go to Mobile that often. But he loved fiddling around with cars so much that the garage and driveway of our three-bedroom house always contained two or three cars to be worked on at all times.

Though we lived in the deep South and there was an occasional incident involving the Ku Klux Klan and other run-of-the-mill racists, we all got along well with the white folks we had to deal with. But Mama and Daddy, who had both served in Vietnam and marched with Dr. Martin Luther King Jr. during the sixties, never let us forget how far Black folks had come. I couldn't count the number of times I heard from Daddy, "When me and your mama was young, we couldn't even eat or go shoppin' where we wanted to down here. We even had to ride on the back of the bus. Y'all kids nowadays got a lot to be thankful for." I usually heard comments like that when I got lazy about going to school.

Daddy made good money, but Mama worked, too. She was a hair-dresser and, like a lot of the older Black women who dressed hair, she worked out of the kitchen in our house. After she had tended to wounded soldiers in Vietnam, where she had met Daddy, Mama had given up nursing to do hair and stay at home to raise my older sister Babette and me. Mama didn't have a beautician's license and had not been formally trained, but she had a long list of regular clients. She even had a few white women on her list that thought cornrows were so "awesome."

Behind the large, marble-topped table facing the stove in our kitchen was a large wooden chair with a high back. Mama had strapped a pillow to the seat to make her customers more comfort-able while she pressed, curled, permed, and braided their hair. In a drawer in the same cabinet with the silverware were several straight-ening combs, a pair of curling irons, and other assorted hairdressing tools. The smell of exotic pomades that Mama used on her clients' hair overpowered the smell of her fried chicken and collard greens, but that never bothered her or us enough to move the chair and her hairdressing items to the den behind our living room. Besides, by working in the kitchen, Mama could look out of the window over the sink and enjoy nature. She was particularly proud of her flowerbed in our front yard and the oak tree where my Uncle Redmond had tied a hammock.

Mama was a busy woman. She was active in the church and she never missed a PTA meeting. She dragged Daddy to movies, plays, and a few other things he hated. On any given day, she had up to four customers, all of them wanting her to perform magic on their hair. Somehow she found time to keep our house clean and Babette and me out of trouble. I spent a lot of my time in front of the TV in the living room next to the kitchen, listening to conversations between Mama and her customers.

One of Mama's best customers and her best friend was a cook named Mozelle Tupper. Miss Mozelle was almost baldheaded, but Mama dressed what little hair she had once a week. One thing I liked about Miss Mozelle was the fact that she lived in a big beige house right next door to the house where Chester Sheffield lived. In addition to the house he lived in then, Chester's parents owned Miss Mozelle's house and the one a few blocks away that Chester would eventually share with Desiree. Miss Mozelle's son Burl was a grade ahead of me at Belle Helene Junior High. He and I were not really friends, but I used him as an excuse to go to Miss Mozelle's house, just so I could be closer to Chester. This was especially important after I had hit Chester with the canned goods. Part of my punishment was, I couldn't visit Chester's house to hang out with his sister Kitty.

Chester stayed mad at me for over a year after the incident with the canned corn. When I saw him at church or on the street, he just rolled his eyes at me or ignored me completely. When he worked in his daddy's store, he waited on me, but he wouldn't talk to me and practically hurled my change at me. And when I called his house to chat with Kitty, he'd hang up on me without calling her to the telephone. By that time, Kitty was already into boys big time and didn't have a lot of time to spend with me anyway.

"Girl, Chester ain't never gonna get over what you done. That spot on his head where you hit him gonna be soft from now on," my second best friend, Regina Witherspoon, told me. Regina lived with her widowed mama in a two-bedroom apartment in the Pike Street projects. We'd been friends since third grade. One night at the age of eleven, Regina slipped out of her house to visit me. While her mother was out looking for her, their apartment caught fire and all six of her younger siblings burned to death. I never told her or anybody else, but I felt responsible for that tragedy. I had nightmares for months after the mass funeral. If I had not coaxed Regina into hanging out with me, her mother would have never left the other kids in the house alone. For months, every time I closed my eyes I could still see those six small cream-colored coffins lined up in a flower-lined row at the Second Baptist Church.

About a month after the fire, Regina's mother, Miss Maggie, developed a weird phobia that a lot of us didn't know much about then.

Agoraphobia caused Miss Maggie to be too afraid to leave the house. Her fear was so deep, she wouldn't even stand too close to a window. Regina felt obligated to spend as much time with her mother as possible. I visited Regina and Miss Maggie a lot, helping them take care of their apartment and doing chores for them that I'd rather get a whupping for than do at my own house. I felt it was my job to help them ease the pain that I had helped cause.

My plan to help Regina deal with her depression helped her but it depressed me. When I couldn't deal with that, I turned my attention to Mimi Hollis, another girl with a disturbing background. Mimi was two years older than me and lived five blocks away from us. Everybody I knew was familiar with Mimi's painful history, but I had heard it firsthand from her mother while she was sitting in our kitchen getting her hair done. In her fifth month of pregnancy, Mimi's mother, Miss Odessa, had tried to abort Mimi. But Mimi had survived, and for the first five years of her life she seemed as normal as Miss Odessa's other five children. Right after Mimi started school, she started behaving strangely. She would go for days at a time not talking, and she ate rocks and mud pies. One Sunday during church, she stood up in front of the whole congregation and exposed her private parts while Reverend Poe was preaching. Miss Odessa took Mimi from one county doctor to another, and not a one of them could put a name on Mimi's condition. Odd, slow, and confused were just a few of the adjectives used to describe the girl's behavior. It was no wonder we all called her Crazy Mimi. When she was nine, Miss Odessa took Mimi out of school and started teaching her herself at home.

When I was eleven and still in my tomboy mode, I had stumbled across Crazy Mimi one September evening in an alley giving blowjobs to some of Chester's friends. I chased the boys away with a plank and escorted Crazy Mimi to my house. Even though I had taken her under my wing, she still ended up pregnant three years in a row by males she couldn't or wouldn't identify.

I spent a lot of time baby-sitting Crazy Mimi's kids or helping her haul them around in a red wagon loaded down with Pampers and toys that we had purchased from either Sheffield's Market or the nearby Piggly Wiggly.

It seemed odd that a mentally challenged girl like Crazy Mimi would take it upon herself to give me advice. "Carmen, there's a lot of other cute boys around here. You need to quit mopin' around about that Chester Sheffield. I used to be crazy about him myself, but I got over him real quick when other boys started payin' me attention. Look at me now! I got three babies!"

I stared at Crazy Mimi's narrow peach-colored face, big, glazed black eyes, and keen nose. I wondered how so many boys could overlook her long, flat breasts; her bell-shaped body, and thin, greasy hair that was always worn in a single lopsided braid. In the long, shapeless black duster she had on and with her sharp features, she looked like a black crow lounging on my bed. The thick makeup and sensible shoes she wore most of the time made her look ten years older. Which is what she told me when I asked her why she never wore jeans, T-shirts, and running shoes like the rest of us. Sadly, looking older often got her in trouble with men old enough to be her daddy.

Crossing her thick, knotty ankles, she added with a sneer, "I know for a fact that Burl Tupper likes you. I asked him myself." Crazy Mimi cackled and lifted her voluminous outfit, revealing a stiff-looking white girdle but no panties.

Getting over Chester was not something I wanted to do. Even though he had me at the top of his shit list, I still had my crush on him. I planned to do whatever it took to turn his feelings toward me around.

"I don't want no potbellied pig like Burl," I said emphatically.

Crazy Mimi and I were in my bedroom that sultry Saturday afternoon in late October, trying to decide what to wear to Kitty Sheffield's Halloween party a week away. A mask of a scowling red demon left over from the Mobile Mardi Gras we'd attended in February lay upside down on the bed next to me. Crazy Mimi and I had both decided that we were too old and cute to be wearing masks that ghoulish. And the last thing I wanted was for Chester to see me as something evil. I had decided to go to the party dressed as a queen wearing a crown.

Crazy Mimi was sitting on the side of my bed next to her drooling, moon-faced two-year-old son, Boogie. I was peeping out of my bedroom window, parting the curtains with my head, hoping to get a glimpse of Chester. I had seen him earlier outside talking to Daddy. Mama and my sister Babette were in the kitchen cooking up a storm. So was every other woman on our block. With the window and my door slightly open, I could smell macaroni and cheese, collard greens, buttered cornbread, pork chops, peach cobbler, and smothered chicken coming from every direction.

"Well, Chester don't want you," Crazy Mimi reminded me. She then delivered a well-orchestrated snap of her thick fingers, swatting Boogie's hand with her other hand as he unraveled a thread on my new chenille bedspread. "Behave, Boogie, or Carmen won't ask us to stay for dinner so we can help eat them screamin' pork chops. Girl, your mama cooks a mean pot of greens, too." Crazy Mimi looked at me and nodded; I nodded back. She sucked in her breath before continuing. "One other thing you need to know, girl." She paused and waved her finger in my face. "The best way to get a boy to want you is to make him think another boy wants you. And didn't I just tell you that Burl wants you?"

I carefully considered Crazy Mimi's words. To be so crazy, she sometimes made a lot of sense.

CHAPTER 8

Thanks to Crazy Mimi's advice, I decided to pay more attention to Burl. It sounded like he could be a valuable tool for me to use. Now that I knew he liked me more than I thought, I decided that it would be a shame not to take advantage of the situation.

Burl rarely came to my house, but I decided to increase my visits to his, anyway. Through Kitty, I would make sure her sexy brother, Chester, heard about Burl and me spending so much time together. She loved reporting hot stories almost as much as she liked boys. And knowing how melodramatic Kitty was, I had enough faith in her to believe she would add just enough spice to whet Chester's appetite.

I had no idea how high a price I would end up paying for using Burl.

I was not fickle like some of the girls I knew. I was focused. Other than Chester, I had other boys on my mind, but not in the same romantic way. My cousin Baby Red, who lived in Mobile, was Chester's age. Baby Red was the only boy I really felt close to at the time. He was the smartest, most generous, most free-spirited boy I knew. Other than his bike, fine wine, good marijuana, and a few philosophy books, he didn't care about money or many other material things. Baby Red had a lot to do with the mess I eventually made of my life, but I'll get to him later.

A few days after Crazy Mimi's last visit, I decided to visit Burl after school for the third time in three days. I dropped my books on his front porch glider as he led me into his house, grinning and motioning for me to be quiet because his mother was resting. I tiptoed behind Burl through a narrow, gloomy hallway to the living room. Burl had a nice round face with dimples and big gray eyes, but he was a head shorter than I was. He waddled like a penguin, and from behind he looked like one. Thick, curly hair covered his head like a ball of black cotton. His hair, his dimples, and his pretty gray eyes saved him from a life of shame and victimization, a position so many other unpopular kids had to endure.

Once you saw and got to know Burl's mama, it was easy to see why Burl was the way he was. Miss Mozelle was old enough to be Burl's grandmother. When they moved to Alabama from Detroit seven years ago, that's what we all thought. According to the gossips, Miss Mozelle had left her husband for another man. Once they got to Alabama, the man left her for another woman. That made Miss Mozelle so bitter, she had not been with another man since. She now devoted all of her attention to Burl. She still combed his hair and picked out all of his clothes. "If Burl was to die, they better dig a hole deep enough for Mozelle, too," Daddy commented one evening over dinner.

Miss Mozelle looked like a full-grown seal. She was stretched out on her couch with her head resting on two pillows, barefoot and wrapped up in a long, throat-high brown flannel robe. She was eating pickled pig's feet straight out of the jar with her fingers. There was a foot tub full of sudsy water on the floor in front of the couch where she had been soaking her feet. A fluffy yellow towel, some Corn Huskers Lotion, and a box cutter used as a toenail clipper were on the floor next to the foot tub.

Miss Mozelle made a good living cooking for the country club, and she liked to spend it on the things she liked. Each room in her house was full of bizarre furniture, mysterious unmarked boxes, and dime-store odds and ends nobody but her would want. She even had a fake canary in a cage in her dining room, swinging from a rope above a life-sized bust of Dr. Martin Luther King Jr. In her living room, with its floral wallpaper, were a battered plaid sofa, two different TVs, some wicker chairs, a red velvet love seat she didn't allow any kids to sit on, and huge green plants reaching halfway across the room. Hanging from the doorway leading from the living room to the kitchen were orange beads that touched the floor. On the end tables in the living room were framed pictures that looked like mugshots of Miss Mozelle, Burl, and other members of their family. They looked out of place sitting next to pictures of John F. Kennedy, Diana Ross, Jesse Jackson, and Jesus.

Other than Burl, Miss Mozelle didn't have any other relatives in Alabama. She had a mean older brother in Detroit that I had never met, and from what I had heard about him, I didn't want to. This beastly man had such a long reach, he was able to control Miss Mozelle and Burl all the way from Detroit. They rarely made a decision without consulting Burl's uncle first.

Lifting her head a few inches off the arm of her sofa, she cleared her throat and set the pig's feet jar on the coffee table and squinted at me. Still smacking on the last pig's foot, she asked in a voice that rattled, "Carmen, how is your mama these days?"

"She's fine." I shrugged and blinked stupidly.

Miss Mozelle nodded and cleared her throat again before continuing. "And your daddy?"

"He's fine, too, Miss Mozelle. My whole family is fine."

She looked disappointed. She dipped her head, lifted her thick gray eyebrows, and started tapping her fingers on the top of her coffee table, waiting like I was holding back something she thought I should have shared with her. I grinned some more and shrugged again.

Finally, Miss Mozelle dismissed me with a wave of her hand and returned her head to the pillows and growled, "Gal, before you leave here I want you to help this boy fold them clothes I left on the counter in the kitchen. Do you hear me?"

Miss Mozelle's skin was the same butterscotch brown as Burl's, but hers was as rough as sandpaper. She was short and thick and had a large, heavy-cheeked face with black, hairy moles dotting her chin like ants. Once a week Mama pressed and curled Miss Mozelle's thin black-and-gray hair, hiding bald spots that decorated her head like manholes. Miss Mozelle was no queen of Sheba, but she was a proud Christian woman and I liked her. In fact, everybody liked her. Even Chester. Last Mother's Day, he insisted that she go out to dinner with him and his mama and some of his other female relatives.

"Yes, ma'am," I said, afraid to sit down. I stood timidly in front of the larger of the two TVs until Miss Mozelle waved me to the side.

"You want to make some taffy?" Burl asked me, still grinning. The more he grinned, the deeper his dimples looked. He didn't look too comfortable, and it didn't surprise me. I knew that my mysterious visits confused him. He had his friends and I had mine. He didn't ask, but I was sure he was wondering why I suddenly started visiting him twice as much as I had before.

"You seen Kitty?" I asked, following Burl into the kitchen, the only room in the house that didn't smell like cod-liver oil. The soothing aroma of baked goods still lingered from pies and cakes that Miss Mozelle had cooked from scratch several days earlier.

Once he reached a counter that was covered with Mason jars, things floating in them that Miss Mozelle had canned, he abruptly stopped.

Whirling around to face me with a puzzled look on his face, he asked, "Kitty who?" Burl had on the same brown corduroy pants and loose white shirt he had worn to school that day. A few dime-sized mustard stains covered the front of his shirt. I had witnessed him gobble up four hot dogs in the cafeteria that afternoon.

"Kitty next door. Chester's sister," I said, motioning with my head toward the Sheffields' house. "She's having a Halloween party next week. You going?"

"She didn't invite me," Burl said sadly, bowing his head and shaking it. When he was unhappy, his bouncy curls didn't look like a black cotton ball to me. Instead, his hair looked like a black cloud above his face. He was the only boy I knew who wore his hair parted on the side like an old man. Whether his hair looked like a black cotton ball or a black cloud, it was a shame to see all those curls go to waste on a boy like Burl. I would have traded my long, floppy, nappy ponytail for his hair any day.

"You can go with me. Kitty said I could bring a guest." Chester was going to be at that party. It was essential for a prop like Burl to be there for me to lean on. "They'll have a lot of food—buffalo wings, ribs, cracklins', deviled eggs. All you can eat."

Burl's eyes blinked rapidly and his tongue slid across his bottom lip. "All you can eat, huh?" He cocked his head to the side and asked, "What about peach cobbler?"

"All you can eat," I repeated. My stomach started growling, and I couldn't wait to get home to dive into the rump roast that Mama was cooking for dinner. "It's just a Halloween party, but you know how Kitty's mama likes to cook." I sniffed. "I'm going dressed as an African queen. Come on, Burl, go with me *pleeease.*" Begging was out of character for me, but I was not too proud to do it for something I really wanted.

"I guess I'll go," Burl said tiredly, smoothing his hair back with his thick fingers. He sighed and stared at me with his head tilted to the side. There was a look of uncertainty on his face.

"You can go as a Zulu warrior. I got a spear you can use," I said quickly and firmly.

Burl flashed me a smile and bobbed his head, his curls dangling like grapes. "I got some paint we can put on our faces," he announced excitedly. Just then the red telephone on the wall next to the stove rang. Still smiling, Burl grabbed it. Within seconds his smile faded and he started mopping sweat off of his forehead with the back of his hand. "Uh-huh . . . no . . . uh-huh . . . no . . . uh-huh. No, sir. Yes, sir. Bye," he mumbled. As soon as he hung up, he turned to me with a hopeless look on his round face. "That was my uncle Mogen callin' from Detroit."

"The scary one?" I asked, scooping up a handful of hush puppies from a cracked plate on the counter and tossing them into my mouth.

"Uh-huh. He calls every evenin' to make sure we doin' all right."

"Oh." I shrugged. "You wanna go with me to visit Kitty now?"

"Naw." Burl waved his floppy hand and shuddered. "Not while Chester's in the house. He don't like me."

It was easy to understand why Burl didn't want to be around Chester. Four years ago Chester had made him eat a rock during a church picnic.

"Well, if we go over there together, Chester won't bother you," I said seriously.

Burl sniffed. "Ain't he still mad at you for hittin' him that time?" As if he had been told to do so, he grabbed a damp dishrag off the counter and wiped up some crumbs I had dropped on the floor. Then he started looking around the room, like he was looking for something else to clean.

I shrugged. "I don't care. Kitty is my friend and I am not going to let Chester stop me from visiting her. Shoot!" I exclaimed, stomping my foot.

Burl let out a deep groan, neatly folded the dishrag, and gently placed it back on the counter. "Chester got his girlfriend over there now anyway."

I gasped. A rage-clouded shadow passed across my burning face, and for a minute I thought I would lose control of my bladder. "Girlfriend? What girlfriend?" I snarled, moving back a few steps with my hands on my hips.

"Sandy Baptiste. She just moved here from New Orleans. A real tall, pretty girl so light she look white. I seen him take her in the house just before you got here. He was hugging her around her neck." Burl sniffed again, this time so hard his whole body shuddered.

My jealousy about Chester being with another girl made my head swim, and I knew I had to come up with a stronger plan. "Oh, you mean that old Creole girl with the bad breath?" I dismissed the thought with a wave of my hand. "Anyway, Kitty told me to stop by today before I go home," I lied. I didn't have any problems with telling lies. From what I had observed so far, lying was the quickest and most effective to get what you wanted.

But as I would soon find out, lies got more people in trouble than did sex.

CHAPTER 9

Burl decided not to accompany me to Kitty's house even after I told him about the candied apples Kitty had brought home from our home economics class. With his eyes sparkling, he licked his plump lips hungrily and explained with regret, "I gotta stay home to scratch and grease Mama's scalp."

Why in the world a woman who was practically bald paid so much attention to her head was a mystery to me. A wig would have solved all of Miss Mozelle's problems.

"How come your mama can't scratch and grease her own scalp," I asked, forcing myself to keep the anger out of my voice. "She got two hands."

"She got grippe," Burl explained with a heavy sigh.

"Oh." All I knew about grippe was that it was one of the many things my grandmother complained about having. And that was all I wanted to know.

Since it was a school night and I had to be home in time for dinner, I knew I had to work fast. I made a quick phone call from Burl's house to Mama and told her a bald-faced lie about having to give Kitty a homework assignment she had accidentally left at school. I grabbed my books off of Burl's front porch and sprinted across his lawn, leaping over a lawn mower in the Sheffields' front yard.

Thank God Kitty's parents were still at their store. I didn't feel like answering a bunch of questions about my family's health, and everything else they discussed with me was just as dull. Unlike most of the people who came to our house for Mama to do their hair, Mrs. Sheffield didn't have a lot of juicy gossip to entertain us with. The only good stuff I had picked up from her was that there were some fast, brazen women hanging around the store, grinning and flirting with Mr. Sheffield right in front of her. Mr. Sheffield often brought his shiny black Lincoln over for Daddy to work on, but he never revealed anything worth repeating. Like Miss Mozelle, the only places Mr. and Mrs. Sheffield usually went to were church and work. When they were home, all they did was sit around and read dull books and watch dull TV programs. I guess they were too wrapped up in their books and TV shows to see all the fun Kitty was having right up under their noses.

Not counting Crazy Mimi, Kitty was the only friend I had who had already given up her virginity. A year earlier, she had spent the night with me one Saturday. To keep Mama and Daddy from asking too many nosy questions, Kitty and I had volunteered to do the dishes after dinner. Right after that, we announced that we were going to my room to study Scripture so that we could be prepared for church the next morning. Mama was busy winding herself around the house, straightening up things in case unexpected company showed up. Daddy was still in the garage, doing whatever it was he did in there. My sister, Babette, was taking one of her hour-long bubble baths. While my family was occupied, I helped Kitty slide out my bedroom window. She had agreed to meet up with a boy that her brother had warned her about because the boy had just been released from a reform school. Against my better judgment, I often conspired with Kitty even though I knew it was wrong. Knowing about my crush on her brother, she kept me under her control by telling me on a regular basis how much prettier I was than the girls Chester dated.

"Girl, I'll be glad when you and my brother hook up. We'll be real sisters then. Chester's hotter than a six-shooter, see. I hope you can handle him," Kitty told me with a wink, adding the obligatory "Shit."

"I hope I can, too," I said with nervous apprehension. I didn't have a clue as to how I was going to keep Chester once I got ahold of him. Though the thought excited me, it frightened me at the same time. "Shit, girl. You think he likes me?" I didn't really like to cuss, but I had done it enough to where I was used to it by now. "Should I wear my blue denim dress when I come over to your house next time so he can see me in it?"

Kitty nodded eagerly. "Uh-huh. He likes pretty girls with long legs. And blue is his favorite color." I watched in awe as Kitty sprayed her crotch with Charlie cologne.

Kitty was as dark as I was and almost as tall. She had a nice, curvy body, but she still stuffed her bra with toilet paper. Her long black hair was always in neat cornrows, complete with beads. She was pretty enough, but she was not nearly as good-looking as her brother was. Her face was too long and her nose and chin were too sharp. She minimized her flaws with makeup tips she learned from my sister. Kitty had braces on her teeth and she complained about that all the time. "Girl, I have to stand on my head to give blowjobs so this damn metal in my mouth don't scratch nobody's pecker." I admired Kitty for knowing what she wanted and going after it. She didn't let anybody or anything stop her. She was my role model and I was working on being just like her. Her role model was Alexis Carrington, the ball-breaking character that Joan Collins played on *Dynasty,* our favorite nighttime soap opera at the time. Kitty's bedroom walls were covered with pictures of Joan Collins that she had torn out of magazines.

As volatile as Chester was, he adored his sister Kitty. He rode her around piggyback until she got too big, and he made furniture in his shop class for her dollhouses. Unlike a lot of the girls I knew, Kitty shared a lot of information with her brother about everybody but herself. That's why, after she told me she was fooling around with a couple of boys, I told her about Burl, counting on her to share this information with Chester.

"Since when did your mama let you keep company?" Kitty wanted to know, walking me back to my house. Just ten minutes had passed since I'd left Burl's house to visit Kitty. It turned out to be a wasted trip, anyway. Because just as I got there, Chester was leaving with that foul-breathed Sandy Baptiste, ignoring me completely.

"I can't have a boyfriend until I'm sixteen, but what Mama don't know won't hurt her," I said smugly. "Besides, Babette's only fifteen and she's got a boyfriend. And what about you?"

"Oh, I ain't allowed to date yet neither," Kitty said in a low voice.

Just as we reached my house, a rusty Mustang crawled down the street and stopped in front of us. A long, thin, hairy brown arm, decorated with cruel scars and a tattoo of a dagger, was hanging out of the window on the driver's side. A wolf whistle came from the driver.

"That's Buzzy. Listen, I left my mama a note that I was goin' to eat dinner at your house," Kitty told me, climbing into Buzzy's old car. "Cover me," she ordered.

Mama was busy in the kitchen fixing dinner as I floated into the living room and plopped down on the sofa. I could hear her fussing at Daddy about leaving some dirty car parts on the kitchen counter. My poor daddy. He was such a complicated man, drifting through our big house like a ghost. Sometimes all I saw of him was his shadow. He had been raised by a housefull of domineering women and now he had to deal with us. But Daddy had cooked his own goose by spoiling us. After every time he whupped Babette or me or got into an argument with Mama, he took us shopping and bought us something nice and expensive.

My sister, Babette, two years older than me, pranced into the living room wearing a shower cap and a new silk yellow bathrobe that Daddy had just bought for her. Like Mama, Babette was slightly plump and had light-brown skin. Babette and I had the same large dark-brown eyes, narrow-bridged nose, and lips that Mama's white clients had to buy from a plastic surgeon. Babette had thick dark-brown hair worn shoulder length; mine was black and a few inches longer. I had Daddy's smooth dark skin and height and his high cheekbones. Daddy's parents had passed on before I was born, but he had two sisters in Florida and one in Huntsville that we rarely saw or heard from. Mama's parents, both retired schoolteachers, lived in Montgomery. My grandparents sneaked into Belle Helene every now and then to make a fuss over Babette and me. Using bad grammar in their presence was the quickest way for us to get a whupping. Speaking properly was a small price to pay to avoid my grandparents' wrath. However, I did sprinkle my speech with enough foul language when I was around my friends to let them know that I was still basically a homegirl.

"That new girl Desiree Lucienne, she said for you to call her," Babette told me, sitting down on the love seat facing me, carefully smoothing the tail of that fancy housecoat. Babette had slapped my hand when I tried to touch the housecoat right after she slid it out of the newly wrapped gift box it had come in. "Desiree said she wants to borrow your black leather jacket," she added, crossing her legs with caution. I didn't know that Daddy had given her new mules, which looked like fluffy yellow bushes, to match the housecoat. "Look how dainty my feet look," Babette squealed, wiggling her feet. After my sister stopped admiring her feet, she turned to me with a serious look. "Carmen, go on and call that Desiree girl back. She sounded desperate."

My choice of friends annoyed my sister. She should have been used to it by now because I'd always been drawn to the kinds of companions who needed a strong friend like me. Before I'd even started school, I had taken in a three-legged dog and a blind cat. I grieved for days when they died the same week. I felt like I had let them down in some way. I didn't want to disappoint any of my human friends and lose them, too. Desiree was my newest project, and I couldn't wait to incorporate her into my life.

CHAPTER 10

Unlike me, Desiree Lucienne didn't have any close friends. She was just as unpopular as Burl. Like with Burl, the only friend who ever called her was me.

She had a telephone in her room, and when I did call back that night, she answered on the first ring. "Carmen, you want to come over Saturday afternoon?" If red robins could talk, they would sound like Desiree. That girl had such a nice, melodic voice. It was one of the things I liked most about her. Especially compared to Regina and Crazy Mimi. They had the harshest voices I had ever heard coming out of teenage girls. More than one person had mistaken Regina for a man over the telephone.

"Uh . . . I don't know. I might be going to the movies with Burl." As much as I liked this new girl, I had to get to her when I could. It didn't really bother me having to put her on hold. I knew she wasn't going anywhere.

"Oh. Well, if you change your mind, let me know. I got some new patterns I want to show you. After that, I have to go down to my daddy's office to help clean up. His cleaning lady has been sick for two days."

Desiree had moved to town three months ago from Birmingham. She was in my homeroom and three of my classes. She was shy and kept to herself, but some of the other girls at our school mistook her for a snob. They picked on her until I took her under my wing. Knocking Chester to the ground that time had earned me quite a reputation. Nobody messed with me, so naturally the kids I befriended were safe. I liked hanging out with Desiree, even though we didn't have a lot in common. She liked to read romance novels and she made most of her own clothes from patterns she created herself. She brought sandwiches to school made with bread that she made from scratch, while I ate lavish meals I purchased from the cafeteria. I rarely cracked open a book, and when I did it was a murder mystery or something by Stephen King. I certainly didn't have the patience or time to fuss with patterns and sewing machines for myself, but I liked watching Desiree do it. She hinted that she wanted to be a designer when she grew up, or a chef. Mama and my grandparents and all of daddy's relatives wanted Babette and me to be teachers. Daddy said, "I don't care what y'all do as long as it ain't illegal."

A career was so far down the road, I didn't give it much thought at the time. I didn't know what I wanted to pursue, but it wasn't teaching. For the time being, just being a teenager was enough to keep me occupied. It was a full-time job hanging out with my friends and trying to capture Chester.

I learned the rest of Desiree's history by listening to Mama gossip on the telephone with Miss Mozelle. Desiree's daddy, Dr. Andre Lucienne, was a gynecologist, a Creole, an alcoholic, and a brute. He had beaten his wife so much, she had run off with just the clothes on her back, leaving Desiree and her older sister, Colleen, with Dr. Lucienne. Now he was beating Desiree and Colleen. Even though I had heard a lot of negative stuff about the doctor, I liked him almost as much as I liked my own daddy. I never told anybody, but I often wished that my daddy was more like Dr. Lucienne. Daddy was younger and better-looking than Desiree's daddy, but sometimes he embarrassed me in front of my friends by using bad grammar and wearing the greasy overalls and lopsided, outdated Afro he wore most of the time. Dr. Lucienne was a short, jowly-cheeked, lumpy man with a moon face and wiry gray hair. And even though everybody said he looked like Fred Flintstone, he had the kind of light skin and straight hair combed back like a duck that a lot of the women I knew liked. I looked forward to riding the bus with Desiree to her daddy's downtown office. I watched in awe as he rolled around his office on his stubby legs, barking at his nurses and patients with the tails of his long white smock flapping like wings.

Mama didn't like me going to the doctor's office because she didn't like his head nurse. Bertha Cross, called Nurse Bertha, had been on staff when Mama worked at the county hospital years ago. Very few people liked this woman. Each time Daddy worked on her truck, she complained about his prices and would only pay him with post-dated checks. Once she tried to pay him with food stamps that somebody had paid her with for an abortion she had performed. (I'd overheard that hot piece of gossip from Kitty, who had heard it from the pregnant girl's mother.) Nurse Bertha was a good Christian lady, but nosy and manipulative according to Mama, and the main reason Mama had given up nursing to do hair. Ironically, Nurse Bertha was now one of Mama's best customers.

The last time Mama did Nurse Bertha's limp, dyed-black hair, Nurse Bertha complained about the style. "Sister Taylor, you got me lookin' like one of them jezebels on *Soul Train.*" Nurse Bertha always wore too much expensive perfume, but she was a heavy smoker and had the breath of a moose. I could smell it from where I stood, peeping from around the doorway a few feet away.

Mama told her, "Didn't I tell you that style was too young and wordly for you?"

Nurse Bertha, a petite woman with delicate brown eyes that looked out of place on her leathery bronze-toned face, glared in my direction as I said, "Patti LaBelle wears her hair like that. Those flat bangs make you look younger, too." My comment made her smile.

"Well, if Patti LaBelle can wear a do like this, so can I!" Nurse Bertha hollered happily.

Mama sprayed the kitchen with pine-scented Glade after Nurse Bertha left. Then Mama advised me not to pass out compliments to people who didn't deserve them. "Lying only leads to more lying. A girl like you has no reason to go around telling lies," Mama added.

"Yes, ma'am," I muttered, crossing my fingers behind my back.

I rarely told Mama about my trips to the doctor's office, and I certainly did not tell her about all the nosy questions Nurse Bertha asked me about our business every chance she got. After the time I blabbed to Nurse Bertha about the man from IRS paying Daddy an unexpected visit—which made Daddy maul my head—I usually kept quiet around her. Desiree was probably the only young person I knew who liked Nurse Bertha. However, she always tried to gather up a posse to escort her to her daddy's office so she wouldn't have to face Nurse Bertha and her daddy alone. Everybody knew that Desiree was terrified of her daddy. I would be too if he lit into me the way he lit into her. I had witnessed him bounce a coffee cup off of her head one day because he said the coffee she had just served him was too cold. His attacks on her bothered me more than they bothered Desiree. While I'd get mad at her daddy after one of his rampages, she'd pick herself up off the floor, dress her wounds, then trot off to the bar in their living room and fix him a highball. I wondered how I could fit Desiree into my schemes. I was glad she was on the other end of the telephone. I didn't want her to see the look on my face.

With so many people around me doing so many strange things, sometimes I felt like I was the only sane person left. At least all I was guilty of was being a fool over Chester Sheffield. He was the highlight of my life. But my life was about to change dramatically. "I promised Burl I'd go to the movies with him on Saturday," I said with my fingers crossed.

"You can come over here after the movies," Desiree pleaded. "You can bring Burl if you want to. He can help us clean my daddy's office. Daddy has to go out to the hospital to deliver a baby by C-section on Saturday." Desiree continued. "Poor Daddy. I feel so sorry for him. It's not easy for him to be prodding around with his fingers inside women's stinky pussies five days a week. No wonder he drinks."

I cringed. "We don't have to clean up nothing real nasty, do we?"

"Oh, no! I just go by to like straighten up magazines, check on the plants, stuff like that. Nurse Bertha and the cleaning lady take care of the real nasty stuff. We can make Burl rearrange the furniture in the waiting room. Daddy would be so pleased," Desiree said breathlessly.

"Uh . . . I'll have to ask Burl. You know how boys are," I replied. As soon as I got Desiree off the phone, I called Burl. "You wanna go to the movies Saturday afternoon?" I had no desire to help clean up Dr. Lucienne's office and field his nosy head nurse's questions, and even without asking I knew that Burl didn't want to either.

"With who?" Burl gasped.

"With me," I said.

"I ain't got no money." He laughed. I could hear Miss Mozelle's muffled, plaintive growls in the background. "I gotta get off the phone. Mama needs for me to scrape the dead skin off her feet," Burl said excitedly.

Burl was such a fool for his mama. It was bad enough that Burl's mean uncle in Detroit had such a toehold on him, but the things he did to keep his mama happy crossed the line. I felt sorry for the girl who ended up marrying Burl.

"Okay, I'll pay your way," I snapped. "But you can't tell nobody." Paying a boy to spend time with me was a level of disgrace so low, I had a hard time believing my own words. As soon as Burl agreed to go to the movies with me, I forgot all about calling Desiree back.

That Saturday, I took my walk of shame to Burl's house right after lunch, reminding myself that Burl was really a nice boy to have for a friend. Besides, he could pass for seventeen, so I needed him to get me into the R-rated movie I wanted to see.

If things didn't work out between Chester and me, I'd still have Burl to fall back on.

CHAPTER 11

Belle Helene had only one movie theater and it was downtown across from the police station. But it had ten screens, so there was always something for everybody. It was always fun to go even though there were several scowling security guards roaming around trying to catch people sneaking into more than one movie without paying. Instead of taking a cab, Burl and I walked the seven blocks to get to the movies. We could have taken the bus, but it was a haven for the bullies Burl wanted to avoid.

As hard as it was for me to believe, Burl was the best-looking boy standing in line waiting to get into the movies. A few brazen girls flirted with him right in front of me. The Turner twins—the two boys who had been playing ball with Chester that day I hit him—rolled their eyes at Burl. They tried to push ahead of us in line, knowing Burl was not the kind of boy to fight. But once they realized he was with me, they backed off. Even kids I didn't know had heard about the time I hit Chester Sheffield, and over the months the story had spun out of control. It had become a legend that even I didn't recognize anymore. Somebody had told a version that included me attacking Chester with a switchblade!

Burl was so busy running back and forth to the snack bar—spending more of my money—he missed the first part of the movie. I couldn't believe that with all the bloodcurdling screams throughout the the-

ater, Burl slept through a deep movie like *Halloween II*. But once I got
close enough to him to smell his breath I knew why. Miss Mozelle
brought a lot of wine home from the country club where she worked.
More than once, I had sat in Burl's living room with him while he
lapped up wine by the jarful.

I glared at him leaning sideways in the seat next to me with his
meaty head on my shoulder. After the movie ended, I was tempted to
leave him sitting there in the dark. But a meddlesome usher turned a
flashlight on us and threatened to call the manager. It took me two
minutes of shaking Burl to wake him up. He was so groggy, we had to
take a cab back across town, which took another three dollars out of
my pocket.

Since I had lied to Mama that I was going to visit Desiree and eat
dinner with her and Dr. Lucienne, I couldn't go home right away
after Burl and I left the movies. I figured the cool air would help
sober Burl up. And because I didn't want to waste any more of my
money, I dragged him out of the cab after a few blocks and we walked
down Jersey Street.

Other than the movies and the mall, there were a lot of recreational activities available to us. I spent a lot of time swimming at the
Y with Regina. And Crazy Mimi's parents owned a video store in the
mini-mall two doors down from the store Chester's folks owned.
When Crazy Mimi was in the store, she sneaked X-rated videos to her
friends. Burl and I could have chosen any one of those places to go to
that afternoon. If we had, it would have made all the difference in the
world in both of our lives.

"Where you wanna go now?" Burl sounded bored, but I gave him
the benefit of the doubt, knowing he had been sipping wine earlier at
the movies. "You got some more money? Wanna go swimmin' at the
Y? Wanna go get some dirty movies from Crazy Mimi?"

I shook my head. "Let's go to the train yard over by the freeway," I
suggested, clutching my almost empty coin purse.

We had all been repeatedly warned to stay away from the train yard
after Georgie Fisher's arm got cut off when he tried to crawl under a
train three years ago. There were **DANGER** signs all over the train
yard in English and Spanish, but none of us paid any attention to
that. Because it was just two blocks from Second Baptist Church,
sometimes when we got bored during Reverend Poe's sermons, we
sneaked to the train yard. We'd hide in boxcars that often sat in the

same spot for weeks at a time without moving. I knew from Kitty that Chester hung out there with his friends smoking weed. The train station was several yards from where the boxcars sat littered with dingy blankets and used condoms somebody had left behind inside. But when the trains were in use, they traveled back and forth to Mississippi and other parts of Alabama.

A strange assortment of men, Black and white, worked at the train yard. When they were not busy chasing us and a few interstate-traveling hoboes away, they patrolled the grounds with sticks and walkie-talkies. Every now and then, a couple of the middle-aged men tried to lure young girls to secluded spots between the boxcars by waving dollar bills at us. More than once, Captain Hook, a scraggly white man with cold blue eyes and a hand with a missing thumb, tried to pay us a few dollars to feel on us. The only girl I knew who ever took him up on it was Crazy Mimi. In fact, when Crazy Mimi's last baby was born, with the same cold blue eyes and a missing thumb and light skin, we all knew that Captain Hook had gotten more than a feel from Crazy Mimi. Like with her other pregnancies, she told her parents she didn't know who made her pregnant. None of us ever told about the blue-eyed, one-thumb man at the train yard, because we didn't want to stop going there.

I didn't know if it was because Burl was clumsy or still drunk, but I had to help him climb up into the boxcar. It was the one at the end of a row of four rust-orange-colored boxcars. The same one that Desiree and I had hopped into the week before to smoke cigarettes. It had been an awful experience for me. The smoke and the taste of tobacco made me sneeze, itch, and vomit. That was the first and last time I ever put a cigarette between my lips.

As soon as Burl and I got situated on the dusty floor of the boxcar, Burl whipped out a Pepsi bottle from his inside jacket pocket, bit off the top with his thick teeth, and took a huge sip. Then he handed the bottle to me. As soon as I realized it was wine, I handed it back to him. He promptly finished it in one gulp and let out a belch that was so tremendous, his eyes rolled back in his head.

I don't know what made me mad the most: Burl acting like he was bored with my company, or him falling asleep on me *again*. But whatever it was, it was enough for me to tie his shoestrings together and leave him lying there on the boxcar floor, folded up in a knotty ball, clicking his teeth in his sleep. I leaped to the ground and with a lot of effort, I shut the heavy door to the boxcar. I stumbled like I was drunk, too, but I was able to steady myself long enough to keep from falling on the rails and knocking something inside me loose.

On the side of a set of tracks connected to the ones where the box-car was that Burl was in was a metal turnstile. I had seen the men who worked on the railroad turn it when they wanted a train to go in a different direction. I knew that the boxcar that Burl was in had been sitting in the same spot for weeks, but I twisted and wrestled with the turnstile until it shifted.

I left the train yard running and laughing, trying to imagine the look on Burl's face when he woke up in Mississippi.

CHAPTER 12

I wasn't ready to go home after I left Burl in the boxcar. I didn't feel like going to the projects to visit Regina. Crazy Mimi was in Mobile visiting her grandmother. So the only close friend I had left was Desiree, but I didn't have the nerve to go to her house. I didn't want to face her too soon after choosing to spend the afternoon with Burl instead of her.

It was getting late. The gloomy sky looked like a cheap gray blanket. I eased my way across the train tracks, kicking up sand and rocks with my new Nikes. Ten minutes later, wending my way toward downtown, I ended up on Main Street admiring all the Halloween displays in the store windows. I stopped in front of Sheffield's Market, located between a bakery and a shoe shop. I guess if I had not seen Chester through the window, working behind the counter, I wouldn't have gone in. The air in the congested little store was full of spicy smells from the meat counter in a corner. The Darth Vader costume Kitty had told me Chester was going to wear to her party was hanging on the wall next to a calendar from Sibley's Funeral Home.

There was a bell dangling from a string at the top of the door. Every time the door opened, the bell rang. As soon as I entered, Chester looked from behind the cash register, where he was checking out a customer. He blinked at me first, and then to my surprise he smiled. It had been so long since he had looked at me without scowling. I had to get as much mileage out of his unexpected smile as possible.

As luck would have it, the customer he was finishing up with had to start up a long-winded conversation about every mundane thing in the world: the upcoming church dinner, Chester's parents' health, how much higher the Sheffields charged for certain items compared to Piggy Wiggly, and on and on. Over the customer's shoulder, Chester gave me a conspiratorial look of exasperation. That was another good sign that I was getting closer to reeling him in. If drunken Burl had staggered into the store throwing up and naked at that very moment, I wouldn't have even noticed him.

In addition to the fully stocked meat counter and a wine rack, the neatly arranged store also sold the usual "mom and pop" items: everything from Dentu-grip to enema bags, and all the latest magazines. I stood at the magazine rack for fifteen minutes, leafing through comic books, waiting for that motormouth customer to leave so Chester could devote his attention to me. I wanted to invite him to my fourteenth birthday party even though it was *five* months away. I prayed that no other customers would come in. My prayer was answered, because no other customers came in, but Chester's mean daddy did. Willie Sheffield, a tall, red-skinned hatchet-faced man with wiry gray hair, came out of nowhere and marched up to me and glared at me like I had stole something. Then he started fussing.

"Gal, every time you come in here you make a mess of them magazines and you don't never buy nary one of 'em." At this point Mr. Willie reared back on his legs and placed his long hands on his hips before he finished me off. "I want you to straighten up them magazines just like you found 'em and then get your tail up out of here, girl! You ain't got no business roamin' up and down the street by yourself no-how with all them randy boys on the loose just waitin' to take advantage of you. You want one of them sodomites to snatch you into a alley and take advantage of you?" He waved Chester to a back room while I straightened up the magazines. I couldn't get out of the store fast enough after that. But Chester had shown me a positive sign by smiling at me, and that had made my stop worthwhile.

Patterson Street intersected Heggy Street where I lived. As soon as I turned the corner, with less than a block left to go to my house, I stopped in my tracks. In the cul-de-sac in front of Burl's house were two police cars. Before I could absorb that, a policewoman led Miss

Mozelle by the arm out of her house. I sprinted down the sidewalk just as a crowd of neighbors started gathering outside in front of Miss Mozelle's house. Miss Mozelle, wearing her familiar brown flannel bathrobe buttoned up to her neck, was crying and waving her arms as the policewoman wrestled her big body into the back of the police car. Now, I knew that Miss Mozelle was a strange woman, but she was a good woman. I could not imagine her doing anything that would get her arrested. The plump retired airline pilot who lived next door to us was standing alone away from the crowd. I stopped next to him.

"Mr. Royster, what did Miss Mozelle do?" I asked, trying to catch my breath.

The ex-pilot gave me a dry look and sucked on his teeth before answering. Then, with a tortured look he told me, "She didn't do nothin'. It's her boy, Burl. That fool was foolin' around on one of them boxcars and fell off when it started movin'. I hope the boy didn't suffer none."

In less than a minute, my whole life flashed right before my eyes like it happens to people about to die. It seemed appropriate for me now. Because the life I had known up to this point was over.

CHAPTER 13

Even though I clearly saw events that had already occurred in my life flash right before my eyes that evening on the sidewalk in front of Miss Mozelle's house, I don't remember much of what else was actually taking place. One minute I was standing there, the next minute I was in my kitchen at the dinner table listening to bits and pieces of an emotional conversation taking place between my parents and my sister.

"I knew something like this was going to happen sooner or later. That's why I've been telling you two to stay away from that train yard for years," Mama said, shaking a fork at me but looking at my sister. "And I'll never forget how that Fisher boy got his arm sliced off when he tried to crawl under that train a few years ago." Mama stopped shaking the fork and stared off into space for a moment with tears in her eyes. It was hard to believe that while Mama spent so much time making other people's hair look so nice, she practically ignored her own. Limp, dry graying curls dangled down the front and sides of her face. A large, clumsy hairpin held a lopsided bun at the nape of her neck in place. "Poor Mozelle. She lives and breathes for Burl." Mama sighed heavily and shook her head as she speared a large piece of fried liver off a platter in the center of our dinner table.

"Is Burl dead? Was he dead when they found him?" I asked. I had not touched much of the food on my plate. It was just as well. A lump had formed in my throat that was so big I wouldn't have been able to swallow anything anyway.

"Naw, he ain't dead," Daddy said with his mouth full of food. "But I bet he wish he was."

"I heard Reverend Poe say they found an empty pop bottle with Burl but he smelled like a winery," Babette added. Keeping her weight down was one of her biggest concerns, but you would not have been able to tell that by the way she was gobbling up liver and cornbread. She released a muffled but powerful belch that forced her to lift herself a few inches off of her seat and back down.

"Carmen, I want you to help Babette clean up the kitchen after dinner. I'd better get over to the hospital where they took Mozelle." Mama paused and turned to Daddy. "Charles, finish up and go crank up the car."

The next few hours were a nightmare for me. While I was drying the dishes, I peed on myself. Babette was too busy talking on the telephone in the kitchen to notice the puddle forming on the floor around my feet. I was in such a serious daze, I didn't even know who she was talking to. While her back was turned, I snatched a huge sponge out of the kitchen closet and mopped up my mess. As soon as I finished doing that, Babette hung up the telephone and turned to me. "That was Mama calling from the hospital."

"Is Burl going to be all right?" I asked anxiously.

"It doesn't look like it," Babette said grimly. Then she narrowed her eyes and tilted her head and added angrily, "It's his own fault! That stupid shit! He shouldn't have been out there messing around in that boxcar in the first place drinking wine! Now none of us will be able to hang out at the train yard again. Shoot!"

After my sister's outburst, I calmly asked, "Did Burl tell anybody what really happened?" My voice was so weak and low I could barely hear myself.

"Oh, he's dog meat." Babette paused and a puzzled look appeared on her face. She looked at me and scratched the side of her neck. "And just where were you all afternoon? Burl rarely leaves his house unless he's with you. Mama thought you went to Desiree's house, but that Desiree called here for you three times this afternoon—with her crybaby self!"

I felt trapped. I knew I couldn't continue the lie about visiting Desiree, and I certainly could not tell my sister the truth.

"Uh . . . when I got to Desiree's house, I heard her daddy inside fussing at her about something. You know how mean he is. Last time I was there when he whupped Desiree, he was so blind drunk he accidentally cracked *me* with his belt a few times," I said hotly, holding up my arm to show a faint scar.

"That fat old fart needs to pick on somebody his own size," Babette growled, inspecting my arm.

"Anyway, I was too scared to knock, so I went to the movies," I added, glad that at least part of my story was true. But my goose was cooked anyway. Burl was in the hospital, maybe even dying, because of me.

CHAPTER 14

I figured the safest place for me to be was anywhere out of sight. I spent the next two hours in the gloom of my bedroom, on my back on my bed, wallowing in my own sweat and tears. With the lights out, at that. That way, nobody could see the guilt written all over my face. Not knowing the exact status of Burl's condition was unbearable. At that point, I didn't know if he was going to live or die. I didn't know if he would remember what happened in the train yard or not. What I did know was, if Burl blabbed on me my life would be over at thirteen. There was a fourteen-year-old boy from our church who was in jail for life. During a visit to Huntsville this boy had shot and killed an elderly woman he had tried to rob. Against the protests of a lot of Black folks, my parents included, they had tried the boy as an adult. As much as I liked Burl and wanted him to be all right, I could not help myself from thinking about how much easier my life would be if he died and took my secret to the grave with him.

I don't know exactly how long I stayed in my room with the same thoughts and fears dancing around in my mind. In addition to Burl, I started thinking about what had happened to Regina's brothers and sisters and how they would not have been left alone if Miss Maggie had not come looking for Regina and me. But at least in Regina's case, I wasn't the only one responsible. I remembered that night well. More than once I had advised Regina to go home or at least call her

mama to let her know where she was. I found out later that the fire
had swept through the apartment so fast, if Regina and her mother
had been home, they would have died, too. In a bizarre way, I had
saved Regina's and Miss Maggie's lives. Realizing this, I turned the
light in my room back on and everything seemed brighter.

Mama and Daddy had returned from the hospital and were sitting
at the table in the kitchen with faces as long and sour as pallbearers.
Babette was dragging herself around in the kitchen making coffee
and conversation. Mama had had a large pizza delivered, but nobody
had touched it.

"I heard Miss Mozelle's brother in Detroit has already started calling lawyers," Babette announced. "He could at least wait long enough
to see if the boy is going to live or die. And if that's not scandalous
enough, I heard Reverend Poe called up the funeral director and told
him to stand by."

"Is Burl going to die?" I asked, pulling out a chair.

"We don't know yet," Mama sniffed. Her whole face was red from
all the crying she had done for Burl and Miss Mozelle. Being light-
skinned had its disadvantages. With my dark skin, and a few drops of
Visine in my eyes to get the red out, nobody could tell that I had been
crying, too.

"Did Burl say what happened?" Babette asked the question that I
had planned to ask next.

Mama looked at Daddy. "Charles, what was that the police told
you?" she asked.

Daddy took a deep breath first and sat up straight in his chair.
Daddy shaved every morning. It was late at night by now, and bristles
had started sprouting on his chin. He scratched his face with dry, ashy
fingers attached to brown nails threatening to turn into claws.
Looking at me he announced, "The boy was drinkin' wine and passed
out. When that train started movin', he woke up and tried to jump
off."

"What else did the police say?" I asked, rubbing my nose.

"Unless Burl pulls through, that's all we'll ever know," Daddy told
me, caressing the side of my face. My skin already felt like it was on
fire, so I could barely feel his rough fingers. Daddy let out a sigh,
glanced at Babette, and then to Mama. "Lizette, ain't we blessed to
have two young'ns that know how to mind?"

I didn't know how Babette was reacting, because my eyes were on my hands. I was wondering how something as simple as me tying Burl's shoelaces together could have caused so much trouble.

"Carmen, don't you worry. And be strong, child. You're Burl's best friend. If he pulls through, he's going to need you more than ever," Mama told me.

That night I had more nightmares than all the other nights put together.

CHAPTER 15

Burl remained in the hospital in a coma for a week. And during this week, almost all of the rest of Miss Mozelle's hair fell out. She couldn't eat or sleep. There were a lot of people who thought she needed to be in the hospital right alongside Burl.

I felt just as sorry for her as I felt for Burl. I had no idea how important the boy was to Miss Mozelle until now. Her older brother Mogen, the white people who owned the country club where Miss Mozelle cooked, and just about everybody we knew from church and our neighborhood came to visit her at her house.

Miss Mozelle was so overwhelmed with grief, she couldn't even bathe or feed herself and certainly could not go to work. Her boss firmly and repeatedly announced that she could take off as much time as she needed with pay.

The neighborhood women, three at a time, took turns lifting Miss Mozelle's large, clumsy body in and out of the bathtub. Mr. Mogen, her mean brother from Detroit that I had heard so many horror stories about from Burl, wrapped himself in one of Miss Mozelle's bib aprons and did most of the cooking. We young people, even Chester, ran errands for Miss Mozelle, like running to the store, doing the laundry, and taking out the trash. My daddy offered to do Miss Mozelle's banking, but her brother made it clear that he didn't want anybody's hands but his touching his sister's money. Mr. Mogen's interest in money explained why he had done research on lawyers in Belle Helene by telephone all the way from Detroit the day after Burl's accident.

Reverend Poe, the spry little gray-haired preacher I dreaded listening to every Sunday in church, came over every night to pray for Miss Mozelle. He also went to the hospital to pray for Burl. Mama did more than anybody did. She helped take care of Miss Mozelle's house and her female needs like changing her bras and her panties. I was amazed at how brave Mama was. The first morning she went to change Miss Mozelle's underwear, I went with her. While Mama wrestled with Miss Mozelle's naked, blunt body, I stood behind Mama, staring in horror. From her neck down to her wide, flat feet, Miss Mozelle's skin was so dry and ashy, it puckered like scales on a carp. Even though she was naked, I could not locate her lower female parts. A flap of loose skin covered the valley between her huge, spongy thighs like a fig leaf.

Miss Mozelle was in no shape to keep her weekly appointment with Mama to get her hair done. Knowing how important it was to Miss Mozelle, Mama went over once a week to do the few tufts of brittle hair she had left. But still trying to hide the bald spots was a waste of time. By now, Miss Mozelle's head looked like a dried-out coconut that somebody had peeled and left out in the sun too long. It took Mama twice as long to style her hair in a way that made it look presentable. Other than myself, I don't think any of the people occupying Miss Mozelle's living room noticed how unbearably sad she looked from head to toe until Babette opened her mouth.

"Miss Mozelle, they have some real nice wigs at the Mitchell Sisters' Beauty Shop on Liberty Street," Babette said in a shaky voice. "That's where Mama gets that human hair she braids with." My sister occupied a large orange hassock on the floor facing the sofa where Miss Mozelle had been placed. Her head had been propped up on three large pillows. From the angle she was in, her eyes staring off into space, her face looked lopsided. I couldn't believe that I was the cause of all of this sweet lady's pain. I felt like I didn't deserve to be in the same room with her, but I was glad I was. Her pain was my pain and I deserved every bit of it.

Out of respect for the preacher in the house, everybody got silent when Reverend Poe cleared his throat and snorted to get everybody's attention. We all turned to him standing in front of the living room window, hugging a huge Bible, a stern look on his face. "Since when did a head of hair serve a spiritual purpose?" he began in the same thunderous tone he used when he delivered his sermons. "Especially a head of hair borrowed from somebody else." Reverend Poe, still handsome at seventy-two, was the most respected Black preacher I knew of. If he had some of the same bad habits as some of the other preachers I knew, like living a lavish double life on the church's money and keeping a woman on the side, at least he was slick enough not to get caught. It was easy to see why "borrowed" hair didn't impress Reverend Poe. He still had all of his. And it framed his square-jawed face like a curly halo.

"At least she'd look better," Babette said impatiently. "And if I were you, Miss Mozelle, I'd pick out the most expensive hair in the store and send the bill to that railroad company."

Reverend Poe narrowed his shiny black eyes and glared at Babette, who didn't know enough to shut her mouth before she said the wrong thing. Even though she was fifteen, Daddy had assured us both that no matter how old we got, we would never be too old to get a whupping. "Shaddup! And get in that kitchen yonder and grab a broom or a dishrag," Reverend Poe hollered at Babette, slapping his Bible against the side of his crooked hip. He scanned the room with a menacing scowl on his face, looking from one young person to another, growling, "Just a generation of vipers!" I bowed my head when he aimed his attention at me. "Carmen, you one of the few young'ns I know that still got good sense. Continue to be a credit to your generation, girl."

I looked up so fast the bones in my neck made a popping sound. Mama and Daddy beamed proudly; Babette let out an exasperated sigh and folded her arms. Sweeping Miss Mozelle's kitchen was the furthest thing from her mind.

In a dim corner stood Mr. Mogen, Miss Mozelle's dreaded brother from Detroit. I didn't know until he floated to the middle of the floor that his huge body had been blocking the view of two other kids. Wearing a cheap blue serge suit, he was just as lumpy and squat as Miss Mozelle. He even had the same hairy moles on his butterscotch-colored face. They looked enough alike to be twins. However, the same features on a man didn't look as gruesome as they did on a woman.

Mr. Mogen had moved to Detroit from Montgomery, Alabama,

when he returned from the army, taking Miss Mozelle with him so he could "keep a eye on her." Like Chester did with Kitty. I was glad I never had a big brother. Meddling seemed so common with them. Mr. Mogen had worked for Ford Motors until a runaway car mowed him down. According to Miss Mozelle, the car had sustained more damage than her brother had, but Mr. Mogen had filed a lawsuit anyway. He'd used his out-of-court settlement to open a dry-cleaning store. He supported an ex-wife and three lazy adult sons. He lived a comfortable life, but he was still not satisfied and wanted even more. Even I knew about the lawsuit against the railroad company he was cooking up, because everybody was talking about it. He had arrived in town three days after Burl's accident and had already met with three different lawyers. He sniffed and gave Babette a look that would have been interpreted as a pass coming from any other man. Then he announced in a booming voice, "Babette, baby girl, by the time I get through with that railroad outfit, they'll be eligible for welfare."

CHAPTER 16

I could not wait for the evening to end so I could get out of Miss Mozelle's gloomy house. It was one of the longest days of my life. I glanced at my watch and groaned. I had been in this miserable place for two hours. Up to that moment, I had not paid too much attention to Chester sitting on the arm of the couch with his long legs crossed and his shirt unbuttoned at the top. Just seeing the silky black wisps of hair on his chest and the muscles across his breastbone made my heart skip a beat. His sister, Kitty, was sitting on the floor at his feet, her face burning with anger and impatience as she observed the activities and conversations in the room. Mr. and Mrs. Sheffield had visited earlier but had already returned to their house and turned in for the night.

"Crazy Legs," Chester said.

My head snapped around to look at him so fast, my neck cracked like a whip. "Huh?" It seemed like Chester had everybody else's attention, too.

"I know you and Kitty hang out in that train yard a lot. I seen y'all crawlin' around over there. But if I find out Kitty's been back over there, after what happened to Burl, I'm goin' to beat her brains out," Chester snarled. All of the grown people nodded and hummed their approval. Even though Kitty's parents were oblivious to Kitty's behavior, Chester stayed on her case. And according to a rumor that

Desiree had shared with me, her own daddy had performed an abortion on Kitty a month ago. Chester had escorted Kitty to Dr. Lucienne's office himself. Chester paused and turned his head to the side and looked at me out of the corner of his eyes as he continued in an even louder voice. "Y'all might not be as lucky as Burl was." He shook his finger at Kitty, who was clearly horrified. Then he turned to me again and looked at me with intense eyes that, in the shadows of the dim lamp in Miss Mozelle's living room, resembled the eyes of a cat.

"You ain't nobody's daddy," Kitty muttered, glaring at her brother. "And you got some nerve tryin' to tell Carmen what to do!"

"And she better listen to him!" My daddy said, nodding at Chester. I figured the best thing for me to do was to keep quiet and look at the floor. Everybody knew how crazy Chester was about his sister. Naturally, he didn't want anything bad to happen to her. Apparently, he felt the same way about me. A warm feeling came over me and the first chance I got, even though Chester didn't see it, I smiled at him.

My other close friends, Crazy Mimi and Regina, stood next to each other off to the side of the door leading into the kitchen. One thing I was happy about was the fact that neither Crazy Mimi nor Kitty showed any jealously toward my newly formed relationship with Desiree Lucienne. Desiree had squeezed into a spot on a red velvet settee across the room between her daddy and Nurse Bertha. Crazy Mimi was too busy being crazy to be jealous of my friendship with Desiree. She was now writing steamy letters to love-starved men in prison. But every time I said something to Desiree, Regina let out a disgusted sigh and rolled her eyes.

Each time the front door opened, Kitty's head swiveled around so fast to see who was coming in the house, her braids slapped against her brother's legs. I was the only one in the room who knew she had planned a rendezvous with Buzzy Hawkins, her latest boyfriend.

Right after Daddy stopped talking, the door opened again and in strode Buzzy, frog-eyed and cone-headed ugly, but one of the most popular boys in town. That Buzzy. When it came to girls, he got around like a record. Even I found him strangely appealing. I guess it was the fact that he thought he was such a prize. His cockiness made a lot of girls curious. Especially Kitty. I didn't know what special talents Buzzy had, but whenever he came around, Kitty drooled like a puppy. Nobody but me noticed how fast Kitty got up from the floor and started smoothing down the sides of her short pink skirt and then squirting lotion in the palms of her hands to shine up her ashy legs. Since the room was so crowded, nobody but me saw Kitty lead Buzzy into the kitchen by the hand. With her other hand, she beckoned me to follow.

Nobody noticed when I slid through the crowd into the kitchen. Dressed in black leather from head to toe, Buzzy had stopped in the middle of the floor with Kitty already clinging to his arm and looking at him like he was something good to eat. She pulled me close enough for her to whisper toward the side of my face, "I need a favor from you."

When I didn't respond right away, she placed a hand on my shoulder and glanced to the side at Buzzy. Buzzy Hawkins's real name was Marion but only grown folks called him that. His friends knew better than to call him by what he considered a sissified name. I used to think that Buzzy's looks proved that Mother Nature had a sense of humor. His head was so long he couldn't even wear a cap like the rest of the boys I knew. Even Burl, with his globe of a head, could wear a cap. But at the same time, nature was nice enough to let Buzzy be tall and have a nice body. From the neck down he looked as good as Chester. And Buzzy had the smoothest bronze-toned skin I'd ever seen. It more than made up for his looks.

"What do you want me to do?" I asked Kitty, not taking my eyes off Buzzy. Even with Kitty standing right next to him, his eyes were all over me, too.

"I can't deal with all that weepin' and wailin' in Miss Mozelle's livin' room. These people are fools, actin' like somebody died! Me and Buzzy goin' out for a little while," Kitty panted. "I'm goin' crazy up in here."

Puzzled, I looked from Buzzy to Kitty. "So? What's that got to do with me?" I asked.

"If anybody ask, you say Kitty was with you," Buzzy said in a voice that was still squeaky at seventeen.

"Huh? But I'll be in there with everybody else and Miss Mozelle," I reminded him, nodding toward the living room.

Kitty shook her head, then told me in a conspiratorial whisper, "No, you won't. I need you to do me a favor."

"Not with my mama and my daddy sitting in there," I wailed, hold-

ing up my hand. I shook my head, which, by the way, had been ringing like a bell from the minute I walked into Miss Mozelle's house.

Kitty sighed in exasperation. "You go on home and hide out in
your room, see. Me and Buzzy will leave out the front door with you.
After you get home, don't leave your room until you hear from me."
Kitty exhaled and stuck out her chest. That Kitty. She had stuffed
fresh wads of toilet paper in her bra that morning and it had slid to
the middle of her chest. It looked like she had one big tittie. She saw
me looking at her bosom, so she reached under her sweater and re-
arranged herself, ignoring Buzzy's crude muffled remarks and laughter. She continued talking to me in a slow, serious manner. "That pop
bottle crate still on the ground under your window? I'll hop on it and
tap on your window after me and Buzzy . . . uh . . . you know." Kitty
paused and winked at me, thick balls of black mascara rolling around
inside the corners of her eyes. Then a serious look appeared on her
anxious face and she looked at me like she was seeing me for the first
time. "I know that Desiree Lucienne goin' around tellin' folks she is
your new best friend, but I ain't worried. I know you still got my back,
ain't you?"

I nodded. "Yep."

Kitty looked over my shoulder toward the living room; then she
looked in my eyes. For a moment, she seemed unbearably sad, and
that didn't make any sense to me. She was with her man and they
were about to go off and have a good time. Then she smiled and told
me, "I love you, girl. Don't you never ever forget that."

I looked at Buzzy. He looked just as confused as I did over Kitty's
last comment. His eyes darted from Kitty to me and then he shrugged.
He didn't even try to hide his impatience. He kept letting out his
breath and shifting his weight from one foot to the other. I refused to
look in Buzzy's eyes as I wondered what Kitty would say or do if she
knew about all the times he had called me up begging me to meet
him behind a deserted building or in the bushes behind his house. I
didn't want to know what Kitty would say. All I wanted was for my girl
to be happy.

"I love you, too, Kitty. Y'all go on and have a good time. You know
you can count on me to cover for you," I said humbly.

Kitty was in front as the three of us made our way back to the living
room. I was behind her. Buzzy was behind me, purposely breathing

on the back of my neck and making sucking noises. That Buzzy. With
Kitty less than a few feet away, he reached out and pinched me on the
butt so hard I stumbled the rest of the way. The world belonged to
boys like Buzzy and Chester. They made up the rules as they went
along when it came to girls. Too wrapped up in their own lame
schemes, they didn't know that girls schemed just as much as they
did. I never expected mine to backfire in such a profound way.

As soon as we reached the living room, I announced that Kitty,
Buzzy, and I were going to my house and that Kitty was going to spend
the night. "And Buzzy's going to go get Kitty and me some chicken," I
lied. An undercurrent of tension throbbed through the crowded
room. Desiree gave me a blank look, then lowered her head. Nurse
Bertha's eyes furrowed. At the time, nobody but me knew that Kitty
was the one fooling around with Buzzy. Chester must have thought
that I was the one Buzzy had his hooks in, because he shot Buzzy and
me one of his dirtiest looks. Then Chester looked at me and gave me
a weak smile. It didn't even faze me. My twisted logic had me convinced that Chester was just as guilty about Burl's accident as I was.
Chester was the reason I had started hanging out so much with Burl
in the first place.

"My goofy brother couldn't take his bug eyes off you," Kitty teased
as she and I and Buzzy walked off of Miss Mozelle's front porch. "Girl,
Chester crazy about you."

Chewing on a toothpick, Buzzy snorted and glared at me. Then, in
his Mickey Mouse voice he announced with a shriek that pierced the
air, "I doubt that! The only dark meat Chester like is on a turkey leg!
He like his women high-yellow mellow." Buzzy added with a wet-
lipped smirk, "Chester don't mess around with no dark-skinned girls!
Shit."

I flashed Buzzy a severe look of exasperation and increased the
speed of my steps. I walked a cautious distance ahead of him and Kitty
until we reached my front porch.

Sucking on a thick joint and drinking a can of beer, Buzzy waited
for Kitty outside my bedroom window. He was sitting on that empty
pop crate Kitty and I had placed on the ground a few weeks ago.
Every time I peeped out to make sure he was still there, he blew me a
kiss, and once he even told me, "You next."

Kitty took a quick shower and slid into one of my best dresses. I
wouldn't let her mess with Mama's Chanel No. 5 perfume, so she

sprayed her crotch with vanilla extract she found in the kitchen. She didn't want to borrow a pair of my panties and told me, "That'd be just one more thing for me to take off." Since Buzzy already knew what was in her bra, she didn't bother with the toilet-paper titties. By the time she was ready to go, she was so anxious she didn't even slide out of the window like a real lady was supposed to. She literally jumped out and landed in Buzzy's arms. They took off running and giggling.

I was glad Kitty was gone. I needed to be alone to think about what Buzzy had told me about Chester's preference for light-skinned girls. I was not proud of the fact that I was still thinking about my own needs so soon after Burl's accident. But I needed something to get my mind off of Burl even for just a moment. If what Buzzy said was true, no matter what I did with Burl, I would never be Chester Sheffield's girlfriend. Not because of the fight we had had, not because he flat-out didn't like me, but because my skin was too dark. I had known Chester all of my life and I had seen him with a lot of girls. I had not given it any thought until Buzzy's comment, but I had never seen Chester with a girl darker than a pecan.

For the first time in my life, even though people commented all the time about how pretty I was, I felt like I had just arrived on Earth from the Planet of the Apes.

This was as good a time as any for me to put my feelings for Chester on hold. I had not given him much thought since I had heard about Burl's accident anyway. Right now my main concern was Burl and what would become of him. And what would become of me.

If Burl died, I knew that I would never be able to forgive myself. And it would be a shame if I had to carry the burden of guilt all by myself. But no matter how I looked at it, I knew that was exactly what was going to happen.

CHAPTER 17

Helping Kitty jump out of my bedroom window was a lot easier than helping her climb back in. Especially when she was high from smoking weed or drunk from drinking whatever it was her boyfriends poured into her. Even with Buzzy hoisting her up on his broad shoulders and then pushing her chunkified butt, it was a struggle trying to get Kitty back into my bedroom from outside in the middle of the night. Her babbling gibberish, passing gas, belching, and twisting her body like Rubber Woman made it just that much harder.

It was late October, so the night air was cool. But both Kitty's and Buzzy's faces were covered in sweat. My cotton nightgown, one side hanging off my shoulder, felt as thin as tissue paper. I was sweating like a pig myself.

I had heard that people weighed more dead than when they were alive. The same must be true of drunken people. Kitty felt like she weighed a ton. Both of my arms felt like they were about to fall off. That was bad enough, so the last thing I needed was an audience. Especially with me standing in my window with my newly forming bosom half exposed.

"Shit! Ain't that that old pilot man?" Buzzy hissed, glancing over his shoulder toward the house next door.

"Oh, God; oh, God—it is Mr. Royster," I stammered. "What in the world is an old man like him doing out this time of night?" I snapped as I continued to grip Kitty by her shoulders. Kitty had jumped out of the window around eight P.M., promising me that she would be back from her "date" with Buzzy within an hour.

It was now midnight. My family had returned from Miss Mozelle's house around nine. I had convinced them that Kitty and I were so distraught over Burl's accident that we just wanted to stay in my room and pray for him in private.

Under the light provided by the moon and the streetlights, I saw a shiny blue Camaro crawl like a worm into the driveway next door. A young blond woman wearing a cowboy hat was driving. To my surprise, the normally sedate retired pilot who lived next door sat in the passenger's seat, grinning in the woman's face. His arm was around her shoulder. I'd known the ex-pilot all of my life. I had never seen him with a woman until now. The only female I had ever seen him hug was his old cat, Lucille. The way he was looking at the blonde, I believed that if it had been broad daylight, my neighbor would not even have noticed us. I was wrong. Right after the woman pecked him on his bloated jaw, he looked over her shoulder in my direction. For a moment, our eyes locked. Even in the night light, I could see a look on his face that combined surprise, suspicion, and amusement.

I lost my grip on Kitty, and she and Buzzy went tumbling to the ground, flattening the pop bottle crate that had served as a ladder. Buzzy and Kitty, giggling like fools, wallowed on the damp ground for a few moments. I dropped to my bedroom floor below my window and cloaked my face with the hem of the curtain. We all stayed in our positions until we heard the Camaro leave and the ex-pilot's front door slam. After that, all we could hear was the low whistle of the warm, gentle wind that was so common at night in Alabama this time of year.

Just as I popped back up from the floor and put my face in the window, Buzzy jumped up from the ground. His long legs straddled Kitty as she lay on the ground like a rug. "Aw, shit!" Buzzy whispered anxiously. "I just seen a light go on upstairs!" he informed me, motioning with his head toward the bedroom above mine.

"It's Babette!" I hissed.

The lone downstairs bedroom on the side of our house had belonged to Babette up until she turned nine. One night right after she had turned in, a huge bat flapped in the window and squatted on the pillow right next to her head. That was the last night Babette slept in the room.

I had just turned seven at the time of the bat's visit. And being the tomboy that I was then, to me a bat in my room would have been a feather in my cap. I had envied all of the attention that Chester and some of the other neighborhood boys received when they showed off the butterflies, crickets, and grasshoppers that they had captured and imprisoned in jars. However, with the exception of a few armies of flies and gnats levitating over apple cores and banana peelings that I had left on my nightstand, no interesting creatures had visited the bedroom since. As soon as Babette entered her teens and discovered boys, she decided that the downstairs bedroom had a unique advantage: a side window. It was low enough to the ground that even a clumsy ox like Babette would have no trouble climbing in and out in a critical situation involving a boy or anything else that required desperate measures. But I had refused to give up the bedroom she now coveted. I knew that it was just a matter of time before I'd get some practical use out of it myself. Ironically, Kitty was the only one who had benefited so far.

There were several blabbermouths in my life. Regina and Crazy Mimi were at the top of the list. Regina liked to stay up in other people's business, then spread it around simply because it was a recreational outlet for her. As far as Crazy Mimi, well, anybody who was still fool enough to tell their business to her deserved to be exposed. She was known for flagging down strangers on the street to share with them something she had promised to keep a secret. Running close behind these two with her big-mouthed self was my sister, Babette. I knew that if she ratted on me for helping Kitty use the window, I'd not only get my head mauled by Daddy, but I'd be forced to switch bedrooms with Babette.

"Buzzy, get this girl out of here before Babette comes downstairs. I'll click my light off and on twice to let you know when the coast is clear," I whispered. I winced as Buzzy slapped Kitty's face a few times so hard, she sobered up enough to open her eyes and start looking around. "Go on, now. Go drive around for a while or something," I ordered. I watched as Buzzy crouched low and disappeared toward the back of our house, pulling Kitty by the arm. Not less than a minute later, Babette steamrolled into my room. I had not had a chance to close the window and return to my bed.

"What are you doing?" Babette asked. She kicked the door to my room shut and folded her arms, looking at me out of the corner of her eye. Even with the slimy face cream she had slathered all over her face, I could see that her eyes were red and rimmed with dark circles from all the crying she had done at Miss Mozelle's house over Burl's tragedy. Knowing that she had cried more than I had—and she was not nearly as close to Burl as I was—was just one more thing for me to feel guilty about.

"Nothing!" I stammered, moving toward my bed. "I couldn't sleep."

Babette glanced around my room, resting her eyes on my bed. "Where's Kitty?"

"Uh . . . she was depressed!" I croaked.

Babette lowered her head and gave me a dry look. "Excuse me?"

"She got real depressed after we left Miss Mozelle's house. Burl's accident upset her," I said weakly.

Babette's eyes rolled from side to side a few times before she returned her attention to me. By now I was back in my bed with the sheets pulled up to my chin.

"Is that why she's with Buzzy Hawkins?" Babette asked, her hands on her hips, her eyes on the open window. "I saw them from my room tipping across the lawn a little while ago."

I gasped. I was so close to the edge of my bed that when I shuddered, I almost rolled to the floor. I coughed and cleared my throat for about half a minute, hoping to buy myself enough time to come up with a plausible explanation. "Buzzy was depressed, too."

"Where did they go?" Babette paused, narrowed her eyes, and looked toward my closet, then quickly back to me.

"I think they went to that all-night mini-mart to get some aspirin."

Babette cocked her head to the side. Before she could say another word, we heard a crash that was so tremendous, the light in my room flickered off. Babette and I got to the window at the same time. There was not much to see from the side of the house, so we ran to the living room. Before we could make it to the front window, Mama and Daddy bolted from their bedroom upstairs and flew downstairs into the living room with their nightclothes flapping. Within seconds, all four of us were outside on our front porch. The ex-pilot and a small crowd of other horrified, barefoot neighbors in their nightclothes had come out onto their porches and lawns.

Buzzy had crashed the front of his old car into the largest of the oak trees in front of our house. He was frantically sliding on his side out of the driver's window. He half staggered, half crawled into the plump arms of the ex-pilot standing on the sidewalk. There was so much blood on Buzzy's face, I couldn't tell what direction it was coming from. When he stretched open his mouth to scream, he had red teeth. Within seconds the car was in flames. It lit up the night like a giant torch.

Somebody yelled, "Kitty is still in that car!"

I screamed so hard, it felt like my insides were trying to come out through my mouth. I ran behind Daddy out to the sidewalk. We arrived in time to see Kitty's terrified face pressed against the window on the passenger's side. Kitty and I looked in one another's eyes for what I knew was the last time. I think she knew it, too. She pressed her lips together and bravely waved farewell to me as the flames licked the window, making her resemble the flickering jack-o-lantern on her front porch that I had helped her carve. Then she started screaming as she tried desperately to open the car door.

Just as I attempted to move closer to the burning car to help her, somebody grabbed my arm and tackled me to the hard ground. A split second later, the car exploded and became a raging inferno. The noise was indescribable, and the heat was so intense it melted a lawn chair near Mama's flowerbed. The impact of the explosion made me black out for a moment. Whoever it was who had pushed me to the ground was now on top of me.

Even after I opened my eyes, it took me a few seconds to realize it was Chester who had prevented me from reaching the car. Realizing that it was too late for me to help her, he had saved me from dying with her.

CHAPTER 18

When I returned to my room that night, a blouse that I had borrowed from Kitty mysteriously slid off a hanger on the back of my door by itself.

My window was still open and the wind was blowing the curtain in such an eerie way, I ran and didn't stop until I reached my sister's room. I sat up on the side of her bed until morning. I had prayed for something to happen that would take my mind off Burl's accident. I never expected something as profound as Kitty dying—and in such a horrific way.

Other than Regina's siblings, death was an intruder that had mercifully stayed out of my life. The cruel way it had just separated me from Kitty was unbearably painful. I could not begin to imagine my life without her. If she had simply run off with some guy to another state, like she had jokingly fantasized about doing a few times, I could have handled that. There would have always been a chance that I would see her again. But she was gone from my life forever, and I didn't know how I was going to deal with that.

Since the one funeral I had ever attended in my life had included six caskets, I felt that I had more than paid my dues in that area. Other than my family, the only other funeral I ever planned to attend was my own.

"Mama, do I have to go to Kitty's funeral?" I whined. Ironically,

Kitty's funeral had been scheduled to take place on Halloween, the same day she had planned to have her big party. I knew that I would never wear my African queen costume now. To make sure, I doused it with some kerosene I took from the garage and burned it in our back-yard and scattered the ashes in the wind.

I was crouched in a corner in the backseat, directly behind Mama in our station wagon, on the way home from the calling hours at the Sibley Funeral Home that Thursday, four days after Kitty's death. My face was shiny with sweat and tears. My nose stung and ached from me blowing and rubbing it throughout the wake. Somebody had pressed a rose-scented handkerchief into my hand. It was still balled up in my fist.

Before Mama could respond, my sister gave me a surprised look from the corner opposite me. "I thought Kitty was your best friend." A red-checked scarf covered Babette's hair. She had lost one of her hoop earrings. She looked like a pirate.

"Desiree Lucienne is my best friend," I said firmly. My lips had been so dry, I had borrowed a tube of Babette's lip gloss. But during the wake, I had licked it all off. My lips were so dry again now, they cracked when I spoke. I didn't care what my hair looked like, but I had covered it with a black beret.

An overturned beer truck had caused a traffic jam on Third Street. Cars, trucks, vans, and bicycles were lined up like a thick snake for three blocks. At the corner of Third and Harrison Street, two blocks from our house, a frustrated policeman stood at the corner blowing a whistle and directing traffic. Directly in front of us was Dr. Lucienne's shiny blue Cadillac. Peeping over Mama's shoulder, I could see Desiree crouched into a corner of the front seat in the Cadillac. Every few moments Dr. Lucienne turned to Desiree. He was moving his lips in a way that convinced me Desiree was being chewed out about something and would no doubt receive a whupping when she got home. Sitting behind Desiree with her head neatly wrapped in a white scarf was Nurse Bertha.

Mama turned around to face me with red, swollen eyes. A flowered scarf was knotted around her head. She stared at me for an uncom-fortably long moment.

"Mama, do I have to go to Kitty's funeral?" I asked again, gripping the back of Mama's seat, my other hand resting on the hump between the seats.

Mama cleared her throat before responding. "I'm sure all of Kitty's other little friends will be there. How will it look to the Sheffields if you don't come? We especially need to show them some respect. They thought their daughter was safe with us that night and she wasn't," Mama croaked, rolling down her window. "Lord Jesus."

"Carmen, you ain't got to go if you don't want to," Daddy said over his shoulder. Our car had been sitting in the same spot for over five minutes. With a heavy sigh, Daddy turned to Mama. "Lizette, I know you don't want to be up all night with this girl like you was after them kids of Maggie's died." Mama ignored the comment about Regina's siblings dying in the fire, but I knew it was something she never stopped thinking about. I still had an occasional nightmare over that myself, and it was always Mama who ran downstairs to my room and sat up the rest of the night cradling me in her arms.

Mama's eyes were still on me. "You can wear that pretty blue suit your daddy's sister sent you for your birthday last year from Fort Lauderdale," she told me. "And what about poor Chester? Don't you care enough about him to show him some respect and sympathy? He worshipped that sister of his. How do you think he'll feel if you don't show up to honor Kitty? This'll be your last chance to be in her presence, you know." Mama finally turned back around, still addressing me. "If for no other reason, do it for poor Chester."

"All right," I muttered. I remained silent the rest of the way home.

For the rest of the ride, Mama kept repeating how our family owed the Sheffield family so much respect because they had expected Kitty to be safe with us. I didn't tell anybody about Kitty jumping out of my window to go be with Buzzy, or that I had helped her carry out her plan. It didn't matter anyway, as far as I was concerned. The girl had made up her mind. If I had not gone along with her plans, she would have figured out another way. And she might have even got herself killed a lot sooner. She took more chances with men than Crazy Mimi, and Crazy Mimi was crazy! But God must have been looking out for Crazy Mimi because He knew she didn't know any better. Kitty did know better. She had been flirting with death for years. In the back of my mind, I always knew that a man would be the death of Kitty, as reckless as she was. I no longer wanted to be like her. She died the same way she lived: fast.

I didn't faint at Kitty's funeral the way I did at the big funeral for Regina's siblings, but a few other people did. Kitty's grandmother from Dallas not only fainted, she had a mild heart attack and had to be carried out of the church on a gurney by paramedics.

Nobody was surprised when Crazy Mimi jumped up from her seat and delivered one of the most melodramatic crying fits we'd ever seen at a funeral. She yelled and screamed and clawed at her clothes until she was half-naked in front of the horrified congregation. Two ushers grabbed a robe out of nowhere and wrapped Crazy Mimi, then wrestled her to the floor. Another set of paramedics had to strap her to a gurney and haul her out of the church, too.

Regina handled Kitty's funeral better than I expected. She sat near the front of the church, sharing a third row pew with her mother's younger brother, Melvin. I was two rows behind them, staring at the program to keep from looking at the closed casket. Halfway through the service, a sharp pain shot through my side and I had to wrap my arms around myself to hold my insides in place.

Daddy was one of the pallbearers. By the time Kitty's casket was to be removed from the church, my body betrayed me again. I bolted from my seat and ran down the aisle and didn't stop until I reached the bathroom in the basement next to the kitchen. A trail of vomit followed me all the way. I returned upstairs just in time to see Reverend Poe and an usher trying to restrain Chester. The boy was delirious. He was screaming Kitty's name and he was bucking and rearing like a bull. Brother Dixon's jaw got broken, and poor old Reverend Poe got pushed so hard, he stumbled all the way across the room. He hit his head on the wall so hard, he had to have stitches. Chester got loose anyway and ran out of the church and threw himself on top of Kitty's casket. It took four more men to drag him away.

I refused to go to the graveyard and watch them lower Kitty into the ground, and I'm glad I didn't. Desiree's report of what happened at the gravesite sent me to the bathroom again.

"Chester tried to open poor Kitty's casket. He sucker punched Deacon Burriss for trying to stop him. It took your daddy, Burl's great big uncle Mogen, and Chester's granddaddy from Dallas to get Chester out of the way long enough for them to put that girl in the ground," Desiree told me. She hovered over me as I kneeled over the toilet with my head hanging so low to the commode, my lips touched the seat. "Oh, girl, it broke my heart to see Chester like that. I didn't know he was that emotional when it came to somebody he loved. Did you?"

"No," I muttered, frowning at the metallic taste of the bile still lingering on my tongue.

"And do you know what insensitive thing Buzzy's daddy had the nerve to say? That dick! He was spewing some shit about Kitty dying by the sword because she lived by the sword! Shit. The girl didn't die in a gang battle or in a shoot-out with the cops. She died because his mole-faced son was drinking and driving! If I was Chester, I'd skin Buzzy alive and ride that daddy of his out of town on a rail!" Desiree roared, staring thoughtfully at the side of my face. "Carmen, it was a beautiful service, but I'm glad it's over. My daddy said it best. He said it was Kitty's time that's all. And poor Burl, everybody thought his funeral would be the next one Reverend Poe preached." Desiree sighed and gave me a hug.

CHAPTER 19

Mama told me that when she was my age, she thought of death as a slack-jawed old man wearing dark, dreary clothing. He always visited people at the wrong time. She had based her belief on a situation that she had experienced when she still lived in Montgomery. "There was this old retired country preacher that nobody liked. Once they ran him out of the pulpit, he moved to Birmingham. A few months after he left, he started showing up back in Montgomery unannounced about once every couple of months, visiting a particular family. Every single time, about a week after his visit, somebody in that family died. Nobody but me ever brought it up, so I was probably the only person in town who believed that that old man was death in disguise." I knew from the way Mama got tears in her eyes when she told me that story that she believed it. I didn't believe it. With all the old men bringing their vehicles to our house for Daddy to work on, I would have gone crazy trying to figure out which one was the grim reaper.

Nothing made my parents as angry as one of us saying something negative about Black folks. That's why I never brought it up that I thought it was a crying shame how superstitious some Black folks were. I did have some superstitious beliefs of my own, though. I sincerely believed that everything happened for a reason. Not that I wanted Kitty to die, but what happened to her diverted my attention away from my role in Burl's accident. I needed my whole brain to think about Kitty's death and the *small* role I had played in that!

I found out three days after Kitty's funeral that around the same time and on the same day she died, Burl came out of his coma. But with all of the confusion going on over Kitty's untimely death, the same people who had held a vigil at Miss Mozelle's house were still too overwhelmed to be there when Burl's uncle brought him home from the hospital two days later.

My entire body had turned into a sieve. I couldn't keep anything inside. My thoughts drifted out of my head. Everything I tried to eat squirted out of either my mouth or my bowels and ended up in the bathroom toilet or on my bed. Desiree was the only one of my friends who managed to keep a level head.

"At least Kitty didn't suffer," Desiree told me as we sat on the edge of my bed. "My daddy told me she had so much alcohol in her system, she was too disoriented to even know what was happening to her. Just like Burl."

"You seen Burl yet?" I mumbled. I had not taken the time to give much thought to Burl's dilemma until now.

"Daddy and I popped over there for a few minutes before he dropped me off over here," Desiree told me with a weary sigh.

"Did Burl say anything about what happened to him?"

Desiree gave me a puzzled look. "No. He must have blocked it all out."

"Oh. Well, how is he otherwise?"

"He'll be okay, I guess. Did you hear about his legs?"

"No. What about his legs?"

Desiree rubbed the side of her face and sighed again "Well, when he fell off that train he landed on his back on the train tracks. He damaged his spine." At this point, Desiree paused and wiped a single tear from the corner of her eye. She sniffed before continuing. "As long as he lives, he'll never walk again."

CHAPTER 20

The house that Burl lived in and the one the Sheffields lived in looked almost identical on the outside. But inside was a completely different story. While Miss Mozelle furnished her rooms with odds and ends that would have looked out of place anywhere, the Sheffields' living room looked like a magazine ad. A high-backed, fluffy powder-blue sofa faced a matching love seat. On the walls there were impressive paintings of great Black leaders, and dozens of framed pictures of family members on the smoked-glass end tables. There was a huge easy chair in a corner facing a large floor-model television set. Before and after Kitty's funeral, a lot of people went to the Sheffields' house to drop off food and to regale the grieving family with cute stories about Kitty. I didn't go to the Sheffields' house before the funeral, but afterward I did. Along with a crowd of over fifty people, half of them weeping and wailing, I joined the endless mourning in the Sheffields' living room. Somebody had brought over folding chairs, but there were still not enough seats for everybody to sit down. I alternated from a spot in one corner to another, leaving the seats for the adults and old people. I figured I had cried enough, so I was one of the few present with dry eyes.

One of my observations about Black folks—one I would never bring up in front of my parents—was the way we reacted when somebody died. As wild and corrupt as Kitty Sheffield was, now that she was dead, everybody made her sound like Saint Teresa. Mr. Blake, the principal from our school, that Kitty had called a "black-ass mother-fucker" to his face the last time he suspended her, cried like a baby when he spoke of all the times Kitty had been sent to his office. "The girl had more energy than a fly," he wailed, ignoring the big tears splashing on his liver-colored face.

Reverend Poe, a small man with a big voice, could make the devil sound like a cherub. "The girl was a disruptive influence, but I have to give her her due for keepin' them other young'ns from sleepin' through my sermons."

In addition to keeping my mind occupied so that I didn't devote all of my time to thinking about Burl, Kitty's death had also diverted my attention away from another profound situation: my obsession with her brother, Chester. It had been a week since Buzzy's comments to me about Chester's preference for light-skinned girls. But with all that had happened, I had not given Chester much thought, except for sympathetic ones over him losing his sister.

I had not seen Chester since we'd left the church after Kitty's gut-wrenching funeral. I wanted to hug him like everybody else had al-ready done.

"Where's Chester?" I asked his daddy, Willie, as he stood next to me mopping his face with a handkerchief that looked like a diaper. "I just want to hug him," I confessed, my heart thumping.

"He's restin' in his room," he replied, his voice cracking. He let out a sigh that must have been painful judging from the way he screwed up his face and shook his head. "This whole thing done ruined my boy." Mr. Willie paused and took several deep breaths. Then he started talking in a labored voice. "Chester'll never get over this. Carmen, go in the kitchen yonder and help your mama."

Before I could leave the room, Crazy Mimi and Desiree accosted me and backed me into another corner. They were both balancing plates piled high with fried chicken, crowder peas, corner bread, and the ever-present greens. Even funerals didn't stop Black folks from enjoying a feast. As a matter of fact, it was a good excuse for us to have a feast.

I had not seen or talked to Burl since he'd come home, but most of my friends had. From what I could piece together from Crazy Mimi's

convoluted report in the Sheffields' living room, Burl could not remember much about what had occurred that Saturday afternoon during the few hours leading up to his accident.

"All I got to say about Burl fallin' off that train is, he shouldn't have
been there in the first place," Crazy Mimi said, sucking her teeth.

Desiree had visited Burl only once. "He slept the whole time," she
informed me with a heavy sigh. "I'm not going back over there by myself. Let me know when you want to go, Carmen, and I'll go with you.
I'm dying to hear what Burl has to say about his accident. Aren't you?"

I nodded gloomily and responded with a voice I did not recognize,
"I sure am."

CHAPTER 21

I stumbled around like a zombie in the Sheffields' kitchen, helping my mother dip large helpings of macaroni and cheese onto paper plates. I couldn't stop thinking about how similar Chester's reaction to Kitty's death was to Miss Mozelle's reaction to Burl's accident. Even though Kitty's death was a bigger tragedy than Burl's accident, I felt equally sorry about both. Especially since Kitty's death had overshadowed Burl coming out of his coma and being sent home from the hospital.

While we were all in the Sheffields' living room, Miss Mozelle, her brother Mogen, and Burl entered the house. Like a trained seal, Miss Mozelle, her head bowed, shuffled in silence behind her brother. Mr. Mogen, with a grim expression on his face, was pushing Burl in the wheelchair the railroad company had donated. It was the first time Burl's tragedy and Kitty's tragedy were part of the same mourning ceremony at the same time in the same place.

The conversation drifted back and forth from all the "cute" things Kitty had said or done to how "blessed" Burl was to still be alive. It was a good twenty minutes before I was able to wade through the crowd over to where Burl was parked in front of the living room window. He looked like he was going to break down and cry at any moment. As soon as I got close enough, he lifted his head and smiled.

"You look good, Burl," I said hoarsely, touching his shoulder. It was a lie. He looked terrible. He had lost so much weight, I could see his cheekbones for the first time. His eyes had the same glazed look of a blind person. His hands, folded neatly on his lap and looking like crooked bones, shook. Even though he had on a pair of thick gabardine pants, I could see that his legs and thighs were now bony. His knobby knees touched each other. The thought of him sitting there in that wheelchair, so helpless he had to wear diapers, almost made my legs buckle.

"You look good yourself, Carmen," Burl told me. He smiled broadly and touched my arm. "I been meanin' to call you." His voice was as weak as a kitten's.

"I've been meaning to call and visit you, too." I lowered my head. "But this thing with Kitty . . ."

"Oh, don't feel bad. I know how close you and Kitty were."

In a fever of anticipation, I stammered and returned my attention to Burl's face. His hollow eyes made me want to look away again, but I couldn't. "Uh . . . do you remember what all happened that day you had the accident?" I held my breath and waited, ready to faint in case Burl told me what I dreaded hearing. I felt that the sooner I found out if he knew that I had caused his accident, the easier it would be for me to take responsibility for it and move on.

Burl sucked in a deep breath before answering. "The last thing I remember about that day was me and you goin' to the movies." He paused and toyed with a loose thread on the hem of his shirtsleeve.

I leaned closer to him. "Oh? Is that all you remember?"

"*Halloween II* was the movie we went to see," he sighed. "I slept through most of it."

"I guess everything else is a blank, huh?"

Burl nodded sadly, then rolled his chair back a few inches. "Not everything. It's all comin' back to me in bits and pieces, a little at a time. I do remember you paid my way into the movies, and I still owe you for that."

"Don't worry about it," I said, waving my hand.

"There's something else."

"What?" I gasped.

"Didn't me and you get in a cab after we left the movies?"

"Uh-huh." My heart started beating so hard and fast, I thought I was going to pass out. I looked around the room. Other than Desiree and Crazy Mimi watching Burl and me, the only other person looking in my direction was Mr. Mogen. I held my breath as Burl continued.

"That's the last thing I remember so far," he muttered.

I breathed a sigh of relief and squeezed his shoulder. "Well, if there is anything I can do for you, all you have to do is ask me. I promise I'll be there. I don't care what it is," I said firmly. Burl smiled and nodded. I would live to regret the commitment I had just made to Burl, and I knew it even then.

But it was too late to take it back.

CHAPTER 22

It seemed like as soon as I stomped out one fire, another one flared up. Even though I regretted making that promise to Burl, knowing about his memory lapse had made it easier for me to cope. If he couldn't remember even going to the train yard and climbing into the boxcar, there was no way the world would ever find out that I was the one responsible for his accident. I would certainly never tell anybody if I could help it. I felt it was safe for me to relax now. That feeling didn't last long.

It was my sister, Babette, who first spotted Chester running down the street toward our house, howling and swinging an ax just before noon the next day after the gathering at the Sheffields' house.

"Daddy! Mama! Chester's lost his mind!" Babette shrieked from our living room.

Daddy was downstairs in the basement. Mama was in the kitchen. Babette's voice was so loud, it sounded like she was in my bedroom with me. I fell twice trying to get from my room to the living room fast enough to witness the latest catastrophe associated with somebody close to me.

By the time I reached the living room, Babette was hopping around in front of the window waving her arms. Mama and Daddy had already made it out to our front porch. I stopped when I reached the window. Chester was standing with his legs spread apart and bent at the knees in front of the tree where Buzzy's car had crashed. Before Daddy could get off the porch, Chester started swinging the ax maniacally at the trunk of the tree. Mama had stopped in the middle of our front yard, screaming loud enough to wake up the dead.

"Chester, take it easy, son!" Daddy yelled. "Somebody call the police!" Daddy continued, holding up his hand, but keeping a safe distance. A few other neighbors peeped out of their windows, but nobody else was brave enough to come outside and try to wrest the ax out of Chester's hands.

Chester ignored Daddy and kept hacking away at the tree that had claimed his sister. The tree's long branches didn't even budge as Chester cursed and attacked its trunk with the ax. Other than a few spots where the weather had eroded a few postage-stamp-size pieces of bark, the soot that the fire in Buzzy's old car had left, and a crooked row of superficial whacks from Chester, the tree remained intact. It seemed like a long time, but it was only a few moments before the ax broke. With the blade embedded in the tree's trunk, Chester cursed at it again before he dropped the ax handle and then started kicking the tree. When he dropped to his knees on the ground, Mama ran out to him and cradled him in her arms. He cried like a baby until his half-dressed, shoeless parents arrived a few minutes later.

Two days after Chester's outburst with the ax, the Sheffields closed their store, locked up their house, and went back to Texas with the relatives who had come for Kitty's funeral. They had planned to stay for a few weeks, at least.

Before long, it was business as usual in our neighborhood. Miss Mozelle returned to her job at the country club, wearing a wig and twenty pounds lighter. Mr. Mogen hired a caretaker to be on call for Miss Mozelle when she needed help with Burl. From what I had heard, the boy needed help getting in the bathtub and into his clothes. Miss Mozelle seemed to be doing all right the first few weeks, but after that a redheaded woman in a white uniform showed up to help Burl every day before I went to school.

People had stopped talking about what had happened to Burl and Kitty, but it was something I thought about day and night. For me it was hard not to. Every time I walked out of our front door, the first thing I looked at was that singed tree. I never returned to the train yard, but with Burl living just a few doors away, it was impossible for me not to think about what had happened.

Before Mr. Mogen returned to Detroit, he and Daddy built a ramp off the side of Miss Mozelle's front porch for Burl to enter and leave the house in his wheelchair. Also in Miss Mozelle's house, they installed a crude elevator that looked like a cage. It was for Burl to go back and forth upstairs when he wanted to.

Before he returned to Detroit, Mr. Mogen stopped by our house for dinner, eating like it was his last meal. Sitting next to me, spraying my face with juice off the collard greens Mama had cooked, he fished out a piece of paper from his pocket and waved it like a flag. "See there, y'all. These is all the things I done listed up that that railroad company gwine to get the bills for. Everybody responsible for what happened to my nephew is gwine to pay big for it! *Real big!*"

I almost choked on the hush puppies Mama had placed on my plate in a neat pile like marbles. That Burl. I sat there wishing that I had never befriended that boy. For a whole hour we had to sit at the dining room table listening to Mr. Mogen's mercenary ramblings. He was still eating peach cobbler out of a cup when we all moved to the living room.

"Yeah! I ain't leavin' nary stone unturned. *My* name will be on every bank account that railroad company got when I get through with 'em." That was the last thing Mr. Mogen said as Daddy walked him to the door. I went to bed feeling sorrier than ever for Burl and myself. I knew now that if I said something about my role in Burl's accident, Mr. Mogen would come after Daddy with a lawsuit.

I had missed the whole week of school after Kitty's funeral, but I was glad when I went back. Desiree and Regina were in some of my classes, and I had some fun teachers, but things would never be the same at school again without Kitty's disruptive presence.

Since Crazy Mimi was taught at home, and only when she felt like it, she had a lot of time on her hands during the days the rest of us were in school. She would sit on the ground in front of my house and wait for me to get home from school and wouldn't leave until she was good and ready.

Against Miss Mozelle's wishes, Burl's uncle had enrolled him in a school for handicapped kids. Burl got out of school before I did and would sit in his window waiting for me to come visit him. Often on the same days and at the same time as Crazy Mimi. While Babette and I were in school, and on the days Daddy worked in his garage in Mobile, Mama was in the house almost every day by herself. More than once she had invited Crazy Mimi to wait for me inside. But the girl insisted on sitting on the ground to wait for me, rain or shine. And Burl insisted on sitting in his window until he saw me, no matter how long it took for me to get home. Some days I went to the Y and didn't get home until almost dark. Crazy Mimi would still be sitting on that hard ground, and Burl would still be sitting in that window under a lamp. They were waiting for me to fill a void in their lives that only seemed to be getting bigger.

As much as I liked Regina, I preferred spending most of my free time with Desiree. Regina was still my girl and I cared about her, but it still sometimes depressed me to be around her. Something always seemed to remind her of her dead siblings. "Carline would be old enough to start school now. . . . Dobie would be in second grade," she lamented one afternoon when we passed a kindergarten class out for a stroll on our way back to school after a trip to Burger King.

I looked forward to spending time with Desiree. When I went to her house, the worst thing I had to put up with was watching her daddy beat her. As painful as it was for me to watch, it didn't seem to bother her. Over and over she would do the things she knew she'd get a whupping for. Like sassing her daddy, not cleaning up the house, and even for giving him a mean look. Sometimes when he came at her with a switch or a belt, she would run out of the house and down the street. She knew he didn't have enough nerve to beat her outside where the neighbors could see. I felt like a complete fool running down the street with her. When she felt she was ready to take her punishment, she excused herself, took a deep breath, and went back in the house to get it over with. One time when Dr. Lucienne couldn't find the belt he liked to beat Desiree with, she went outside and got a switch off a tree herself. Like I said, it was painful for me to watch, but I got used to it.

After a while, the few kids that Burl had hung out with stopped coming around. I was one of the few friends he had who still visited him on a regular basis. With him being in a wheelchair, there were not a lot of things we could do to keep ourselves occupied. I spent a lot of time sitting with him in his living room after school while he sketched sorry pictures. Mostly of me, flowers, snakes, and naked women. He had developed an interest in art since his accident.

During conversations where we sometimes had to struggle for things to discuss, he rarely mentioned his disability. By now I was convinced that my part in his accident was a secret I shared only with God.

I tried not to think about Kitty, because every time I did, a pain shot through my side. It was hard not to think about her with that tree in my front yard. And with Buzzy in his new car barreling up and down the streets.

Some days when Burl wanted to see me, he didn't wait for me to come to him; he came to me. It got to be annoying to look out and see him zipping across the street toward our house in his wheelchair. Since our house was not wheelchair accessible, the only way he could get in was for Daddy to lift him out of the wheelchair and carry him in first, then go back and get the wheelchair. And even though Daddy never complained in front of me, I knew it was hard on him. That's why when Burl came, I usually met him at the door, then escorted him back to his house.

During Thanksgiving break, Burl and I were on his front porch when a long cab stopped in front of the Sheffields' house. Chester's parents tumbled out with their luggage. They had been in Texas since the week of Kitty's funeral.

"Where's Chester?" Burl called out, wheeling himself to the edge of the porch.

I was glad to see that the Sheffields were able to smile again.

"Oh, he's goin' to stay on with his grandfolks in Dallas," Chester's mother called out. "I doubt if he'll ever come back this way."

"Oh," Burl said. He turned to me and whispered, "That's the best news I heard in a long time. You too, I bet. Chester had been plottin' to get his hands on you for a long time."

I gasped and whirled around to face Burl. "Chester didn't like me that way. Did he?"

Burl nodded. "Oh, yes, he did. He told me to my face, on your last birthday, that he couldn't wait for you to get old enough so he could jump on you. That nasty dog."

I didn't hear much of anything else Burl or Chester's parents said, because a sharp pain in my side took all my attention. It was then that I realized I still had my crush on Chester. But if what his mother had just said was true, like Kitty, I would never see him again either unless I moved to Texas. I looked at the side of Burl's face and then at the wheelchair. I smiled sadly, glad that Chester was out of my life. I recalled the hours leading up to Burl's accident. I had thought then that if I never got to be with Chester, I would always have Burl to fall back on.

It was not a choice now; it was an obligation.

CHAPTER 23

Like me, Desiree was not allowed to date yet. But that didn't stop her from seeing boys every chance she got. We were both still virgins. I had fooled around with a few boys at parties, kissing and hugging and even letting one or two play with my titties. But since Burl was the closest I could come to having a boyfriend, I didn't have any trouble keeping my legs closed. Since Chester was the only boy I had ever wanted to be with, boys weren't that important to me yet. Desiree didn't feel that way.

"Who was that cute boy with the dreadlocks I saw getting in the car with your mama?" she asked, entering my room. She shut the door and joined me on my bed, where I lay propped up with two pillows holding a hot-water bottle against my stomach. At fourteen, I was just getting my first period, accompanied by a mild case of cramps. It had been a year since Kitty died and a year since I'd last seen Chester.

"My cousin from Mobile. His name is Redmond Junior, but we call him Baby Red," I mumbled, struggling to sit up, still holding the hot-water bottle next to my stomach. "Why?" I glared at Desiree out of the corner of my eye.

Desiree shrugged and gave me a tight smile. "Well, he sure is cute." She shook her head and rolled her eyes back in her head. "How come I've never seen him until today?" She had not even shown me the patterns she had brought over for the dress she was going to wear to a wedding she'd been invited to. Her sewing bag was on the floor.

"He just got back from Canada. What color are you going to use for your dress? Go shut the window."

Desiree hadn't even mentioned the dress she planned to make since she'd arrived. She rose to go shut my window, stepping over her sewing bag, talking over her shoulder. "What was he doing in Canada of all places?" She marched back to my bed and stood over me with her arms folded. It was amazing how much Desiree had changed since she'd slid into my life. She was a head shorter then me, but her body was a cascade of curves. She was the only one of my friends who wore a C-cup bra. It seemed like the only thing happening to my body was, I was getting taller. She covered her flawless skin with makeup she didn't need, but only when her daddy was too drunk to notice. Because he would grab her and roughly remove her makeup with a dishrag, telling her only whores painted their faces and that it was only to hide their shame.

"He graduated two years ago when he was sixteen. The day after graduation, he and some girl rode their bikes from Mobile to Canada." I was feeling better now. I flung the hot-water bottle to the side of my bed.

"Oh. So he's got a girlfriend?" Desiree's smile disappeared and she sat down hard at the foot of my bed, finally opening her sewing bag.

"I don't know." I shrugged. "He's way too old for you, so don't even think about hooking up with him. Besides, he's not normal. . . ."

Desiree gasped and leaned toward me. "What's wrong with him?"

"Well, he doesn't eat meat and he likes to roam around like a gypsy on his bike. He's going to Asia next."

"Is he rich?"

"Hell, no. His daddy works for my daddy. His mama, she ran off when Baby Red was little. Baby Red does odd jobs to survive. On his way to Canada, he made money digging graves. He even slept in the same cemetery to keep from paying a hotel. He even followed a circus for three months, him and that girl. They made money cleaning up elephant shit."

Desiree shuddered and let out a long sigh. "Well, he's still cute. I hope I see more of him while he's here. What kind of a bike? A Harley? A Suzuki?"

I shrugged. "Just a bike bike. An old ten-speed I think. That boy is dirt cheap. Even if he had money, he wouldn't spend it on something as expensive as a Harley or a Suzuki or any other motorcycle."

"Hmmm. A real earth brother, huh?"

"I guess." To change the subject, I pulled out all of the sewing materials from the bag and spent the rest of Desiree's visit pretending I was interested in helping her make her dress.

Regina had given up her virginity to a boy she had met at a party. She couldn't even remember his name. Crazy Mimi was still writing steamy letters to lonely men in prison. A month ago, she left her house on her way to visit me. She never made it. She had checked into a motel with one of the recently released prisoners she had been corresponding with, and according to Regina, "he fucked the hell out of her."

Desiree never told me all the details, but a month later she made a startling confession: she had started a relationship with my eccentric cousin. They were an odd couple, to say the least. Baby Red was tall and sharp-featured. He had droopy, round eyes, reddish-brown skin, and shoulder-length dreadlocks almost the same shade as his skin. He wore clothes that he fished out of bins in secondhand stores. He smoked marijuana almost every day. When he visited us, Mama made him smoke outside. Most of the time when he came for an overnight visit, he slept under a cardboard box in our garage. Desiree was a doctor's daughter. She had nothing in common with my cousin. I was shocked and saddened, and I told her so.

"You can just mind your own business!" she snapped, almost biting my head off.

My cousin Baby Red told me basically the same thing when I got in his face. "Shaddup! This ain't got nothin' to do with you, girl."

Desiree got a whupping from her daddy later that day for not decorating the Christmas tree he had bought. I saw the whole thing. As a matter of fact, Dr. Lucienne whacked me a few times with his belt when I tried to interfere.

"Carmen, mind your own business," Dr. Lucienne calmly told me, escorting me out the front door as Desiree lay on the sofa crying and bleeding from the welts on her legs. "You should know enough by now to stay out of things that don't concern you." He was right and I knew it. But minding my own business seemed like the one thing I couldn't do. Meddling was my biggest flaw.

Every chance Desiree got; she sneaked Baby Red into her daddy's house while he was at his office or in bed asleep. She had even allowed my cousin to take her virginity on her living room sofa on Christmas day. Afterward, she called me up and begged me to come over. She was still spraying rose-scented Glade in every room by the time I got there.

"Daddy would have a fit if he found out about us smoking weed in here. I'd be in enough trouble if he found out about me having a boyfriend," she said nervously. She started laughing as she stumbled across the floor. I rolled my eyes at her when she grabbed her crotch. "Let me tell you right here and now, sex is not what it's cracked up to be." She stopped and snatched up a glass from the coffee table and drank whatever was in it. "But it was a nice Christmas present from your cousin."

There was a Jack Daniels bottle on the same table. Desiree had barely paid attention to the new sewing machine her daddy had given her for Christmas. It still sat in its box on the floor next to the clock radio I had given to her.

Desiree lived on Blecker Street, six blocks from my house. The big green house she shared with her daddy reminded me of a cheap hotel. It had been furnished with a lot of outdated furniture that it took Desiree and two cleaning ladies to care for. Velvet maroon curtains draped the windows in the living room, but the curtains and the windows stayed closed all the time. It was no wonder the living room plants were always dead or dying. Two of the four bedrooms were totally empty. After Desiree's sister, Colleen, had fled, Dr. Lucienne had angrily removed all of the things from her room and dumped them in the garage. There was no room left for the doctor's car. It was always in the driveway, just like Daddy's. The things that Desiree's mama had left behind had been stuffed into boxes and placed in the garage, too. Even pictures that included Desiree's sister and mama had been dumped in the garage. I glared at the Jack Daniels bottle on the coffee table.

"So," I began, "you drinking, too, now?"

"Only when I need it. That's one thing I can do right up under my daddy's nose and he wouldn't know the difference. Poor Daddy."

Desiree paused and tapped the liquor bottle. Then she tilted her head and looked at me with a dreamy expression on her face. "Carmen, you are the luckiest girl I know. You got that pretty mama, a real cool daddy, a sister, and you don't have a care in the world. I never told you this, but I wish I was you."

The last part of her comment almost made me laugh. "No, you don't, girl. No, you don't," I told her.

Growing up was hard. It presented a whole new set of problems. The one I had the hardest time accepting was that my friends were not only growing up, too, but they were growing away from me. I was too young and limited to realize that at the time, my friends' actions would eventually force them to turn to me even more. Especially Burl and Desiree.

CHAPTER 24

Somehow I made it through the first half of my teens in one piece. Throughout that tense period of my life, I'd spent almost every day expecting the world to come crashing down around me because of what I'd done to Burl.

To other people I was just like any other normal teenager. I hung out at the mall, the movies, and at parties, where I allowed possible future boyfriends to fondle me. For Halloween and Mardi Gras I wore the most bizarre masks I could find. But after I removed the freak masks, the mask of a fake smile took over. I couldn't hide my lying eyes, but I obscured them with heavy makeup, making Dr. Lucienne roll his eyes at me with contempt when I visited Desiree, because he still believed that only whores wore makeup. Sleep was no longer an escape for me. At night, alone in my room, the reality of the pain behind the "mask" I wore haunted me almost every time I dozed off. In one of my frequent nightmares, I was in Burl's place. Except it wasn't a wheelchair, it was an electric chair. That was what I subconsciously saw as my punishment. I made a bargain with God that if nobody ever found out what I had done to Burl in the train yard that day, I'd continue to keep Burl as a priority in my life for as long as he needed me.

There was a hint of a reprieve when Burl made friends with some of the students from the handicapped kids' school he attended.

"I don't feel so bad no more about bein' disabled," Burl told me with a broad smile and misty eyes. Seeing his lips curl up at the ends made me smile along with him. He had gained back all of his weight and then some. His hips and thighs strained against the sides of the seat of his wheelchair.

One thing I liked about Burl, he didn't let his disability stop him from being stylish. He had on a pair of Calvin Klein jeans and a bright-red polo shirt. A sparkling gold chain hung from his thick neck. He was eighteen now and shaving. He even had the nerve to splash Eternity cologne on his cheeks and neck every morning. For some odd reason, the soft curls that had once adorned Burl's head had now become hard and thorny. Even though Miss Mozelle still combed his hair, when she didn't oil it, the curls looked and felt like cockleburs. I rubbed the back of Burl's knotty head as he continued. "Some of them kids at my school are a lot worse off than I am. They were born with their disabilities, or something happened to them when they was a lot younger than I was. At least I had me fourteen good, normal years before I got myself in this mess. And if them other kids ain't bad off enough, they got stuck with the wrong color skin, too." I gave Burl a dry look and then we both cracked up laughing. All of Burl's new handicapped friends were white.

Among Burl's school friends was a beautiful girl with huge blue eyes and hair like corn silk. Debbie had been born with no arms. There was a freckle-faced boy named Dennis with a hawk's nose. His legs had been amputated during an elevator accident when he was seven. And there was Wendy, afflicted with cerebral palsy. I could not tell if she was pretty or not. Her mouth was screwed up like a coin purse, and her face was so lopsided and twisted, from a distance it looked like she had only one eye. Wendy had all but replaced me as Burl's closest friend. I was jubilant!

I figured it was a safe time for me to start weaning Burl off of me. But I began the transition with caution. After not visiting or calling him for a week, I invited myself to go to the park with him and the no-armed girl in a van driven by one of his counselors. I ended up regretting it. Burl and his new "girlfriend" paid very little attention to me. They seemed relieved when I decided to leave the park early with Crazy Mimi when she wandered by wearing a diaper for a scarf.

"Carmen, why you always hangin' out with them ill-formed kids? Don't it depress you?" Crazy Mimi asked with a frown on her face.

Her innocent concern gave me something to think about. "Sometimes it depresses me," I told her. Lying to somebody in Crazy Mimi's state of mind seemed like a waste of time. But I did it to distract and confuse her. She got agitated, but it got her to move on to another subject. I spent the rest of that afternoon helping her unpack new videos at her parents' video store.

Even though I was the one responsible for Burl's disability, it was not up to me to act as his guide dog for the rest of my life. He still needed his own space. Once when I went to visit him and while the girl with cerebral palsy was there, I felt like the ugly stepsister. The girl practically ignored me, speaking to me only when I spoke to her. Burl seemed uncomfortable the minute I walked in the door.

"Uh . . . Carmen, I think I just seen Crazy Mimi headed to your house," Burl promptly told me, unable to hide the excitement in his voice. It took me a moment to realize he was trying to get rid of me.

"Oh—well, I better go on back home," I stammered.

Burl practically ran over my feet rushing to get me out of the door so fast that day. If any of my other friends had brushed me aside like that, it would have upset me. I didn't know if Burl was feeling guilty about taking up so much of my time or if he really was trying to cultivate relationships with other kids. It gave me a lot more to think about. Such as, I was the one who'd offered my open-ended assistance to Burl. He hadn't asked for it. Now, if he could get along without me, I'd let myself off the hook and move on with my life. I could even pursue a real boyfriend.

One Friday after school, I ran into Burl and the girl with cerebral palsy at the mall. It could have been my imagination, but it looked like Burl was trying to hide from me behind a cassette display in a record store.

"Burl, is that you?" I yelled, squeezing between the display and his wheelchair. The girl, with as straight a face as she could manage, stared at me with contempt. Her twisted lips quivered, and the eyelid on her one good eye flapped like a shutter on a window when I kissed Burl on the cheek.

He became visibly nervous. "Uh . . . me and Wendy, we on our way to get pizza," he stammered.

I had been headed for pizza, too. "I'm on my way to get my nails done," I lied. "I'm late, so I'd better run." I knocked over the cassette display trying to get away so fast.

Knowing that he had friends more like him now, I reduced my

phone calls and visits to Burl and started spending more time with my other friends. Even though Chester had become part of my tortured past, I still thought about him from time to time. I often wondered what our children would have looked like. My equilibrium didn't last long. I heard from Chester's daddy that Chester had married a Dallas Cowboys cheerleader.

"God took one daughter away from us, but he didn't waste no time blessin' us with another one. Praise the Lord," Mr. Willie told me during one of my infrequent visits to his store. Now that Chester was gone, I didn't go there as much. Even though the food prices at Piggly Wiggly got higher and higher and it was out of the way, I preferred going there when I wanted something for myself. But Mama kept reminding me how important it was for us to support Black businesses. When she asked me to go pick up something from Sheffield's Market, I went. Mr. Willie was glad to see me and couldn't stop talking about Chester. "And Chester is just crazy about Madeline—that's my new daughter-in-law's name. But then, the boy's always been partial to pretty girls with long legs. Heh, heh, heh. Just like his old man." Mr. Willie paused long enough to mop sweat off his forehead with the back of his hand. He looked so much older these days. Mama had told me that nothing aged a person quicker than grief. Mr. Willie had apparently neglected his teeth since the last time I was close enough to notice. The bottom part of one of his front teeth was missing. His snaggle-tooth grin was distracting, but I was happy to see him so happy. "The good Lord done already blessed 'em with a brand-new baby girl! Chester so proud he could outshine a Christmas tree." Mr. Willie sniffed and handed me the neatly wrapped duck Mama had sent me to get.

A twisted smile crossed my face. "That's nice, Mr. Willie. I hope Chester will be happy with his new wife and baby," I said, actually meaning it.

"Me and the missus, we gwine to shoot over to Texas in a few weeks to visit him. Here—have a dill pickle on the house." Mr. Willie snatched the lid off a large jar on the counter and speared a pickle with a plastic fork and handed it to me. "When I talk to my boy again, I'll tell him I seen you and that you just as pretty as ever."

"You do that," I mumbled, stumbling out of the door, nibbling on the pickle. I almost walked out in front of a bread truck, I was in such a daze.

What I had just heard saddened and intrigued me at the same time. Chester was no longer one of my goals, but I often wondered what it would have been like to be with him. I was sorry that I would never feel his arms around me again the way I did the night Kitty died when he grabbed me and threw me to the ground.

Sadly, once Burl graduated, his handicapped friends drifted out of his life. The legless boy committed suicide, the no-armed girl moved to another state, and the girl with the lopsided face got married! The girl getting married depressed Burl for days. How did he deal with it? He started calling me twice as much as before when he wasn't sitting in his window staring toward my house.

There were times when I wanted to kill that boy with my bare hands, and there were times when I wanted to hug him and never let him go. I felt sorry for him, but I could never love him the way a woman was supposed to love a man. God knows I don't know why I said what I did.

"There is no reason in the world why you can't still get married one day, too. You have so much to offer. As a matter of fact, I will personally dance at your wedding." That made us both laugh.

Before I knew it, I had allowed myself to slide back into Burl's dark world. But this time I felt more like a guide dog than ever.

CHAPTER 25

Even with her bizarre mental condition, Crazy Mimi got a job. To a lot of people, that was not much of an accomplishment, since it was Crazy Mimi's parents who allowed her to work full time and with pay in the video rental store they owned. Before being put on the payroll, she had just hung around the store sneaking dirty movies to her friends.

One of Regina's few talents included hair-braiding, and she was good at it. Like my mama, she had a long list of regular clients. At seventeen, Regina was stashing away over a thousand dollars a month in tax-free money. Her "seed money," she called it. She hoped to have her own beauty parlor someday. She thought it was a woman's obligation to look as good as she thought she did. Her eyes were the most noticeable and attractive thing on her. They were shiny-black and large. She was a butterscotch brown with off-black hair nobody could remember because she had been wearing hairpieces since the sixth grade. Her small teeth seemed lost behind her full lips. She was of medium height, but too thin for her frame. No matter what she wore, it hung on her like a curtain.

A few months earlier, a mild stroke had forced Desiree's daddy to retire. His head nurse, the meddlesome Nurse Bertha, had moved in with him and Desiree, taking over the house like a taskmaster. I knew that if I felt like a prisoner when I visited Desiree now, she must have felt like she was in hell. We had to tiptoe and whisper the whole time we were in the house.

Nurse Bertha, always dressed in her white uniform when I visited, usually attacked me the minute I waltzed in the door. "Carmen, you ain't in the Hilton. Don't you be sittin' around here with them long legs propped up on that coffee table like you just paid off a mortgage." The private moments I had once shared with Desiree in her bedroom had become a thing of the past. The whole time I was in Desiree's room with her, Nurse Bertha darted in and out, giving us suspicious looks and even finding chores for us to do. I spent more time helping clean Dr. Lucienne's house than my own.

I spent the evening of my seventeenth birthday, March 7, 1987, helping Desiree and Nurse Bertha shampoo a carpet just so Desiree could go out with my family and me to celebrate my birthday later that night.

Desiree's justification to her daddy for getting an after-school cashier's job at the Piggly Wiggly was so she could help with the household expenses. But her real motive was, she needed money to cover the many motels she and my cousin checked into when they couldn't use her daddy's house. She didn't deny it when I confronted her, and reacted almost violently.

"Get outta my face, Carmen!" She shook her finger so close to my face, she pricked my nose with her sharp fingernail. I backed away as she continued. "It was bad enough having just Daddy in the house all the time. Now I have to deal with Nurse Bertha! So what if I spend *my* money on a motel to be with *my* man! You'd probably do the same thing if you were in *my* shoes, girl!"

"You're right," I said contritely. "I just didn't want you to get hurt."

"Hurt? The only thing hurting me is your attitude about my personal life."

"All right. I get the message. I just . . . I want you to be happy. That's all."

"I am happy, and I can't wait for you to fall in love so I can see you happy, too," Desiree told me.

The rule that my parents had set, the one about me not being officially allowed to date until I turned sixteen, had expired more than a year ago. Other than a few more boys fumbling around with my titties at parties, I had no "physical" contact with boys. I was still a virgin. And that had become a source of ridicule among my friends.

"Girl, we got to get you busted before graduation," Desiree told me, a few hours after her latest interlude with Baby Red. Her face was still flushed, and there was a hint of rapture in her eyes that I could not ignore.

It was God's never-ending presence that played a major role in my clumsy development. But even knowing that God was watching every move I made didn't stop me from ignoring a siege of telephone messages from Burl the Saturday of Regina's eighteenth birthday party, in December during our Christmas break from school.

It had been a long time since I had really had a good time with my friends without Burl breathing down my neck. As a courtesy, Regina had invited him to her party, too, but she and I both knew he would decline because the apartment building she lived in was not wheelchair accessible.

"Now if you really want to drag Burl with you, I can arrange for our super, *the one with the bad back,* to carry Burl up them three flights of stairs to my apartment," Regina told me a few days before her party.

"Uh . . . that sounds like too much trouble," I groaned.

Burl was happy to get the invitation, but he promptly declined like we had predicted and hoped he would.

Since this was a milestone birthday, Regina wanted to make sure she and her closest friends had a good time. "Other than you, Desiree, and me, there ain't gonna be no other cute girls up in here," she told me.

"What about the boys?" I asked, not really caring. Chester was the last of the good-looking, sexy Black boys in Belle Helene, and now he belonged to Texas and that cheerleading heifer he married.

"Well, since my man is goin' to be at my party, I can't risk too many male distractions. But don't worry, I will have plenty of alcohol. After enough sips, looks don't matter no how. Everybody looks the same when you blind drunk," Regina replied.

To me, it didn't really matter if I had to dance with a roomfull of plain boys. All I was interested in was having a good time, and some of the ugliest boys I knew were a lot of fun.

My sister, Babette, now lived near Alabama State, where she was studying to be a teacher. Rather than come home for the holidays, she had decided to go on a weeklong cruise to the Caribbean, frolick-

ing with a guy from Nigeria she had agreed to marry right after the
New Year.

One of my old maid great aunts on Daddy's side had been in bed
with some unidentified malady since Thanksgiving. Mama and Daddy
had agreed to spend the whole month of December and the first
week in January with Aunt Rose in Montgomery. It had been Mama's
idea. When she proposed it to Daddy, he got so upset he had a chest
pain he insisted was a mild heart attack.

"I was gwine to drive over to Mississippi and go fishin' in the Gulf,"
he whined, clutching his chest with one hand, a can of beer in another. Because he never stopped drinking during his "heart attack,"
Mama and I knew he was all right.

"Now, you look here, Aunt Rose your family and you are going to
Montgomery with me even if I have to haul your black ass in an ambulance," Mama said. "Besides, we can spend some of that time with
my mama and daddy."

"Why don't I go with you instead, Mama? I can spend the whole two
weeks of Christmas vacation in Montgomery," I offered.

"No way, sugar. I know you'd rather be with your friends. And this is
an especially painful time for poor Burl. How would he get through
the holidays without you?" Mama gave me a smile and a hug. It
seemed like the black hole that I occupied with Burl was getting
deeper and deeper.

Baby Red had been invited to stay at the house with me and sleep
in Babette's old room. Daddy made him promise not to smoke any
weed in the house. But before Mama and Daddy could leave our
driveway, Baby Red had lit up a joint as thick as a cigar and was on the
telephone in the kitchen calling Desiree. With me sitting just a few
feet away, he and Desiree plotted a romantic evening in front of our
fireplace and later in Babette's bed. I was horrified. I didn't tell
Regina about Desiree and Baby Red's agenda, but something told me
that Regina's party was the last thing on their minds.

As soon as Baby Red hung up the telephone, he turned to me with
a suspicious smile, rubbing his hands together. "Say, cousin." He
paused and clapped his hands once and smiled even broader. "What
time are you goin' to make yourself scarce this evenin'?"

I loved my cousin. The way he approached life intrigued me. As
loose as he was, he did things that made us all proud. He had partici-
pated in a mass bike ride to raise money for cancer research a month

ago. He often helped serve free meals to the homeless. And no matter what Daddy asked him to do around our house, he did it with a smile.

I gave Baby Red an exasperated look and I took my time responding. "Regina's party doesn't start until nine." He looked at his cheap watch and groaned. It was only six P.M. "You and Desiree don't have to worry about me. Pretend you don't see me," I said, my voice dripping with envy.

"Oh," Baby Red said, not bothering to hide his disappointment. A callused hand smoothed back his unruly dreadlocks.

He glanced over my shoulder out the window over the kitchen sink. I knew he was looking toward the cul-de-sac where Burl lived. I had peeped out of the living room window from behind the curtain twenty minutes ago. Burl had parked himself in the middle of his front porch and stared sadly toward my house like a neglected puppy. I followed my cousin's gaze. Now Burl had moved from the porch but was in his living room, sitting in front of the window. Like a sentinel, he sat without moving, his eyes aimed in the direction of my house. Shit! The thorn that Burl represented in my side had grown to the size of a basketball. To keep from adding to his despair, I had already planned to leave the house by either the back door or the window in my bedroom. No matter how late I returned, I'd reenter the house the same way.

I was not proud of how deceitful I had become, but I had no immediate plans to change my course of action when it came to my personal life. I had put a lot of the things on hold that I normally would have done. It was so unfair that the foolish prank I had played on Burl in the train yard had altered my life so dramatically. I was going to make sure that Regina's party made up for some of the things that it was too late for me to experience and enjoy.

CHAPTER 26

Daddy and Mama had driven to Montgomery in Daddy's two-month-old Taurus. Even though our second car, a year-old Camry, was left behind for Baby Red and me to use, I knew Baby Red would not use it. The way he treated his bike, you would have thought it was a chariot. He rarely drove a car and had vowed that he would never own one. I don't know why it surprised some people when he rode all the way from Mobile on his bike to visit Desiree or us. Especially after he had ridden it from one end of the country to the other on up to Canada.

The only times I saw my cousin in a car were when Desiree hauled him back and forth to motels in her daddy's Buick. Desiree thought it was cute one time when a desk clerk at one of the cheap motels they frequented mistook her for a well-known prostitute.

"Can you imagine somebody thinking I'd fuck for money?" she mused. She was not being paid to fuck my cousin. She was paying to fuck him. And I told her so.

"It's the other way around," I said, making Desiree cuss me out and not speak to me for two days.

I couldn't imagine there being a man I wanted to be with so desperately I'd pay for a motel room. I would soon find out that I was no better than Desiree was.

Other than Desiree's house, motels were the only places she and Baby Red went. Baby Red had not eaten in a restaurant since elementary school, and he considered movies "capitalistic propaganda." And the only things he watched on TV were educational programs and the news. Desiree loved going to the movies, and she ate out several times a week with me. I could not figure out what a girl like her saw in my cousin, and vice versa. But they spent as much time together as possible.

An odd expression often appeared on Desiree's face when she talked about Baby Red or when she was around him. Her eyes watered up and glistened like a wet fish, and her lips curled up at the ends, forming a stiff smile that looked like it had been painted on.

Before I left to go to Regina's party, Burl called again. Baby Red grabbed the telephone on the first ring and answered with a roar that made my head throb. I didn't even have to instruct him. He knew by now what to say.

"Brother man, didn't I tell you Carmen wasn't here? I don't know, dude. Yeah, I will tell her to call you when she comes home." Baby Red hung up and looked me up and down as I entered the kitchen. "Civilians!" he complained, flashing his matted dreds. Then he looked at me and did a double take. "You lookin' might tasty there, cousin," he said seriously. "If I didn't have this abscess in my mouth, I'd bite you."

"I'm not showing too much, am I?" I asked, turning around in front of him. I finally had an impressive bosom and other curves I liked to show off. The black leather pants and matching vest I had on clung to me like another layer of skin. It was cold outside and it was going to get even colder, but the leather was thick enough I didn't need a coat.

"If you ask me, you ain't showin' enough. It's a damn shame when a foxy chick is related. In your next life, come back ugly," Baby Red teased, rubbing his hands together.

I rolled my eyes at him. "The last thing I want to do is die and come back and go through a bunch of shit again," I said seriously, meaning every word.

My cousin shrugged and gave me a curious look, scratching the side of his head. I heard Desiree pull into our driveway in Dr. Lucienne's car. Before she could turn off the motor, Baby Red bolted out of the door to go meet her.

I left out the back door so I would not have to see that familiar glazed look on her face. And so I wouldn't have to see Burl sitting in his window like a statue, looking toward my house.

CHAPTER 27

Regina lived in the Mahoney Street projects with her mother, Maggie, in a Section 8 apartment. With the money that Miss Maggie got from disability and with what Regina made braiding hair, they could have afforded a place in a much nicer neighborhood. But because of Miss Maggie's severe case of agoraphobia, moving was out of the question. Miss Maggie was now to the point where she wouldn't even stand too close to a window. Her going outside even for a minute was still out of the question.

A lot of the people I knew thought all projects were run-down hellholes occupied by nothing but criminals and other low-level individuals. Those same people had never even been to the projects Regina lived in. To me, every visit to the projects was an adventure. And even though it was dangerous, the only murders we'd had in Belle Helene that year were in a nice, quiet white neighborhood full of doctors and lawyers. Regina's neighborhood was the only place where I could sass a grown person or cuss out loud and get away with it. The five shabby, graffiti-tagged buildings faced an empty lot. Before the drunks took over the lot, we used to play ball there. Inoperable and abandoned cars always lined the street. When I was younger, I used to jump up and down on the tops of the abandoned cars with the other kids. "Ghetto kids have all the fun," I used to tell Regina. Even though she agreed with me, she spent as much time in my neighborhood as she could.

Each time I visited Regina, aggressive individuals greeted me as soon as I entered the neglected grounds. They tried to sell me hot jewelry, meat still in the package, pirated videotapes, T-shirts, incense, dope, cookware, and hair products. Some of them got hostile if they saw you too many times and you didn't buy anything.

After a scar-faced woman blocked my path and told me one day, "Miss Thang, I hope don't nobody jump you and take them Nikes you got on when you leave," I started buying a thing or two. It was never something I needed or wanted. What I didn't pass on to Regina, I tossed in the first trash can I saw.

I loved attending "social" events in the projects. When it rained, the residents barbecued in the bathtub! We could get as rowdy as we wanted and not have to worry about the police. The few times people did call the police, by the time they showed up—*if* they showed up—the party was over.

Because I knew I'd do some drinking, I took a cab to Regina's party. I arrived around nine-thirty that night with a slab of cellophane-wrapped ribs that I had purchased from a man hiding in the shadows between two apartments on the ground floor.

"'Bout time you got here," Regina slurred, snatching the ribs out of my hand. "Is this suppose to be my birthday present?" She laughed, waving a can of generic beer in my face.

I had had so much on my mind, I had forgotten to buy Regina a present. I gave her a sheepish grin and nodded toward the ribs. "Oops. I left your other present at home."

"I'll get it tomorrow, and it better not be nothin' cheap." Regina winked and pulled me by the arm into the crowded living room.

In addition to Regina's mother and her mother's baby brother, Mel, there were at least forty other sweaty people in gaudy outfits present. After only ten minutes of mingling, I realized most of them were couples. Even Regina's pecan-colored mother, with her flat face and lopsided wig, had some man hanging on her ashy, spidery arm. "Smooth Operator" was blasting from four different speakers. Seeing Regina with her current boyfriend, a cute light-skinned brother who drove a bus, and all the other couples swaying against one another in the dimly lit living room made me feel lonelier than I'd ever felt before in my life.

Regina's uncle Mel, even with his receding hairline and extended belly, was beginning to look good to me. Even in his yellow suit and white shoes. Mel was only twenty-eight, and his flawless dark-brown skin reminded me of a Hershey bar. He flirted with me for an hour, winking his small, beady black eyes, before I decided I'd grab him and run as soon as he got close enough. But Buzzy Hawkins got to me first. That Buzzy. Now, he was a story within itself that had no ending. He had written a letter of apology to Kitty's parents a week after she had died in his car. The very next day, some other girl's daddy chased him down the street with a crowbar for messing with his fourteen-year-old daughter.

I didn't even know Buzzy was at the party until he surprised me by grabbing me around my waist from behind. Not knowing who it was almost scared me to death. My heart felt like it was trying to leap out of my chest.

"Damn, Carmen," he chirped, twirling me around. "Damn, Carmen," he repeated, this time looking me up and down, nodding his approval. I had only seen Buzzy a few times since the night Kitty died. From what I had heard, he had made himself scarce to avoid the wrath of Chester and some of Kitty's other male relatives. I had also heard that the accident had caused a major change in the way Buzzy behaved. He had gone to night school and earned his GED. Now, at twenty-one, he had his first job, working for a construction company. The thing I found hardest to believe about Buzzy that I had heard was that he had curtailed his womanizing. Especially the way he was all over me now. "What you up to these days, girl?"

"Just hanging in there, I guess. Looking forward to graduation," I told him, taking a sip from a can of beer. I had already eaten two rib sandwiches and shared a margarita with Regina. Not wanting to get too drunk, I had decided to drink only beer for the rest of the night.

"Well, I finally slowed down long enough to get myself back on track." He leaned back a few inches and inspected my face. "Where your man at tonight?"

"I don't have one," I admitted. Burl's image flashed through my mind, but he certainly did not qualify as my man.

Buzzy tilted that long head of his and blinked his eyes a few times. A gold tooth he now displayed did nothing to enhance his appearance. He was still ugly. "If you had been my girl, Kitty would still be alive," he casually informed me.

I gave him an incredulous look and gasped. "What's that supposed to mean?" I asked, waving my beer can in his face.

"I asked her for your phone number one time."

I gasped. "Why did you want my phone number?"

He let out a deep breath before continuing. "You was my first choice. I tried to get your phone number from her. I finally got it from Crazy Mimi."

"Kitty never told me," I said stiffly, setting my empty beer can on the table next to the stereo, forcing a plump roach to scurry off.

"Yeah. She fed me some ass-backwards story about her brother tryin' to get next to you."

"Chester never in his life tried to get with me," I said firmly.

Buzzy drank from his beer, belched, and said dryly, "I didn't think so. You ain't his type."

CHAPTER 28

"I know I'm ugly, Carmen. But it don't make no difference, 'cause I'm cool. I can get me any girl I want. And do you know why? I know how to treat 'em, that's why . . . if you know what I mean." Buzzy winked at me and slid his tongue across his bottom lip.

Of all the guys I knew, including Chester, Buzzy had dated the most girls. Like Kitty, his other girlfriends had chased him all over town like dogs in heat. Even with his miserable face, Buzzy displayed the confidence of a true ladies' man. Several girls had informed me that one way to tell if a guy was good in bed was by the frequency of his dates with the same girl. Especially a homely guy. Once Kitty had gotten beyond Buzzy's face and gone to bed with him, it seemed like she had slid into a river of no return.

Buzzy had pulled me into Regina's kitchen so that he could talk to me in private. I stood with my back against a noisy, hot, vibrating, round-shouldered refrigerator. Like every other room in the apartment, the kitchen had been filled with cheap items. Only two of the eyes on the stove worked. A battered hot plate sat on the counter next to the stove to make up for the two eyes that didn't work. Pictures of white kids with sad, bulging eyes decorated the kitchen walls. Thin plastic curtains covered the one grease-splattered window over the kitchen stove. The heat had melted the bottom parts of the curtains, and the sun had bleached them to where I couldn't determine the original colors. Mama would have been horrified to see such a tacky display. Except for the greasy window, everything else was clean and neatly arranged.

Buzzy had me pressed so hard against the refrigerator, I could barely breathe. His face was so close to mine, I could see faint scars on his face. He had sustained just a few cuts and bruises from the accident that had killed Kitty.

"Girl, this party ain't hittin' on nothin'. I had more fun at church last Sunday. Why don't me and you go to a real party," Buzzy growled in my ear. His brutally foul breath, a combination of alcohol and garlic, made me cough.

The party was not nearly as much fun as I had expected. Half of the people had already left to go to a rowdy club down the street. All of the beer was gone, and people were fighting over the last of the barbecue. That and the huge, hard bulge of Buzzy's crotch against mine, which felt quite good, helped me make a quick decision.

"Let me go tell Regina I'm leaving," I managed. Buzzy leaned back a few inches, but when I wrapped my arms around his waist and pulled him back to my crotch, a satisfied look appeared on his face.

I grabbed Regina off the dance floor and pulled her into the dim hallway outside her bedroom. Balancing a can of beer in one hand and a hot-link sandwich in the other, she listened as I told her my plan. She had on a red dress, but I could see sauce on it. There was even sauce on the tips of her braids.

"I am not surprised. Buzzy's been lookin' at you all night. I think he wants to try somethin', girl," Regina told me.

"I hope so," I whispered.

Regina guffawed. "Well, go on, Miss Hot Pants. I could sure use some myself, so get enough for me."

"What about what's-his-name in there?" I nodded toward the living room.

Regina dismissed that notion with a wave of her hand, then rolled her eyes. "That frisky, one-nut, one-minute motherfucker. He don't do nothin' but frustrate me. He don't know it, but tonight is the last night he'll be up in my face. I'm gonna find me a real man after

Mary Monroe

tonight." Regina paused and a serious look appeared on her face, making me uncomfortable.

"Why are you looking at me like that? You don't think I should go off with Buzzy?" I asked, glancing toward the kitchen, where I'd left Buzzy smoking a joint.

"If you don't, I will. Shit." Regina slapped my shoulder and gave me a thumbs-up. "Call me first thing tomorrow mornin'. I want to hear all the details. If what I done heard about Buzzy is true, I'll be the next girl to ride on his train."

Buzzy shared a one-bedroom apartment with a friend of his that I had never met. "Eddie sleeps like a possum. We ain't got to worry about him," Buzzy told me as I followed him to his car. The door on the passenger's side had been welded shut. I had to crawl in from his side. My seat belt was a knotted rope. On the floor were a tube of mascara and a few bobby pins next to a wadded-up bag from Burger King.

"Uh . . . can't we go someplace else other than your apartment?" I asked as the noisy old Pinto shot out into the street, almost sideswiping an oncoming car.

"Well . . . I guess. As long as you don't mind coverin' it. I just paid my rent and I'm broke as a haint till payday," he chirped.

I had never been to a motel, but I knew from Desiree that even a sleazy motel was at least twenty dollars.

"Oh," I replied, disappointed. "What about protection?"

"I'm all the protection you need, baby. Ain't nobody gonna try no shit with you while you with me. I will dick-slap 'em! And I don't leave my house 'less I'm packin' my piece—and I know how to use it," Buzzy said, patting his pocket. Knowing that Buzzy had a gun in his possession was the bad sign I should have paid more attention to, but I didn't. I was now too busy wondering if the gun had been the hard bulge I had felt when he'd pressed his pelvis against mine.

I cleared my throat and groaned. "That's not what I meant, Buzzy. I meant . . . protection like . . . condoms or something."

"Now, that's another three dollars." We stopped at a red light and he turned and looked me up and down, licking his bottom lip. "Girl, somethin' tells me we gonna need us a whole package of them motherfuckin' condoms." Poking the side of my arm, he grinned salaciously, then growled, "Look at you! Girl, you sharper than a serpent's tooth."

I laughed. "Buzzy, you are making this sound like a game."

Without warning, Buzzy reached over and massaged the inside of my thigh. I could feel myself getting wet between my legs for the first time in my life. As much as I wanted to finally see what all the fuss was about, I didn't want to spend too much of my money on it. The last time—which had also been my first time—I had financed a date was the fateful day I paid Burl's way to the movies. And the cab fare that had transported us part of the way to the train yard. Still paying the consequences for that date was enough for me.

"I don't have enough money for a motel and a whole package of condoms," I snapped. "Can't we just go somewhere dark and park behind some bushes? That's what Regina and her boyfriends do," I added sweetly.

Buzzy sighed. "That's so . . . so uncool," he scoffed. "I want this night to be special. What about that all-night drive-in theater off the freeway?"

"How much is that?"

"How much you got?"

I reached for my purse on my lap and fished out my wallet. I cracked it open and glanced at the contents, holding the wallet too low for Buzzy to see in it. "Just ten dollars," I lied. I had close to a hundred dollars on me. It was part of the money that Daddy had left to cover expenses for Baby Red and me.

"Hmmm." Buzzy caressed his chin. "Three dollars apiece to get into the show . . . snacks . . . rubbers." He slapped the steering wheel with the palm of his hot, hairy hand. "Shit." Then he talked and belched at the same time. "We can save three of them dollars and use it on some beer. I'll get you into the drive-in for free!" To save three dollars, Buzzy talked me into letting him sneak me into the drive-in movies in the trunk of his car.

Even though I didn't feel comfortable about hiding in a trunk, I agreed to do it. But I still cringed at the thought of having to pay for everything else. My long-overdue first taste of passion was only going to cost me ten dollars. I hoped that my ten dollars would be well spent. If it wasn't, I would never forgive myself. I promised myself that if I ever spent another dollar again to have a good time, it would be on a vibrator!

In a strange way, I hoped that Buzzy would be a lousy partner. That way, I wouldn't be so quick to stoop so low in the future.

Desiree's face entered my thoughts. She paid for sex all the time and she never complained. Not only did she pay for it; she glowed and risked all kinds of beatings from her daddy if he ever found out. It saddened me to know that this was what the world had come to for us girls.

CHAPTER 29

Buzzy and I stopped at the open-all-night mini-mart near the drive-in to pick up the beer and a burrito for him. While I sat in the car, I saw Chester's daddy drive by. He was going in the opposite direction, so he didn't see me, but I still crouched down in my seat. In my confused mind, I could hear Mr. Willie telling me all over again about Chester's getting married to the cheerleader and having a baby girl. I had not seen Chester in over four years. And even when he was still in Belle Helene, he went his way and I went mine. So I can't explain why I suddenly lost interest in Buzzy.

I looked through the window of the mini-mart. Buzzy was turned to the side as he leaned over the counter. His head looked like a missile. His lips were flapping like leaves in a strong wind. The clerk waiting on him, one of his friends, snapped his head around, held up a pair of horn-rimmed glasses to his face, and stared out the window at me. I sighed when he gave Buzzy a high five. Even though I couldn't hear the conversation, I assumed it was similar to the one I had had with Regina before I left her party. I realized right then and there that Buzzy would blab sooner or later about me having sex with him. I suddenly lost my nerve.

As soon as Buzzy made it back to the car, I had another lie ready to roll off of my lips. "I got some bad news," I began.

He just grunted and started the car without even looking at me. He had dropped the bag with the forty-ounce bottle of beer and condoms on the floor on top of my foot, almost smashing my toes. "Them damn condoms done gone up a whole dollar! Damn crooks. I don't know what the world is comin' to! I couldn't get a whole package like I wanted to. We'll have to make do with just two, I guess."

"We won't be needing condoms," I said quietly.

"The hell we won't. Shit, girl. I ain't wantin' to catch no disease they can't cure. I mean, you look clean and healthy and all, but that don't mean nothin'. I'm too young to die over a piece of tail." We sped the wrong way down a one-way street toward the freeway. "I'm horny as a motherfucker. My dick is harder than times in 'thirty-nine. We gotta make the best out of them two rubbers till I get paid."

"I'm a virgin, Buzzy!" I snapped. It angered me more to hear that his only concern was catching a deadly disease from me. "How could you catch something from me? You ought to be more worried about getting me pregnant."

"Now, I ain't about to be nobody's daddy, neither." He laughed and stepped on the gas even harder, not even concerned about the highway patrol car we passed parked on the side of the freeway. "What's the bad news you got to tell me?"

I sucked in my breath and fiddled with the strap on my purse. "My period just started," I said, pulling a package of tampons out of my purse.

Buzzy didn't even look at me. He just sighed and slapped the steering wheel. "I knew this was too good to be true. Shit." He sighed again. "Well, since we already got the beer, and the drive-in is the next exit, what say we go on, watch a movie anyway? Lemme pull over by them bushes so you can get in that trunk. All right?"

I nodded and shrugged. "What the hell . . ."

CHAPTER 30

Buzzy cussed under his breath when I got out of his car and went to go squat down on the ground to slide in a tampon. We had parked along the tree-lined road outside the drive-in theater. He stuck his head out of the window and watched me.

"I oughta' fuck you anyway," he said casually. "A bloody pussy is better than nothin'."

"Uh-uh. I got cramps, too," I said, forcing myself to groan.

"And what the hell is that? That like the clap?"

I gave him an exasperated look and stood up, zipping my pants.

"Hurry up so you can get your butt in that trunk, girl," he yelled.

"I'm ready," I hissed.

I was glad I had on a leather pants outfit. I could not imagine crawling into the trunk of a car in one of my nice dresses. The trunk was just as dark, musty, and spooky as I had imagined it would be. It would not have been so uncomfortable if I had had more room. I had to fold myself almost in half to keep the greasy tools and old clothes that Buzzy had in the trunk out of my face. Luckily, there were enough holes in the trunk for me to get a lot of air as the car crawled down the dark road.

After a few minutes, I felt the car stop briefly. I assumed Buzzy was paying for the one ticket. Then the car moved in a zigzag manner for another few minutes. Each time, the nasty tools shifted and got closer to my face. Finally the car stopped, and I heard Buzzy's key in the keyhole of the trunk. It jiggled for more than two minutes before it stopped. I expected the hood to pop open, but it didn't. I heard the key jiggle in the lock some more, but the door still did not pop open. Five, ten, fifteen minutes went by and I was still locked in the trunk of Buzzy's car. I stayed there curled up and feeling like a fool for half an hour before I started pounding on the roof of the hood.

All kinds of crazy thoughts ran through my head. Was Buzzy playing a cruel joke on me because my period had cheated him out of a good time? Had some other girl's boyfriend or daddy attacked him? I didn't know what to think. My hand was throbbing, so pounding some more didn't appeal to me. I just waited. About another half hour later, just as I was about to start crying and yelling, I heard more jiggling in the keyhole and some muffled voices. At last, after I had peed on myself, the trunk of the door popped open. There were faces of men in police uniforms staring at me. The only one I recognized was Chester Sheffield.

"What the hell—Crazy Legs, is that you?" Unlike Buzzy, who still had the high-pitched voice of an adolescent, Chester's voice was unbelievably deep now. *He sounded like Barry White!* Chuckling under his breath, he grabbed my wrist and pulled me out onto the ground. My legs buckled, but his arms went around my waist to keep me from falling.

"Girl, what in the hell were you thinkin'?" Chester boomed. There was a young white officer with Chester, and another scowling white man chewing on a thick cigar. I assumed he was the theater manager. They all chuckled. Chester just looked me up and down, frowning and shaking his head. I could not believe how much more handsome he looked in a uniform. The years had been good to him. He was bigger and better than ever. His hand on my arm felt like a vise. Gone was the scowl I'd seen on his face more times than I cared to remember. His crooked smile was a welcome relief.

"Chester Sheffield? You're back? You're a policeman?" I asked all in one breath. This was all the information I had failed to get sooner by avoiding his daddy's store.

"I'm still in trainin'," he mumbled, squinting his eyes to see my face. "Girl, look at you. You look like you been mauled."

"I feel like it, too," I said, brushing off the sides of my pants. "Uh . . . where's Buzzy?" I looked around. Several people had climbed out of their vehicles and were standing around grinning and clutching bags of popcorn and other snacks.

"He's where he should be!" Chester snapped, balling his fist. "He had a slew of outstanding warrants and an unregistered gun on him. He'll be off the streets for a few weeks. Come on, girl. I'm takin' you home."

"This was Buzzy's idea," I said quickly, looking from Chester to the theater manager. "I've never done anything like this before."

As it turned out, Buzzy had broken his car key trying to open the trunk. Unable to locate a locksmith, he had been forced to call the police. He was already in the backseat of the police car when Chester escorted me to it. A tow truck pulled up behind Buzzy's car.

"This is fucked up!" Buzzy hissed in my ear as soon as I slid in beside him. "Fucked up!"

I sat with my head bowed submissively during the whole ride, not saying a word until Chester turned onto my street.

"Chester, can you let me out at the corner?" I pleaded.

"No problem," he offered over his shoulder. "Carmen, you know you lucky I got this call," he added gruffly, peering at me through his rearview mirror. "The theater manager wanted us to arrest both of y'all."

"Oh," was all I could say.

As soon as the car stopped, Chester leaped out and trotted around the side to let me out, pulling me by my hand. He slammed the door shut and led me a few feet away from the car.

"They call what you and knucklehead did defraudin' a theater owner. I hope the next time you go out with that loser, he treat you with a little more class. If you was any other girl, I'd run you in anyway." He paused and shook a finger in my face. "You better behave yourself, now. If I catch you tryin' to pull a stunt like this again, I'm goin' to teach you a lesson you'll never forget. Do you hear me?" He grinned.

"Thanks, Chester," I said sheepishly. "Uh . . . are you back here to stay?"

He nodded. I almost peed again when he leaned back and looked me over, smiling and caressing his chin. "Nature's been good to you, huh?"

"You, too," I said shyly, looking at the big black boots on his feet. "Them crazy legs is twice as long, ain't they?"

"I'm five-eight now," I replied, nervously brushing off my clothes. The leather I had on hid the fact that I had peed on myself in Buzzy's trunk. Even though you couldn't see the wet pee spot, I could smell it. I moved away so Chester wouldn't. I cleared my throat and stood up straighter. "Your daddy told me you got married."

His mood changed and a dark look crossed his face. "Well, did he tell you I also got divorced?"

"No, he didn't," I said hopefully. It was hard to believe that this was the same brooding bully I had fantasized about throughout my youth. In the blink of an eye, the puppy love I thought I had outgrown had returned with a vengeance. "That's a crying shame. . . ."

Chester let out his breath and looked away. "Yeah." Then he looked at my face again. "Tell your sister I got her weddin' invitation. I'm sorry I haven't responded. We've been busy as hell tryin' to control all them punk-ass kids around here tryin' to form gangs and shit." He waved his hand in disgust. "I swear to God, them hardheaded moth-erfuckers about to drive me crazy." He shook his head and chuckled. "And I used to be one of 'em."

"I remember," I grinned.

He grinned sheepishly and winked at me. "Well, it was nice seein' you again." Then he tipped his hat and turned to leave.

"You got your own place?" I called after him. I glanced briefly to-ward the cul-de-sac at the big house he had grown up in next door to Burl. The Sheffields' house was dark, but the lights were on in Burl's living room. To my everlasting horror, Burl was peeping out of his liv-ing room window! I experienced a heat wave of disgust.

"I live in one of my old man's houses," he said, climbing back into the police car. "Listen, take care of yourself."

I stood on the sidewalk at the corner looking toward my house. The only light on was the one in Babette's room. Desiree's daddy's car was still in our driveway. As I dragged my feet down the sidewalk, look-ing toward the cul-de-sac, I saw Burl waving like a madman. I waved back. Then I turned my back to Burl and watched until the police car turned the corner.

Not only was I covered in filth from the floor of Buzzy's car trunk, sweat was pouring down my face. As soon as I got inside, Desiree floated down the stairs with that annoying glow on her face that I had come to hate. Funny thing is, it didn't bother me this time, because my face was glowing just as much.

"How was the party?" she asked, marching toward the kitchen, wearing one of Mama's best negligees. I followed her and stood in the doorway as she snatched open the refrigerator and grabbed one of Daddy's bottles of beer and opened it with her teeth, spitting the top into the sink.

"It was all right," I said casually.

Desiree took a long sip, burped, and then gave me a knowing look. "What's his name?" she asked with an accusatory look.

"Who?"

"The guy who put that smile on your face. Anybody I know?"

I smiled shyly. "Did you know Chester was back in town?"

"Chester who?" She drank again, then screwed up her face. "Oh, you mean Kitty's brother. I heard he got a divorce. Was he at the party?"

"Uh . . . no. I bumped into him on my way home." I sniffed. "He's changed a lot," I continued, still smiling. "His voice sounds exactly like Barry White's now."

"Where are the Pop Tarts?" Desiree asked, skipping around the kitchen with her naked body exposed. "Your cousin is always hungry." She grinned and winked. "I think he should nibble on something other than me."

"The Pop-Tarts are in the cupboard next to the stove." I motioned with my hand. "I wonder why Chester got a divorce."

"I hope these damn things aren't fattening," Desiree snapped, pulling a partial container of Pop Tarts out of the cupboard. Then she shrugged and darted out of the kitchen. Over her shoulder she yelled, "By the way, Burl called a few times."

I stared out the window toward the cul-de-sac. Burl was still sitting in his window looking toward my house.

CHAPTER 31

The morning after Regina's party, I rolled out of bed around nine A.M. I had no idea what time Desiree had left our house, but by the time I got myself up and dressed, she was gone. So was Baby Red. His bike was missing, so I knew he was not with her. There was no evidence that Desiree had even been in the house. She had made Babettte's bed, tossed out all of the wine bottles she and Baby Red had emptied, and returned Mama's negligee to the top drawer of Mama's bedroom dresser drawer. And either she or Baby Red had sprayed the whole house with room deodorizer, because there was not a trace of marijuana fumes left. However, they had overlooked the trash can in the upstairs bathroom. Right in plain view were at least half a dozen used condoms. I held my nose and fished out the slimy condoms with a toothbrush I no longer used. I ran back downstairs to the kitchen and pitched the condoms and the toothbrush into the trash can.

One of the many things that kept me from letting myself go and get as much out of life as I could was the fact that I cared too much about how my actions affected other people. I went out of my way to avoid disappointing everybody. And when I did, I went in the opposite direction trying to make up for it.

Burl was surprised but pleased to see me when I showed up at his house the next morning, hugging a large bag containing three take-out breakfasts.

"Mama, Carmen brought us breakfast," he shouted over his shoulder as he let me in the house, grinning and bobbing his head. His hair had been freshly combed and oiled, but the familiar wide part was missing from the bouquet of curls. For the first time, Burl looked his age and not like a man several years older. He had on a crisp, white cotton shirt, but a nasty dark ring had already started forming around his collar. "I tried to call you last night to see if you wanted to come watch *Scarface* with me." He lowered his voice and added, "I rented *Halloween II,* too. Since I went to sleep on it that time me and you went to see it at the movies." I groaned under my breath and stumbled behind Burl as he wheeled furiously toward the kitchen yelling, "Mama, you don't have to cook this mornin'."

Miss Mozelle, standing over the stove, about to pour some instant grits into a pan of boiling water, froze. "Well, do say." She gave me an anxious look as she wiped her hands on her ruffled apron. Her standing next to Burl was a heart-wrenching sight. As soon as she dried her hands, she rested one on Burl's shoulder and started stroking him.

"You hurry and sit yourself right on down, Miss Mozelle," I ordered, removing the Styrofoam containers from the bag and placing everything on the table. "I went by Tommy's and picked up eggs, sausage, grits, biscuits, and home fries. Burl, I got some of that plum jam you like so much. Miss Mozelle, I got you an extra order of sausages."

"You so sweet." Miss Mozelle grinned, waddling around the kitchen, gathering plates and silverware. "I told Burl to stop mopin' around here. You ain't forgot about him." Miss Mozelle's dry, rubbery lips brushed the side of my cheek. She then wiped her hands on the lap of her apron and pulled out a chair for me. I didn't usually eat breakfast, but I forced myself to dive into the grits.

"Did Burl tell you the good news? His uncle is drivin' a special-made van down here for him to get around with. Now he can take you out and do most everything else the other kids do," Miss Mozelle said, beaming as she wiped slime from Burl's lips with a napkin.

"Uncle Mogen's bringin' me a motorized wheelchair, too," Burl added, talking with his mouth full.

"Oh, that's nice," I said sadly. The thought of Burl becoming more mobile could only mean one thing: he'd expect to spend even more time with me. Shit!

"We can even go to the drive-in sometime," Burl chirped.

"Yeah, we can, can't we?" I said glumly, forcing myself to smile.

A pensive look appeared on Burl's face. He sucked his teeth before speaking. "Carmen, why did a police car bring you home last night? I seen you."

"Oh, that? I couldn't get a cab to come pick me up from the projects, and everybody else was too drunk to drive." The words shot out of my mouth like bullets. I speared two link sausages at the same time and stuffed them into my mouth.

"Oh," Burl mumbled, his eyes staring blankly.

"You goin' to church this mornin'?" Miss Mozelle asked, spraying my face with bits of scrambled eggs.

I swallowed first and then wiped juice from my lips. "Uh, no. My cousin left the house in a mess, and it's going to take me all day to clean it up," I lied. It amazed me how ornate my fibs had become. "After that, I have to do about six loads of laundry." Somehow, I managed to eat most of the food on my plate in less than two minutes. "I can't stay long," I added, already rising and still chewing.

"If I was you, I'd make that lazy-ass Baby Red clean up his own mess," Miss Mozelle snorted, spearing another piece of sausage. "Carmen, since you up, could you run out to the front porch yonder and bring the throw rugs in I left to air out last night?"

"Yes, ma'am." I was glad I had an excuse to leave the room. As soon as I got out to the porch, I gasped and stopped in my tracks. A shiny red Corvette was in the Sheffields' driveway. I had noticed it before, but I didn't know who it belonged to. One thing for sure, it was not the type of car Mr. or Mrs. Sheffield drove. They drove the usual station wagons and other ordinary vehicles associated with conservative people like them. As I was about to lift the throw rugs off the porch banister, Chester sauntered out of his parents' house, leading his mother by her arm. They didn't even notice me standing there with my jaws twitching. I ducked into the doorway and peeped through the screen as Chester helped his mother into the passenger's seat of the Corvette. I waited until they drove away.

"So Chester's back in town," I said, returning to the kitchen. Burl and his mother were so involved with the lavish breakfast I had bought them, they didn't even hear me. "Where should I put the rugs, Miss Mozelle?"

"Huh? Oh. Just drop 'em on the floor. I'll deal with 'em later on. Burl, baby, stop eatin' like you at a hog trough. Pay some attention to your company," Miss Mozelle barked. "Carmen's the best friend you got."

Burl looked up at me, chewing so hard his ears wiggled. "I'll have my new van by the weekend," he announced proudly. "And my new wheelchair."

"That's nice, Burl. I want to be the first one to ride in it. The *van*, I mean. I'll call you later on today."

I left and returned home, where I spent most of the day peeping out of the living room window toward the cul-de-sac, hoping I'd see that red Corvette again.

CHAPTER 32

Compared to everything else I was guilty of, being a bald-faced liar, too, didn't seem so bad. My life had become a series of deep, murky rivers with bridges of lies helping me cross over each one without falling in.

"Carmen, this is Andre Lucienne. How's your ankle, child?"

The minute I heard Desiree's daddy's voice on the telephone, I knew I had to think fast. It was obvious that Desiree had used me as a cloak to keep her daddy from knowing that she had spent the night frolicking in my sister's bed with Baby Red while I was at Regina's party, plotting my own escapade with Buzzy Hawkins.

"Huh? Oh! My ankle is fine now, Dr. Lucienne," I said quickly, holding the telephone receiver away from my ear. It seemed like every time I told a lie I wasn't prepared for, my ears burned.

"Well, you'd better stay off of it for a while. And keep soaking it in that Epsom salt concoction Desiree prepared for you. I'm sending her back over there to spend the night with you again. Oh, Desiree!" Dr. Lucienne's voice trailed off. After a few moments, Desiree was on the other line.

"Girl, don't you be up prancing yourself around that house on that ankle. As soon as I get back from church I'm coming back over there," Desiree said breathlessly.

"All right," I mumbled, hanging up the telephone before Dr. Lucienne got too nosy.

It took me a few moments to put the puzzle together. Desiree's daddy thought she had spent the night with me because I'd injured my ankle. Now that she had laid the groundwork for another lie, I had to go along with it. I was not the least bit surprised when the telephone rang again less than a minute later.

"Carmen, it's Desiree," she whispered. "Are you coming to church today?"

"No," I told her.

"Good. I don't want you around Daddy until we've had a chance to talk. Listen, after church I'll take Daddy home. I'll be over to your place as soon as I get him settled in. Baby Red should be back from Mobile by then."

"You're spending the night over here again?"

"Not the whole night. Just a few hours."

"What if your daddy wakes up and comes over here?"

"Girl, Armageddon wouldn't wake Daddy up after he's had a few highballs. I have to go get ready for church. 'Bye, now." That Desiree. She never ceased to amaze me.

I didn't call Regina to tell her about my encounter with Buzzy like I had told her I would. I had no intention of telling anybody about that disaster at the drive-in. The thing that stood out above all the other things on my mind was that Chester Sheffield was back in my life. I knew I had to do something or my obsession would escalate. I just didn't know what.

Still wrapped up in my bathrobe, I watched a few dull TV programs, leafed through *Essence* magazine, and took a brief nap on the living room sofa. I didn't realize the whole afternoon had drifted by until Desiree blew into the house like a storm.

"How was church?" I asked, not moving from the corner I had claimed on the living room sofa. Knowing that my parents were gone, like an obnoxious relative, Desiree had entered the house without knocking. She still had on the prim and proper outfit she had worn to church: a pastel blue suit with matching gloves and shoes. Her hairdo was a neatly braided bun at the nape of her neck.

"A fat woman fainted and fell on Deacon Mays," she told me, falling onto the love seat across from me, peeling off her gloves.

"Other than that, everything was the same; Reverend Poe's sermon put half of us to sleep." She lifted her head and looked around, all wide-eyed and anxious as she fanned her face with her gloves. "Did Baby Red make it back from Mobile yet?"

"I haven't heard from him."

"Did he call?"

"I haven't heard from him," I repeated.

"Well, Daddy's in for the night. Nurse Bertha's at the house in case, getting paid to do next to nothing. The old crone. Anyway, you fell on the steps in Regina's building last night after the party. That's how you twisted your ankle. Got that?" Desiree said, shaking her gloves in my direction like a stern teacher advising a difficult pupil.

"Did I go to the hospital?" I asked, my voice dripping with sarcasm.

"No, you didn't. The Epson salt and hot water I mixed worked. But you stirred around too much too soon, and that's why your ankle is all swollen up now. Daddy insisted that I come back over here to keep an eye on you. We prayed for you at church today."

"Desiree, how can you roll out so many lies after just coming from church?"

Desiree laughed, sighed, and fanned her face some more, this time wiping sweat off her forehead with the gloves. She blinked hard a few times and started chewing her nails. All during this time there was an expression on her face I didn't see too often. She was so deep in thought, it seemed like she was talking to herself. "Remember Kitty's big brother?" she began, her voice low and steady.

I sat bolt upright. "You mean Chester? What about him?"

"He escorted his mama to church today." Desiree paused and a puzzled look appeared on her face. "I never paid much attention to him before today. I didn't know he was so . . . so *fine.*"

"Oh, is he?" I asked casually. I got up and padded across the floor and flipped on the television, hoping to divert Desiree's attention. I was so preoccupied, I didn't realize I had turned on a Spanish-speaking soap opera.

"There was this sister with him, hanging on his arm like a sling. First thing next Saturday, I'm taking my tail to the mall for a serious makeover. She looks like that new singer from England, Sade. I felt like a flying monkey in the same room with a girl that pretty." Desiree paused and shook her head, then rolled her eyes and moaned in a way that embarrassed me. She blinked and then stared straight ahead with a glazed expression as she continued talking. "Either he gave her a real nice Christmas present or she's bowlegged as hell. Umph!" Desiree slid off the love seat and curled up on the floor.

I was glad she couldn't see my face. The frown I made even scared me.

CHAPTER 33

Christmas Day, about a week after Regina's party, was one of the most miserable days of my life. I didn't know what to do with myself. It was the first Christmas I had spent without my immediate family. Baby Red didn't celebrate Christmas—or any other holiday, for that matter. However, he spent it with Desiree, holed up in Babette's room with numerous bottles of fine wine, condoms, and vegetarian snacks.

"And what medical problem am I supposed to have this time?" I asked Desiree as she danced around our kitchen gathering wineglasses, ice, and plates during a break from Baby Red.

"Don't worry about what I told Daddy. I have him under control today," she snorted, frowning as she shattered ice cubes she had wrapped in a paper towel against the edge of the counter. "Hand me a bowl," she ordered, moving around the kitchen so fast I got a cramp in my neck from turning so frequently to keep my eyes on her.

"Your daddy still slapping and punching you around?" I asked boldly. It had been a while since we had discussed the abuse Desiree endured. There was no question in my mind that it was still going on. The frequent bruises on her body, and an occasional black eye, told the whole story.

Desiree dropped her head and stared at the floor. The ice cubes in the towel had started to melt. Huge teardrops of water oozed through the towel and onto the floor. "You don't know men like I do," she told me.

"And what do you know about men that I don't know?"

"It's all about experiences, girl." Desiree sniffed and gave me a thoughtful look. "When I was seven, I went to spend the summer with my aunt Rita in New Orleans, where some of my daddy's folks still live. One day she sent me to the store. On my way back I saw her running down the sidewalk screaming, with no shoes on and curlers still in her hair. Uncle Ed was chasing her with his belt. By the time I reached the house, she was hiding behind some bushes on the side of the house. He beat at the bushes with that wide leather belt until my aunt crawled out. He dragged her by her ankles into the yard, and then he beat her to a pulp because she had threatened to leave him for another man. His belt buckle hit her in the eye and she lost all the vision in it. 'I'm the only man would have your blind ass now,' my uncle told her when he brought her home from the hospital. She never spoke to her lover again, and she had lied to the doctor that a piece of metal had flown up in her eye. A few weeks later, sitting in her parlor with the black patch covering her eye that she'll have to wear for the rest of her life, she told me all men beat their women. It's their real rite of passage." Desiree sniffed and looked in my eyes. I was stunned when a weak smile appeared on her face.

I dismissed her comments with a detached groan and an abrupt wave of my hand, but that was not enough. I cleared my throat so I could say what I wanted to say and get it right the first time. "Fuck that rite of passage shit! The one time my daddy slapped my mama, she laid his head open with an iron skillet, and he's been walking a chalk line ever since," I wailed. "And anyway, Dr. Lucienne is your daddy, not your man."

"A man's a man. Where's the bowl I asked you for?"

I handed Desiree a large bowl from the cupboard over the stove. It didn't bother me that she made herself so comfortable in my house whenever Mama and Daddy were not around. All of my friends did. I did the same thing when I visited their homes.

"Regina told me about that time you busted Chester Sheffield up alongside his head with a brick," Desiree said, grimacing. "I am scared of you."

"It was not a brick. It was some cans of corn," I snapped, poking my bottom lip out. I didn't like being reminded about my altercation with Chester.

"Girl, you must have knocked five years off of his lifespan. Nurse Bertha happened to be at the ER when they hauled him in stretched out on a gurney that day. She told me and Daddy that spot where you hit him would never heal all the way. A 'soft spot' is what Nurse Bertha said Chester has on his forehead from you hitting him. From now on."

"And I haven't hit anybody since," I said proudly.

Baby Red stomped on the floor in the bedroom above the kitchen, then followed that with a whiny yell. "You better get on upstairs. Tarzan's getting restless," I said dryly. "And save me some of that wine."

As soon as Desiree was safely out of the kitchen, I dragged a chair to the living room. I parked myself in the front window, peeping from behind the curtains toward the cul-de-sac. As long as I stayed behind the curtains, I could not be seen from outside. The last thing I wanted was for Chester to be visiting his parents and to see me doing something as desperate as spying on him. Worse than that was Burl seeing me and thinking it was him I was spying on.

Now that I was determined to get Chester out of my system, spying on him didn't make any sense. But then, what did?

CHAPTER 34

I was too afraid to ask around about Buzzy Hawkins and what had happened to him after his arrest at the drive-in. Since I hadn't heard from him since our ill-fated date, I assumed he was in jail. But during a casual conversation with Regina a week later, she mentioned that Buzzy had paid off his fines and moved to Nashville to live with his grandparents. In a way I was glad. I knew that if Buzzy had approached me about finishing what we had started, I would have agreed. Lord knows Buzzy was a piss-poor substitute for Chester, but by now I was just that anxious to let myself go.

On New Year's Day, 1988, I learned by peeping from behind the living room curtains that Burl's uncle delivered the Ford van Burl had been so excited about during my visit the morning after Regina's party. After more than a week of hour-long window-peeping sessions, I had seen Chester just once. The Corvette he drove had cruised past my house and stopped in the Sheffields' driveway. Seconds later, Chester leaped out, wearing jeans and a denim jacket. He didn't even look in my direction, but I still jumped to the side of the window and held the curtains together with both of my hands, leaving just enough of a crack for me to still be able to see out. I almost turned into a pillar of salt when I saw Chester open the passenger's door and help out the Sade look-alike that Desiree had told me about. I blinked hard to make sure my eyes were not playing tricks on me. I watched until they disappeared into the house, his arm wrapped around her shoulder like a python.

Burl's new dull-brown van and Chester's sleek red Corvette were solid symbols of how different these two men were. It seemed so ironic that they would both be on my mind so much these days, and at the same time.

It made Burl so happy to have me ride in the front seat of his van next to him. It did no good for him to explain to me how the van had been designed for a person who could not use his legs to drive. Even though I was grinning and making a few obligatory comments, my mind was not on Burl sitting there in a plain gray flannel shirt buttoned up to his chin in his new van that first Sunday into the new year. He had started wearing his hair parted again. The part was now in the middle of his head instead of on the side. Now his hair looked like a divided highway.

Somehow I managed to live through a double feature at the same drive-in theater that I had gone to on that disastrous date with Buzzy. To this day I could not remember the two movies Burl and I watched. I do remember that after we returned to our street and parked in front of my house, Burl hauled off and kissed me on the mouth! I immediately drifted into a brief state of shock. He had washed down a garlic-laden pizza and a pickled pig's foot with a few cans of Budweiser beer. His foul, hot breath made me cough. Burl had never been this forward with me before. Not even in the boxcar that day in the train yard. He guided my hand to his crotch. I massaged a soft golfball-sized lump. A lump that would never get hard again. I had to keep reminding myself that Burl had no feeling below his waist. I removed my hand and blinked stupidly, saddened by the frustration and sweat on his face.

"Carmen, I hope you know just how much I appreciate havin' you for a girlfriend. I'm blessed," Burl croaked in my ear, scratching the side of his neck worriedly.

Girlfriend?! That Burl.

I hugged him before I responded. "I'm blessed, too, Burl."

"You are the only real friend I got left around here," he said sadly.

"You have more friends than you know, Burl. If you were a little more outgoing you would know that." I slid my fingers through his hair.

"Well, now that I can get around better, I won't spend so much time sittin' in the house starin' out the window at your house," he informed me, laughing dryly.

A casual smile crossed my face. This time I leaned over and kissed Burl. My chest tightened as he parted my lips with his rubbery tongue and stuck it in my mouth so far back I almost gagged.

He was looking at me in a way that made me nervous, confused, and sad. A sleeve of moonlight beamed on his face, and his tongue probed even farther into my mouth. Tilting my head back, I asked, "Just how long is your tongue?"

"Long enough to make you very happy," he replied in a throaty voice, lightly patting my crotch. I had never witnessed Burl act in such a bold manner. It took me a moment to realize what he was proposing. I was still a virgin. I had not even performed the sexual basics. Oral sex was way too advanced for me.

"It's late. School starts up again tomorrow," I said, already opening the door. "I have to finish up a book report Mrs. Curry gave for us to do over the holidays."

Burl sniffed and pursed his lips before speaking again. "My offer stands from now on," he said firmly.

I nodded. "That's good to know." I jumped out of the van and took off running. I didn't stop until I was in the house and had locked the door.

CHAPTER 35

Before I had left to go to the drive-in with Burl, Daddy called to say that he and Mama would not return home until the first week in February. "But Babette's getting married this month!" I wailed.

"No she ain't, praise the Lord," Daddy snickered.

"What happened? Did she break up with . . . what's his name?" I had only met the Nigerian once that my sister had met at college and planned to marry. Not only was he good-looking, prosperous, and classy, he seemed like a nice guy. He was the most polite man I'd ever met in my life. Mama adored him. Daddy liked him, too, but was suspicious that he might be gay because he was way too perfect.

"Naw, she didn't break up with that African." Daddy snorted and snickered again. "He must be a pretty smart boy to be able to talk her into putting the wedding off until March. I told that girl she had to be out of her mind to be plannin' a weddin' on Superbowl weekend! Did I tell you that African got me season tickets? I guess I was wrong about him bein' a sissy, huh? Anyway, don't you and Baby Red burn that house down."

Baby Red spent so much time in Babette's bedroom with Desiree, it was like I was alone in the house. Even though I could hear the bedsprings squeaking and smell the familiar sweet aroma from the joints they sucked on, it still felt like I was in the house all by myself. With

Regina and Crazy Mimi spending so much time with their families and male friends, it had not been that hard for me to make up my mind to go to the drive-in with Burl when he asked. Besides, I didn't have anything better to do. Sitting around like an old maid watching TV by myself had become stale. But I was glad that the date was over and that I was back in the house. With us having to return to school the next day, I assumed that was why Desiree was not at my house.

Baby Red's bike was gone. So I was really alone. Before I could make it to my room, the telephone rang. I trotted across the living room floor and grabbed it, falling onto the sofa. I was facing the window that I spent so much time peeping out.

It was Crazy Mimi's mother and she was frantic. "Carmen, did my daughter leave your house yet?" Her voice choked and she moaned under her breath before continuing. "She didn't take her medication with her!"

"Huh? I just got home, Sister Jenkins. I've been at the drive-in movies all evening. I haven't seen Crazy Mimi, ma'am."

"Oh, Lord . . . that girl's been gone for hours. She disappeared while the rest of us was eatin' dinner. Then she called me from a pay phone and she said she was comin' to see you. Lord, she got all them babies with her, too."

"I haven't seen her. Do you want me to call the police?" Before Sister Jenkins could answer, I saw Crazy Mimi walking casually down the sidewalk toward my house, her three toddlers marching behind her like little soldiers. "Sister Jenkins—Crazy Mimi and the kids are coming up the walkway right now!" I hollered.

"Carmen, child, will you hold 'em till I can get over there? I declare, it's gettin' harder and harder to keep a eye on that girl. The last thing I want to do is put her away, but I'm gettin' too old for all this mess." Two years ago Crazy Mimi's parents had signed her into a facility where they thought she'd be better off. They took her out after only a week. There was a big scandal about some of the male orderlies taking advantage of the female patients. A woman who had been in a comatose condition for five years came up pregnant. Crazy Mimi insisted that none of the men had touched her, but when a doctor checked her out she had a venereal disease. One of the smartest things Crazy Mimi's parents did was to have Dr. Lucienne sterilize her.

"Oh, please, Sister Jenkins, you can't put Crazy Mimi in another one of those asylums. She'll go crazy—or worse. As long as we all look out for her, she'll be all right. Listen, I got my daddy's car. I'll bring her and the kids home right now," I insisted.

I hung up the telephone and ran to the front door. I didn't even wait for Crazy Mimi to knock. I jumped off the porch. "Girl, where have you been?" I asked, bending down to gather her whining, snotty-nosed kids around me. "Your mama is on the verge of a nervous breakdown!"

"Where I been is my business," Crazy Mimi said seriously, looking past me toward my house. "Can you call me a cab?" Her face was smudged with sand. Her brown corduroy jumper had grass stains and there were dead leaves stuck to the back of her head. Her hair, in two long, thick braids, looked like horns. Crazy Mimi was nineteen now, but just as confused as ever. A continent of tiny pus-filled pimples dotted her forehead. It was the first I ever saw pimples on a Black teenager. Half of the white kids I knew had complexions that looked like pale peanut brittle, but it saddened me to see such a blight finally claim Crazy Mimi, a girl whose feeble mind seemed destined to destroy her and the people who loved her. I was so glad to see her and the kids, I hugged them all.

"I'll take you and the kids home," I said, my arm still around Crazy Mimi's shoulder.

I loaded her and her dazed babies into the car and shot off like a bullet down the street in silence.

About a block away, the hefty ex-pilot from next door was out walking his cat. He was taking his good old time crossing the street, forcing me to slow down.

Before I could stop her, Crazy Mimi rolled down the window and screamed, "Get your black ass outta that street!"

I swerved around the stunned man and his cat and shot off again, turning the corner on two wheels.

"Carmen, why you drivin' so fast?" Crazy Mimi asked, rolling the window back up. She was in the front passenger's seat, cradling Samantha, her four-year-old daughter in her arms.

"I got to hurry up and get back home so I can get to bed. I got school tomorrow," I explained, yelling so I could be heard over all three of Crazy Mimi's kids' screaming. There were so many distractions inside the car, I could not focus on what was going on outside. I guess that's why I ran that red light.

A police car, it's siren yipping loud enough to wake the dead, roared out of nowhere.

"Goddamn it!" I shrieked, pulling over to the side of Main Street across the street from Sheffield's Market. The police car stopped directly behind me, and I immediately started rooting around in my purse for my driver's license. I still had my head down when there was a sharp, single tap on my window.

"Chester? What in the world—" I mouthed, rolling down the window. The air was cool, but my denim jacket felt as heavy and hot as a military blanket. I could already feel the sweat sliding down my back like night crawlers.

"May I see your license and registration, please? You just ran a red light." I could not believe how cold and distant Chester sounded. He blinked slowly and then stared at me with so much intensity, a chill went through me all the way down to my bones. I blinked, too, and he must have interpreted it the wrong way, because he let out a disgusted breath, rolled his eyes at me, and shook his head impatiently. "Miss Taylor, will you please show me your driver's license and registration?" he said gruffly and with a straight face.

"Miss Taylor?" I gasped, narrowing my eyes to see his face better in the dark.

"May I see your license and registration, please," he repeated, looking at me like I was a rank stranger. Now he was shining a flashlight in my face.

"Chester, what's the matter with you? That damn job done gone to your head or what?" Crazy Mimi muttered, shaking her finger at Chester.

"Would you be quiet, Miss Jenkins," he said, shining the flashlight on the documents I had just handed him.

"Don't you 'Miss Jenkins' me, you black-ass nigger! I know where you live!" Crazy Mimi shrieked, then started sobbing so violently all three of her children stopped howling at the same time, their eyes staring curiously at her now.

"Miss Jenkins, one more word from you and I'll cite you, too," Chester threatened. "I advise you to be quiet."

"And I advise you to lick my pussy, motherfucker," Crazy Mimi sobbed, wiping her nose with the back of her hand.

Chester grunted and stomped the ground once. Then he looked around before he returned his attention to Crazy Mimi, shaking his flashlight in her direction. With his head cocked to the side he roared, "Girl, shaddup!"

I glared at Crazy Mimi myself. She stopped talking but she kept on crying as I turned back to Chester. "Um . . . now, you know all about her mental condition. She doesn't know any better," I said in a low voice, my hand cupping my mouth.

Chester eyed me sharply, a trace of contempt in his eyes. Finally, but slowly, he nodded. "I am well aware of your friend's mental state." He paused and stood up straight, like he was showing off his tall frame on purpose. "And if you don't mind me sayin', I have some serious concerns about *your* mental state, too." He paused long enough to watch my mouth drop open as I gave him the most incredulous look I could come up with.

"Excuse me?" I managed, rotating my neck for emphasis.

"It seems like you are havin' difficulty choosin' friends," he snorted, handing me the ticket he had scribbled. "This is the second time in less than a month that I've come across you in the company of . . . well . . ." He paused again and let out a disgusted breath. "For old times' sake, do me a favor and get yourself a better class of friends. The ones you got now seem to keep draggin' you into one mess after another. Believe me, jail ain't no place for a girl like you, Crazy Legs. Y'all have a nice evenin', now." He tipped his hat and turned to walk back to his squad car.

I was stunned, angry, disappointed, and speechless.

Crazy Mimi said what I was thinking about Chester: *"That nigger's crazy!"*

CHAPTER 36

Babette ended up canceling the lavish wedding Mama had been looking forward to. Instead, she and her Nigerian eloped the same night Mama and Daddy returned from Montgomery. Relieved, Daddy was grinning all over the place. He was going to save a lot of money. But Mama cried off and on for three days.

"The dress that Sister Meachum was going to make is a duplicate of the one Princess Diana wore when she married Prince Charles," Mama reminded me, blinking her swollen, red eyes at me from across the kitchen table. She suddenly stopped crying and gave me a critical look. Then a smile appeared on her face. "Maybe we can still get that dress made and *you* can wear it!"

Such a jolt went through me, I accidentally knocked a saucer full of bacon to the floor. "I'll probably never get to wear it either," I said seriously.

Mama screwed up her face like she was going to start crying again. Instead, she snapped her fingers and told me proudly, "Of course you will. I see the way these boys around here look at you."

I bowed my head, my eyes on the bacon I had just picked up from the floor. "Well, I doubt if I'll land a prize like Babette did."

"You don't have anything to worry about. I've been praying for you," Mama told me.

Before Mama could stop grieving over Babette's canceled wedding,

Babette threw another monkey wrench into Mama's plans. She dropped out of college and moved to Nigeria to become familiar with her new in-laws and their culture. Mama was inconsolable.

Again she held me hostage at the kitchen table in a pre-dinner discussion. She told me in a voice barely above a whisper, "When you do get married, the least you can do is marry a local boy. One that won't grab ahold of you and drag you to some faraway-off place like Babette's husband did." Mama stared at me for an uncomfortably long time and it made me nervous. But not nearly as nervous as what she said next. "I'm so proud you didn't turn your back on poor Burl the way his other friends did after he became disabled. Devotion is a virtue. People know they can always count on a truly devoted friend." Mama patted my hand and gave me a conspiratorial smile as Daddy entered the kitchen from the garage.

"Whose goose y'all cookin' now, and how much is it gwine to cost me?" Daddy asked, wiping his hands on an oily, wrinkled rag. The evening shadow of brittle whiskers, more gray than black, almost covered the bottom half of his face.

"Carmen just promised me we don't have to worry about her marrying and moving halfway around the world," Mama chirped. Her eyes sparkled; her lips curled up at the ends.

Complete exasperation was the best way to describe the look on Daddy's face. After a quick peek into the oven, he dismissed us with a brief but effective scowl and a wave of his hand.

I chose not to have a party to celebrate my eighteenth birthday a few weeks later that March. My last year of school had not been what I expected. I spent too much time being depressed and worried to enjoy it. Several boys had asked to take me to the prom, but I'd chosen to attend the all-night Marx Brothers film festival with Burl. Desiree turned down a few boys and spent prom night with Baby Red. Afterward, she had convinced her daddy that she and I had gone to the prom with two boys from our graduating class. Regina went to the prom with a mailman she had been eyeing for months. "Girl, senior prom is a once-in-a-lifetime thing. You gonna regret not goin' when you get old," Regina insisted.

Old? At eighteen I felt like I had already lived a hundred years.

I was in no hurry to continue my education. School had been a necessary burden, but it was one I wanted to put aside for a while. Surprisingly, my parents did not pressure me to go to college. They had ridden Babette's back like a mule throughout her high school years until she broke down and decided to go get her teaching credential. I figured out why they didn't jump on my back, too, when I overheard part of a tense conversation between my parents the last week in May. They had been giving me suspicious looks during dinner one evening, so I decided to investigate by lurking outside their bedroom door to see if I could hear what they were cooking up. From what I could piece together, they were afraid that if I went off to Alabama State like my sister Babette did, I'd run off with a foreigner, too. I waited a few days after I'd heard that conversation, and then I revealed my interest in pursuing a nursing career in a few years. Mama was pleased with my decision. Daddy's reaction was still "Girl, I don't care what you do as long as it ain't illegal."

In June, a week after graduation, I got hired as a junior secretary at Holtsmark and Leefe, a law firm in downtown Belle Helene. Eric Holtsmark was Daddy's lawyer and the kind of boss most people dream about. He was generous, fair, sensitive, and out of the office a lot. I settled into a small cubicle with a window, next to a nervous spinster with eyes and a shapeless wardrobe as gray as her hair. Miss Lutie Peterson was the senior secretary that I had been hired to assist.

She spent most of her day making sure I was happy. I never saw a person so happy to buy another's lunch, and I let her treat me as often as she wanted to. She once took me to an old restaurant in a part of town where the only Black people you saw were maids and butlers. Daddy was stunned when I told him I'd eaten lunch at Lester's Kitchen. "I was one of the ones that helped integrate that place. After I ate there I heard from one of the nicer rednecks that worked in the kitchen that when Black folks started eatin' there, the cook spit in their food!" After Daddy told me that, I stopped eating in restaurants in all-white neighborhoods. Miss Peterson was puzzled about me turning down her invitations to have lunch at those particular restaurants. But she was more concerned about me running off with a man, like the last few girls had done.

"The last girl ran off and got married on us. To a Mexican, at that," Miss Peterson told me with tears in her eyes one day as she handed me a huge bear claw she had baked the night before. "The girl before her didn't last that long, but at least she did take off with one of her own kind. You colored girls are not that flighty. Erline, the colored girl who cleans the office, she's been with us for thirty years. But," she paused and sighed sadly, "Things have changed. Our young coloreds have a lot of new insight these days, and you are kind of cute. Don't you get too used to these bear claws, now. I wouldn't want you to lose your shape—in case you do get an itchin' to get married." Miss Peterson clucked, wiping crumbs off my cheek with a towelette.

"I don't date," I told her, clearing my throat.

It was an easy job, and the pay was good, considering I had no experience. Daddy being one of the law firm's clients and Mr. Holtsmark's mechanic had a lot to do with it, I decided. Miss Peterson ended up doing most of the work while I played around on the computer most of the day. I didn't have to worry about Burl popping into the office unannounced like the boyfriends of the other young secretaries who had run off. I had told him that Mr. Holtsmark was a racist beast who had only hired me to fill an Affirmative Action quota.

"Why you want to work for a peckerwood like that?" Burl wanted to know.

"Well, we are going to have to deal with these kinds of people from now on. Working with them is the best way to get used to them," I explained.

With my first three paychecks, and with some financial assistance from Daddy, I moved into a two-bedroom apartment on Lansing Street, six blocks away from the neighborhood I had grown up in. I had looked at several apartments, but the only one my parents approved of was this one—mainly because Nurse Bertha's thirty-five-year-old gay son lived in the building and he had everybody's back. Jimmie Lee Cross, better known as Sweet Jimmie, was one of Mama's best customers. She kept his shoulder-length locks looking fresh. Unlike Nurse Bertha, Sweet Jimmie was one of the most likable people I knew. He considered himself Crazy Mimi's godmother, so naturally he had a lot of affection for her friends. I didn't mind Sweet Jimmie entering my apartment without knocking, which he did almost every day. Some days when I wasn't home, he entered my apartment and made himself at home, taking whatever he wanted. Even after I noticed the slow disappearance of my makeup, underwear, food, videos, fashion magazines, and toiletries, I still welcomed his visits. Other than being a good friend, Sweet Jimmie kept me from getting bored by entertaining me with gossip and margaritas.

I liked living alone, but it was lonely enough for me to eat out in public places three to four times a week. Two blocks over from my street was Hanover Lane. It was a street lined with nondescript buildings that included several restaurants, a few bars, and other businesses. I had become a regular at Adam's, a popular barbecue joint by day and a dance club by night. That's where I went after work that Friday evening. Burl had called me before I left work and asked me to pick up a chicken dinner to go for him, which I had already purchased. Just as I was about to finish my meal, Chester entered the restaurant. With him was the same beautiful woman I had seen him with before. The one who looked like Sade. Even though Chester didn't even notice me humped over my plate when he passed my table, I had the waitress wrap the rest of my meal and I left.

The video store Crazy Mimi's family owned, Mo' Movies, was a block away on the same side of the street as Adam's. I had selected two movies and was about to check out when I felt somebody's hot breath on the back of my neck. I could see Crazy Mimi behind the counter, so I knew it was not her breath sending shivers up and down my spine. Startled, I dropped the movies and Burl's fried chicken dinner to the floor and whirled around. Chester was standing over me with his arms folded.

"What you so jumpy about this time?" he asked. Before I could answer, he dropped to his knees and helped me pick up the movies. *"Nightmare on Elm Street* . . . now that's a classic," he mouthed, inspecting the movies I had selected. "And . . . hmmm . . . everybody should watch *The Leech Woman* at least once." He sighed and handed me the videos, then grabbed my arm and helped me up.

"Hi," I managed, looking around for his lady friend. "What are you doing in here?" I snapped, still angry with him for giving me a ticket for running that red light.

"Well, believe it or not, I rent a few movies from time to time myself," he smirked, nudging me with his elbow. He held up the video of some Western and waved it in front of my face. "Ever rent *High Noon?"*

"I'd rather get a whupping," I mumbled, walking away, still looking around for the woman he seemed so fond of.

"Well, Gary Cooper ain't half as interestin' as Freddy Kruger, but *High Noon* is the Cadillac of shoot-'em-up flicks. You'd enjoy it," he told me.

I just smiled and blinked stupidly. I wasn't able to breathe normally until he turned down a different aisle. After I paid for my movies, I rushed out, but not before glancing over my shoulder. Crazy Mimi and Chester were in a conspiratorial huddle. Looking in my direction, they laughed.

Trying to balance my purse, the food containers from the restaurant, and the movies was not easy to do. I stopped once I got outside on the sidewalk. Before I could rearrange all of the things in my hands, Chester darted out of the video store and caught up with me.

"Come on. I'm goin' in your direction," he said, beckoning me to follow him to the Corvette parked at the corner.

"I only live a couple of blocks," I said, hesitating.

"I know where you live. Get in the car, Crazy Legs."

I never expected to ride in his car, and I figured this would be the only time I had the chance. When he opened the door on the passenger's side, I slid in. I had no idea that the high price I'd end up paying for this one ride would literally include blood. . . .

"Uh . . . where did your lady friend go?" I mumbled.

He shrugged. "I didn't ask her," he replied, strapping me into my seat. His touch made me shudder in a way I had never shuddered before, and I liked it.

"And what were you and Crazy Mimi laughing about?"

He laughed before answering. "She told me that the shoplifters about to put 'em out of business. She just asked me to keep a eye on you." He laughed again.

"Oh." That vague, overused word seemed like the best thing to say.

He stopped laughing and gave me a serious look. "You mind if I smoke?" Not waiting for me to respond, he started the motor and snatched a cigarette from a pack on the dashboard and lit it. A plume of smoke blinded me for a second. Once my vision returned, I stared at him from the corner of my eye, and I experienced a hot flash.

"I told Crazy Mimi to let me worry about you," he grunted, talking with the cigarette dangling from his lips.

"Oh," I said again.

CHAPTER 37

"This is a really nice car," I said once we pulled out into the street. I looked straight ahead, hoping he wouldn't see how rigid my cheeks had become.

"I like nice things," Chester said crisply, glancing at me. His expression was steely. I froze like a block of ice when his big hand patted, then massaged my knee. "Crazy Legs," he grunted. He was still the only person who ever called me by that nickname.

I was as stiff as a slab of concrete as we rode in silence the rest of the way to my apartment. I was glad that I had on a sweater so he couldn't see that my silk blouse was limp with sweat. I started opening the door on my side even before the car stopped moving.

"Uh . . . thanks for the ride, Chester," I managed, fumbling with all the bags in my lap. He responded by leaping out of the car and dashing around the side to open my door. He made a grand sweeping gesture with his hand as I stumbled out, my bones cracking like a woman four times my age. "Thanks," I said again, walking toward the steps leading to my apartment. Sweet Jimmie, my busybody gay neighbor, was sipping from a huge coffee cup as he stared boldly out of his front window, fanning his face with a flyswatter.

"Well, for old times' sake, you can at least invite me in," Chester decided. "We are still friends, aren't we?" He cocked his head and raised an eyebrow, staring at me with amusement.

"Of course we are," I said sharply. I stumbled some more and he grabbed my arm and led me upstairs to my apartment.

As soon as we got inside, I waved him to the sofa as I dropped all of the bags onto the coffee table. "Uh . . . would you like something to drink? I don't have any alcohol," I said nervously, moving briskly around my living room, opening windows, gathering up empty glasses, and kicking cassettes and magazines out of my path. Some leftover chicken on a saucer, gnawed down to the bones, sat on the floor by the end of my sofa. While he was looking around, I slid it under the sofa with my foot. I could tell from the expression on his face that he was impressed with the way I had decorated my apartment. I was proud of the African artwork displayed on my walls, and my plush beige sofa and matching love seat. It was too late for me to grab and hide the empty rib containers on top of the large TV I had just purchased. But while he was still looking around, I managed to slide another plate full of bones under the love seat facing the sofa.

He let out an exaggerated gasp and gave me a sideways look. "You better not have no alcohol up in here, girl. If I remember correctly, you're still underage." He laughed. Then he whipped out a bottle of tequila from the inside pocket of his jacket. "But if you don't tell, I won't."

"So did you catch any criminals today?" I couldn't think of anything else to say.

"I'm off today." He sniffed and rubbed his nose. Then he goggled at me and patted the seat next to him on the sofa. I groaned when I noticed the strap of a discarded bra sticking out from under his butt. "You can sit down. I ain't goin' to bite you. Come put a bug in my ear." Before I could comply, he glanced at a stack of magazines on the coffee table and lifted the one on top. It was open to a page with one beautiful Black model included in the display with half a dozen blondes. "Is this *you*?"

"I wish!" I exclaimed, jumping back. I sniffed so hard my nostrils stung. "That's this year's Black model. Naomi Campbell's her name, I think," I said over my shoulder as I walked toward my kitchen. When I returned to the living room with two glasses, he had already unbuttoned his shirt and removed his shoes. He brazenly swung his long feet up on the coffee table and made himself at home. He patted the sofa again and I sat down.

Chester took a few sips from the glass he had poured for himself and started talking in a low, controlled manner. Tears formed in his eyes when he mentioned Kitty and how much he missed her. I had to blink to hold back my own tears when he told me how he took fresh flowers to Kitty's grave once a month. What really stunned me was him telling me how he went around talking to school kids about drugs and gang violence. I had known this man all of my life, but in many ways he was like a stranger. His demeanor changed when he talked about his ex-wife. "She calls me up in the middle of the night threatenin' to send her daddy over here to jack me up for me callin' her. She says I'm harassin' her—like hell. I call to check on my kid. She won't even let me see my baby girl," he growled, spraying my face with specks of hot, tequila-laced spit.

"I can't believe she won't let you see your own flesh and blood," I sniffed, casually wiping his spit from my face. The only times I tasted tequila was when it was in a margarita. But when he handed me the bottle, I poured some into my glass and took a deep swallow. Right away my head start spinning like a wheel.

Chester let out a deep sigh and frowned. "Come to find out, the baby ain't even mine," he continued, his jaw muscles twitching.

"What?" The alcohol had made me so disoriented, I had to blink hard to keep from seeing double. I set my glass on the coffee table and covered my mouth to soften a huge belch.

"That heifer was already pregnant when I met her, but that's somethin' I didn't know at the time. Anyway, Katherine's my daughter as far as I'm concerned. I was the one there the night she was born. I'm the man she calls 'Daddy.' I'm the one who pays child support—every goddamn month!" He went on to admit that he wished he had never left Alabama after Kitty's death. He told me a lot of other things that I had not heard until now.

"I didn't know you'd joined the navy, too. Where were you stationed?" Even though I was already slurring my words, I took another swallow from my glass. I hated drinking straight tequila, but the burning sensation in my throat was worth the mellow buzz I now had. My arm was firmly on the arm of the sofa, keeping me from sliding to the floor.

"Hawaii first. Then they shipped my ass to Australia. That's where I met my wife." Chester finished what was left in my glass and then tapped his chest with his fist before he let out a tremendous belch. "Aw, shit," he groaned, frowning and then belching again.

"I thought she was from Texas." I wanted to ask him what his Dallas Cowboys cheerleader ex-wife looked like, mainly to see how I stacked up compared to her. But after I thought about it, it didn't seem to matter anymore. He was no longer with her, and the way he screwed up his face when he mentioned her, it didn't sound like he wanted to go back to her.

"She was born and raised in Dallas." He paused and looked at me with a pensive expression on his face. "You and her could be twins. Same face, same shade, same *crazy legs . . .*"

"Oh," I said lamely.

"She was in Sydney on vacation with some of the other cheerleaders." He paused and shrugged tiredly. "One day she got tired of bein' married, at least to me."

I sniffed and blinked some more, even though I could see clearly now. "What did you do to her?"

"I didn't do shit!" he snapped, shooting me a harsh look. "If you really must know, she wanted to be with that other dude. Katherine's real daddy. I loved that girl so much, I let her do pretty much whatever she wanted. Boy, had she whipped me good. My crazy black ass was hidin' in bushes and duckin' behind trees like I was goddamn George of the Jungle tryin' to keep up with her. When she brought that other nigger to the house, I had to leave. That heifer!" He slammed his fist down on my coffee table, almost knocking it over. This was the Chester I knew.

"Uh . . . can I have another drink?" I asked, now nervous. My biggest concern was trying to figure out what his visit was leading up to.

I only had to see Burl on my terms and I liked it that way. I was in the control of what he and I did or didn't do. Chester was in control of everything now. At least for this one night. I was not prepared for what he did next. He put his arm around my shoulder and pulled me onto his lap and kissed me long and hard. In a way it was like my first kiss from a man, because it was the only one I'd received so far that mattered. Other than Daddy, Baby Red, Sweet Jimmie, and the pizza deliveryman, Chester was the only other man who had been inside my apartment since I'd moved in. I had been approached by a lot of men. I had been fondled at a few parties and bars, but that was as far as I had gone. With the exception of the quick pecks I'd given to

Daddy, Baby Red, and Reverend Poe on their cheeks, Burl was the only other man I had kissed in the last year.

"I've been wantin' to do that for a long time," he whispered in my ear.

"Why didn't you?" I managed. He responded by kissing me again, longer and more passionately. I wanted to stay in his embrace. I felt so safe and so . . . *desirable*. His heart thumping against my chest made me dizzier than the tequila did. I had to force myself to remember my curious position in his life. He seemed surprised when I pulled away. "Who is that woman I keep seeing you with, and what is she to you?" I slid my tongue across my bottom lip, still tasting him.

"What woman?"

"The one who looks like Sade," I said glumly.

"Oh, that woman. She's just a friend." He sucked in a deep breath before continuing. "She teaches ballroom dancin'. She got mugged on her way home one night and I took the call. Well, you know . . ."

"No, I don't know," I said firmly.

"She's just a friend, that's all. I wanted . . ." He stopped talking and stared at a photograph of Kitty and me on the end table next to him. His hand started shaking, and without thinking I reached over and squeezed it. That's when he pulled me even closer. He let out a strange chuckle and shook his head, his eyes still on his beloved dead sister's picture. "That Kitty. That girl just about drove me crazy."

"I know," I mumbled.

"Now that she's restin', I can rest."

"I know." I felt stupid saying what I said, but I didn't know what else to say. But it seemed more appropriate than 'oh.'

He turned to me and winked. "And you, you did a lot of cloakin' for that wild-ass girl. I was on to you, too, you heifer, you." He jabbed the side of my arm. "And don't you sit here again and say 'I know.' "

I just smiled stupidly, turning my face away from him for a moment. I shuddered when I turned back to him and saw him looking at me with a blank expression on his face. He stared at my face longer than I wanted him to, making me self-conscious. Since I didn't have a lover in my life to impress, I was not that careful about making sure my makeup looked good all the time. Burl didn't know when I had on makeup and when I didn't. I knew that my lips were dry and my mascara was in clumps. But that didn't seem to bother Chester.

"You're a beautiful woman, Carmen."

"You're not so bad yourself," I muttered, wetting my lips.

"I know," he told me.

I was as limp as a dishrag when he lifted me off the sofa and looked around the living room, cradling me like a baby.

I nodded in the direction of my bedroom.

CHAPTER 38

Chester was already naked and in my bed on top of the covers, grinning and looking me up and down as I stood by the side of the bed, peeling my clothes off. I was glad I had on naughty but nice underwear. Even without a man to appreciate it, that was all I ever wore. Desiree ordered a lot of sleazy, provocative stuff from a Frederick's of Hollywood catalogue that she had sent to my address so her daddy wouldn't find out. The stuff she decided was too tame for her she passed on to me. Chester whistled when he saw that I had on crotchless panties.

"I've never done *it* before," I admitted.

"You're kiddin'." Then he guffawed long and loud and sat bolt upright, motioning for me to get closer to him.

I shook my head, moving toward him, slapping his hand. "I'm not kidding."

He caressed my fingers and grunted, "You're nineteen now, right?"

I nodded as he slowly and gently unbuttoned my see-through bra, the only thing I still had on. "You won't tell anybody, will you?" I asked.

"What? That you're a virgin or that you're with me?"

"Never mind." I grinned, covered my mouth with my hand, and coughed to clear my throat. From what I had seen going on in some of the raunchy adult movies Crazy Mimi had slipped to me, I didn't know what to expect. I wasn't sure how a man really carried on in bed with a woman in real life. I had seen movies that had been downright disturbing, with horny people screaming and flipping and flopping all over the bed. "You're not real loud are you?"

Chester threw his head back and laughed; then he leaned toward me and in a mock whisper he asked, "Why?"

"Well, the walls, the floors, and the ceilings in this building are thin. I don't want to entertain Sweet Jimmie."

"Sweet Jimmie won't hear nothin' he ain't heard before," he told me in a steely tone, all the while fondling the bosom I was so proud of now. "Come on here now, Crazy Legs." That was the last time we spoke for the next hour.

Instead of a wild stallion practically splitting me in two, like Desiree, Regina, and Crazy Mimi had told me to expect the first time, Chester was gentle and patient. I was embarrassingly frisky, grabbing and pulling at him. I was acting like I had just been let out of prison! He told me in a level voice, "Slow down, girl. You got my attention."

It was a night to remember. I entered a world of pleasure so intense, I forgot about almost everything else that had happened in my life so far. There was nothing holding me back from enjoying myself, and I did in ways that embarrassed me. The first time I cried out in ecstasy, he covered my mouth with his hand. But after that, he didn't care how loud I got, and I didn't care either. I was totally unaware of everything else in my bedroom except Chester until the telephone rang during our first break. Not thinking clearly, I grabbed it on the second ring. It was Sweet Jimmie.

"Girl, what in the world is goin' on up there? Sound like you wrestlin' with a bear!" Sweet Jimmie hollered.

"I can't talk right now," I panted in a whisper. "I'll call you—" Chester promptly interrupted the call by reaching over my shoulder and unplugging the phone, and that was all right with me. We then exchanged conspiratorial glances.

Like he was in his own house, he got up and waltzed to the living room and returned with the movies we had picked up at the video store. He slid one into the VCR on top of the portable TV facing my bed and leaped back into the bed. I only made it through *High Noon* because I stayed in his arms throughout the whole movie. He fell asleep ten minutes into *The Leech Woman*.

I liked watching him sleep. He actually looked innocent. My head, with my hair standing up like knotty horns, was on his shoulder. In his sleep, he wrapped his arms and legs around me. I waited another hour before I untangled myself and eased to the bathroom to wash away the blood that had oozed out of me. I trembled from the pain between my thighs when I sat on the toilet to pee. The reality of what I had just done hit me when the condom he had used slid out of me. I lowered my head and trembled even harder. I had a mild hangover, and I was aching in other parts of my battered body. My rumbling insides felt like snakes crawling around in my stomach.

"You all right?" Chester asked, entering the bathroom, squatting sideways in front of me. He lifted my head and kissed me before I responded with a smile anyway. I couldn't tell whose tequila-stale breath was the foulest, his or mine. Other than in a few X-rated movies, I had never seen a grown man's body before until this unplanned encounter. Chester was naked except for his wristwatch and socks. The line of his back, hips, and butt was perfect. There was a lump of awe in my throat as I looked him over. I didn't know what other naked Black men looked like, but there was a purple birthmark on the inside of his right thigh and he had no pubic hair.

"I'm fine," I whispered. "But . . . uh . . . that condom you put on came off," I told him, rising so he could see it in the toilet. He flushed the toilet and pulled me into his arms.

"You ain't got nothin' to worry about, Crazy Legs. I just got tested. I'm HIV-negative," he told me with a sigh of relief, squeezing me hard.

"What if I'm pregnant? I don't believe in abortion."

"I don't either," he declared emphatically.

"What if I am pregnant, though?" I asked worriedly, searching his penetrating eyes.

"I'll take care of you," he chuckled. He rubbed my back and pulled me even closer to him. "Till death do us part," he said seriously. "I'd treat you like the queen you are."

A warm feeling came over me. "Then you have thought about me—us—before tonight?"

"I have. Even before you damn near sent my crazy black ass to kingdom come with them goddamn cans of whatever that shit was that day." He laughed and rubbed the spot on his head where I had hit him so many years before.

"It was corn," I said gently. "Jolly Green Giant."

He carried me back to the bed and placed me down on my side. Then he curled up next to me, wrapping me in his arms in a viselike grip. That's where I was when the sun peeped in through a crack in my curtains the next morning. He was already awake and leaning on his elbow with his face just inches from mine. I had never seen him smile the way he was smiling at me now. For the first time in my life, I felt like the most beautiful girl in the world. I didn't remember him removing his clothes the night before, but they were now on the handlebars of the bicycle-like exercise machine in the corner that I had been using as a clothes rack.

He sniffed and tapped my cheek. "I think I always knew that someday you and me would end up together," he told me.

When I reached over and touched his shoulder, I saw the same kinds of electric sparks I sometimes saw when I stepped on a carpet a certain way. After the sparks disappeared, for a split second, it was Burl's face just inches away from mine. That Burl. The man I had unofficially allowed to control my destiny. All because of one stupid teenage prank. My breath caught in my throat and I snatched my hand back and balled it into a fist to keep it from trembling. I wished that Burl had died on the train tracks that day. I *immediately* regretted having such a macabre thought about poor Burl. Right then and there I knew what I had to do, and I had to do it fast.

I took a deep breath and cleared my throat to make sure my words came out right. "Chester, get up and get in your clothes and get the hell up out of here. I never want to see you again," I said seriously. He thought I was kidding, because he just laughed. "I mean it," I said gruffly.

Chester's body stiffened and he gasped. In a voice thick with disbelief he roared, "What the hell brought that on?!" He was understandably angry and containing himself with a mighty effort.

"You shouldn't be here. I . . . we shouldn't have done this." I was already up, sliding into the bathrobe I kept at the foot of my bed. "What about that ballroom-dancing woman?" I asked, my eyes staring at the wall.

"What about her? She don't mean shit to me," he said bitterly.

"Well, I'm . . ."

"You involved with somebody else?"

"Yeah!" I turned to face him. "I am. It's Burl!"

He leaped off of the bed like a cricket, slapped his hands on his hips, and gaped at me in slack-jawed bewilderment as I blinked stupidly. Suddenly, he snatched his clothes off the handlebars of the exerciser near my window, grumbling unintelligible gibberish under his breath. I turned away, because the sight of his nakedness was working against me. He stomped out of the room without saying another word. I didn't move from the bed until I heard him slam the living room door on his way out. He had left his belt on my exerciser.

I glared at the telephone. Not more than a minute after I plugged it back in, it rang. To my everlasting horror, it was Burl.

"Carmen, what happened to that chicken dinner you was supposed to bring me last night? I ended up havin' to eat neckbones for dinner," he whined.

I was surprised at how composed I was. "Uh . . . they were out of chicken, and when I got home my phone was temporarily out of order, so I couldn't call you. It just started working again," I lied. The more I lied, the better I lied. I had gotten so good at it, even I had started believing my own lies.

"Oh," Burl breathed. "You sound funny. Is everything all right? I been thinkin' about you."

I rubbed my eyes. The belt that Chester had left behind was dangling like a snake on the handlebars of the exerciser, grimly reminding me of what I had become. While Burl was still talking, I placed the telephone on the bed and stumbled over to the window. Chester was standing in front of his car, looking up at my bedroom window with the most disappointed look on his face I had ever seen. Our eyes met for a moment. Then he shook his head and slammed the palm of his hand against the top of his car before he left. When I returned to the bed and picked up the telephone, Burl was still talking.

He hadn't even missed me.

CHAPTER 39

Iwas still standing in front of my window when Sweet Jimmie stormed into my apartment in his bathrobe with his hands on his hips, ten minutes after Chester's departure. Unlike his petite, birdlike mother, Nurse Bertha, Sweet Jimmie was a tall, medium-brown, nicely built man with sharp features, large black eyes, and wavy shoulder-length hair. He wasn't into long-term relationships. Between his many frequent one-night stands, he spent his time socializing with young females like my friends and me. Some of the things I refused to share with Desiree and my other friends I eagerly shared with Sweet Jimmie. Gossip and secrets were like nourishment to him, but I knew that what I told him in confidence he kept to himself. Even so, I had never told him about my lengthy obsession with Chester, or the real reason I was so devoted to Burl.

"Do you know how close I came to bustin' up in here and joinin' y'all last night?" Sweet Jimmie said, bobbing his head as he pranced across the floor and joined me at the window. "I would appreciate it if you would let me know in advance the next time Chester's comin' over here, so I can put in my earplugs. Shit."

"There won't be a next time," I said solemnly, moving toward the kitchen with Sweet Jimmie on my heels. I sat down hard at the kitchen table while he moved about the kitchen making coffee.

"I'm not surprised. Even I could have told you that Chester was out of your league." Sweet Jimmie talked to me over his shoulder as he searched for coffee cups. "I remember my first time. Girl, I couldn't sit down for three days. I felt like I had been fucked by a train." Sweet Jimmie put his arm around my shoulder and sucked his teeth. "I go to the same gym as Chester. I see him naked all the time, so I know you had your work cut out for you last night. He hurt you much?"

"I'm fine," I replied, waving my hand. I didn't have a problem discussing other people's sex lives with Sweet Jimmie, but it embarrassed me to be talking about mine.

"Then what's the problem? Why you sittin' here lookin' like somebody done stole your pocketbook?"

"I can't turn my back on Burl." My voice was shaking as I continued. "Burl needs me more than Chester."

"Well, why can't you have 'em both?"

"I couldn't do that to Burl. And you know Chester well enough to know he wouldn't put up with me seeing him and Burl at the same time."

Sweet Jimmie placed a cup of coffee on the table in front of me; then he sat down and cupped my hand. "Let me tell you somethin', baby. Ain't no such thing as a happy martyr. The people we try to save is the ones havin' all the fun while we sit around and boo-hoo, hopin' somebody will come and take care of us for a change. It don't happen that way, sugar." Sweet Jimmie released my hand and drank from his cup.

"What would you do?"

"I'd go for Chester. As far as I know, he don't swing my way, but if he ever decides to, I'll swing him like a baseball bat." Sweet Jimmie was trying to make me laugh, but it didn't work. He got serious again. "I know Burl is your friend, but you don't owe him shit! He got a mama. Besides, he's a cripple, girl. What can he do for a woman like you?"

I shrugged. "It's too late."

Sweet Jimmie continued in an even more serious tone. "You still young, baby. Take advantage of that. Life is too short. I spent half of my life tryin' to look out for Crazy Mimi. That girl don't listen to me no more than she do the man in the moon. Or anybody else for that matter—and if it wasn't for me, she'd be dead."

I looked at Sweet Jimmie with renewed interest. "You know about what happened to her?"

"I was there! Mama used to make a few extra dollars on the side helpin' girls and women in trouble get out of trouble. Cheap abortions. I'd help her clean up the mess afterwards. I'd wipe up the blood and shit and haul it to this big old trash can behind our house. Well, somethin' went wrong with Crazy Mimi. Her mama was too far gone. The girl slid out of her mama, kickin' and screamin', right into that bucket I used to hold up under the women to catch everything. I could have kept my mouth shut and dumped that bucket anyway. I didn't. Now, the girl got some serious mental problems, but she leadin' as good a life as anybody else. Nobody never told her about that night and my part in it, but I think she knows." Huge tears oozed out of Sweet Jimmie's eyes and slid down his face like bubbles. He paused to wipe them away with the tip of his finger. "From the day she learned to talk, Crazy Mimi's called me Uncle Sweet Jimmie."

Before the conversation could continue, somebody knocked on my door, but I didn't answer it. Wiping away the rest of his tears and clearing his throat, Sweet Jimmie ran with me to the living room window. We got there just in time to see Chester walking back to his car. Sweet Jimmie shook his head and gave me a look of concern.

"Girl, you been in the storm too long. You ain't never goin' to be dry again," he told me.

CHAPTER 40

Two days later, my romp with Chester was still so fresh on my tortured mind that I called up Burl that Sunday morning and practically begged him to pick me up and take me to brunch at Hammie's, a white-owned pancake house. I could have gone alone, but it was important for me to see him in person. Not only was his presence a potent distraction, but seeing Burl helped keep me focused on my commitment to him.

"It'd be cheaper if we ate at the church," Burl informed me. It did him no good to attempt to sound like he was annoyed with my suggestion. He loved hearing from me and I knew it. "Besides, you know them crackers at Hammie's can't cook a lick. Remember how they scorched the bacon the last time? And who else but white folks would serve *white* toast?"

I insisted on eating at Hammie's. It was too dangerous for me to go near Second Baptist Church. Chester would more than likely be there with his parents. Hammie's, strategically located in a low-income Black neighborhood, was a good choice. Even though the prices were low, most of the Black folks I knew avoided it. I knew that I would never run into Chester there. He was even stricter than my family about supporting Black-owned businesses.

I used menstrual cramps—bogus, of course—as an excuse to keep me from spending more time than it took to eat brunch with Burl.

It helped having Miss Mozelle go with us. After we maneuvered Burl into the restaurant and parked him on the side of our table, Miss Mozelle squeezed into the booth next to me, growling complaints about the dingy tablecloths and gummy floor. She was convinced that white folks were naturally unclean. A sign in bold letters faced us: "WE GLADLY ACCEPT FOOD STAMPS." Miss Mozelle stared at it in disbelief, then turned to me and gasped, "What kind of squalor is this y'all done dragged me into?" she whispered. Without knowing it, she enhanced my lies to Burl. Inspecting a spoon, then blowing on it and wiping it with a napkin, she mumbled, "Carmen, you look like you swallowed a fishhook. You want me to whup up you some ginger tea when I get home? That's the best thing in the world for cramps. I'll send Burl back to your place lickety-split." Miss Mozelle had on one of her more elaborate hats. It was a loud orange, wide-brimmed lamp-shade with a long brown feather dangling off one side. It matched the voluminous, baggy-sleeved orange dress she had on. A ruffled sash tied carelessly around her middle divided her massive body into two equally large lumps. Burl was conservatively dressed in a black suit, a plain white shirt, a maroon tie, and a black fedora. I had on a limp gabardine skirt and a baggy T-shirt with a brooding illustration of Bob Marley on the front. A baseball cap turned sideways hid the helmet of naps on my head. I didn't have any clean turtleneck sweaters, so I had hidden the numerous marks that Chester had left on my neck with a scarf.

"Uh . . . I'm allergic to ginger," I claimed. I loved ginger tea. I felt bad about lying, but I didn't want to give Burl a reason to visit me later that day.

"Well, when you get home, stretch out with a heatin' pad on your belly. You got some brandy?" Miss Mozelle asked, staring at me lovingly. While waiting for me to respond, she wiped off the top of the table with a napkin. All around us, dingy, shabbily dressed patrons, Black and white, loudly enjoyed their meals. Slovenly waitresses trotted back and forth. Like trained seals they barked their orders to an unseen cook. It was almost like being at a circus. Burl and Miss Mozelle were clearly uncomfortable, and so was I, but for a different reason. I had things a lot more disturbing on my mind than this crude restaurant.

"Mama, Carmen don't drink yet," Burl said hotly, glancing toward me. He lifted his eyebrows and asked anxiously, "Do you, Carmen?"

I shook my head vigorously. "I'm going to take some Midol and hop back in bed when I get home," I announced weakly, adding a moderate groan for emphasis.

We rushed through our meal and left as soon as we finished, ignoring the cups of beige coffee our waitress had dropped off on our table.

"Carmen, you go straight to bed when you get inside," Miss Mozelle ordered as we neared my apartment. "Cramps ain't nothin' to play with. That's the very reason my niece in Memphis can't have kids."

"I wish y'all would stop talkin' about female problems," Burl complained, not taking his eyes off the road. He tried to be as normal a man as possible. Driving his van was one of the highlights of his day. "Carmen, if you feel better later on, call me and we can go eat at a *real* restaurant and maybe go to the drive-in movie afterwards."

"I don't think so," I mumbled, practically crawling out of Burl's van onto the sidewalk. It didn't surprise me to see Sweet Jimmie staring out of his window with an inquisitive look on his face.

I continued my charade when Sweet Jimmie followed me into my apartment. "I can see you in too much pain to talk, so I won't stay long, baby," he told me, patting my shoulder. I slid into my bed and left him in my kitchen, cleaning up a mess from the night before. Afterward, he made my bed up with me in it and didn't leave until I pretended to fall asleep. I was glad to be alone again. I had a lot of thinking to do now that I had appeased Burl.

It was so ironic that after the years and years that I had spent lusting after Chester Sheffield, he was now the last person on Earth I wanted to see. He had left two messages on my answering machine while I was having brunch with Burl and his mama. I did not return Chester's calls. After spending that passion-filled night with him, my feelings for him were stronger than ever. Getting over him was going to be twice as hard now. Not communicating with him was the only choice I had if I wanted to wean myself and get over him completely and permanently.

An hour after Sweet Jimmie's departure, I moved from the bedroom to the living room. Wrapped up to my chin in a sheet, I balled up on the sofa and sipped a weak margarita. Before I could finish it, Chester called again.

"Crazy Legs, this is Chester." I can't explain why just hearing "Barry White's" voice on my answering machine made certain parts of my body go numb. I couldn't even feel my hand and didn't realize I had dropped my margarita until the glass crashed to the floor. Still wrapped up like a mummy, I lifted my head and listened to him continue talking to my answering machine. But first I heard him let out a long, deep sigh, and then nothing but silence followed for the next few moments. Finally he announced, "I have a few more things I need to say to you before we lay this thing to rest. Now, either you call me back or expect to see me real soon, goddamn it. Have a nice day."

CHAPTER 41

I had forgotten to set my alarm the night before, but I woke up in time to get ready for work the next morning. Before I left my apartment, I made sure I had erased the tape on my answering machine.

I was unspeakably horrified when I got off the bus at the corner from my apartment after work and saw Chester's Corvette parked boldly on the street across from my apartment building. I shaded my eyes as I dragged my feet toward my apartment. Chester, with a blank expression on his face, was sitting on the bottom of the steps on the side of the building. Sweet Jimmie, his white nurse's uniform glistening in the evening sun like wet fish scales, was standing over Chester, flapping his arms and lips. If it had been Regina, Crazy Mimi, or Desiree chastising Chester, it would have bothered me. But Sweet Jimmie was known for exhibiting this type of behavior. And since he had assumed a position of authority in his friends' lives, we all expected him to make our business his business.

As soon as Chester looked away from Sweet Jimmie in my direction and spotted me easing down the sidewalk, he rose from the steps, brushing off his tight black jeans. By now, Sweet Jimmie was waving his long, neatly manicured finger in Chester's bewildered face. For a split second Chester smiled at me. When I didn't respond favorably, his face went blank again.

"Carmen, I want to talk to you," Chester called out, raising his hand like an anxious schoolboy. An impatient frown quirked across his dark face.

With his hands on his hips now, Sweet Jimmie whirled around and continued to control the situation. "Well, Carmen don't want to talk to you," he said to Chester, winking conspiratorially at me.

"I want to hear that from Carmen," Chester said calmly, moving slightly to the side. "Talk to me, Crazy Legs."

Sweet Jimmie gasped and leaned back on his legs. He kept one hand on his hip as he shook his finger in Chester's face again. "Didn't you hear what I just said? Carmen don't want to hear nothin' you got to say, black boy."

My head started spinning as Sweet Jimmie gnashed his teeth, even threatening Chester with "legal action" for "stalking" me. All during this tense time, Chester's eyes were on me. He didn't speak again until Sweet Jimmie paused.

"Carmen, I told you a long time ago, you needed to get yourself a better class of friends." Chester paused and nodded toward Sweet Jimmie. "You didn't take my advice, hmmm?"

I lowered my head and let out a deep sigh. My life had spun completely out of control. "Let's go inside," I said, looking at Chester. Sweet Jimmie had already geared up to follow, but I shook my head as soon as he took his first step toward my apartment. If he had had a tail, it would have been between his legs as he rushed toward his ground-floor apartment shaking his head.

As soon as Chester and I entered my living room, he charged toward me, kissing me up and down my neck, squeezing me so hard I could barely breathe. I couldn't believe that I had to choose Burl over Chester. But I had to. Before I pushed him away, my arms went around his neck like a noose, and I kissed him back so hard my teeth bit into my bottom lip. Just as he was about to lift me off the floor and wrap my legs around his waist, I untangled myself and pushed him away. But before I could move beyond his reach, he grabbed my wrists and pulled me back against him.

"You said you wanted to talk," I rasped, licking the lip I'd bitten to stop it from aching.

He cupped my face in his hands and forced me to look into his eyes as he ground his pelvis against mine. "What are we goin' to do about this thing we started?" he asked hoarsely, still grinding against me.

"I told you, Chester." I pulled away from him and attempted to move across the floor. He lunged at me again and pinned me against the wall between my TV and a huge floor vase filled with plants, thirsty because I had been too preoccupied to notice them lately.

"I don't like to start things I can't finish," he informed me. A stream of evening sun coming through a crack in the curtains on the window behind the TV made his face glow. His wet lips glistened. "And don't think I believe that sorry-ass story about you and Burl." I covered his mouth with my hand and he promptly pushed it away. "Do you love him?" he asked quietly.

I nodded.

"And me?" he asked with his eyebrows raised. "Do you love me, too, Carmen?"

It was the one chance I had to come clean. If for no other reason, I had to let Chester know how I truly felt. *"All my life,"* I whispered. It felt good to tell the truth, and it was about time. I didn't know about the tears on my face until he kissed them off.

"But you choosin' Burl over me? Come on, Crazy Legs. Don't be playin' with me."

"I have to choose Burl, Chester. It's . . . it's not important why. But believe me, I have to." I was waving my hand and shaking my head.

"Girl, you better tell me what the hell is goin' on and you better tell me quick! I can take but so much of this shit!" Chester snorted and took a few steps back. Suddenly, his mouth dropped open and he guffawed and slapped the side of his thigh. "Why didn't I see this before!" He then slapped the side of his head and gave me an incredulous look. "Burl's got that megabuck settlement comin' through from the railroad company as soon as he turns twenty-one." He glared at me, bobbing his head and shaking his finger in my face at the same time. "It all makes sense now. Well, Carmen, I figured you was above that kind of gold-diggin' shit." He laughed dryly and headed for the door.

"This is not about Burl's settlement. I don't need Burl's money," I insisted, stumbling behind Chester and tapping his shoulder. He lifted my hand, squeezed it, and pushed me away. "And I meant what I said about loving you all my life. From the time we were kids . . . I've loved you so much it hurt," I declared, my voice cracking. "When you left town and got married, I—I never thought we'd get together. That's why I got into this thing with Burl. I didn't think I would ever be with you. I can't just turn my life upside down now."

"What if you find out you're pregnant with my child?" he said softly, his eyes searching mine. "Will you let me know?"

I nodded and said doubtfully, "I'll let you know."

"And then what? You goin' to let Burl think it's his?"

"Burl will never be a father or a lover," I said sadly.

With his hands on his hips, Chester stared at me, slack-jawed and confused. "You don't want his money, or so you say. He can't make love to you. And if you don't mind me sayin', he ain't about to win no blue ribbons for his looks. Yet you choose him over me." He laughed. "Now it all makes sense, the friends you choose. I'll never tell you to find a better class of friends again. After what you just told me, the ones you already have are the best you can do. I don't belong in your life." His hand was on the door as he half-turned to look at me. Shaking his head he told me, "Listen, I . . . I hope you have a nice life, Carmen. I really mean that."

"I hope you do, too, Chester." I smiled. He gave me a quick peck on the cheek and then he opened the door. Sweet Jimmie, who had been leaning against the door outside listening, fell on his face, banging the top of his head against the door. Chester sighed, shook his head and stepped over Sweet Jimmie's prostrate body, and left.

I helped Sweet Jimmie up and he staggered into my living room, brushing off his uniform. "I oughta make that nigger pay my dry cleanin' bill," Sweet Jimmie growled and followed me to the sofa and sat down hard next to me. "Girl, that was some conversation. And what is it about Burl that's done roadblocked you?"

"I am the only close friend Burl has. He considers me his girlfriend. I don't like to see him suffer, so I try to help him lead as normal a life as possible."

Sweet Jimmie clapped his hands together and gasped, giving me a sharp look. "Suffer? You think Burl Tupper is sufferin'? Girl, you got it all wrong. Burl ain't the one sufferin'! You go to work with me at that hospital one day and I'll show you what sufferin' is. Folks floppin' around on beds with AIDS and so many different cancers we can't name 'em all. They would trade places with Burl in a heartbeat. Let me tell you somethin' right here and now." At this point, Sweet Jimmie shook his finger in my face. "If you didn't never hang with Burl again after today, he would still go on livin'. He ain't dead. He got family. He got a brain. And once he get his hands on that half-a-million-dollar settlement, he'll have more women around him than

Alabama State Women's Prison. When them greedy heifers look at Burl, they won't see no man in a wheelchair like you do. They'll see a goose that done laid a golden egg. I bet you a dollar and a donut, Burl won't think he sufferin' with all that attention. You the one sufferin'. Shit." Sweet Jimmie rotated his long neck and rolled his eyes. "Hangin' around you straight folks is 'bout to do me in. I need a drink." He leaped up from the sofa, waving his arms in exasperation.

I gave Sweet Jimmie's words some thought, knowing in my heart that what he said was true. "Well, Chester didn't like what I said, so it wouldn't make any difference now anyway. It's over," I said evenly, following Sweet Jimmie into my kitchen.

He flung open the cupboard above my sink and snatched out a fresh bottle of tequila and a can of margarita mix. "How come I can't never find the salt in your place?" He paused and looked around. There was a disgusted look on his face as he plucked a box of salt off the floor. "Let me tell you, you ain't seen the last of that Chester. Trust me. I know men a lot better than you do." Sweet Jimmie let out a tremendous sigh and gave me a sincere look of pity. Speaking in a high-pitched voice, he told me, "That devil ain't through with you yet. He'll be back."

CHAPTER 42

Sweet Jimmie promised me that he would not blab my business to the rest of my friends. It was too dangerous to share information this sensitive with women who made a sport out of gossip. I didn't care what they thought and said about Burl, but I didn't want to hear anything unflattering about Chester. My brief affair with him was something I not only wanted to savor, I wanted to keep it in a certain perspective.

I was glad I had finally had sex, and so were my friends. Now I had a juicy story—well, *part* of a juicy story—to share with them.

"And where did you meet this guy?" Regina asked, her arms folded, her legs crossed. She rotated the toe of her shoe impatiently. She and Desiree shared my sofa the following Friday night. I sat Indian-style on my living room floor with my ever-present margarita in my hand.

"Uh . . . on the bus I used to take home from work," I lied. "Gary."

"Hmmm. Not that lumpy albino with the bulging eyes and the nappy mustache, I hope," Desiree slurred. She was sitting with her hands in her lap, both of them wrapped around the large tumbler holding her margarita.

I shook my head. "Gary's real tall . . . and dark and real good-looking—but it didn't work out between us," I blurted. By now I was telling lies on top of lies. "Now that I have a car, I won't have to ride on his bus anymore." Daddy had cosigned for me to purchase an '89 Nissan Sentra the day before.

Since I was so vague about my phantom boyfriend, the subject quickly changed. Regina dominated the conversation with reports of her latest romantic adventure. "Y'all ain't heard nothin' yet till I tell y'all about this young lawyer I seen. . . ."

Burl was a done deal. By default he was a part of my life, and I had to live with it. But I avoided the places where I thought I'd run into Chester. Particularly the bars and Second Baptist Church, where we had both been baptized. I knew that me being in the church would keep Mama and Daddy off my back. Each time I missed a Sunday sermon, they reminded me that that only brought me closer to "losing my way." I didn't stop going to church, but because of Chester, I started going to a different church so I wouldn't run into him. I never knew when he was going to be there escorting his mama. With my lying self and all of the corruption I had in me, I felt I needed all the spiritual guidance I could get. And I didn't care where I got it as long as I got it.

One minute I blamed Chester for my downfall, the next minute I blamed Burl. But most of the time, I blamed myself.

Between my visits to Burl, I visited a gym around the corner from my apartment, where I worked out three times a week. In Regina's Jeep or my car, she and I cruised to the clubs, plucking guys off bar stools. One week I slid into bed with three different men whose names I promptly forgot.

Without warning, Baby Red decided it was time for him to do some more roaming. He left town on his bike with a backpack containing everything he thought he'd need strapped to him. Desiree wasted no time leaping into a pit of depression and tried to drag me along with her. It soon became a full-time job counseling her. When she came to my apartment and found me gone, she waited for me in the Firebird she had just purchased using her daddy's old car as a trade-in since he couldn't drive anymore. The times she didn't wait in her car for me, she waited in Sweet Jimmie's apartment or on my steps. The times I didn't want to see her, I didn't answer my door. One day when she came knocking and I didn't open the door, she sat in her car for three hours. Twice when I peeped out of my window, she was asleep. It was one of the saddest sights I ever saw. As weak as I got when I thought about Chester, I was proud of the fact that love had not reduced me to such a sorry state. Finally she left, but she called me as soon as she got home.

"I can't believe Baby Red's gone," she whined to me over the telephone. "I don't know what I'm going to do."

"I told you to go with him," I snapped.

"He's going to Mexico on a bike, girl! He's going to live in tents, sleep under bridges, and eat all kinds of greasy, slimy shit! And what about Daddy? I can't leave him. He's so old and sick now. Oh . . . I got to find something to do with myself before I go crazy." I admired Desiree's devotion to her father. Like me, she had put her life on hold in certain ways. All through school she had talked about going to culinary school so she could operate her own catering service. She had not mentioned that in years, but I knew it was still on her mind. I felt she had a lot more to offer than working at that Piggly Wiggly supermarket. But since I had not yet made any moves toward attending nursing school like I had promised Mama, I kept my opinions to myself in that area.

"Well, Regina and I tried to get you to go out with us last night," I reminded her. "The best way to get over one man is to get another one." I flinched at my own words. I'd been with several other men by now, but Chester was still the only one on my mind. The belt he had left in my bedroom was a constant reminder that he had been mine for a whole night. I refused to store that belt away in a drawer or return it to him. I saw nothing wrong about wanting to keep it near me since I couldn't have him. If people had known all of this, they might have felt that I was as big a fool as Desiree was. Desiree's whining was enough to make anybody sick. I felt that if a woman was going to be a fool over a man, the least she could do was keep it to herself *like I was doing.*

"Baby Red is not dead. He'll be back in a couple of years, he said. And I'll wait for him. I won't let another man take his place," Desiree vowed.

Three years floated by and Baby Red was still cycling his way through Mexico and other Third World locations. What the boy was searching for was a mystery to me. I wondered if he even knew himself. In one of his infrequent letters, written on the back of a hotel napkin, he informed Desiree that he was going deeper south. He also told her that he didn't know when or if he would ever see her again, reminding her that she was the one who had shattered their relationship by not going with him. It was the push Desiree needed to return from the living dead. "Let's go on a cruise and have some real fun," she chirped, tearing Baby Red's letter into a dozen tiny pieces. I was proud of her.

So far, 1992 had been a tense year. In April the Rodney King mess had us all on edge. By the end of May things had quieted down. We were all looking for something on a less serious note to focus on.

After three week-long cruises to the Caribbean and more than half a dozen lovers later all within one year, Desiree finally got over my wayward cousin. She was happier than I had seen her in a long time. But her equilibrium was short-lived. A month after our last cruise Dr. Lucienne had another stroke, this one more serious than his first one. He needed round-the-clock attention. Nurse Bertha was a big help, but helping Desiree take care of the old man was even too much for her. The bulk of the work landed in Desiree's lap—even though Nurse Bertha was getting paid! Desiree's depression returned with a vengeance.

"I feel so trapped. I just know that I am going to spend the best years of my life tied down taking care of Daddy," Desiree complained. Then she made a bold surprise move. She made arrangements to put Dr. Lucienne in a nursing home. She lured me to her house to be there when she told him. She timed it perfectly. She planned to tell him on the same day that she had arranged for the paramedics to pick him up and transport him to the home. While he was watching a TV program, Desiree and I slipped into his bedroom and packed some of the personal items he would need in the home. He was stunned when he turned around and saw us standing in the doorway with his suitcase.

"What are you two stooges up to now?" Dr. Lucienne asked, a puzzled look on his face slowly turning to suspicion. I could not believe how pitiful he looked. He no longer had the round, jowly face of Fred Flintstone. With his sunken eyes and bony features, he looked emaciated and neglected.

Desiree moved back a few steps before responding. "Daddy, I've been talking to a lot of people." Clearing her throat and moving back a few more steps, she paused and looked at me. I nodded for her to continue. "Daddy, they—we all feel that it would be better for you, and us, for you to go to one of those nice homes."

"I'm in a nice home," the ailing doctor managed, glaring at the suitcase on the floor. "And it would be even nicer if you kept it clean. . . ." His face was horribly twisted from the stroke, and he could barely talk for more than a couple of minutes at a time. But he could still get around with his cane. He could use one hand, and that was all he needed to fix the highballs he lived on. He narrowed his drunken eyes and glared at me, then back to Desiree. She moved back a few steps when his jaws started twitching. "I'll be dead within a month if you lock me away in one of those places," he said in a shaky voice.

"It would be cheaper than us trying to hold on to this big house. Besides, it's time for me to move out on my own." Desiree was now managing the Piggly Wiggly, where she had been working since high school. She was making good money and could easily afford her own place. For some reason I thought that Dr. Lucienne owned his house. Without going into detail, Desiree had mentioned to me just a few days earlier that they were renting, not buying the house they lived in. She had been vague and evasive, so I had not pressed for more information.

Dr. Lucienne nodded and lifted his gnarled hand, clutching his cane. Without a word, he brought it down across Desiree's leg so hard; she fell screaming to the floor. It was the first time he had attacked her since his last stroke. He struggled to lift himself from his recliner and hobbled over to Desiree and cracked her leg again with his cane. Then he hit the suitcase, knocking it to its side. I stood there frozen in horror. Before he could do any real damage, I managed to pull him back to his chair, where he bowed his head and started shaking and crying like a baby.

"Carmen, I am sorry you had to see that. The paramedics should be here any minute to take him to the home. But can you do me a favor and go call Nurse Bertha? She's at Sweet Jimmie's. I have a feeling things might get pretty ugly around here," Desiree managed, rising from the floor, rubbing her leg.

I gave Desiree a big hug and a brief peck on the cheek before I dialed Sweet Jimmie's number to coax his mother, Nurse Bertha, to come to our aid. Before I could finish my call, Dr. Lucienne weaved across the floor and grabbed the telephone out of my hand and hung it up. Then he called 911. What he told the dispatcher stunned me. "My lesbian daughter and her bitch just assaulted me! I'm a dying man! I want both these two wenches arrested!"

CHAPTER 43

While Desiree, Nurse Bertha, and two beefy paramedics were wrestling with Dr. Lucienne, trying to strap him to a gurney, I answered a knock on the door. Standing behind a sharp-featured white policeman was Chester. It had been over three years since my brief unplanned rendezvous with Chester. I had glimpsed him from a distance driving around in his shiny red Corvette, but we had not communicated since. My breath caught in my throat and almost choked the life out of me. I motioned the two police officers into the living room. Chester smiled, tipped his hat, and patted my shoulder as I stumbled through the house with him close behind me. In the blink of an eye, my dormant feelings for him returned and all but consumed me. I could no longer feel my feet in front of me.

"Sounds like a real mess goin' on here," Chester said, surveying the house. He was more handsome than ever before, but there was a dark, grimly determined set to his face now. It made him look older than twenty-six. He lifted his cap and scratched his head.

"It's about time y'all got here. Somebody could have got killed," Nurse Bertha snarled. She had moved away from the fracas and was now on the sofa, fanning her face with an *Ebony* magazine. Dr. Lucienne had ripped the front of her uniform. She held it together with her other hand, blinking to hold back her own tears. It saddened me further to see her in such a weakened state. This was a woman who had once fought off a mugger with her purse.

Dr. Lucienne realized he had made a mistake by calling the police. It was Chester and his partner who finished helping the paramedics strap him to the gurney. "You devils! Turn me aloose!" Dr. Lucienne yelled until he lost his voice. It was so sad to see a man who had once been so full of fire reduced to such a whimpering heap. Desiree was relieved when Nurse Bertha volunteered to be the one to ride along with the paramedics to get the doctor checked into the nursing home. I stayed inside while everyone else watched from the front porch as the ambulance screamed down the street. Desiree was crying. Chester put his arm around her and pulled her head against his chest. I jumped back from the window when he started leading her back into the house. His long arm was still around her narrow waist when they returned to the living room.

"What was your name again?" he asked Desiree, finally releasing her, wiping her face with a handkerchief he had fished out of his pocket.

"Desiree." She sniffed and offered a weak smile, blowing her nose into the handkerchief before handing it back to him.

He nodded. "Oh, yeah. I remember you now. You work at Piggly Wiggly. You came to the house with my sister a few times before she died." Chester sucked in his breath and continued, stuffing the soiled handkerchief back into his pocket. "It's a good thing I like your old man. Otherwise, I'd cite him for bitin' me," he grinned, licking his hand where I could see a clear print of Dr. Lucienne's false teeth. "Listen, don't worry about your daddy. He's goin' to be much better off now." Chester turned to me. "Do me a favor, Crazy Legs. Make sure Desiree takes it easy for a few days." He turned to Desiree, resting his hand on her shoulder. "Take a few days off from work. Get your nails done. Buy a new dress. Get drunk. You like tequila?"

Desiree sniffled and nodded, her eyes now on Chester's face. "Carmen makes the meanest margaritas in town," she mumbled. "You ought to taste one sometime," she told him, her voice cracking.

Chester nodded uneasily in my direction. "Carmen . . . uh . . . maybe you can keep your friend at your place at least for tonight. You still live in the same apartment?"

"Uh-huh," I muttered uncomfortably.

"Y'all like smothered chicken?" Chester asked, walking back toward the door, not waiting for Desiree or me to answer. "I'll drop by after my shift ends and we'll all get shit-faced." He tipped his hat and strutted confidently out of the front door. Desiree ran to the window and watched as Chester joined his partner.

After the police car drove off, Desiree turned to me with a sigh, talking out of the side of her mouth. "Can you believe that Nurse Bertha? She was out there going on and on about somebody scratching her truck." Desiree paused and chuckled. It was good to see her laugh. "I'm going to need a whole pitcher of your margaritas tonight all to myself." Desiree laughed again, then gasped, one eyebrow raised. "Girl, Chester was flirting."

"With who?" I asked, blinking stupidly. I sprawled out on the sofa, crossing my legs at the ankles.

"Are you blind? He was flirting with *me.*"

"Oh." It seemed like the day was getting darker and darker for me. I couldn't wait to be alone so I could assess the latest situation involving Chester. The possibility of him getting with Desiree was remote, but from what I had just witnessed, I didn't know what to expect now. I couldn't even fathom the thought of two of the most important people in my life getting together. I refused to believe that God would allow that to happen to me, too. I was already so overloaded with burdens, some days I felt like I couldn't go on. I gave Desiree a guarded look.

"Chester's way too busy to give you the kind of attention you need," I insisted. "Knowing him, he's got more women on his agenda than a women's college."

Desiree sniffed smugly and waved her hand. "I know. He's dating a lady lawyer, you know."

"Who told you that?" I asked, wondering vaguely.

"Oh, I don't remember. Probably Regina or Sweet Jimmie." Desiree wiggled her nose, rubbed it, and continued. "I didn't know he was so nice. You think he was serious? You think he's really coming to your apartment tonight to get us drunk?"

"I doubt it. You know how men lie," I said evasively. "Listen, I'll go with you to see your daddy when you're ready."

Desiree sat down hard next to me and patted my knee. I pushed her hair off her sweaty face.

With a serene look on her face now, Desiree started talking in a low, controlled voice. "When I was eight I took my daddy out on a date. It was his birthday. I had sold cookies for a whole week to raise enough money to take him to lunch to celebrate him turning fifty. He grinned all through that soggy Happy Meal. Ronald McDonald sang happy birthday to him. That was the last time I saw him happy." There was a sad, faraway look on Desiree's face now. "Maybe I can concentrate on that culinary school now. I'm going to get me an apartment, go out and meet somebody, and get myself out of this rut I've been in for too long. Maybe now I can have a *normal* life like you," Desiree chirped.

"Maybe you can," I told her.

By ten P.M., Desiree and I were both pretty tipsy and singing along with Barry White in my living room.

"Carmen, listen . . . Barry White's voice sounds just like Chester's," Desiree squealed.

"Not to me," I slurred.

Sweet Jimmie banged on his ceiling, but we ignored him as we lay on my living room floor, soiling the plush brown carpet with our drinks. When we heard heavy footsteps on the stairs outside my apartment, we turned off the music.

"Chester!" Desiree squealed. She leaped up and staggered across the floor. Before she could open it, Sweet Jimmie stumbled in, clutching a margarita of his own. "Oh, it's only you." Desiree dropped back to her spot on the floor, punching the pillow she had been using to prop up her head.

"Well, who was y'all expectin'?" Sweet Jimmie pouted, strutting into the kitchen, looking like a black crow in his black floor-length housecoat.

"Chester Sheffield's coming by to party with us," Desiree announced. "Or so he said," she added with a yawn.

Sweet Jimmie darted back to the doorway with his mouth hanging open. He looked at Desiree before he gave me a puzzled look. "Oh?"

"Uh . . . he helped us get Dr. Lucienne ready to go to the nursing home. It was hard on Desiree and he said he'd come by to have a drink," I explained.

Suddenly, Desiree looked from Sweet Jimmie to me with a confused look on her face. "Carmen, how did Chester know where you lived?"

"I told him one night at Rocco's bar when we was discussin' old times. He was so drunk that night, I bet he wouldn't remember our conversation," Sweet Jimmie blurted. "Carmen, bring your happy ass in here and help me find the salt. Your kitchen is about as organized as a crime scene. I bet you couldn't get a chain gang to clean up after you." I leaped up and trotted into the kitchen behind Sweet Jimmie. He pulled me into a corner by the stove and whispered, "Is there somethin' you ain't told me?"

"It's nothing," I replied, waving my hand. "Uh, Chester was just trying to be nice to Desiree. He's not coming over here," I said with confidence, waving my hand.

Sweet Jimmie gave me a suspicious look. "Did you ever tell her about that fuckfest you had with Chester that traumatized me so bad that night? And don't you lie to me, you happy bitch. I been had your number." It disappointed me the way Sweet Jimmie made things sound so crude. Especially with me knowing that his tawdry personal life included threesomes and video cameras in his bedroom.

"No. And you'd better not tell her, either," I hissed under my breath.

Desiree was staring out of the window when Sweet Jimmie and I returned to my living room. She turned to me with a long face and tired eyes. "Will you call me a cab? I want to go home." She sighed heavily and added in a hopelessly sad voice, "Chester's not coming."

Right after Desiree's departure, Sweet Jimmie finished his drink and left. Ten minutes later, Chester knocked on my door. I immediately got so nervous, sweat covered my face like a veil.

"There was a five-car pileup blocking Lansing Street," he told me, blinking at the trembling hands I couldn't hide.

"Uh . . . Desiree had to leave." I had turned out the lights and had dressed for bed. Standing there in a shapeless, throat-high Cookie Monster gown that my grandmother had sent to me, I still felt exposed.

He shrugged. "That's more for us to drink." He grinned, holding up a huge brown-paper bag. "I picked us up some smothered chicken, too."

I had cracked open my door just far enough to lean my head out and shake it. I glanced over my shoulder and motioned toward my bedroom. "I have company," I told him in a firm whisper.

His smile froze. He nodded and let out a deep sigh. "I see." He didn't even try to hide the disappointment in his voice. He let out another deep sigh and blinked. "Well, it was good seein' you again, Crazy Legs." He shrugged and nodded toward my bedroom. "Don't do nothin' else in there you'll regret."

CHAPTER 44

Dr. Lucienne kept his word and died two weeks after being admitted to the Molly Stark Nursing Home, less than fifteen minutes away from the house where he had terrorized Desiree for so many years. He passed away right after refusing dinner as Desiree cradled him in her arms like a frail little bird. I was glad to be there with her when it happened. One minute he was cussing us out, the next minute he was gone, right after Desiree had lied and told him she was going to take him back to his own house.

"The last conversation with my daddy and I had to lie to him," she sobbed. "What makes us lie when we know it's wrong? What's wrong with us, girl?"

"Sometimes we *have* to tell lies to keep the people we love happy," I told her, forcing myself not to think about the mountain of fibs I had piled up. I was the last person in the world to be trying to make sense out of telling lies. I almost laughed out loud when I thought of what I would have looked like if my nose grew the way the cartoon character Pinnochio's did every time he told a lie.

In a way, the doctor's death was a relief to almost everybody who worked at the home. Within his first week there, he had assaulted half of the staff. Two days before he died I had also accompanied Desiree to the home. That day Dr. Lucienne had thrown a full bedpan at us and assured us both that we would suffer and then burn in hell. After an orderly helped sponge us off, I returned to my apartment with my hair, face, and blouse soiled with Dr. Lucienne's urine and feces. In an odd way, I was glad he was finally gone. Anybody that mean and burdensome in life was better off dead.

After I thought about it, I felt bad about my feelings toward Desiree's daddy. I tried to make up for it by spending as much time as possible with Desiree during the first few days after his death. I was even the one to attend to his final arrangements. That surprised me because I still had occasional nightmares about Regina's dead siblings and the horrific way Kitty died. I didn't think I could do enough for Desiree, but I tried.

Other than a few distant relatives from various cities throughout Alabama and Louisiana, none of Desiree's other family members showed up. Not even her own sister, Colleen.

The crowd from the funeral entered Desiree's house like a swarm of flies. My daddy and two other men lifted Burl onto the porch and wheeled him into the living room. Desiree was overwhelmed. After the first hour, she lured me to the back porch, where I held her in my arms and she cried for ten minutes. Once she composed herself, we sat down on the back porch steps. We briefly discussed the fact that Dr. Lucienne had left all of his life insurance to a distant cousin in Baton Rouge, Louisiana, a relative who didn't even attend the funeral. It took all of Desiree's savings and part of mine to bury the old man.

"I'll have to work my fingers to the bone, but somehow I will pay you back the money you donated," Desiree told me in a surprisingly firm voice.

"You don't owe me a dime," I assured her. "I was glad to help out." I had been saving for another cruise, but I didn't mind making the sacrifice. Looking out for my friends had become a way of life for me. But as much as I cared about Desiree, I refused her offer to move into the house she had shared with her daddy when she revealed to me that she was afraid to live alone. And she was tired of paying the high rent on that big house. "I am sure you'll be able to find somebody to room with," I told her.

Since the beginning of my friendship with Desiree, I had always been the stronger one. It was a position of power that I enjoyed. I felt validated. People *needed* me. But I had to draw the line somewhere. I needed my own space. Sharing a place with one of my needy friends was out of the question. I was glad that Desiree didn't push it.

"I am so lucky to have a friend like you, Carmen. I hope I never let you down."

"I hope you don't, either," I said distantly. "It's a shame nobody could locate your mama. But I don't understand why Colleen couldn't let bygones be bygones and come to her own daddy's funeral," I said.

"Daddy used to beat her until she couldn't walk," Desiree said hoarsely. She sniffed and wiped away tears and snot with the sleeve of the plain black dress she had worn to the funeral. The cuffs were already soaked.

"Well, he's still her daddy, too. He can't hurt her anymore now. She could have come just so she could be here to support you. He treated you like hell, but you stayed on with him anyway. If I'd been in your shoes, I'd have left as soon as I got out of school," I stated emphatically.

"What? Why, I couldn't leave my daddy when he needed me the most. He wasn't responsible." Desiree faced me with contempt. "That's a selfish thing for you to say, Carmen Taylor."

"I don't mean to speak ill of the dead, but if he wasn't responsible for beating the shit out of you, who was? I'm sorry." I shook my head in disgust. "I can't understand why you were so loyal to him."

Desiree looked up and let out a deep breath. "I ask myself that all the time about you and Burl."

I whirled around to face her. "What?"

"Your life revolves around him, and for the life of me I can't figure out why."

"I'm his friend," I reminded her. "His only true friend."

"Well, the doctor was my daddy. At least in my case, I owed him something."

"What's that supposed to mean?"

"My daddy couldn't beat me enough to make up for what I did to him," Desiree announced. I looked at the side of her face as she continued. Her voice rose from a whisper to a roar. "I had a good life before we moved here! We lived in the biggest, finest house in our neighborhood! My sister and I both attended private schools! We went to Europe or somewhere abroad every summer." Desiree paused and let out a short chuckle, lowering her voice. "My sister lost her vir-

ginity to a cute young Italian waiter on a beach one night. I was their
lookout. The boy paid me hush money in lire. The equivalent of ten
dollars." She got serious again. "We had a maid clean our house and
cook for us five days a week. Mama, Colleen, and me were too busy
being beautiful to clean floors and wash clothes. On one of the
maid's days off, Daddy told me to sweep the kitchen. I didn't do it and
I sassed him. So he gave me a whupping. He also made me cancel my
tenth birthday party that I had been looking forward to all month. He
even threw my cake to the floor, then made me clean it up. I got so
mad, I stayed awake all night trying to come up with a plan to make
him sorry. I lost a lot of friends over that canceled party. A week later,
I told my teacher that Daddy had molested me." Desiree paused, held
her head in her hands for a few moments, then continued, staring at
the high fence behind her house. "Things really spun out of control
from that point on. Daddy got arrested and Colleen and I had to go
into a foster home—that same day! It was all over the newspaper.
They suspended Daddy's license. Poor Mama had a nervous breakdown and everybody turned against Daddy. His patients and even his
own family. He got out of jail on bail and hired a high-priced lawyer.
He had to sell our house and use up all our savings to pay that lawyer and all of the bills that had got behind. It was a mess, but the
lawyer got him off. Lack of evidence, they said. Daddy never recov-
ered financially. As a matter of fact, he was still paying that greedy
lawyer up to the day he died. That's why we lived in a rented house."

I was so stunned, I had to breathe with my mouth open to keep
from hyperventilating. "Your own daddy molested you and you still
took all that shit off him? He must have done some serious apologiz-
ing to you." I placed my arm around Desiree's shoulder, but she
pulled away.

"He didn't," she responded in a voice so low I could barely hear
her.

"He didn't even apologize?" I was stunned even more. This was a
heavy story to be hearing on the same day as the funeral.

Desiree looked in my eyes and whispered, "He never touched me
in the first place."

The muscles in my face got so tight, it was a strain for me to keep
talking. "You lied?" I asked, giving her the most incredulous look I
could manage. It was like I was seeing Desiree for the first time. This
was not the woman I had admired for so many years. Sitting next to

me was an evil stranger. "How could you put your own daddy through something like that?" I shrieked, moving away from her. "And you call me selfish!"

"I was a child when I lied on my daddy," she replied firmly, blinking her eyes so hard her nose wiggled. "When I finally told the truth, it was too late. My family, my life, Daddy's practice: everything I loved was ruined. That's why we moved to Belle Helene. But nothing was ever the same again. Some days we would all be walking around the house crying at the same time. Sometimes Daddy would start crying at the dinner table and the only thing that would shut him up was a highball. Before too long, he had to have highballs just to get through the day. But he was so angry by then, he had to take it out on somebody. He started beating Mama first. She was never the same after her breakdown, so nobody was surprised when she took off. Then he started beating Colleen and me. As soon as Colleen got old enough, she took off, too. She begged me to go with her, but I couldn't. I had to stay behind to try and make things right again for Daddy. His life was ruined because of me. I couldn't see any other way to make it up to him but to stay there with him so he wouldn't be alone. So when you wonder why I do the things I do, that's the reason."

"Let's go back inside," I sighed, starting to rise.

"I've wanted to tell you all this for a long time, but I was too concerned about what you would think of me. Can you keep something this deep a secret? I hope so, because I don't want anybody else to know," Desiree said, struggling to stand back up.

"I can keep a secret," I replied, giving her a brief but firm hug. "I'm real good at keeping secrets." Before we could get all the way back inside the door, Burl zipped into the kitchen.

"I was hoping you hadn't left," he told me. "I wanted to give you a ride home."

I looked at Desiree and she smiled and nodded. Ending the day with Burl seemed like the fitting thing to do after a funeral.

CHAPTER 45

"Carmen, I seen Desiree at Rocco's bar last night. We missed you."

"Regina Witherspoon, you called me at seven A.M. on a Sunday morning to tell me that?"

It had been a week since Dr. Lucienne's funeral. I had left Desiree a few messages, but she had not returned my calls. I had been worried about her. But now, hearing that Regina had seen Desiree in a bar, I decided that she was doing all right. I sat up in bed, rubbed my eyes, and scratched my itchy scalp. I was immediately sorry that I had answered the telephone. An early-morning call from Regina was always a bad omen.

"Well, at least I missed you." Regina paused long enough to catch her breath; then she continued in a slow, steady manner. "Me, I don't think Desiree missed you, though. She was too busy. . . ."

"Why do you say that?" I sighed, angry with myself for letting Regina get this far.

"Oh, that sister was all over Chester Sheffield like a cheap wig. That heifer called me a heifer when I tried to hang with her. But Chester was so sweet. He carried her out of that place in his arms like a baby. It was so romantic . . ."

Romantic? Regina could watch a Godzilla movie and find something in it "romantic." But hearing this still disturbed me. Suddenly, I was wide awake.

"The girl must have been really drunk for him to do that. I hope he didn't arrest her, too. I've told her about getting too drunk in public," I offered.

"I just hope he didn't do nothin' nasty after he got her alone. If every time you crack open a newspaper and read about some horny priest molestin' somebody, ain't no tellin' what a cop would do to a pretty woman if he had the chance. These days you can't tell a cop from the boogeyman. Eeeyow! You goin' to church today?"

"Uh . . . maybe later. I better check on Desiree." I hung up the telephone and sat staring at my hands for a few seconds. Chester's belt was still on the handlebars of my exerciser, more than three years after he had left it. Without giving my next move much thought, I dialed Desiree's number. She answered on the third ring. "Are you all right? I heard you had a bad time at Rocco's last night."

Desiree hiccuped before answering my questions. "I'm fine now. Listen," Desiree's voice became a whisper. "I'm kind of busy right now. 'Bye, girl."

It took me five minutes to leap out of my bed, wash my face, and slide into my clothes. I drove like a bat out of hell to Desiree's house. I parked across the street and sat there as stiff as a rock. I had to roll down the window so that the fresh air would help cool me off. There was a steel gray Volvo in her driveway behind her royal blue Firebird. I looked up and down the street for Chester's red Corvette. When I didn't see it, I started my car. It was obvious to me that if Desiree had a man in her house, it was somebody other than Chester. I knew his Corvette so well I had memorized the license plates.

I don't know what made me look up toward her bedroom window just as I was pulling off. Standing there, naked to the world, with his arms folded defiantly, was Chester. It was unspeakable! I was horrified beyond belief. He just stood there, looking at me with a smug expression on his face until I stomped on the gas and turned the corner on two wheels. My car felt like it had suddenly sprouted wings, because I couldn't even feel the ground anymore. Frantically, I rolled my window up and drove two more blocks before I had to pull over to the side of the street so that I could compose myself. My life had been turned upside down so many times, I could have walked on my hands just as well as I walked on my feet.

"Oh, no, not *him*, Desiree. Of all the men in this town, why Chester?" I didn't realize I was talking to myself until a scowling woman came out on her porch, slapped her hands on her hips, and stared at me. I drove for another block and stopped again. This time I placed my head on the steering wheel and just sat there staring at the dashboard. For the next ten minutes I remained in the same spot in that trancelike state. It was only when I rolled down my window again and felt the wind on my face that I returned to reality. I was ashamed of myself. Chester had wanted to be with me, but he couldn't because I wouldn't let him. I cared enough about him to want him to be happy. I loved Desiree and I wanted her to be happy, too. Baby Red was gone, and he had left an indelible mark on her life. I knew that she would never really get over him. She had endured so many guilt-ridden years after destroying her family with her careless lie. If there was a chance that Chester could make her happy, that was a chance she deserved. And, if she could replace me in his life and make him happy, he deserved her. I sucked in my breath and drove slowly back to my apartment, where nobody could see the tortured look on my face.

"Did Chester get a new car?" I asked Sweet Jimmie later that day when he barged into my apartment.

"Girl, where you been? He been drivin' around in that Volvo for almost a month."

"I didn't know cops made the kind of money for him to buy a Corvette, now a Volvo," I said thoughtfully.

"They don't. But the man lives rent-free in his daddy's house. And, his granddaddy found a little oil on his farm in Texas. Chester's the only grandchild, so he ain't goin' to never be hurtin' for money," Sweet Jimmie revealed, grinning smugly. "I heard all that straight out of my mama's mouth. You passed up a good thing, girl."

"Oh, well," I sniffed. "Anyway, Chester's involved with Desiree now," I said dryly.

"That's good. Now we know we won't never have to worry about him draggin' his tail back over here to stalk you." Sweet Jimmie dashed into the kitchen and started slamming cabinet doors. "Where is that damn salt this time?" he yelled.

I was glad when Sweet Jimmie left to return to the hungover lover he had left in his bed. It was easier for me to talk to Desiree when she called.

"Desiree, Regina told me about you and Chester. Is it true?" I asked with caution, deliberately leaving out the part about me sitting in front of her house. There was a long pause before she answered.

"He said we were meant to get together. He told me everything that happened to him and me in the last few years had been leading up to us getting together." Her voice was low and hollow, but her words still stung my ears.

I wondered if his belief included my contribution. "That's deep," I remarked.

"And ooh, girl, the sex was the best ever." Desiree moaned and so did I.

"What about Baby Red?" I asked, my voice so hoarse my words came out in a croak.

"That was different. He was my first. He will always have a special place in my heart. Don't you feel that way about Gary?"

"Gary who?"

"That bus driver that finally cracked you open!"

"Oh, him. I think about him from time to time. But he's not special."

"Hmmm. Well, your first sex must not have been that good."

I chuckled first. "But my *first* time was a night to remember," I said smugly, wondering what she would say if she knew that Chester was the man who had taken my virginity. I couldn't wait for this awkward conversation to end.

"I am so tired now, but I feel so damn *good* all over. Ahh . . . you could knock me over with a feather. I didn't know great sex could be so humbling." Desiree burped. "And my little trip to Margaritaville didn't help. I'm hungover, too."

"Oh. When are you going to see him again?" It was hard for me to believe that the sad, small voice coming out of my mouth now belonged to me.

"Oh, didn't I tell you? We've already moved some of my stuff into his place. I should be all moved in by Wednesday. You can have that Ming vase you've always been so fond of."

I gasped, almost swallowing my own tongue. "You're moving in with Chester?"

"Isn't it wonderful? You were right when you said I'd get a roommate, and the timing was perfect. Being in that gloomy house was hard. I could still feel Daddy's presence there, you know. Now I know there is a god. Now I got a real man, and he's going to take care of me from now on! And don't get mad, but I won't be able to hang with you too much anymore. He's real possessive. He doesn't want me in the bars unless I'm with him. He promised he wouldn't crowd us, though. I mean, I can still go out with you and Regina and even dance with other men, but Chester will be there. Oh—about that cruise we were planning to take. That's out—unless you agree to let Chester go with us. He said that's the only way I'd be able to go. . . ."

I was fit to be tied. It never occurred to me that Chester would continue to interfere with my life through Desiree. "I can always go on my next cruise with Sweet Jimmie," I whimpered.

"That's good to know. Sweet Jimmie is a lot of fun. If you do decide to go with him, I want you to invite his mother, Nurse Bertha, to go. I'll pay her way. She was so good to Daddy till the very end. One more thing, though. Remember that time you let Chester have it with those cans when you guys were kids? He told me to tell you it was no big deal. He had it coming. Even though he has to live with a soft spot on his forehead where you hit him. He said you're welcome to come to the house anytime you want and make yourself right at home. And you know me, what's mine is yours."

Poor Desiree. If she only knew how true that was.

"Desiree, I am happy for you. No matter what happens, don't you ever forget that."

It took her a few moments to respond. "Why did that sound so ominous?"

"I'll always be there for you if you need to talk or something. I love you, girlfriend."

"I love you, too, Carmen. Let's get—I have to go; my man is back!" Desiree hung up before I could say another word.

I sat there holding the phone in my hand, going over her words in my head, hoping that she would never find out that Chester had been *my* man, too.

CHAPTER 46

My job at Holtsmark and Leefe was so mundane and boring, I could have done it in my sleep. But I loved it. It was the only consistent thing in my life. When I was there, it kept me from thinking about the spiritual warfare that was threatening to consume me. Whenever Mr. Holtsmark let me, I worked overtime just so I could delay stepping out into the real world. Besides, the extra money came in handy. I lived high on the hog, and it was time for me to stop falling back on my parents.

Now that I was out of the house, it was time for Mama and Daddy to do some of the things they had been putting off. I was glad when Mama told me after Sunday dinner a few days after my last conversation with Desiree that she and Daddy were going to do some serious traveling.

"After we get back from that cruise in the Mediterranean, we are going to go visit your sister in Nigeria for a couple of weeks," Mama told me. Then, giving me a sharp look, she said, "You don't mention Desiree much these days. Why?"

"I've been spending a lot of time with Burl," I replied, shifting uneasily in my chair, rolling some leftover hush puppies around on a plate with my finger.

"That's nice." Mama tilted her head to the side and peered at me out of the corner of her eye. "Now, don't you take what I'm about to say the wrong way." I could feel my body getting tense as Mama smoothed my hair off my face and continued. "I'm not saying Burl is a scoundrel or anything like that, and I feel for him being confined to that wheelchair, but he's still a man. I hope you know by now that men come from a totally different planet than us. Please don't let a man come between you and Desiree."

"I won't, Mama."

Desiree had given me the number to the house she now lived in with Chester. She had been living with him for almost two months, and I had not called her yet. She had only called me three times. I wasn't about to invite her out and have to look at Chester, too. I had to visit Piggly Wiggly when I wanted to see her in person. I finally called the house for the first time as soon as I returned to my apartment after having dinner with Mama and Daddy. I almost dropped the telephone when Chester answered.

"Crazy Legs, how you doin', girl?" he asked guardedly. It sounded like he was holding the telephone away from his face so there would be a slight echo. That gave me an eerie feeling.

"I'm fine. Is Desiree home?" I said quickly. "I wanted to invite her *and you* to my apartment this Friday night for drinks. Sweet Jimmie, Crazy Mimi, Regina, and their boyfriends will be there." Sweet Jimmie was the one who had encouraged me to throw a get-together, telling me that I had to meet Desiree more than halfway now if I wanted to maintain my friendship with her.

"What about *your* boyfriend?" Chester asked, his voice dripping with sarcasm. Now his voice was so loud and clear, it sounded like he was in the same room with me.

"Uh . . . Burl won't be there." No matter how many times Sweet Jimmie offered to help haul Burl up the stairs to my apartment, Burl refused to visit my place for that reason. "We all miss Desiree, and we all thought it would be nice to include her . . . and you."

"What's in it for you?" he asked sharply, breathing so hard I could almost feel his hot breath on my face.

"Desiree is still my best friend, Chester. I want her to be happy. Spending time with me and the rest of our friends makes her happy," I said firmly, careful not to sound too impatient. The last thing I wanted was to give Chester a reason to manipulate Desiree out of my life completely.

"Well, she's my woman now. Don't you think I can make her

happy?" It was strange hearing him pout, and more than a little un-settling.

"I know you can make her happy, Chester," I said seriously. There was an uncomfortably long moment of silence before he responded.

"I could have made you even happier, Carmen."

"Chester, that was a long time ago. I've forgotten it and I thought you had, too."

"I'll never forget that night, Carmen. Don't you forget *that.*"

"Look, Desiree loves you and she thinks you love her. I'll never tell her about us and I hope you won't, either. She'd never understand, and I don't want to lose her over . . . uh . . ."

"Go on and say it. You don't want to lose your best friend over a man."

"Now you're putting words in my mouth, Chester. But will you tell her to call me, please. I'd really like to see her."

"We'll be there," he said gruffly. A long silence followed before he hung up.

I was so glad that things turned out the way they did. Desiree had planned to come over, but she had to cancel. At the last minute she had been asked to work late. I talked to her on the telephone in my kitchen around eight-thirty that Friday night. Sweet Jimmie and the rest of the crew were all in my living room.

"But Chester said he'd still like to join you guys," she told me, clearly disappointed. "That is, if you don't mind. He's trying so hard to be friends with my friends. Especially you, Carmen."

"Uh . . . I canceled the get-together," I lied, covering the telephone receiver with my hand so she couldn't hear all the noise coming from the living room. "Maybe we'll all get together next weekend." I hur-riedly got off the telephone and returned to my guests. Sweet Jimmie, Regina, Crazy Mimi, and their current boyfriends had come to party with me. And so had my nomadic cousin, Baby Red. He had on a stiff plaid shirt and a pair of torn brown corduroy pants that he had stolen off a scarecrow in Pearl, Mississippi. He stood moodily in front of my living room window, glancing out every time he heard a car. He had just returned from his latest globe-trotting adventure, and from what he had shared with me, he was back in Belle Helene for good.

"Do you plan to see Desiree?" I asked, talking loud to be heard over all the noise.

Baby Red gave me an incredulous look before he snapped, "Of

course I plan to see my baby—if she wants to see me!" He got quiet, and an unbearably sad look appeared on his face. "She's the only reason I came back."

I had already guzzled two margaritas, and my head was doing a slight spin. A cup of strong coffee was in my hand now. "She's seriously involved with Chester Sheffield. They live together and he's crazy about her," I blurted, my voice cracking.

Baby Red shrugged, smiled, and waved his hand. "That's Chester's problem."

CHAPTER 47

After the rest of my drunken posse left my apartment, I sat up until dawn listening to some of my wandering cousin's travel stories. He paced around my living room floor regaling me with one snippet after another.

"I got chased by a racist motorcycle gang in L.A., seduced by a sexy Native American grandmother on a reservation where I spent the night in New Mexico, and bitten by a pit bull named Lancelot that I had been hired to baby-sit in Amarillo, Texas."

The best story was the one involving the scarecrow.

"Why did you steal clothes off a scarecrow?" I asked, eyeing his tacky ensemble from the spot I occupied on the floor. Black thread hung from the hem of his stolen jeans, and the shirt was so thin I could see through it.

"I was taking a dip in a creek when a big old bird swooped down and landed next to my shit on the creek bank. Well, my bike was on top of my backpack; he couldn't get to that. But my pants and shirt were just on top of the bike. That big-ass bird grabbed my shit and hauled ass. I waited until it got dark before I moved on, cycling down back roads naked. Thank God the first scarecrow I came across was my size."

"That's what you get for traveling with just one set of clothes," I scolded.

"I don't like baggage or anything else cluttering up my life. Except a good woman," Baby Red exhaled and motioned toward the kitchen. "Now, why don't you go call up your friend?" He slid his hands in his pockets and finally stood still, giving me a hard look.

"Are you crazy? It's the middle of the night. And I am not about to call Chester's house to ask Desiree to talk to you." I held up my hand. "Cousin, there is enough of an uproar going on in my life without you stirring up a mess with Desiree. It's been a long time and she's changed. If she walked in that door right now, I bet she wouldn't know you from Moses."

Baby Red shifted his weight from one foot to the other and let out a deep sigh. "She still workin' at that Piggly Wiggly?"

"Yeah," I replied, rising. "She's the manager now."

He nodded. Then he stretched and yawned. "Uh-huh. So that means she can pretty much come and go as she pleases?" he asked, offering a mysterious smile.

"I wouldn't know," I said, too tired to show my exasperation.

Baby Red chose to spend his first couple of nights back in Belle Helene sleeping on a pallet on my living room floor as opposed to sleeping on my sofa. "I feel more comfortable sleepin' closer to the earth," he explained. But as soon as Mama heard he was back in town, she ordered him to come take over my old room, which he promptly did.

I prayed that Desiree would call me so that I could alert her about Baby Red's sudden return. After my last conversation with Chester, I didn't have enough nerve to call the house again too soon. Desiree was too busy at work to take personal calls, so I couldn't call her there. My only choice was to pop into the Piggly Wiggly and take her aside for a few moments. I left my job early that following Monday, but by the time I got to her work, she was gone.

"She went home sick," one of her coworkers told me.

I didn't know Chester's schedule, but knowing that Desiree was at home gave me the courage to call. Chester answered.

"Hi, Chester," I chirped. "This is Carmen. May I speak to Desiree?"

He hesitated for a moment. "Are you callin' from the hospital?" His voice had become even deeper over the last few years. Each time I talked to him I had to remind myself that it was not really Barry White's sexy, thunderous voice speaking to me.

"Excuse me?" I squeaked. "Hospital?"

"That's where Desiree is supposed to be—with you and that nasty female infection you got so bad you couldn't drive. I guess you delirious, too, hmmm?"

"Oh." I did the dumbest, most damaging thing I could possibly do. I hung up without saying another word. I called my mother and she confirmed my worst suspicion: Desiree had come to the house and picked up Baby Red that afternoon! That Desiree. She was like a fart in a windstorm.

Within an hour, Crazy Mimi and Regina had stormed my apartment.

"I seen Desiree and Baby Red sneakin' pass my daddy's video store," Crazy Mimi revealed. "If I was that Chester, I'd give her a whuppin'."

"Well, if Baby Red wants her back, Chester can forget it. Desiree will never get over your strange cousin. What she sees in him is beyond me." Regina paused and gave me an apologetic look. "Sorry, girl. But I'd pester Chester over a bed with Baby Red in it any day."

By the time Sweet Jimmie joined the mix, the mood in the room was as dark as it was going to get. Or so I thought. While I was in the kitchen heating buffalo wings, Crazy Mimi answered a knock on the door. Nobody was surprised to see Chester.

"Chester, we know somethin' you don't know," Crazy Mimi teased, stabbing Chester in his chest with her finger. He brushed past her and strutted into my living room, stopping in the middle of the floor, folding his arms.

"What's that?" he asked, scanning the room with a look of contempt on his face. I was in the doorway leading to the kitchen, bracing myself. My heart felt like it was about to leap out of my chest.

"Uncle Sweet Jimmie checked out some real real nasty videos today," Crazy Mimi hollered, looking behind her at Sweet Jimmie. He lowered his head to hide his embarrassment. "There was a white boy with him, kissing up and down his neck," she added.

"Is that right?" Chester asked with a crooked smile.

"And guess what else me and Uncle Sweet Jimmie seen while he was there? We seen your lady friend, Desiree. That hussy went to that *mo-tel* across the street today with Baby Red. Me and Uncle Sweet Jimmie was peepin' out the window and we seen 'em." Crazy Mimi sighed triumphantly and returned to her seat on the sofa between a stone-faced Sweet Jimmie and a horrified Regina.

My eyes were on the floor. I ignored the buffalo wings burning in my oven. When I looked up, Chester was looking at me, biting his bottom lip. He opened his mouth to speak, but nothing came out at first. Finally he said, "Y'all have a nice evenin'." As if he didn't know what else to say or do, he nodded in my direction and then left.

Sweet Jimmie, clearly frazzled, grabbed Crazy Mimi by the hand and escorted her out the door. Regina started gathering up her things.

Not a minute later, I was in my living room alone with a plate full of charred buffalo wings, wondering when the bomb was going to explode.

CHAPTER 48

I had been working at the same job for four years now. Even though I had done nothing extra, I had received nice annual raises and a larger cubicle. Miss Peterson, the old-maid senior secretary, was still worried about me running off with a man. Sweet Jimmie dropped by often, acting more effeminate than Miss Peterson and me put together. "At least I don't have to worry about *him* hijacking you," Miss Peterson remarked, offering a rare chuckle. But when she heard me talking to Burl on the phone one day, she stood over me with tears in her eyes.

"Was that a *boyfriend* I overheard you say you'd go to the drive-in movies with this weekend?" she asked nervously, fingering the buttons on her staid plaid jumper.

"Yes, ma'am. But he's gay, too," I lied.

She smiled with relief, clapped her hands, and yelled, "Fags, fags, fags!"

During the four years, I had never called in sick. As a matter of fact, I went to work even when I really was sick. That's how important the distraction of having this job was to me. I took off only when I absolutely had to. Like when Desiree and I took those three Caribbean cruises, and a few days here and there around the holidays when relatives were in town.

In addition to nursing school, I had been putting off visiting my sister in Nigeria for years. Now seemed like a good time to make myself scarce. As much as I cared about Desiree and my cousin, I did not want to get caught up in the explosion that I was expecting to happen any day.

I didn't relish the idea of traveling all the way to Nigeria alone, but this was one time I truly believed that being away from my friends for a couple of weeks would do wonders for my morale. By this time I was convinced that everybody in Alabama was crazy, especially me.

"Carmen, are you crazy?" These were the first words to come out of my sister's mouth when I called her at her home in Lagos, Nigeria, two days after Chester's surprise visit. "Don't you know it's four in the morning down here?"

"Oh," I mumbled, wrapping the telephone cord around my finger. "I keep forgetting about the time difference. You want me to call back?"

"I'm awake now," Babette squawked. "How is everybody?"

"Everybody is fine. Mama's dragging Daddy, kicking and screaming, all over Europe, and Baby Red's back in town," I replied.

"Oh, is that where he is? He snuck out of here last month with a pair of Odell's best shoes. I bet he'd steal from a dead person."

I laughed for the first time in days. "I bet he would, too. Listen," I paused and sat up straighter on the sofa, where I had been parked for the past hour with my door dead-bolted and my curtains drawn. "I have a lot of vacation accrued. I was thinking about coming down there for a week. I'll be off for the next two weeks."

"Good. You can take care of these wild-ass kids so Odell and me can go to the Sudan to visit his uncle. Now let me warn you, we live in a Muslim neighborhood, so don't bring any shorts, because these women might stone you. These people are very sensitive and will make you suffer big-time if you offend them. Besides, some of these women down here practice witchcraft and would just love to cut up a chicken and fling it at you. They found a dead British woman—who had been warned—in shorts and a see-through blouse lying next to a headless speckled hen alongside the road last week. White folks are so hardheaded when they visit a Black country. And don't even think about coming down here and drinking alcohol or fooling around with any of these men. Some of them are mighty aggressive and good-looking, so ignoring them won't be easy. When are you coming?"

"Uh . . . let me call you back on that," I mumbled, hanging up. Suddenly, my problems at home didn't seem so big. I nuked the idea of spending two weeks in Nigeria—or anywhere else, for that matter. Besides, Sweet Jimmie had told me more than once, "Ain't no hidin' place when it come to tryin' to get away from your problems. Best thing to do is deal with 'em head-on."

After my conversation with Babette, I wandered around my apartment to keep from looking at the telephone wishing it would ring. Sweet Jimmie was working a night shift this week, so I couldn't count on him to come upstairs to keep me company. I was so anxious to hear from Desiree, I was afraid to leave my apartment to go visit anybody else. Finally, around midnight, the telephone rang.

"Carmen, it's Desiree." Desiree sounded disembodied. I was glad that she had identified herself. Otherwise I would not have recognized her voice. She sounded like a frog.

"Girl, I hope you're not calling me from beyond the grave," I said seriously. "Have you lost your everlasting mind? Crazy Mimi told Chester about you being with Baby Red." I gasped. "Have you seen Chester yet? You sound *hellish!*"

"Carmen, I'm at the hospital," she choked.

Something flashed in front of my eyes—spots, stars, I couldn't tell. My heart started beating a tattoo against the wall of my chest. "What did he do to you? Are you all right?"

"I'm fine." I heard some voices in the background and then the next person to speak on the other end of the line was Sweet Jimmie.

"Carmen, Chester's been shot," he sobbed.

CHAPTER 49

I don't even remember driving to Belle Helene General Hospital, but somehow I got there in one piece. Once I got inside, scowling police officers were crawling all over the place like ants. I almost got arrested for mowing people down trying to get to the receptionist desk near the first-floor entrance. A long-faced, gum-smacking woman peered up at me from a dog-eared novel just long enough to tell me she had no information on Chester Sheffield yet.

I roamed around the first floor of the hospital for more than an hour, not knowing if Chester was dead or alive. Just as I was about to leave, Sweet Jimmie appeared out of nowhere. I was frantic by now, my face covered in tears and snot. I didn't know that I had not buttoned my blouse before I left my apartment until Sweet Jimmie buttoned it for me, all the way up to my neck.

"Carmen, you all right, baby?" he hollered, placing a firm grip on my arms, then wiping my cheeks with his fingers. His eyes were red and threatening to spill more tears.

"Did my cousin kill Chester?" I managed. An image flashed in my mind that chilled me down to the bone. I could see poor Baby Red rotting in a murky cell and Chester rotting in the ground.

Sweet Jimmie led me to an orange vinyl sofa across from the receptionist desk. "It was no such a thing, praise the Lord," he declared with a nod. "Chester tried to apprehend a carjacker and things got real ugly."

I gasped so hard I almost choked on my tongue. Sweet Jimmie slapped me on the back. "Is Chester dead?" I croaked.

Sweet Jimmie shook his head furiously. "Hallelujah, no. He just got a little shoulder wound. But the suspect . . . well, he won't be goin' home for Christmas. He just died."

"Chester killed a man?"

"Chester killed a low-down, funky black motherfucker that was tryin' to kill him. He didn't have no choice. I wish I'd a been there. Come to find out, the police was lookin' for that booger in three states. Chester did the world a favor by takin' out that devil."

I breathed a sigh of relief. "Where's Desiree?" I asked in a squeaky voice, covering my chest with my hand, hoping to make my heart stop beating so hard.

"I sent her home. She was such a mess, she was upsettin' my other patients," Sweet Jimmie wailed, fanning his face with his hand. Beads of sweat dotted his forehead.

"Well, can I see Chester?" I asked gently, looking over Sweet Jimmie's shoulder. Chester's parents, his mother bent over and weeping, got out of an elevator down the hall and disappeared around a corner before I could get their attention.

Sweet Jimmie caressed my face before he responded. "Not tonight, baby. He's still in the recovery room, so groggy he wouldn't know you from me. You can see him tomorrow."

I was up all night, staring at the wall and pacing from one room to the other. Every time I looked at Chester's belt on my exerciser, I shuddered. Desiree didn't answer when I tried to reach her by telephone. I didn't feel like talking to anybody else, so I turned off my telephone. My plan was to catch up with Desiree in the morning and go with her to visit Chester.

I tried to call her from eight A.M. to one P.M. On a whim, I called every motel in town, trying to locate her with no luck. I didn't think to call the most obvious place: my parents' house, where Baby Red was lodging for free for as long as he wanted it. Mama and Daddy were still in Europe and Baby Red was alone in the house. At least, he was supposed to be alone. I refused to believe that Desiree was brazen enough to shack up with my cousin in a house a few yards away from where Chester's parents lived. If Chester's parents didn't see her sliding in or out of the house, I was convinced that the nosy retired pilot next door would.

Instead of calling my parents' house, I drove over there. I sighed with relief when I didn't see Desiree's Firebird anywhere in the vicinity. The house was as silent as a tomb when I entered through the door leading from the garage to the kitchen.

I found Desiree just where I thought I would: in Baby Red's arms in my old bed. He was sleeping like a baby, but she was lying there with her eyes wide open. She barely blinked at me, standing over her with my hands on my hips. I motioned with my hand for her to follow me. She reluctantly slid out of bed, just as naked as she could be. I led her out into the hallway, quietly closing the door to my room.

"Have you completely lost your mind, girl?" I asked in a coldly hostile voice.

"What?" she asked, blinking stupidly.

I gaped at her in total disbelief. "Why are you up in *here?*" I snarled, making a sweeping gesture with my hand. "Naked at that."

She folded her arms and moved back a few steps, grinding her teeth. Her breath, reeking of alcohol and my cousin's juices, was as foul as jackal shit. "What is your problem? I am not doing a damn thing I haven't done before. Why do you have a problem with me being in this house now?"

I gasped. "Desiree, what about Chester?"

"What about him?"

"Shouldn't you be at the hospital with him? The man's been shot!"

Yawning, she dismissed me with a wave of her hand. "Chester's going to be fine. It would take a *silver* bullet to bring him down—just like Dracula." She combed her tangled, matted hair with her fingers.

"The silver bullet was for the werewolf," I corrected.

"Whatever." She shrugged and rolled her eyes.

"When and if you do go back out to that hospital, you need to look into some therapy for yourself," I told her, giving her a look that was a combination of anger, pity, and disbelief.

Desiree's eyes got wide and she rotated her neck. "Why are you making such a fuss?"

I let out an exasperated breath and glanced sharply toward my old bedroom. Even with the door closed, I could hear Baby Red snoring and blasting piercing farts. "You're leaving Chester to get back with Baby Red, aren't you?"

Desiree dropped her head and then shook it. "Before Chester went on duty last night, we sat down and had a deep conversation about our relationship."

"I bet you did. Crazy Mimi let the cat out of the bag about you and Baby Red checking into that motel when Chester came to my apartment looking for you," I hissed. "I sat up all night expecting the coroner to call me to come identify your body. How is it you managed to get out of getting an ass-whupping? Chester was as mad as a Russian when he left my place."

"Oh, he was foaming at the mouth when I got home, too. He cussed up a storm and threatened to drink my blood. Then"—Desiree leaned forward and lowered her voice—"we made a pact. Well, it was really his idea. One last fling for him, one last fling for me." Desiree smiled dryly and nodded toward my bedroom door. "This is it for me."

"And then it's Chester's turn to have one last fling, right?"

She nodded. "I told him I didn't want to know when he did it and with who." A fierce scowl crossed her face. "I already know who he's got his dick aimed at."

I moved back a step and held my breath. "Who?"

"That ballroom-dancing bitch he used to drag around town," she snapped, her eyes blinking angrily.

"The Sade woman?" I cleared my throat, waiting for Desiree to respond. She remained silent. "Do you love Chester?"

Her hesitation confused me. First she shook her head; then she nodded. "I guess I do," she confessed with uncertainty. "He's strong and dependable, like you. I need him in my life as much as I need you. He's the first man to ever give me flowers. He's not perfect, but he's perfect for me. Other than you, I am all alone." There was a pleading look in her eyes that I could not ignore. The only other times I'd seen such a desperate look were on Kitty's face just before she died and on Burl's the times I'd seen him sitting in his window in his wheelchair watching me drag myself down the sidewalk to his house.

I hugged my troubled friend and patted her back. She abruptly pulled away from me and offered a dry, weak smile as she continued talking with her eyes staring toward the wall. "Chester's not anxious to get married again, but he thinks a baby would help our relationship."

A baby! What was the world coming to? My legs almost buckled. I couldn't stand to hear another word on the subject. "Uh . . ." I started moving away, talking over my shoulder. "Y'all better clean up your mess and leave this house just like you found it." I bolted from the house and ran all the way back to my car.

I didn't even acknowledge Burl as he whizzed by me in his van and blew his horn at me.

CHAPTER 50

A moon-faced receptionist gave me an annoyed look when I asked for Chester's hospital room number. Two hours had passed since my conversation with Desiree and I had not heard from her since. I had no choice but to visit Chester alone, and in a way I was glad. Knowing that he cared enough about Desiree, that he wanted her to have his baby, saddened me more than anything did. It was going to take me a while to be able to stand in the same room with the two of them together at the same time now. Desiree's information alone had made me feel like a volcano about to erupt. Seeing them together too soon after hearing their devastating plans probably would have made me explode. Desiree and Chester were the last two people in the world I wanted to witness my meltdown.

"Are you a relative?" the receptionist asked. Before I could respond, Sweet Jimmie, clutching a chart, trotted over and did it for me.

"She's his wife," he told the receptionist, turning to me with a wink. "Come on with me, Mrs. Sheffield," he grunted, patting my disheveled hair, frowning before he told me, "Time for you to get a perm." He grunted again. "You doin' all right, baby girl?" Then he led me down the hall. Our heels sounded like castanets on the hard tile floor as we made our way to a bank of elevators.

I shrugged. "I've had better days," I mumbled. "How is Chester?"

"Oh, he's fine. He'll be goin' home this evenin'." Sweet Jimmie opened the door to Chester's second-floor room and ushered me inside. "Don't stay too long, now," he advised before he disappeared back down the hallway.

When I was seven, Daddy's favorite uncle checked into a hospital in Huntsville to have a cyst removed. Nobody knows what went wrong during the surgery, but Uncle James had ended up in the morgue. From that point on, I looked at hospitals the same way I looked at haunted houses: I had to have a damn good reason to go into one on my own.

Chester was lying on his side with his back to the door. I gently shut the door and padded to the side of the bed and touched his shoulder. He was asleep. I rooted around in my purse and fished out a get-well card that I had picked up in the hospital gift shop. I was as quiet as a mouse, so I was surprised when he turned over and opened his eyes. He blinked a few times and then a wide smile appeared on his face. He lifted his limp, cold hand and grabbed my wrist. His grip was so hard it almost cut off my circulation.

"You look terrible," I teased, prying his hand away from my wrist. Dark circles outlined his eyes, and dried matter that looked like balls of lint filled the corners. The luscious lips that I had lost so much sleep over throughout my life were ashy and chapped.

"You lookin' good, Crazy Legs," he said. As weak as he looked, his voice was as deep and strong as ever. A thick coat of makeup hid the fact that I had been up all night and had circles around my eyes just as deep and dark as his.

"I'm glad you're going to be all right," I said, clearing my throat.

He lowered his eyes and nodded. "Where is Desiree?" he asked in a faltering whisper.

"I think she went to work. She was really upset when we talked yesterday."

His eyes looked up at me and shifted accusingly. "Is that right?" The sarcasm in his tone was so thick I could have sliced it with a sword.

I took a deep breath before I continued. "For the record, I don't appreciate that . . . that thing she and my cousin cooked up, and I told her so to her face." I paused and cleared my throat. "I hope you two work things out. Desiree is a lonely woman and she needs a lot of love."

He nodded again and blinked. "We could all use a lot of love," he said hoarsely. He stunned me when he lifted himself up high enough to reach my head. He cupped my face and kissed me on the forehead, the way Reverend Poe did, short and impersonal. That made a statement I never really wanted to hear from him: I was nothing to him anymore. Even after all the drama he had performed in my bed.

"Thanks for comin' by, Carmen," he told me. "Could you shut the door on your way out?" He dismissed me with a wave of his hand. Then he turned over on his side, his back to me.

CHAPTER 51

About a week after my visit to the hospital, I came home from the nail shop to find that Burl had left a message on my answering machine. He informed me that he and his mother were flying to Detroit that night to attend somebody's daughter's wedding. Knowing Burl and Miss Mozelle, I was certain that this was something that they had talked about profusely in my presence. But I couldn't remember if they had or not. That's how preoccupied I had become.

Regina and Crazy Mimi were in Gulfport, Mississippi, feeding coins into the slot machines and looking for a few good men.

Desiree had called me only once since our tense conversation outside my old bedroom. She reported that Chester was doing fine and had returned to work. What she didn't tell me was that she had spent even more time with Baby Red in my daddy's house. An eyewitness, the nosy ex-pilot next door, had revealed this information to me in a roundabout way when I ran into him at a nearby gas station. "Carmen," he said, "tell Desiree to stop tramplin' my bulbs in my yard to sneak into your daddy's house. She need to walk on the sidewalk like everybody else. She lucky I didn't call the law on her narrow behind last night."

I was extremely disappointed with Desiree, but I had to accept the fact that what she did was her business. However, whenever I did hear from her again, I planned to let her know in no uncertain terms what I thought about her doing her dirt in my parents' house.

The weekend before I was to return to work from my so-called vacation, I spent a few hours helping Sweet Jimmie lick envelopes. He had volunteered to help his church mail out flyers to some local businesses announcing a bake sale to raise money for AIDS research.

"I'm running out of spit and my tongue is starting to ache," I complained, rising from his kitchen table. "I'd better stop now."

Sweet Jimmie's apartment was a sight to behold. Huge erotic posters of men with men covered almost every wall. Expensive, impressive furniture filled every room. He smoked a lot of weed, but you couldn't tell, because in every corner was a bowl of potpourri. His floors were so squeaky-clean you could eat off of them.

Sweet Jimmie laughed. "I understand, baby. I'm fixin' to throw in the towel myself." He paused and glanced at his watch. "I got this cute little sailor comin' over tonight and I'm goin' to need a nice, wet tongue. Seafood can be right salty." He winked. I blushed and looked away.

Around eight that night, I drove to Adam's to pick up a rib-and-chicken combination dinner. On my way, I passed Chester hovering over some unfortunate individual's car, writing a ticket. He tipped his hat at me as I cruised by. When I came out of Adam's, he was leaning against my car with his arms folded.

"You made an illegal turn," he piped, glaring at me through narrowed eyes. For the first time, I noticed that in the glow of yellow streetlights, his eyes glistened like black diamonds.

"Well, I didn't have my seat belt on when I did it, so you might as well get me for that, too," I said nastily, wondering with fear where this encounter was going. He moved to the side and allowed me to open the door on the driver's side of my car and pitch my neatly wrapped dinner onto the passenger's seat.

Then he smirked. "Crazy Legs, if I was a real dog I could make your life a livin' hell."

"You're doing a pretty good job already." I smirked back. I knew just how dangerous the police could be. The Rodney King mess was still fresh on my mind. Not to mention a few new cases about roguish police officers abusing their power. During Baby Red's latest cycling odyssey, a *Black* highway patrolman had stalked him for miles through Montana, forcing him to hide in some bushes for two hours. With this unsettling information on my mind, I smiled at Chester. "I am so happy to see you looking so well," I told him, meaning every word. "I prayed for you." My last comment knocked him off guard. A broad smile replaced his menacing scowl and he stood up straight, folding his arms.

"Thanks, Crazy Legs. Uh . . . it looks like you picked up a mighty big plate." He motioned with his head toward my dinner, which, by the way, was so potent it could be smelled from outside of my car. "You goin' to eat all that by yourself?"

I nodded. "What I don't eat tonight, I'll eat tomorrow." I started my car, looking straight ahead. He stood back and I carefully eased away from the curb with my seat belt securely fastened.

Once I made it home, halfway through my dinner Desiree called.

"I was in your neighborhood. I was going to stop by, but I noticed your lights were out," she told me. There was static on the line, making her voice sound like a rattle.

I slid the huge Styrofoam container to the side of my coffee table, wiping grease and sauce from my lips with the sleeve of my nightshirt. The ribs, the bones gnawed almost in two, were in a neat pile on a blanket of paper towels on the floor.

"Oh, yeah? Where did you go?" I mumbled, chewing on gristle.

"I had to drop off a change of clothes down at the precinct for Chester. He's spending the night with a couple of his fishing buddies and they want to get an early start tomorrow morning to get to Mobile Bay."

"Oh. Well, talk to me, girl. I don't see much of you these days," I chided. "How's your love life?" I asked frostily.

She let out a deep breath first. "He asked me to marry him."

"Who?" I asked dumbly. My mind refused to accept this startling piece of news.

"Chester," she mumbled.

I could not believe my ears. If I had had false teeth, I would have swallowed them right then and there. My stomach did a flip-flop and the food that I had already eaten threatened to make a return appearance. My head felt as light as a balloon. My voice came out in a squeak. "So Chester's ready to settle down again?"

"Hell, no! If he is, it's not with me. But Baby Red is. He'll be twenty-seven on his birthday in June. He's finally come to realize that the gypsy life is not so great anymore."

"Well, are you leaving Chester for Baby Red?" I asked hopefully.

"I can't. I really do care about Chester, and he's offering me real security. Now that Kitty's dead, he'll inherit all of his daddy's property: the store, three houses. Not to mention some of that oil well money from his granddaddy in Texas. And ooh, girl, he's trying so hard to make things work between us. He is so anxious to have another child. That bitch in Texas goes out of her way to keep him from seeing his daughter. Poor Chester."

What I had just heard was unspeakable. I was devastated. "So what are you going to do? Are you going to continue seeing Baby Red?"

"Well, he wants me to whether I leave Chester or not. Chester, he thinks I'm over Baby Red. Remember that pact I told you we made? I don't know for sure, but I think he's cooking up something with that ballroom-dancing bitch. I have a feeling that's the so-called 'overnight fishing trip' he's going on tonight." Desiree laughed. "I am not worried about that bitch making my shit look bad. If she was that good, he wouldn't have broken off with her in the first place."

"You really don't mind him seeing other women?"

"Hell, yeah, I mind. But I can't stop him from creeping." Desiree paused and laughed again. "And he can't stop me."

It was my turn to laugh now and I cackled like a witch. "I think you both need some serious therapy."

"I'm glad you're laughing, because that's funny coming from you." Desiree didn't give me a chance to reply. "You could be married by now or at least living with somebody. Instead, you roam around with that Burl. Even Chester thinks you're wasting your best years. Every last one of his male friends has tried repeatedly to get him to set them up with you. But he's not into matchmaking and getting into other people's business. For some reason, Chester's got all his friends thinking that you're unapproachable." Desiree clicked her teeth. "You with that gorgeous body, that face—what a waste. Girl, I feel so sorry for you."

Desiree's comments disturbed me. Mainly because they were true. "Well, don't. There's more to life than sex. It doesn't bother Burl that we can't have sex, and it doesn't bother me. Besides, I've been with other men and I will continue to be with them—when I feel horny." I felt cheap making that comment, but I felt good because I was being honest.

"Well, I got a date so I'm going to haul ass," Desiree said smugly.

"Tell my cousin I said hi." I sighed.

CHAPTER 52

My telephone conversation with Desiree had taken away my appetite. I wrapped what was left of my dinner and shoved it into the refrigerator, then stood looking around the kitchen, wondering what to do next. It was a sad way for a young, single woman to spend a Saturday night. I had become far too familiar with alcohol, but that didn't stop me from snatching open my cupboard and grabbing my margarita mix in one hand and a fresh bottle of tequila in the other.

Half of a glass was all I could stand. And I drank that bending over the counter. Right after I returned to my sofa and starting leafing through *TV Guide*, somebody knocked on the door.

"Who is it?" I yelled with my ear pressed against the door, holding my unbuttoned nightshirt together with one hand.

"You know who it is. Shit." There was no mistaking that voice.

The door felt as heavy as lead as I cracked it open. "Chester, what in the world are you doing here?"

Still in uniform, he sighed and lifted his cap to scratch his head. Then he gave me a dry look. "Do you want me to come back with a search warrant? If I do, I'm sure I'll find some weed layin' around up in here. And I'll be able to add resistin' arrest and assaultin' a police officer, no doubt. You lookin' right vicious tonight," he teased, looking over my shoulder. I moved back as he gently pushed the door open with his foot and entered my living room.

"What do you want?" I asked nervously, still clutching the front of my nightshirt. "Desiree said you were on your way to go fishing."

"I am." He sniffed. "But I didn't say what I was goin' fishin' for." He let out a wicked laugh before he got serious. "I never thanked you properly for visitin' me in the hospital." He wrapped his fingers around my wrist and held on hard.

"You could have called to tell me that," I snapped, slapping his hand away. "You stop that and get your ass out of here!" In the blink of an eye, the handcuffs he kept dangling from a loop on his belt when he was on duty were locked around my wrist.

"Behave yourself!" I advised, trying to shake my wrist loose. "I know all about that so-called pact you and Desiree cooked up. She thinks you want to do it with that ballroom-dancing woman one last time."

"Desiree was wrong again," he said with his lips just inches away from mine, amused at me trying to pry off the handcuffs with my teeth.

Reluctantly I moved my face back a few inches, breathing so hard my eyes burned. "I don't ever want her to know about us."

He shrugged. "She'll never hear it from me," he said firmly.

I took a deep breath and dropped my head, resting it against his chest, muffling my words. "Chester, Burl and I are getting married." It was the biggest lie I had ever told, and the most painful. My jaws started aching as soon as I got the last word out. "All you and I will ever be from now on is friends, not lovers." He stared at me, blank-faced and mystified. I lifted my hand. "And I'd appreciate it if you would un-ass my wrist from these damn handcuffs."

"Married? You and Burl? Aw, come on, Crazy Legs. Don't do that to yourself, girl." He seemed genuinely disturbed. "You know damn well you do not love Burl."

"It's none of your business," I hissed. "Can't you get that through your head?"

With a frighteningly still face, he produced a key and unlocked the handcuffs. "What is the point of you marrying a man like Burl? Why would you want to bog down yourself with a load that heavy?"

"I love him and he loves me, and that's all that matters," I replied, massaging my wrist.

"What about kids?" he asked, dipping his head.

"We can adopt."

"What about . . . you know?"

"There's more to sex than intercourse," I said vaguely. "You'd be surprised what you could do with a towel if you know how to use it. Now, you go—go on and find somebody to arrest." I shooed him with my hand toward the door.

He nodded. "You askin' me to leave?"

"I'm telling you to leave, Chester. Now get."

He didn't budge. Instead, he folded his arms defiantly. "I just want to know one thing, and then I will leave you alone with your favorite towel. One time you told me you cared about me. Was that just lip service or did you mean it?"

"I meant it then and I mean it now."

A hopeful looked appeared on his face. "You still have feelin's for me, but you don't want to be with me?"

"You chose Desiree. You moved her into your house. You want her to have a baby with you," I firmly reminded him.

"Goddamn it! I tried to choose you! Then outta nowhere you gave me that gobbledygoop story about you and Burl!"

"I'm going to marry Burl, Chester."

He sighed with defeat and asked wearily, "You really mean that? You choosin' him over me?"

I nodded.

"This is the last chance for us, Carmen. I do care about Desiree, but we both know what's goin' on with her and your cousin. She already told me that if I wanted to break it off with her, she could be moved out in five minutes. I don't think she'd be too upset about us gettin' together. After all, it was me and you first. She needs to know that anyway."

I shook my head.

Holding up a hand, shaking his head like he had trouble believing me, in a suddenly hostile voice he asked, "So that's it?"

I nodded, and when I tried to kiss him for the last time, he turned his head. Then he left.

CHAPTER 53

That Burl! He had become an albatross around my neck, and I wanted him dead more than ever now. Or at least attracted to another woman. He was the biggest obstacle preventing me from experiencing a normal life.

On one hand, I was proud of myself for rejecting Chester. It was living proof that I was not as weak as I thought I was.

Desiree was my best friend, and I did not want to lose her, especially over a man. As far as Burl was concerned, well, I was no closer to relieving myself of him now than I'd been more than ten years ago when I promised that I'd always be there for him. I was sick and tired of arranging my love life around Burl. And the other forgettable men I went to bed with didn't come close to satisfying me. But five minutes after Chester left my apartment that night, I prayed that he would turn around and come back to finish what he had started. When the doorbell rang, my heart skipped more than a few beats. Sadly, Desiree and Burl suddenly didn't seem so important. I broke three nails trying to open the door so fast.

"You oughta be ashamed of yourself." Sweet Jimmie, in his night-gown, his hands on his hips, blocked my doorway.

Looking past him I asked, "Who are you talking to?"

He shook a finger in my face. "I'm talkin' to you, girl! Do you see anybody else standin' here besides me and your nasty self?"

"If you mean Chester, nothing happened." I retreated to the sofa, too exasperated to get upset with Sweet Jimmie. "We just talked."

"Is that all?" Sweet Jimmie seemed disappointed as he joined me on the sofa, eyeing me with suspicion.

"Chester and Desiree are going to really work on their relationship," I bleated. I had to swallow hard and take a deep breath before I could finish. "They are going to try and have a baby."

Sweet Jimmie looked like he was going to pass out. "My Lord," he moaned in a high-pitched voice. He fanned his face and shook his head, his eyes still on me. "How do you feel about that?"

"What do you mean?"

"Girl, don't play with me. I know you still got a thing for that man and I can't blame you."

I smiled and took another deep breath. "Didn't I tell you? I'm going to marry Burl."

Sweet Jimmie gasped and leaned back to look at me through narrowed eyes. "Like I said, you oughta be ashamed of yourself, girl."

CHAPTER 54

"Carmen, what's this I hear about me and you gettin' married?!"
"When did you get back?" I asked Burl. This was the first time
he had called me at work in over a month. Not only had I told him
not to visit me at work, I had told him in no uncertain terms not ever
to call me at work unless he absolutely had to.

"I'm still in Detroit," he said anxiously. "Lord have mercy—*you* wanna
marry *me?*"

I was dumbfounded. Things were happening way too fast for me.
"Who told you that? Chester?"

"Regina called me up here at five o'clock this mornin'. She heard it
from Crazy Mimi. She heard it last night from that old use-to-be pilot
next door to your daddy."

Sweet Jimmie had been busy burning up the telephone lines. It
had been two days since I shared this information with him. "I—we
can talk when you get back," I managed. The next voice I heard from
was Miss Mozelle's.

"I'm so pleased! I prayed for my baby to settle down with a up-
standin', Christian-hearted girl like you. Can't beat this with a whip.
God sure is good to me," she squealed. "Listen, baby, we'll be home
tomorrow night."

I had really cooked my goose this time. By the end of the week,
everybody I knew was talking about Burl's and my upcoming mar-

riage. My telephone was ringing off the hook. Desiree called me five times in one day. "Chester can't stop laughing," she told me, laughing herself.

Mama called me from Nigeria, where she and Daddy were visiting my sister and her family. I never did find out who had called her to tell her about Burl and me planning to get married. "Girl, what in the world is going on back there? Your cousin got you smoking some of that mess? Don't you do a thing until your daddy and I get home!"

As soon as Burl returned to Belle Helene from Detroit, I went to visit him. He was beside himself. I could have knocked him over with a feather. "You done made me the happiest man in Alabama," he swooned, almost in tears.

Miss Mozelle couldn't have picked a better time to have a massive stroke the very next day. In a way, it got me off the hook. At least for a while.

CHAPTER 55

As much as I loved Miss Mozelle, her health problems made things mighty convenient for me. She spent two weeks in the hospital hovering between life and death. Burl was too upset even to think about marriage. His uncle Mogen fired the nurse who had been coming to take care of Burl and hired Nurse Bertha to move in so that she could take care of Burl and Miss Mozelle when the hospital released her.

"Carmen, let's hold off with our plans until Mama gets well enough to know what's goin' on," Burl told me. "She's been waitin' on me to get married for too long to have to miss out on it."

During the next four excruciating years, Miss Mozelle was practically confined to her bed the whole time. On some days, she could not even talk. I resumed a few shallow relationships with some of the men I'd met over the years even though I was "engaged" to marry Burl. It had been months since anybody mentioned Burl and me getting married. I prayed that something else would happen that would force us to cancel it altogether.

Time had lost its meaning to me. While the rest of the world continued to change, I felt like I had come to a standstill. I had little interest in current events. O. J. Simpson's arrest, trial, and verdict were nothing more to me than an annoyance interrupting my television viewing.

The years continued to roll by. My friends were all moving forward. Regina finally talked her mother into getting the therapy she needed so that she could get over her devastating phobia about leaving the house. On the same day that England buried Princess Diana, Miss Maggie left the house for the first time in over fifteen years to see Regina marry a lawyer. A small-time lawyer, but to Regina, a lawyer was a lawyer. Crazy Mimi, a woman so mentally unbalanced she was now walking into walls, met a visiting preacher and was threatening to get married, too. It was like the whole world was spinning out of control. I knew that if I didn't watch my step, I was going to fall off and none of my friends would be there to catch me. I felt totally abandoned, and it didn't help matters when Nurse Bertha told me, "At least you still got Burl. He ain't goin' nowhere."

Desiree had been trying to get pregnant for years. She went to Dallas with Chester every other month to see his daughter and always came home depressed. Her failure to have Chester's baby was the one thing I could not show her any sympathy for. When I did have to face Chester, he was distant but cordial. I felt it was safe for me to start calling Desiree on a regular basis at home again even when I knew he was in the house.

Time continued to pass me by. My twenty-ninth birthday was approaching. By now, Miss Mozelle was finally doing a lot better, but her prognosis was grim. It was her wish to see Burl get married while she was still alive, but she wanted to be lucid enough to enjoy it. I was not proud of the fact that I was glad that she had remained so sick for so long.

Still, Burl and I had planned to get married within the month. I felt that the sooner I got it over with, the easier it would be for me to go on with what was left of my tempestuous life. Somehow, someway, I would learn to accept being married to Burl. It symbolized the end of a burden I had carried around for too many years. But it also symbolized the beginning of a new one. I really needed to talk to Desire as soon as possible. Even though my mind was made up, there was still a chance that I'd allow Desiree to talk me out of marrying Burl. After all, it had been five years since I'd concocted my clumsy plan to marry him.

I dialed Desiree's number from work three days into the new millennium. "Chester, I'd like to speak to Desiree," I began, wrapping the telephone cord around my fingers.

"So would I," he said gruffly.

"She's not home?"

"She's not with you?"

Before I could answer, he grunted something unintelligible and then he hung up. After yet another restless night, I confronted Desiree at the Piggly Wiggly right after I got off work. "You still fooling around with Baby Red?" Baby Red was still living with my parents. He did odd jobs when he needed money, and I saw him around town with different women from time to time. He and I rarely discussed Desiree, and I was glad.

"I don't have time to talk," she told me, looking everywhere but at me. "I'll stop by your place later tonight."

I didn't know what time Desiree was coming by, but I had a pitcher of margaritas chilling in the freezer when she showed up around nine that night.

"I'm leaving Chester. This farce has gone on long enough," she told me right away. She looked wide-eyed and frazzled. Her pursed lips, smeared with candy-apple red lipstick, looked like a bloody beak.

I had heard that Baby Red was planning to move back to Mobile. "You're moving to Mobile to be with Baby Red," I accused.

"I'm through with him, too," she hissed, dismissing me with a wave of her hand. "I'm going to California to live with my sister," she said grimly. "I'm going to bring some suitcases over here for you to keep until I'm ready to haul ass."

"You're planning to leave soon, then?"

"Yes. Why?"

"Burl and I are getting married, and I wanted you to be with me."

She gasped. "What—I—after all these years you're really going through with this?" She seemed amused and was threatening to smile.

I nodded and shrugged. "He—we're going on a cruise for our . . . honeymoon." I smiled weakly. "Being married to him won't be so bad. I won't ever have to work again if I don't want to," I said, sounding like I was reading from a cue card.

"The hell you won't! Girl, you will be working night and day in that house. Do you really want to spend the rest of your life helping take care of an invalid? And what about Miss Mozelle? They will expect you to help take care of her, too. Carmen, don't do this to yourself. You could do so much better! Don't burden yourself with some crazy shit like marrying Burl. He's a cripple!" Desiree ran into the kitchen and returned within a minute with a huge margarita and held it to my lips. "Drink this shit, girl, and talk to me. Drink every drop of it!"

I took a long swallow and let out a painful belch. "I'm getting married. What's there to talk about?" We spent the next two hours talking about Desiree's problems. She was leaving town and that was all there was to it. I don't know if it was the strong drinks that impaired my judgment, but I went home with her and helped her pack two suitcases.

"I want you to take this to your place and put it somewhere," she said, holding up a Smith and Wesson that Chester kept in the house. "I don't want this damn thing in the house as long as I'm still here."

I slid the gun into my purse and then I helped Desiree load her suitcases into the trunk of my car.

CHAPTER 56

A week rolled by and Desiree had not decided when to leave Alabama. As a matter of fact, she and Chester seemed to be getting along better than ever. "He thinks he misplaced his gun," she told me. I shuddered when I thought about the weapon hidden underneath some old newspapers in my broom closet.

To my surprise, Chester encouraged her to throw a bridal shower for me at my apartment a week later. It was the first time in months that I'd had a good time with my friends in my apartment. It was a small gathering and a sad occasion for me. I had invited old Miss Peterson from work, but she had declined.

"Why, oh, why in the world would you tie yourself down with a gay man, dear?" she'd asked. "Are colored boys that scarce?"

"Oh, it's just for tax purposes," I told her, lying to the very end. After I assured her that I would stay on at the law firm, she presented me with a toaster.

Later the night of my shower, Chester came by my apartment with his good-looking friends: Duke, Perry, Nick, and Clyde. It was hard, but I had to ignore every single one of them. We finished the night drinking even more at Rocco's bar and grill, with Burl in attendance, grinning nonstop and hanging on to me for dear life. That night I forced myself to believe that things were not so bad after all. All of my friends were happy, Burl was happy, and just seeing all this made me happy.

I danced with Chester for the first and last time that night. Ironically, it was to a Barry White tune. Chester had approached me after witnessing his friends dancing me off the floor into corners so that they could grope me. I thought I would melt in his arms. His embrace was so firm, I could feel his heart beating against his hard chest.

"Crazy Legs, I still wish it was me and you, and I know you know that," he whispered, grinding against me. Like always, I had to remind myself that it was Chester's voice I was hearing, not Barry White's.

"I know that, Chester. I really do." I meant every word I said. If Desiree had not cut in, I would not have been responsible. I wanted to leave that place and everything and everybody in it that night to be with Chester Sheffield again. This time permanently.

"Loosen up, sister. He belongs to me," Desiree joked, encircling Chester's waist from behind with her arms. He stared at me longingly for a few seconds before he pulled away from Desiree and reached for me again. All eyes were on us as he hauled off and kissed me, pushing his tongue so far into my mouth I gagged. I could hear Sweet Jimmie gagging from across the room. Crazy Mimi whimpered, and Regina just stood there with her mouth hanging open, leaning against Earl, her new husband. I was even more stunned than Desiree was. I was surprised at how graciously she handled such a tense situation. "You never kiss me like that," she pouted, bopping Chester's chin with her fist. "You'd better behave yourself before I tell Carmen about the time you went down on me with gum in your mouth and how you had to shave me to get it all off." Chester bowed his head and followed Desiree into a corner, but throughout the rest of the night his eyes were on me, and so were Burl's. Surprisingly, Burl didn't mention Chester's blatant behavior to me afterwards, and neither did I. Oddly, nobody else did either.

Mama was severely disappointed because I had declined to wear the elaborate wedding dress she had wanted Babette to wear so many years before. "Miss Peterson at work said it would be bad luck for me to get married in a dress like Princess Diana's now that she's dead," I told Mama. Even so, Mama had arranged for Reverend Poe to marry Burl and me in her living room. Babette was pregnant again and experiencing too many complications to travel from Nigeria for the wedding.

Other than the fact that I was getting married too close to the

Super Bowl, Daddy didn't have much to say about me marrying Burl. But he did tell me, "I didn't raise no fool, now. You better make sure you get your name on them power-of-attorney papers, too. If some- thin' was to happen to Burl, I want my girl to be provided for. You know how his uncle is."

Even with that humongous bank account Burl now had, my plan was to keep working. Now more than ever, I needed that distraction. But the closer I got to marrying Burl, the more apprehensive I be- came, and it showed.

"Carmen, you been pickin' at that same pork chop for ten min- utes," Daddy said over dinner a few days before the wedding was sup- posed to take place. "And if your face get any longer, it'll be draggin' this floor."

"It's still not too late to call this thing off," Mama added, pushing my limp hair back off my face. "I got a bad feeling about you doing this."

"Let the girl alone, Lizette. She ain't gettin' no younger no-how. How many more chances is she gwine to get to marry a rich man? Shoot," Daddy snorted.

It was amazing how I had allowed poor judgment to get me into so much trouble. The little prank that I had played on Burl in the train yard over fifteen years ago was going to haunt me until the day I died. Calling off the wedding was out of the question.

Burl's greedy uncle was beside himself with anger. I had heard ru- mors that he considered me a gold-digging Jezebel and that if it was the last thing he did, he was going to make sure I didn't take advan- tage of his nephew. He had spent a fortune the last couple of years fly- ing back and forth from Detroit to Alabama, trying to talk some sense into Burl, but it had done no good. Burl was ecstatic and proud that for the first time he was defying his stern uncle.

Miss Mozelle knew her brother was upset, but the upcoming wed- ding was all she talked about when she could talk. Even though she claimed to be feeling so good, something told me that she was hang- ing on just long enough to see her dream come true. And it would have if Desiree had not called me to come pick her up that night after Chester had attacked her—the night before my wedding.

Because of my years of lying and deceitful ways, the nightmare that I now found myself in was not a nightmare. It was real. I had killed

Chester. Lying there on my bed reliving my life up to this point had only made it seem even worse. I had made so many mistakes in my lifetime, and I was about to make even more.

"Carmen, if we are going go, we have to go now." Desiree's shaky voice cut into my thoughts like a knife.

Grasping at straws, I said, "Desiree, I think I was dreaming. I thought . . ." I gasped. I had not been dreaming. I had killed Chester Sheffield, and Desiree and I were planning to run away to keep from going to jail. I sat bolt upright, my hands shaking like leaves. It was then that I recalled that strange incident in my bathroom right after my shower: ice-cold wind on my face that could not be explained. I realized now that it had been a chilling premonition that something unspeakably bad was going to happen.

"Get up, now," Desiree coaxed, pulling me by my arm. I felt like the child I wanted to be again.

"Wait. I'm . . . I'm . . ." My arm and the rest of my body felt like dead wood, and I had no control over it. Even with Desiree pulling on me, I couldn't move. I just sat in that same spot on my bed, staring toward the mirror on the dressing table facing my bed, looking at the stranger I had become.

Desiree let go of my stiff arm and crossed the room and stared out the window. "I'm taking you with me to California." Turning to me, she added, "Come on, now, we have a bus to catch." Finally, I got up and looked around my bedroom, resting my eyes on the belt on my exerciser that Chester had left behind so long ago. It was hard not to think about why it was there. It was hard not to think about what might have happened if I had not chased him out of my life the night he had left that belt.

It was hard.

CHAPTER 57

Desiree and I walked from my apartment to the nearest intercity bus stop, which was four blocks away. Two blocks from my apartment building was a parking lot surrounded on both sides by a thicket of bushes and trees. A trash can sat at the entrance of the parking lot. I had wiped as much of Chester's blood as I could off of the weight. I tossed it into the bushes. "Put it in that trash can, too," Desiree advised, tossing a plastic grocery bag into the trash can. The bag contained her bloody windbreaker and the blouse that Chester had ripped one sleeve off of. Both had been bleached and shredded before we left my apartment.

"Nobody'll be fooling around in these bushes for anything," I insisted, shifting the overnight bag I had packed to my other hand.

"You are," Desiree shot back at me. "Now, you put that weight in the trash can like I told you. They'll empty it later on this morning. Anything you put in the bushes could be there for a long time. Sooner or later some nosy busybody would find it."

I retrieved the weight and slid it into the trash can between a bundle of old newspapers and the plastic bag Desiree had just dumped in.

"What about your bloody house shoe?" Desiree muttered, looking around.

I gulped and became frantic and light-headed. "Aw, shit! I forgot it! I left it on the bathroom floor! We have to go back—"

Desiree slapped the side of my face. "What's wrong with you, girl? There is no turning back now."

"Well, I did wash the blood off the shoe—remember?" Then I froze. "They'll find Chester's gun in my broom closet. . . ."

Desiree nodded and gave me a steely look, walking off toward our destination. "It won't make any difference. We'll be long gone by the time they do." The rain had stopped, but it had left behind puddles so deep and wide on the sidewalks, it made walking at daybreak just that much harder to do. We moved with our heads bowed and our tired bodies bent forward like elderly refugees. Slipping, sliding, and hopping to avoid stepping in puddles, we still ended up with slime and mud outlining our shoes like halos.

Since I'd been taller than all of my female friends all my life, I had no conception of what it was like to be Desiree's height, five-three, and I had never given it much thought until now. Every few steps, she had to hop to keep up with my long strides. She didn't complain until we had less than one more block to go.

"I have to stop for a minute," she wheezed, leaning against a newspaper truck parked on the street. "My head is spinning." I panicked when she dropped the small suitcase she had been carrying and placed both hands on her stomach. "My stomach feels like somebody is in there churning buttermilk."

Other than a few service vehicles, we were the only ones on the street. But lights were on in most of the houses and apartments along the way. I knew that it was just a matter of time before we had to interact with someone other than ourselves. My biggest concern was that we'd run into somebody who knew us well enough to see a difference on our faces and in our behavior. Somebody who could read the guilt in our eyes.

I stopped and glanced around before speaking. "You don't look good at all," I said softly. "It's still not too late for us to . . . turn ourselves in." Now that the reality had really set in, my attitude changed. I didn't know if I had weakened or come to my senses. I silently prayed that Desiree would insist on us turning ourselves in. At least we would know what we had to look forward to. As bad as a nasty trial, shame beyond description, and jail sounded, at least it sounded better than the unknown did now. Staring at my pregnant friend, I asked, "What kind of a life would two pampered Black women have as fugitives?" I silently reminded myself that the facts were overwhelm-

ing. We couldn't work regular jobs for too long, we couldn't do anything to call attention to ourselves, and we would have to look over
our shoulders day and night every day from now on. And we would
have to live in places probably worse than jail. Developing serious relationships and raising children were out of the question. Children!
Desiree was pregnant. "Desiree, we have to consider the baby." I sucked
in my breath and lowered my head, which felt like it was hanging
from a meat hook. For the first time since I'd killed Chester, I was
thinking about someone other than Desiree and myself. "With a baby,
it would be just a matter of time before things fell apart. And look at
you; you'll never make it to California on a bus in the shape you're in.
You may as well ride on a roller coaster."

Desiree coughed and stood up ramrod straight, offering me a weak
smile. "I'm fine," she insisted, shaking her head. "It was not easy for
me to decide to run. I am not going to back out now. California is a
zoo, a big zoo so crazy anything and anybody normal would look
crazy. As long as we don't look and act too out of the ordinary, it'll be
easy for us to blend in." A dry smile crossed her face. "Colleen told
me one time that San Francisco was full of people from other places,
all running away from something. The first year she lived there, she
shared an apartment with a Mexican woman who had robbed three
banks." Desiree shook her head and cracked an even broader smile.
"The woman lived *la vida loca* until she fell in love and blabbed to a
man who wanted the reward money for turning her in more than he
wanted her."

"Well, if you can still smile, you must be feeling all right," I said levelly, exhaling a stale breath. "I'm still down for this if you are," I declared. Desiree responded with a nod and we started walking again.

CHAPTER 58

Other than about a dozen drowsy, grumbling weekend commuters, Desiree and I were the only ones waiting to board the bus that would get us to Mobile. Once we got there, we would board a Greyhound bus to a connecting destination that we had not decided on yet.

I had not seen much of the South, but I was convinced that the state of Alabama was one of the most beautiful spots on the planet. It was still fairly dark outside, so I could not have enjoyed the scenic view from the bus anyway. The long, dark, winding concrete route that led to Mobile was decorated with small ponds and dozens of snaggletooth trees. When it was dark there were no streetlights to help see the many deer that dashed back and forth across the road. Even in a vehicle with the windows closed, you could smell the scent from the pine and magnolia trees and the scent of polecats and other creatures hiding in the bushes and behind the jagged trees. In the predawn light and with the help of the bus's headlights and the moonlight, I could see a few vehicles zooming past us going in the opposite direction. The only one that stood out was a rusty old Chevy station wagon with a Confederate flag displayed on the front tag. A backseat passenger, lying on the seat, dangled his big, pale, bare feet out of a back window. "That's just like a redneck," I mumbled to Desiree. She responded with a grunt before she placed her head on my shoulder and slept the hour and a half it took for us to get to Mobile, moaning off and on all the way.

Daddy had owned the garage in Mobile since before my birth, but I had only been in it about a dozen times. There had never been much reason for me to hang around such a smelly, greasy place. But Daddy had insisted that Mama, Babette, and I have keys to the place. "Just in case," he told us. I had had the key on my keychain for more than twenty years and I had never used it. I'd kept it, though, just in case. I was glad I did.

"My daddy's garage is just around the corner," I told Desiree, standing by the side of the commuter bus we had just exited.

She gave me a stunned look. "A garage?" she mouthed, her eyebrows raised. "We are going to hide out in a nasty-ass, smelly-ass garage?"

"Well, we can't go check into the Holiday Inn now, can we? The first bus out of the state doesn't leave for a while. It's warm in the garage and Daddy keeps a little ice box there with some snacks and bottled water."

It had been four years since I'd visited Daddy's garage. I hardly recognized **Taylor's Automotive Shop** on Miler Street in downtown Mobile. The sign swinging from a long-necked pole was new, but the windows looked like they had not been cleaned in years. Nobody could see in or out. I could smell oil and dust from outside. My hand was shaking as I inserted the key into the front door.

"What's taking you so long to unlock a door?" Desiree asked impatiently.

"I can't get this damn thing open," I wailed.

Desiree set her suitcase down and snatched the key out of my hand. "Shit. They've changed the lock," she informed me with a look of panic on her tear-stained face. The bruises on her face were much more profound now. Her left eye was so swollen she could not open it, and it looked like a bee had stung her bottom lip. "I am so so tired," she muttered, swaying like a willow tree. I set my travel bag down and wrapped my arm around her shoulder to keep her from falling.

"My uncle lives six blocks from here," I revealed.

When I felt Desiree's body stiffen, I thought it was because of the protracted distance I had just told her we had to walk. She pulled away from me, surprising me with a weak smile and the question, "Baby Red's daddy?" She blinked, forcing a lone tear to roll from the corner of her swollen eye. "If I had bought me a bicycle and pedaled off somewhere with him, I wouldn't be in this mess." Her smile faded and an unbearable sadness covered her face, making it look even more distorted.

Leaning against the musty dusty door of my daddy's garage with my head pounding, I nodded. I was disappointed and disturbed that with all the trouble we had on our hands, Desiree still had romance on her mind!

"This uncle, is he a man we can count on?" she asked, sniffing and rubbing her nose.

Men and our involvement with them had brought us to this point. It seemed reasonable to expect a man to help us.

"He better be," I said nervously.

CHAPTER 59

Uncle Redmond was a quiet man who rarely left the congested apartment he rented on Mason Street above a fish market. He was Mama's only sibling. They rarely saw one another but remained close by talking on the telephone at least three times a week.

Before his marriage to Baby Red's mother, Bonnie Sue, Uncle Redmond had spent several years roaming around the world with the merchant marine. During that time, he had no place to call home and he had instructed the post office to forward his mail to our house. Just like Baby Red did when he was on the move.

Even after Uncle Redmond married Baby Red's mother, he continued to roam. During one of his most extended cases of wanderlust—two summer months in South America sleeping among natives and snakes with seven-year-old Baby Red in tow—Aunt Bonnie Sue started roaming herself. By the time my uncle returned, my aunt had roamed into the arms of another man and accompanied him to an island in the Caribbean.

Not long after that, my uncle packed up Baby Red and left him with us. To keep my aunt from sneaking back into Alabama and snatching Baby Red, Mama guarded that boy like he was the Hope Diamond. By the time Uncle Redmond traveled to Jamaica to beg his wife to come back, it was too late. She had moved on. Everybody that my uncle had talked to gave him different information as to where my aunt had moved. I often wondered if Baby Red's roaming around the world was his way of trying to find his mother.

The building my uncle lived in was not located in one of the best neighborhoods in Mobile. Bones, empty bottles and cans, old newspapers, and other assorted trash spilled out of battered garbage cans. The cans had been lined up in short, clumsy rows on the cracked, uneven sidewalk in front of the fish market below my uncle's apartment. You could smell raw fish from a block away. On the side of the building was a cluttered driveway. In it sat my uncle's low-to-the-ground, rusty old Cadillac with a shabby mattress strapped on top.

Desiree gasped when I stopped and pointed toward a set of steps on the side of the building. The first step had a hole in it big enough for a cat to crawl through, and the railing had been tied together with what looked like an extension cord. "I'm going to be sick," Desiree managed. Before I could respond, she vomited on the ground, barely missing my foot. The stench coming from the fish market was so overwhelming, I almost threw up, too.

"We won't be here long," I promised, leading her up the shaky steps by the arm. "Uncle Redmond likes his privacy and won't want us here too long anyway."

I don't know how long I knocked on my uncle's door, but it was not long before the knuckles on my hand started throbbing.

"Maybe he's not home," Desiree mumbled, sitting on the top step hugging her suitcase. "Didn't I see a pay phone outside that fish place downstairs?"

I left Desiree sitting on the steps. It took me less than a minute to sprint back down to the sidewalk. I wound around the building to the front of the fish market, where there was a pay phone. The telephone book had been ripped in two and graffiti covered half of the booth. I was surprised that the telephone still worked. A woman with a nasal voice answered my uncle's telephone

"Mmmm-hello," she mooed, grumbling under her breath. Before I could respond she repeated herself with more vigor, "Mmmm-hello!"

"Hello, is Redmond Murphy there?" I asked casually, wrapping the telephone cord around my finger until I realized somebody had covered it with something slimy.

"Who is this, this ully in the moanin'?" the woman growled in a profound "down-home" drawl. It was six A.M. and I could hear Reverend Ike's voice screaming Scripture from a radio over the woman's voice.

"Uh . . . I'm Carmen, his niece," I replied, speaking slowly and cautiously. All of the down-home people I knew could get righteously fierce if you offended them. Even a little thing like speaking in a manner that they considered too "uppity" could set them off.

The rude woman didn't say anything else to me, but I heard her mumble something to somebody in the background. The next voice I heard belonged to my uncle.

"Carmen, what's wrong with you, girl? Where you at? What you doin' callin' this house this time of mornin'?"

"Uncle Red—I need to see you," I blurted. "I know it's early and I'm sorry for disturbing you while you have company. I'm downstairs in front of that fish place," I said frantically, noticing that some of the same slime from the telephone cord was on the receiver. I rubbed my lips and chin with the back of my hand and held the telephone a few inches away from my face. "Uncle Red, I need to come in your apartment for a little while."

There was a long, tense moment of silence before my uncle continued. "Girl, what kind of mess you done got yourself into? Ain't you suppose to be gettin' married to that wheelchair boy today?"

"Well, yes—I mean no. I'm not getting married today, Uncle Red. I'm not getting married period." It felt good to finally hear myself say those words.

"Well, what you doin' in Mobile? You done involved yourself with another man, ain't you?"

"Something like that," I said firmly. "Listen, Uncle Red, I need to talk to you real bad. Please come open the door," I bleated, hardly recognizing my own voice.

My uncle opened his front door wearing a thick brown, natty housecoat wrapped around his stout body like a blanket. There was a cut-off, knotted stocking cap on his large head hiding most of his thin, limp gray hair. A profound scowl hid the fact that at one time my uncle had been a very handsome man. His thin lips were turned down so severely they resembled a horseshoe. His bloodshot eyes, with heavy blue sacks underneath and furrowed brows, glared at me so hard I started itching all over. His complexion, once as fair and smooth as Mama's, was now mottled, wrinkled, and pockmarked.

Looking past me at Desiree with his nostrils flared, he snorted, "Ain't you that doctor's girl? The one Baby Red made such a fool out of?"

Taken aback by his second question, Desiree stumbled against me before answering, "Yes . . . sir."

Uncle Redmond shook his head, sucked his teeth, and then waved us into his living room. His eyebrows lifted up when he looked at our baggage. Shaking his head, but without saying a word, he grabbed them and set them on the floor by the door.

Yard-sale castoffs, from wobbly footstools to a large potbellied lamp with no shade, dominated the small room. A fake tree about my height sat to the side of the only window in the room, its branches obscuring the view of a red-brick building next door. On the seat of a three-legged chair was a small TV with a coat-hanger antenna. The hardwood floor, with strategically placed fuzzy throw rugs, sparkled like new money. The smell of raw fish coming from the fish market downstairs was so strong it permeated the room. As depressing as my uncle's home was, he was proud of it. On the wall facing the door was a large "Bless This Home" sign embroidered in red against a white background.

"What y'all done did?" Having schoolteachers for parents had had no affect on Uncle Redmond's diction the way it had on Mama's. Like Daddy, he slaughtered the English language almost every time he opened his mouth. Before allowing us to respond, looking at Desiree with a look of sorrow on his face he added, "Baby Red was raised to respect women. You musta' done somethin' hella' bad for him to jack up your face that bad."

"Uh . . . he wasn't the one," Desiree admitted with her head lowered. "See, I—"

Uncle Redmond interrupted her by abruptly holding up his hand. "Well, I hope whoever you tangled with, they look worse than you do."

Desiree looked at me. I dipped my chin and focused my attention on my feet as my uncle waved us to a lumpy maroon love seat that squeaked as soon as our butts touched it. Standing over us with his hands on his hips, he sucked his thick yellow teeth before continuing. "Now, what's goin' on here?"

"We need some money, Uncle Red. And we need to stay here for a little while. Just an hour or so until the bus we need to catch is ready to leave," I blurted.

Uncle Redmond scratched his chin and narrowed his eyes. "Well, when y'all gwine to tell me what kind of mess y'all done got yourselves in?"

"Well . . ." I didn't even know where I was going with my response. I glanced nervously at Desiree, and she was looking upside the wall like she was in a trance. She slowly turned her attention to me and just blinked.

I could tell from the way my uncle was blowing, he was becoming more exasperated by the minute. He nodded and turned to me. "I knowed you wasn't gwine to go through with marryin' that Burl boy. But is runnin' off the only way you can get out of it?"

"It's more than that, but we can't . . ." I stopped and looked at Desiree. I could almost feel the hot glare from her eyes. I didn't have to read her mind to know we were thinking the same thing. It made sense to let my uncle believe that this mess was all about Burl and me.

"Mr. Redmond, can you help us?" Desiree asked in a strong voice. "We need to go away for a little while." She got silent when I nudged her foot with mine.

I took over the conversation, rising and folding my arms, hoping to increase my level of authority to the point where Desiree would allow me to control the situation. At least until we got on that bus. "Uncle Red, will you promise me you won't tell anybody we came by here? No matter what you hear about us after we leave?" I said.

My uncle shrugged first. "And y'all better start steppin' real soon. Go on to wherever you gwine and don't get me caught up in nothin' I can't get out of. Shit."

"You won't tell anybody we were here, then?" Desiree asked. "We don't want people to know which direction we went in."

Uncle Redmond let out a deep groan and shook his head. "What time that bus leavin'?" he growled.

"We'll leave here in a couple of hours," I said. "We can walk to the bus station." I turned to Desiree and she nodded, looking more exhausted and in more pain than ever. Her arms were wrapped around her stomach. "It would sure help us if you'd lend us some money, Uncle Red."

"How much y'all need?" he grumbled, scratching his neck.

"How much you got?" I asked eagerly.

"I think I got a little over a hundred." Uncle Redmond paused and looked toward the bedroom and nodded. "Essie just got her check. Wait a minute." He disappeared into his bedroom and returned within a minute, clutching a few bills. Looking past him, I saw an attractive dark-skinned woman in her forties, also wearing a stocking cap, peeping from the cracked bedroom door. When our eyes met, she darted off to the side. "That stingy heifer," my uncle mumbled, handing me six wrinkled twenties. "Y'all hungry? I coulda' made y'all some sandwiches if Essie hadn't burned up them beef tongues last night. But there's some Pop-Tarts and gizzards in the ice box, and some Gatorade."

I shook my head, Desiree just blinked.

"Can we stretch out on a pallet until it's time for us to leave, Mr. Redmond?" Desiree muttered with pleading eyes.

Uncle Redmond nodded and disappeared again into the same bedroom. He returned a couple of minutes later with an armload of thin blankets and two flat pillows.

With no real plan and only limited funds, we had enough working against us. But the more I looked at Desiree, the more I realized that one of our biggest burdens was her pregnancy. I forced myself not to think about how that was going to hinder us.

I didn't sleep, but Desiree did. For an hour and a half, she rested with her head against my back, clucking and choking on her own tongue, crying in her sleep. I don't know what my uncle told his lady friend, but she never came out of the bedroom the whole time we were there.

Around seven, we rose from the pallet. We left the apartment before my uncle returned to the living room. Then we continued our fall into the hellhole we had dug, which was getting deeper and deeper.

CHAPTER 60

"Why does my ticket have the name Crystal Freeman on it?" I asked Desiree. She had purchased our bus tickets while I relieved myself and splashed cold water on my face in the bus station bathroom. As luck would have it, my period had started. Menstrual cramps that I had lied about having when it suited my needs throughout my life now forced me to my knees. Desiree, as sick as she was, had squeezed into the bathroom stall with me. She handed me a cup of weak coffee and my bus ticket and helped me to my feet. In that small space, she leaned against one side of the stall and I leaned against the other, staring at the ticket in my trembling hand.

"Nobody's going to be coming after a woman named Crystal Freeman," Desiree sighed and stared at my stomach, all the while rubbing her own. "Or Wanda Jones," she said, fingering the ticket she had purchased for herself.

We had an hour and a half to kill before boarding a bus that would transport us to Sebring, Mississippi. Once we got there we would purchase another set of tickets to another town we had not yet decided on. We had decided not to buy one ticket that would get us all the way to San Francisco. Instead, we planned to purchase a separate set of tickets from one obscure town to another, using different names each time.

Rather than hang around the bus station and the other weary, vacant-eyed travelers, we wound our way around a few blocks and ended up at a shabby diner next door to a foot clinic. Instead of coffee, we both ordered milk and slid into a corner booth in the back near the men's room. That was a big mistake. The stench of pee—and whatever else men did in public toilets—was overwhelming. Desiree's battered face, now looking like a Halloween mask, turned temporarily purple as she coughed and sneezed and held her nose together with two fingers.

"I feel the same way," I said hoarsely, furiously fanning my nose with the stained, dog-eared menu I had lifted from the wobbly table. "We can move to another table or we can go back to the bus station," I offered. The milk, served to us in cracked beige coffee cups, smelled and looked like pabulum, but we drank it.

Desiree shook her head and took a deep breath. Drinking the milk seemed to help. She sighed, let out a mild belch, and then smiled.

We didn't notice the mangy homeless man until he was up in our faces. He was so filthy, I could not tell if he was Black or white. He mumbled something unintelligible and then stuck out his hand, palm up and fingers wiggling. I handed him the dollar I had planned to leave on the table for a tip, and he shuffled across the floor and out of the diner without another mumble.

Desiree gave me an exasperated look. "Now, you are going to have to close down your Mother Teresa act."

I turned so hard to face her, my neck cracked. "What's that supposed to mean?"

Desiree nodded toward the door and frowned. "We might need that dollar before we get to where we're going."

"The man was hungry," I said firmly.

"The man was drunk, and with that dollar he's going to go off somewhere and get even drunker." Desiree coughed and gave me a hard look. "You know, for a woman so smart, you sure know how to do some dumb shit when it comes to dealing with people."

Something that felt like electricity shot through my head. I had to shake it hard to make it stop. I looked at Desiree through narrowed eyes, slack-jawed and confused. "What are you trying to say, girl?"

Desiree sucked her teeth first and moistened a scab on her bottom lip with her tongue. "I never could figure out why you felt the need to be the town mammy. If it wasn't Crazy Mimi or Burl you were fawning all over, it was somebody else."

"Like you?" I shot back, wondering where this conversation was going.

Desiree shifted in her seat and exhaled before she drank from her cup again. Her hand was shaking so hard, milk spilled and trickled all the way across the table next to my hand. I started to reach for a napkin to mop up Desiree's mess until I absorbed her words. "Do you have the nerve to sit here and tell me to my face that I—what are you trying to tell me?"

"I am not *trying* to tell you anything, Carmen. I'm telling you." She paused and glanced around the small diner. When she spotted a waitress looking in our direction, she cupped her mouth and leaned across the table. "All I wanted you to do was come to the house to pick me up. You could have walked away from Chester. It wasn't your fight."

I gasped. "If you didn't want me to get involved, why did you call me?"

"Like I said, I called you to come pick me up; that's all. You coming to the house to commit murder was not what I expected." Desiree let out a deep sigh. Blinking hard, she continued, "How long will I be able to live underground with a child?" She slammed her fist on the table, making it wobble even more.

Talking with my eyes on the door I remarked, "We can't do anything to change what's already happened. The future is what we need to focus on now." I paused and let out a tremendous sigh. My eyes were still on the door, but I could feel Desiree glaring at me. "I know it's going to be hard living on the run with a child," I added.

Desiree cleared her throat and mumbled something unintelligible. This encouraged me to look at her. There was a strange half-smile on her face, and her eyes, as bruised and swollen as they were, glistened under the glow of the weak yellow light above our table. "Baby Red spent a month in Brazil," she said in a mechanical voice. I blinked stupidly and shrugged. Then I motioned with my hand for her to continue. "I think he told me that Brazil doesn't have an extradition thing with the U.S." She sucked in her breath so hard, she whistled. Then she dipped her chin and stared at me in wide-eyed anticipation.

"So?" I shrugged again, shaking my head to add emphasis.

"We wouldn't have to live underground in Brazil. Dionne Warwick bought a house in Brazil, so it must be a nice place to live. And we're pretty. Brazilian men like pretty Black women from America. They'll be good to us. . . ."

My mouth dropped open and my eyes felt like they had doubled in size. "How did we get from hiding out in San Francisco to roaming around Brazil like gypsies? And as far as the men down there being good to us, *men* are the last things we need on our agenda. It's because of men that we are in the mess we're in now! We've fucked up our lives because of men."

"Well, Chester's *dead* because of us. Can't get any more fucked up than that," Desiree said evenly, holding up her hand in exasperation. "Come on. Let's take a walk till it's time to get on the bus. I don't feel too good."

CHAPTER 61

Time and distance had lost their meaning to me. I don't know how long it took to get from Mobile, Alabama, to Sebring, Mississippi. I had slept most of the way with my head against the window and Desiree's head on my shoulder. I woke up when the bus driver jerked the big, clumsy bus to a stop in the noisy parking lot outside a convenience store. The familiar Greyhound bus logo was hanging from a battered sign swaying above the front door.

"I feel like shit," Desiree said hoarsely, lifting her tousled head.

"You look like it, too," I muttered, yawning. "Not much of a town," I remarked, looking out of the bus's steam-covered window with the melting print of my head on it.

Across the highway from the convenience store was a truck stop and a nondescript motel. In the parking lot were several eighteen-wheel trucks and big, beefy-faced truck drivers being pestered by tired, tacky-looking prostitutes. Desiree and I attracted curious stares as we stumbled into the truck stop and slid into a booth. I ordered tea while she searched for a bathroom. She returned within two minutes, still zipping up her jeans, with a look on her face that made me grimace.

"Are you all right?" I asked, touching her cold hand. Her skin felt like leather.

"I was spotting," she whispered, blinking hard.

"Oh, shit!"

Desiree held up her hand. "I'm all right. It stopped."

"Drink this." I pushed a cup of the weak tea in front of her. "You need to eat something before you get really sick."

Desiree nodded, her gaze drifting toward the wall. We sat still for a brief moment before she looked up and stared out the window. "I'll be right back." She left before I could respond. From the window I watched her approach the only Black prostitute we'd seen so far, a husky woman in her late thirties wearing a wild blond wig and a gold lycra dress so tight it puckered around her waist. After about a minute, Desiree fished something out of her purse and handed it to the woman, and then the woman fished something out of her bosom and handed that to Desiree. Then they hugged. After about two more minutes, Desiree returned to the booth.

"We can spend the night in that motel," she informed me.

"We have to show ID to rent a room," I wailed.

Desiree shook her head. "That sister was cool. I gave her twenty bucks for the key to the room she just tricked in. We can spend the night there."

"What did you tell her?" I asked.

"She didn't want to know anything but whether or not I had any money to give her."

At this point, I was too tired and disoriented to put up a good argument, so I followed Desiree to the motel room at the end of the parking lot.

Inside the dreary room were two small, low beds with spreads that looked like horse blankets. A huge wet spot was in the center of one of the beds, and a used condom was on the floor. In silence, we sat down on the other bed and looked at one another. To break the silence, I grabbed the remote control off the cigarette-stained end table between the two beds. I clicked on the small black-and-white television set facing us on a dark-brown dresser. Of all the movies in the world, *Thelma and Louise* was showing. Both Desiree and I had seen this movie several times and had memorized every scene. I had turned on to the part where the Louise character had just shot and killed the man who had raped Thelma.

"Turn that shit off!" Desiree said in a strong, loud voice, holding up her hand.

I wasted no time complying. Looking at her I said, "At least Thelma and Louise had a gun and a car."

Desiree, now stretched out on the tacky bed, offered a weak smile. "And they still died," she reminded me.

The room got uncomfortably quiet. We listened to a conversation taking place in the room next to us. A prostitute was arguing with her trick. Then we heard a scream followed by laughter coming from the same room.

"How would we get to Brazil without passports?" I asked lamely.

Desiree gasped. "You want to go there?"

"I don't want to die or go to jail," I admitted.

Desiree shrugged. "It shouldn't be that hard to get fake documents once we get to California."

I was way too tired to argue or think clearly. "I'll go get us something to eat."

I returned about fifteen minutes later with a greasy hamburger for myself and a cup of alleged vegetable soup for Desiree.

"This shit looks like shit," she said wearily, setting the Styrofoam cup down on the end table. The hamburger was not much better. It ended up on the floor next to my travel bag, where a huge roach was lying in wait.

"I'll go get something else," I insisted, moving toward the door.

As tacky as the truck stop was, it had a clean pay phone near the bathroom. Without thinking, I dialed my parents' number, hoping that I would get the answering machine. I hung up as soon as I heard Mama's voice. Near the exit of the truck stop diner was a rack with some generic postcards. I bought one with a stamp and scribbled: *Mama, Daddy, I am sorry. We are all right. Will call you when I can.* I signed it "C."

When I got back to the room with some cheese sandwiches, Desiree was in the bathroom taking a shower. I could hear her cussing over the running water. She stumbled back into the room with a pained look on her face and a dingy towel wrapped around her wet body. "There are roaches in there bigger than me. This place is a sty!" she exclaimed, stomping her foot. "I can't stand it."

"Well, do you have any better ideas?" I asked. "You are the one that got us in here," I reminded her, setting the sandwiches on the night-stand.

Desiree glared at me and sat down on top of the low dresser next to the television set. Her lips quivered before she spoke. When she did speak, it was with a firm voice, pronouncing each word slowly and carefully. "If you had not been so jealous of me and Baby Red, none of this would have happened."

I stood up from the bed, folding my arms. "What? Don't you sit there and put all the blame for this mess on me, girl. All I did was try to help you. How many more times are we going to go there? And what makes you think I was jealous of you and Baby Red?" I jabbed my chest with my finger. "I had a boyfriend."

"Yeah, right. That Burl was a real prize," she smirked. "Instead of baby-sitting Burl, you should have been trying to find you a real man. Maybe you wouldn't have been so damn frustrated and up in other people's business all the damn time. Chester always said all you needed was a good fuck."

"And he should know," I mumbled, sitting back down so hard the bed vibrated for two minutes.

"What's that supposed to mean?" Desiree hissed.

"Nothing. Look, I had my reasons for being with Burl."

"I bet you did. Half a million."

"I didn't want that money Burl got from the railroad company!" I rose from the bed again and marched across the floor and stood in front of Desiree, hands on my hips. "And I am sick and tired of people accusing me of being after Burl's money. I *had* to stand by Burl. I—I'm the reason Burl had his accident! I was with him in that box-car! I tied his shoelaces together! I tampered with that turnstile! Goddamn it!" I blurted. I was so glad to finally get those words out of my mouth. It was the very first time that I had uttered them out loud, and it hurt. My mouth had heated up with each word, making my tongue feel like it was going to explode into flames. But what stunned the hell out of me was that Desiree did not look the least bit surprised.

"I know," she said evenly, not taking her eyes away from my burning face. "I've known all about it for a long time."

"What?" I moved closer to her, hands still on my hips. "What do you mean, you know? Who told you?"

"Chester told me," she said smugly. Her eyes refused to blink. She stared at me in a way that made me feel even more condemned.

The room started spinning and I had to sit back down on the bed to keep from falling. In a daze, I tried to think back to that night I had spent with Chester, wondering if I had revealed this information to him while I was drunk. Or by talking in my sleep!

"How . . . how did Chester know?" I muttered, pressing my legs together to keep them from shaking.

Desiree sucked in her breath before responding. To my everlasting horror, she looked me straight in the eyes and announced, "Burl told him."

CHAPTER 62

In all of the years that Desiree had known me, she had only seen me cry at funerals.

"It's too late for you to be crying now," Desiree said, rising from the dresser. She moved to the window, pulled back the thin curtains, and peeped out. "It won't help," she added, adjusting the towel around her body.

"You've known about Burl's accident being my fault all this time and you didn't tell me? Who else knows?"

She shrugged and turned to face me as I writhed on the bed.

"I don't know who else knows. But Burl has always known. Chester told me he helped Burl get home one night after he'd run into him drinking at Rocco's about four years ago. Burl had been drinking all night, so it was a convoluted story he told. He told Chester that once he realized you didn't know that he knew what you'd done, he figured he'd use it to his advantage. Knowing you like he did, he knew that you would part the Red Sea for him if you could. Chester woke me up as soon as he got home and told me. He told me to keep my mouth shut and wait and see just how long it took you to tell me. . . ."

I could not believe my ears. I had denied myself a real life on account of Burl, and he had exploited me in the worst way. If he had revealed this information to me years earlier, my life would have taken a different turn. As sorry as I was about what I had done to Burl, I found myself hating him and what he had put me through. Again I found myself wishing that Burl had died on those train tracks. Then I immediately felt sorry about that.

"Burl knew which buttons to push on you," Desiree cracked. "In some ways, you were just as 'handicapped' as he was."

I sucked in my breath and wiped my face with the sleeve of my blouse. "Any more secrets you want to share with me?" I asked, my voice dripping with sarcasm.

Desiree shook her head. "I think I've said it all." She laughed dryly. "Chester always told me that I didn't really know you."

I glared at her. "I could say the same thing about him," I snapped.

"I know you knew him a lot longer than I did, but I knew him better than you."

I shook my head. "Did you know about him and me?" I asked boldly, staring straight into Desiree's eyes.

Her face froze, and for a second it looked like her pupils had dilated. Then her eyes blinked rapidly. She cocked her head to the side, glaring at me from the corner of her eye. "What are you talking about?"

"I guess it's time for *everything* to be out in the open." I sighed.

A strange look suddenly appeared on Desiree's face. She left the window and sat down hard on a metal chair in front of the window, fingering the towel tighter around her bosom. "Are you trying to tell me that Chester tried to make a move on you?"

"There was a lot Chester didn't tell you about him and me, huh?" I waited for Desiree to catch her breath. "If it hadn't been for Burl, I would have been the one with Chester."

"Why, you black-ass heifer, you," Desiree laughed dryly. "You've lost your damn mind. Chester wouldn't give you the time of day!"

"Oh, he gave me a lot more than that," I replied, rotating my neck.

"Are you telling me you slept with my man?"

"He wasn't your man then. It was a long time ago." I refused to look at Desiree, but I could hear her crying. "He tried like hell to keep it going, but I couldn't. All because of Burl. Even after Chester hooked up with you, every chance he got he tried . . ."

"I don't believe you and I don't know what you are trying to prove. Chester loved me."

"Oh, I believe he loved you. But he loved me first. He's got a birthmark on the inside of his thigh and . . . no pubic hair."

I heard Desiree gasp before she jumped up and ran back into the bathroom and slammed the door. She came out a few minutes later wearing the jeans and blouse she had worn before her shower.

"I'm sorry I had to tell you this way," I said. She pushed me away when I tried to embrace her.

"When we get to California, I want you to go your way and I will go mine," Desiree told me. Without looking at me, she started rooting through her suitcase on the floor.

"It'll be harder for us to stay free if we split up," I informed her. "We can end this all right now." I moved toward the telephone.

"You can do whatever you want. I don't give a damn now. Me, I'm going to California," Desiree insisted. She snatched a brush out of her suitcase and started brushing her hair so hard, sparks flew.

CHAPTER 63

I didn't sleep at all that night. Desiree didn't either. She curled herself into a ball next to me on the bed and cried off and on all night.

When morning finally came, we gathered our things in silence.

"Uh . . . we can get tickets to this little town I know about in Louisiana. Baby Red told me about a hostel there that'll take in anybody, no questions asked," Desiree announced in a voice barely above a whisper.

Once we purchased more tickets, we boarded another bus, sitting several seats apart. For the next two hours, I did not move from the seat I shared with a huge Native American with the breath of an ox. Before the bus arrived in the backwoods town in Louisiana we were headed to, we'd made several stops. Twice I sat and watched as Desiree stumbled off the bus and disappeared into seedy restaurants and returned with snacks that she did not share with me.

By the time we reached our next destination, I was so hungry and weary, I was ready to confess to crimes I hadn't committed. She was already off the bus and standing outside hugging her suitcase when I exited.

"I'm going back home," I told her, almost out of breath. "I can't live like this. I don't care what they do to me when I get back to Alabama."

Amazingly, her face softened right before my eyes. She stunned me further when she squeezed my arm and shook her head.

"Don't do that. We've come too far." That was all she said before beckoning me to follow her to a dusty cab sitting in front of the bus station.

The hostel we had planned to spend some time in was nothing more than a glorified homeless shelter. In a large, dank room were about forty beds and just as many grim-faced, shabbily dressed men, women, and confused children.

"This makes that motel look like the Ritz," Desiree said as we set our things down on a lumpy, squeaky bed next to a stack of cardboard boxes.

"Have you spotted any more?" I asked.

Desiree shook her head and smiled. "I'm feeling much better now. We don't have that much farther to go."

After a sloppy dinner of green peas and lumpy mashed potatoes in a dim dining room, a man dressed as a priest—the same man who had escorted us to the large dormitory—approached us with fresh bedding and a warm smile. Shaggy mud-colored hair covered his head and half of his face. I never dreamed that I would have to depend on a Rasputin like him for help.

"We don't have much," he informed us, "but we will share with you all what we do have."

A wrinkled white woman with frizzy black hair and her pinched-faced toddler moved from the beds that they had been assigned so that Desiree and I could be next to one another. It was already bedtime, for which I was grateful. My entire body was aching, especially my head. Not from the long, uncomfortable bus ride, but from the tense conversation I had had with Desiree before we left the motel.

In the darkness, Desiree sat on the side of the bed I had crawled into.

"Carmen, I'm sorry. You have been the best friend I ever had and I appreciate that. What you said about you and Chester, well . . . I had my suspicions for a long time. I used to watch him watching you. . . ."

I sat up. "Nothing ever happened between him and me after he got with you. I hope you believe me."

"I do. I just wish things had turned out differently. I should have run off with Baby Red the first time he asked me to. I'd be living in a tent on a beach sipping margaritas by now." In the dim light coming from the hallway outside the room, I could see her smiling in a way I had not seen her smile in days. "Damn that Burl."

"Well, Burl's got enough of a mess on his hands just being in that wheelchair," I told her.

"You'd be married to him by now if we . . . if we hadn't . . . you know. Do you think about him and how he must have felt when he found out you ran out on the wedding?"

I nodded. "Oh, yeah, I think about Burl. I'll be thinking about Burl till the day I die." It was my turn to smile for a quick moment. Then I got serious again. "Did you mean what you said about splitting up after we get to California?"

"Not if you don't want to. Listen, now that so much is out in the open, I feel so much better." Desiree got quiet for a moment, then turned to me with a guarded look on her face. "If I had been more like you, maybe Chester and me could have had a nice life together."

"You don't want to be like me," I said grimly.

"Did you love him?"

I nodded and chuckled. "Harder than a rock. Did you?"

Desiree shook her head and winced. "And he didn't really love me." She sighed and shrugged. "I didn't want to be alone; he didn't want to be alone. That's all that was about. Chester was . . . Chester was a pretty nice guy. He was funny, he was generous, and he was thoughtful. He would have been good for you. Too bad you had so much other shit weighing you down."

I felt a sharp pain in my side just thinking about all of the burdens that I had taken upon myself and what it had all done to my spirit. Looking out for friends like Crazy Mimi and Regina and tying myself down to Burl had all taken its toll on me and I was tired. As tall as I was, I felt small and confused, but now I felt "free." I didn't know what lay in store for us once we reached California, if we did. But with my renewed strength, I convinced myself that remaining free would be just that much easier to do.

I had not let go of my burdens; they had let go of me. Well, at least some of them had.

CHAPTER 64

Three days and two more "hostels" later, we arrived in San Francisco on a warm morning just before noon. It was refreshing to see that California was actually as magnificent as it had been in my dreams. It seemed odd that a place as beautiful as California attracted so many people with so many ugly secrets. A bright sun welcomed us, but it was cooler than I had expected. I was glad that Desiree and I both had on thick denim jackets.

Desiree's sister, Colleen, was four years older than Desiree was. But at thirty-three, she looked more like a woman in her twenties than Desiree did. Standing in the crowded bus station waiting room with her thick brown hair pulled back into a shoulder-length ponytail, Colleen looked like a bewildered teenager. She had on just a hint of makeup, but even without it she was more attractive than Desiree. Colleen widened her already large brown eyes and gasped when she realized that the tired, disheveled woman stumbling toward her with outstretched arms was her baby sister. She frowned as soon as Desiree got close enough for her to see the bruises on her face.

"Girl, you look like you've been mauled," she mouthed, holding Desiree away from her, then looking me up and down. "What in the world—Carmen, what are you doing here?"

During stops in the last two towns, Desiree had called up Colleen from pay phones and left messages on her answering machine that she was on her way. "Didn't Desiree tell you I was coming with her?" I asked in a hoarse voice. A lump in my throat made it difficult for me to speak. My lips were so dry, they had cracked. I licked at the scabs that had formed the night before. I had not bathed since the night before. My vile body odor was the least of my concerns. I didn't know Colleen well enough to know what to expect from her. Especially when I smiled and she didn't smile back.

Colleen let out a great sigh and took a couple of steps away, rubbing her nose. I got a whiff of Desiree and she smelled just as foul as I did.

"This girl didn't tell me much of anything!" Colleen snapped. "She calls me the other week to tell me she's moving out here. Then I don't hear from her again until the other night, telling me she's almost here." Colleen paused at this point and gave each of us a sharp look. "I want to know what in the world is going on with you two." Moving so close to me her face almost touched mine, she asked, "Carmen, why are you here?"

"I needed to get away," I said dumbly. The stench of my breath made her frown and she moved away again.

"Can we go on to your place and talk?" Desiree began, rubbing her stomach. Colleen, with a blank expression on her face, didn't move right away. Desiree cleared her throat and added, "Colleen, Carmen and I are in trouble. Real trouble. You are the only person who can help us."

A stunned look appeared on Colleen's face and she folded her arms. "If I am the only person who can help you, *you are in trouble,*" she informed us.

During the ride to Colleen's apartment in her battered Toyota, she told us about her own troubles. She'd lost her job, her marriage to a cross-country truck driver was on the rocks, and she was having "female problems." "The doctor wants to put me in the hospital within the next week, where I will be for at least a month. So, don't you two be coming out here expecting me to carry you." She sucked her teeth and glanced at Desiree sitting on the seat next to her. "You ever hear anything about Mom?"

"No," Desiree mumbled, bowing her head.

Desiree never told me, but I believed that her runaway mother was one of the many reasons she and Baby Red had bonded. He had given up on ever seeing his own mother again. I had always wondered what it felt like to walk in their shoes. I had not thought much about the fact that if Desiree and I remained on the run, I might never see my own mother again. The bright side, if it could be called that, was that I at least knew where my mama was. No matter where I went in the world, I could always contact her. Killing Chester was the thing that had dominated my mind the most in the past few days. Now that our ordeal had reached a new level, Mama and Daddy and the rest of my family were on my mind a lot. Even Baby Red.

The one person I forced myself not to think much about was Burl. I was angry and confused. If he knew all along that I had caused his accident, did he think that I was with him out of guilt, or love? Was he so desperate for a lifelong companion that he would marry me and keep me from living a normal life, too? As hard as it was for me to admit to myself, I didn't want to know. I was deeply remorseful about what had happened to Burl, and would be until the day I died. I knew it would be a long time, if ever, but I knew that I had to forgive Burl for his deceitful behavior. I just didn't know when and how.

"We won't give you a hard time," Desiree told her sister. "We'll just stay long enough to get things straight before we move on."

"Robert'll be home next weekend, and I'll be checked into the hospital by then. You two can stay until then." Colleen stopped for a red light and checked her hair in the rearview mirror. "What kind of trouble are you two in?" First she glanced at Desiree, then over her shoulder at me.

"Can we get to your place first?" Desiree asked.

"Well, it must have something to do with Chester. He was barking like a mad dog when I called last night." Colleen sniffed. "Good-looking men can be so arrogant."

Desiree rotated her neck so fast and hard, I heard her bones crack. She gasped and looked from me to Colleen with her jaw hanging open. "Colleen, what did you say about Chester?"

"I said he was arrogant. We can pick up some Big Macs if you guys are hungry," Colleen grunted, turning the corner on two wheels, heading toward a McDonald's at the corner.

"What did you just say about talking to Chester? When did you talk to him?" Desiree hollered.

"I talked to him last Saturday when I didn't hear from you. I had talked to him a few days before that, too. Girl, you should have told me you and him were having problems. I slipped and blabbed to him that you were coming out here, but I thought he already knew. Like I said, I didn't know what was going on. He started babbling about suspecting some kids of stealing his damn gun out of his house and how he was afraid somebody might get hurt. I asked him if it was the gun you had Carmen hold on to." Desiree and I both gasped at the same time.

"Are you sure *last night* was the last time you talked to Chester?" Desiree demanded, bobbing her head. "It had to be before that."

"And why is that?" Colleen wanted to know.

"Because Chester's . . ." I began. A sharp look from Desiree silenced me.

"Because Chester's a fool? Well, last night he was an asshole *and* a fool! As soon as he realized it was me calling, he cussed me out and hung up." Colleen parked the car in the handicapped zone in front of McDonald's and leaped out. Desiree and I sat staring at one another in slack-jawed amazement. Without warning, Desiree opened the car door and vomited on the ground. Then she leaned back in toward the driver's side and slumped facedown. I don't know why Colleen turned around when she did, but she looked in time to see what was happening. She immediately trotted back to the car.

"What's the matter?" she yelled, shaking Desiree.

"She's pregnant," I mumbled.

Colleen sighed. "Is that all?"

"We thought . . . we thought Chester was dead," I added.

"And why would you think that?"

I felt like a piece of stone and surprised myself when I realized I could still talk.

"Because I killed him," I managed.

CHAPTER 65

"I am not leaving this car until I know what the hell kind of shit you two are in," Colleen said angrily. Even as exasperated as she was, she managed to revive Desiree. Desiree sat up and took a deep breath, staring straight ahead. Colleen's lips formed an angry straight line as she glared at me.

"There was a fight and I hit him with one of his weights," I rasped. "I—we thought he was dead. He looked dead."

"Are you sure you talked to Chester *last night?*" Desiree managed, her eyes on the side of her sister's face. I could hear Desiree's teeth clicking together.

"I talked to Chester Sheffield last night around eight," Colleen said firmly.

"What all did he say?" I asked breathlessly.

"Didn't I just tell you he cussed me out and hung up?" Colleen snapped.

"He wasn't breathing or moving," Desiree sobbed. "We thought he was dead and we came out here to keep from going to jail."

"I'll be damned." Colleen slapped the steering wheel so hard the horn blew. "So you two decided to play Thelma and Louise? Are you two crazy?" Colleen rolled down her window and hawked a huge wad of spit. Turning back to me, shaking her head, she added, "Robert is going to shit his pants when he finds out my own sister tried to drag me into some half-assed murder mystery." Colleen threw back her head and let out a laugh that almost pierced my eardrums.

"But Chester didn't die," I reminded her. On top of the many tense emotions that had already nearly crippled me, I had this to deal with now. I started breathing through my mouth. Desiree opened the car door again and got out and leaned against the side of the car. She vomited again, splashing the side of the already dirty car door.

Colleen stopped laughing and turned serious again. "Yeah, but you didn't know that until now." She let out a tremendous sigh and nodded toward Desiree. "Is Chester the father of her baby?"

"Yeah," I mumbled.

As soon as Desiree returned to her seat, Colleen lit into her. "Girl, you've done some stupid shit in your life. After that stunt you pulled with Daddy—" Colleen covered her mouth with her hand and glanced at me.

"Carmen knows about what I did to Daddy. I told her the whole story," Desiree whined. "I've paid for that a million times over by staying with Daddy—after you and Mom ran off—and taking care of him so many years. I gave up a lot for Daddy—which is more than I can say for you."

"Don't you go trying to lay a guilt trip on me. Mama and I suffered just as much as you did with Daddy. He was a beast." Colleen sniffed and wiped a tear from her eye. "I hated him for years and I hated myself for hating him. That's why I didn't come to his funeral. I couldn't face him even in death. That's a load I'll have to live with for the rest of my life."

The car got so quiet inside, I could hear us all breathing, snorting like pigs.

"Can we go to your place now?" Desiree managed, caressing the side of her sister's face.

CHAPTER 66

As soon as Mama heard my voice on the telephone, she started crying and babbling like a baby. I had to hold the telephone away from my ear to keep my head from ringing.

"Mama, calm down," I pleaded. Daddy was barking in the background. I could not understand a word coming out of his mouth, either.

Colleen and Desiree were in the spare bedroom in the small two-bedroom apartment. Colleen lived in the high-crime area of Hunter's Point with her husband and a bowl of potbellied goldfish. Through the open door, I could hear the conversation between Desiree and her sister better than I could understand the one I was trying to have with Mama.

"I didn't expect you to be living in a neighborhood like this," Desiree commented. "We've always lived in nice neighborhoods."

"*We* won't anymore," Colleen replied. "This is San Francisco, girl. The cost of living is a lot higher out here than it is back in Alabama. This dump is a Garden of Eden for fifteen hundred dollars a month," Colleen said, shaking her head and waving her hand around the cluttered, cheaply furnished living room as they returned. She had a large paper towel in her hand that she kept using to wipe her nose and eyes. She had been crying off and on since we left the Mc-

Donald's parking lot. We never did get the Big Macs she had promised, but she had already popped a frozen pizza into the oven.

"You've got to be kidding!" Desiree hollered. "With all these run-down, tagged buildings, and tramps lying on the ground, how can you sleep at night?"

"All of the doors in this building are triple dead-bolted and the windows are bulletproof," Colleen said with confidence. "O. J. Simpson's mama lives not far from here." Colleen and Desiree got silent once they reached the spot where I was standing. Desiree had changed into one of Colleen's terry-cloth bathrobes and covered her hair with a shower cap.

Finally, Mama said something I could understand. "Girl, are you on dope?"

"No, Mama, I am not on dope. Listen, stop crying and screaming and let me talk for a minute," I said, holding up my hand and glaring at the telephone.

"Where are you? Is Desiree with you? Have you quit your job?"

"Mama, I put in for two weeks vacation . . . for . . . for the wedding. Remember. They are not expecting me back until February."

"Where are you, girl? Why is there so much static on this line?"

"I'm in California."

"California! Lord—Charles—Carmen, hold on. Your daddy just hit the floor. Babette get your daddy a pill." Mama returned her attention to me. "Your sister hopped on a plane as soon as she found out about you running off to keep from marrying Burl. She was scared to death that you had had a nervous breakdown and was wandering around in the woods somewhere." Mama paused again and I heard some muffled voices in the background. "Carmen, how could you do this to Burl? You didn't have to run off to get out of marrying him. It's a good thing Mogen was in town after all."

"You think I ran off to get out of marrying Burl?"

"Why else would you pull a crazy stunt like this?"

"Mama, I didn't run off just to get out of marrying Burl."

"What are you trying to tell me?"

"Mama, have you seen Chester Sheffield since last Friday night?"

"Chester? He was here earlier today, helping your daddy haul some damn car parts off a truck. And he's at his daddy's house right now as we speak, washing that car of his. I can see him from the kitchen window. What's Chester got to do with this mess?"

"Is he . . . all right?"

There was a long moment of silence before Mama responded.

"Carmen, you are talking crazier by the minute. Why are you so concerned about Chester? I thought he was Desiree's man."

"He is. Uh . . . he was. Did he say anything about me and Desiree?"

"Like what? I . . . child, are you trying to tell me something I don't want to know? Are you and Desiree . . . doing something *unnatural*? Your daddy always suspected that Sweet Jimmie was a bad influence on you."

"Mama, Desiree and I are not lesbians. The thing is, she had a problem with Chester and I tried to help her; that's all."

"And what's that got to do with you and Desiree running off to California?"

"We thought Chester was dead."

I heard Mama moan and then the next voice I heard was Daddy's.

"Burl was beside hisself last Saturday when he found out you had skipped town. You takin' off like you done was rough on him," Daddy said, sounding relieved. Daddy didn't sound like he needed pills to me. "You all right?"

"I'm fine, Daddy. Listen, I don't want to talk to Burl just yet. I will write him a letter and tell him how sorry I am. But I don't want to talk to him." I honestly didn't know what I would say to Burl about what I had done to him *and* what he had done to me. "And I'll write Miss Mozelle a letter, too. She is one of the last people in the world I wanted to hurt. No, I'll talk to Burl and Miss Mozelle in person as soon as I get back to Alabama."

"If you comin' back to Alabama, you won't be talkin' to Burl or Mozelle," Daddy said evenly. "Mogen played his hand as soon as he found out you had run off. He had that woman and that boy, wheelchair and all, packed up by Sunday evenin'. Monday mornin' the Salvation Army truck hauled off most of that junk Mozelle had been collecting all her life. By Monday evenin' Mogen piled Mozelle and Burl into that fancy van of Burl's and carried 'em back to Detroit with him. Mr. Carter from the bank told me that Mogen had called him the night before and told him he needed to have Burl's money transferred to Detroit."

I stared at my ashy hand and bit my bottom lip. "Uh . . . Daddy, can you wire me some money to fly home?"

Colleen had a puzzled look on her face; Desiree looked disappointed when I got off the telephone. "I'm going back home," I said gently.

An unbearably sad look appeared on Desiree's face. She shook her head, shrugged, and then turned to her sister. "I have nowhere to go. . . ."

Colleen sighed, but I couldn't tell if it was relief or disgust. I felt better when she smiled and gave Desiree a hug. "You can stay with me."

"What about your husband?" Desiree asked in a weak voice.

"He can stay with me, too." Colleen turned to me. "What did your folks tell you?"

I shared what I had learned from Mama and Daddy about Burl first. "Chester is fine," I added.

"You don't think he'll cause you some trouble if you go back?" Desiree asked, screwing her face up and hunching her shoulders.

"There's only one way to find out," I replied, handing the telephone to Desiree. "He's at his daddy's house right now. Call him up."

CHAPTER 67

Colleen chose to leave the room. I stood next to Desiree while she waited for somebody to answer the telephone on Chester's end. She was shaking so hard, she had to hold the telephone with both hands. I put my arm around her shoulder.

"Chester, this is Desiree." She sounded like a weak kitten. When she stretched open her eyes and pursed her lips, I thought she was having a spasm. But she was just reacting to Chester's voice, which was so loud I could hear him myself.

"I know who it is! Shit!" Chester's voice was so loud, it seemed like he was in the room with us. "You mad-ass cow!"

"Uh . . . I am glad you're all right. And whether you believe it or not, I am sorry about what happened. Carmen is, too. She didn't mean to—you know . . . hit you."

"Well, it wasn't the first time she hit me! Damn it!"

"Listen, I'm at my sister's place in San Francisco. Carmen is with me. Colleen wants me to stay out here and get a job. But if I change my mind and return to Belle Helene, I don't think we should get back together. I mean, I still love you and all, but we don't belong together. We can still be friends, though. See, I—"

"Shaddup!" he roared. "Let me say what I got to say! Friends?! You still wanna be my friend? Why, you crazy heifer you! You can come back here, you can go to Mars, and you can go to the goddamn devil for all I care! I don't want your cheesy high-yella ass back in my life! You got that?"

Desiree held the telephone away from her ear and looked from it to me before she spoke to Chester again. "If that's the way you feel, that's the way you feel. I just wanted to let you know I was sorry. Carmen is standing right here. Do you want to talk to her?"

Before Chester could respond, Desiree handed me the telephone. "NO! HELL NO!" he shrieked. "She's just as crazy as you!" Without another word, he slammed the telephone down.

"If you do go back and if he wanted to be a real asshole, being a cop, he could come up with all kinds of ways to make your life miserable," Desiree told me, giving me a weak hug.

"I can take care of myself," I mumbled. "You, you worry about yourself and your baby."

Desiree blinked hard as she stared at me with tears in her eyes. "All that stuff I said about you getting up in my business, forget I said it. I'm glad you were there for me." She let out a strange laugh and then playfully stabbed me in my chest with her finger. "Now that Burl and I are out of the way, you can be with Chester now if you want to. . . ."

I didn't respond to Desiree's last comment. Not because I didn't want to, but because I didn't know how.

CHAPTER 68

As nosy as Sweet Jimmie was, he surprised me by not pumping me for information about my mysterious escapade until I had been home for a week. The truth was too bizarre to share, so I only told him a tale I knew he would appreciate.

"You ran off just to get out of marryin' Burl?" he paused and snorted. "That's just what I figured. And I wasn't surprised. But I'm just sorry to hear about Desiree leavin' Chester. He been lookin' mighty lonesome and pitiful ever since. The night y'all left, he must have got real confused. He dragged hisself into the hospital with a towel on his head coverin' up a bloody risin' he got when he fell off his porch, or so he said. I bet a nickel and a donut he got bopped by some old gal. Pitiful! I went up to him when he came back to the hospital to get his bandage removed and I told him not to worry, he'll find him a good woman one day 'cause I'm prayin' for him."

I nodded.

In my bedroom on the same Exercycle was the same belt Chester had left behind more than a decade ago. It was still hanging there the evening, seven months after my return to Alabama, when Colleen called around five-thirty. I had not heard from her or Desiree in over a month. The few times I had talked to Desiree, she had shared vague accounts of what she planned to do. She planned to have her baby, go to culinary school, get a job, and find a new man.

With Desiree and Burl gone, I had a lot of time on my hands. I still worked at the same law firm, and I had finally enrolled in night classes at the Lyman School of Nursing.

"Carmen, Desiree had a little girl," Colleen told me, her voice so low I could barely hear her. "She looks just like Chester's dead sister Kitty."

A broad smile appeared on my face as I stood up from my sofa.

"Is everything all right? How is Desiree doing?" I asked, smoothing my newly braided hair with my hand.

Colleen sucked in her breath and moaned before continuing. "My sister died giving birth. We won't know what went wrong until they do an autopsy," Collen said.

"No, she didn't! She didn't go through all the shit she went through to die now!" I hollered, frantically pacing the floor. Sweat started dripping off my face immediately.

"Carmen, the girl wasn't happy out here anyway. But she was too proud to return to Belle Helene and fall back on you. The day before she died, she said she didn't know how she would have made it this far without you. She felt bad that she had caused you so much heartache. That's why she never wanted to call you that much." Colleen's voice cracked.

I was so stunned, I couldn't even cry. "What about the baby?" I asked, rubbing my eyes, trying to coax out a few tears.

"Well, that's another thing. Robert never wanted us to have kids, see. So he's not about to raise somebody else's. He's made that clear. If I could, I would leave Robert and raise that baby myself. But . . . that new job I just got at the cannery, a contract fell through, so now they are getting ready to lay us all off."

"What are you going to do with the baby?"

"We have this off-cousin in Moline, Illinois. We've never been really close to her because she has always been looked upon as the family fool. She never could have kids of her own, so she raised a bunch of cats and treated them like kids—talking to them and stuff." Colleen paused and cleared her throat. "Nobody else wants to raise the baby. So it's either Cousin Anna or the adoption people. . . ."

"What about Chester?"

"Desiree never told him she was pregnant."

"Well, don't you think you should let him know? Especially now."

"I'm tired, and to tell you the truth, I don't want to be bothered with that man. If you want to tell him, you go right ahead. And if you plan to, you better do it soon. Cousin Anna said she'd call me back tonight to let me know if she can take the baby. I sure do hate to send a poor little innocent baby to be raised around a dozen cats. In a trailer, at that."

"Oh, good gracious! Listen, Colleen, don't do anything until I call you back tonight."

"I don't know how long I'll be at the funeral home tonight," Colleen sobbed.

"Oh . . . well, call me when you get back. Please don't make any plans about that baby until we talk again. Please."

"All right, Carmen. You take care of yourself, girl. 'Bye."

As bad as I wanted to sit down and have myself a good long cry, I knew I had to postpone it. I did take enough time to drink a strong cup of coffee to make me more alert. I needed it before I called Chester. I had not sipped on a margarita since the night Desiree and I left Belle Helene. The alcohol and all of the unnecessary lies that had affected my life in so many negative ways were both part of my past now. For that I was proud.

The telephone number at the house Desiree had lived in with Chester had been changed. And I got the answering machine when I called his parents' house. I didn't know how he would react seeing me face to face. I had only seen him from a distance since my return, so we had not communicated at all. Even though he had resumed his relationship with the ballroom-dancing woman, I knew from Sweet Jimmie that Chester lived alone now. My choices for locating Chester were limited, but the best thing I could do was to park in front of his house and wait for him in my car. So that's what I did that same night. If his nosy neighbors had not kept peeping out of the window at me, I would have waited longer than the two hours I waited. Finally, I left a note on his door and I went home.

Five minutes after I got inside my door, my telephone rang. It was Regina.

"Regina, I can't talk to you right now," I said impatiently.

"Oh? Well, I guess I'll be to share my good news with somebody else," Regina pouted.

"What is it?" I asked, letting out an exasperated sigh.

"It's a boy," she squealed.

"What are you talking about?"

"I'm pregnant. Earl's outside right now, runnin' down the block passin' out cigars."

"That's great, Regina. Listen, I really have to talk to you later. I need to keep the telephone line open for an important call I'm expecting."

Regina made an exasperated noise with her teeth and then let out a deep groan. "So, Desiree finally got around to returnin' that call you made last month?"

"Desiree died last night."

"Oh, God, Carmen—I'm so sorry." Regina started crying. "What the hell happened?"

"She was pregnant when we left here. She died giving birth. I'm waiting for Chester to call me back because . . . this is his child."

I had to hang up on Regina. Three minutes later my telephone rang again. This time it was Chester. Instead of him grinding his teeth and roaring like a lion like I had been expecting, he was unusually calm.

"Chester, uh, I need to talk to you," I began.

"What about?"

"I'd rather tell you in person, but if you don't want to see me, I'll tell you over the telephone."

"Hang on a minute." He was gone for about five minutes. Then I heard a door slam shut. "What is it?" he said, now sounding distant and annoyed.

"I . . . listen." I stopped. I patted my chest and let out a deep breath. "This is not something I want to tell you over the telephone. I think you should come over to my place and . . . and you can bring your woman with you. I don't care."

"I don't have no woman."

"Well, whether you do or not, I need to talk to you about something really important."

"Can't nothin' be that important between you and me no more. Now, if you got something to say, you say it now."

I sucked in my breath, held it for a moment, then exhaled so deeply my chest hurt. "Desiree died last night giving birth to your daughter."

He gasped. Then the telephone went dead. I didn't call him back. I figured I had done my part. The rest was up to him.

CHAPTER 69

It was almost midnight when I finally went to bed after talking to Chester. I had not heard from Colleen, and Chester had not called me back. I couldn't sleep, so I got back up and moved from the bed back to the living room sofa.

Other than Sweet Jimmie, Crazy Mimi, Regina, and my parents, the pizza deliveryman was the only person who knocked on my door these days. I missed Baby Red and saw him about once a month when he cycled to Belle Helene to keep Mama from worrying about him. I had not been out to any bars much since my return. Since I didn't drink alcohol anymore, the bar scene bored me now. I had been celibate since a disastrous night with a football coach I'd met in Adam's rib joint four months ago. I couldn't even remember his name even though he occasionally left messages on my answering machine threatening to drop by. For a moment I thought it was the football coach knocking on my door, because I knew that Sweet Jimmie and Crazy Mimi were out dancing and Regina was with her new husband and I had not ordered a pizza. Even though I had talked to Chester and practically begged him to come talk to me, I never expected it to be him.

"Can I come in?" he asked, leaning in my doorway. He was in street clothes, so I knew that this was not an "official" visit.

I waved him to the sofa. I flattered myself by thinking that me being in my nightgown might provoke Chester. But it didn't take me but half a second to dismiss that notion.

"Now, can you tell me what the hell happened?" he began, looking unusually weary. I had not seen him look this tortured since his sister's death.

"Desiree didn't want you to know about the baby," I announced solemnly, easing down on the arm of the sofa. "She knew you'd stop at nothing to be with that baby."

"Is the baby all right?" he croaked, blinking rapidly.

I nodded. "Colleen was supposed to call me back after she got home from the—funeral home tonight. She hasn't called me back yet, but if you want to, you can call her from here." Then I remembered what Colleen had said about not wanting to talk to Chester. "But . . . uh . . . I can tell you everything you need to know."

His eyes were red and filled with water. He nodded for me to proceed.

"I don't know why Desiree died from just giving birth. But her sister said she was miserable all the time anyway. It could be that she just lost her will to live and just never woke up from the anesthesia." I paused and exhaled deeply. "Colleen can't keep the baby and raise it herself. They have this cousin, who said she might take the baby and raise it. But from what Colleen told me about this woman, she sounds suspiciously like Crazy Mimi." I held my breath and dipped my head. "And she lives in a trailer with twelve cats."

Chester's mouth dropped open and he narrowed his eyes to look at me.

"There ain't no way in hell somebody *else* is goin' to raise my child!" he snapped. "Colleen better start usin' her head for somethin' other than a hat rack. How could she think I'd sit back and let *her* decide what to do for *my* child?" He paused and angrily shook his head. "I don't know what this world is comin' to."

"I figured you'd feel this way, but I wasn't sure." I paused to clear my throat. "Uh . . . I had made up my mind that if you didn't want the baby, I'd take her and raise her myself."

Rising, he shook his head more vigorously. "This is my responsibility, not yours." He stood looking down at me, his hands on his hips. "Colleen still have the same telephone number?"

I nodded, rising, following him as he headed toward the door.

"Thanks, Carmen. I owe you one," he said, handing me a slip of paper with his new telephone number on it. "In case you need to get in touch with me," he told me with a smile. Then he was gone.

I had never felt more alone in my life than I did that night. Desiree was gone, Regina and Crazy Mimi were continually growing away from me, and Sweet Jimmie was threatening to move to Detroit so he could keep an eye on his aging mother, Nurse Bertha. A week after Miss Mozelle's and Burl's departure, Burl's uncle had wooed Nurse Bertha to join them in Detroit so that she could help take care of Burl and Miss Mozelle.

At age thirty, I knew that my chances of finding someone I wanted to be with for the rest of my life were slim and getting slimmer by the day.

There had been many times in my life when I thought I was crazy because of some of the things I did. That part of me had changed. But even after all that had been said and done, I still had strong feelings for Chester Sheffield.

I stood in my window and watched until Chester got in his car and drove off. He didn't seem surprised when I called his new telephone number an hour later.

"I just wanted to let you know that you can call me if you need anything. You know, like help with the baby," I offered.

"That's good to know, Crazy Legs."

"Did you talk to Colleen yet?"

"Yeah, I did. We just got off the telephone. It's too late for me to catch a red-eye tonight, so I'm headin' out there around six in the mornin'."

"Oh. Well, did Colleen say when the funeral's going to be? I'd like to be there for that."

"She wasn't sure yet. I need to go over that with her when I get out there. Desiree didn't have any insurance . . . so . . . I need to do what I can to take care of her . . . final expenses."

I never thought that I would see the day when I would be discussing burial expenses for my best friend.

"I'd like to help, too," I offered. "I'll call Colleen again in the morning." I was beginning to feel awkward. "You have a safe trip, now."

"You sure you goin' out there, too?"

"I have to be there," I said firmly, holding back my tears. "I'd like to hug my girl one more time."

"Well, I wouldn't mind havin' some company if you want to go together. First-class on me."

"I'd like to, but I need to go in to work tomorrow and arrange for the time off. Maybe we can come back together, though. It's not easy traveling with a baby."

"I'd like that. I'd like that a whole lot. Uh . . . maybe you can invite me and my daughter over to your place so I can pick up my belt. . . ."

I held the telephone away from my face and smiled at it. Then I looked at the belt that he had left in my bedroom the night he had spent with me. "It'll be right where you left it," I told him. "Good night, Chester."

"Good night, Crazy Legs. I'll see you soon."

I guess I always knew that one day he would use that belt as an excuse to get back into my life.

GONNA LAY DOWN MY BURDENS

MARY MONROE

ABOUT THIS GUIDE

The following questions are intended to enhance your group's reading of GONNA LAY DOWN MY BURDENS by Mary Monroe. Award-winning and National Bestselling Author Mary Monroe once again delivers a powerful story of deceit and redemption set against the backdrop of a colorful community.

DISCUSSION QUESTIONS

1. Carmen was wrong to conceal her role in Burl's train accident. Was Burl justified in keeping his knowledge of Carmen's guilt a secret from her?

2. Even though Burl was confined to a wheelchair, he was a manipulator and a pest. Should handicapped people be excused for this type of behavior?

3. If Desiree had known about Carmen's obsession with Chester, do you think Desiree would have started a relationship with Chester anyway?

4. If Carmen had gone through with her plan to marry Burl, do you think she would have eventually stopped loving Chester?

5. Desiree's lie about her father sexually abusing her destroyed her family. Was her guilt enough of a reason for her to continue living with her violent father?

6. Desiree loved Baby Red because he was a free spirit. What attracted her to Chester?

7. Chester was a fool when it came to females. Was he also a fool to claim the daughter his wife gave birth to, knowing that the child was not his?

8. Chester used his position as a policeman to harass Carmen, but Carmen never reported him. Do you think it was because it was more important to Carmen to keep Chester "close" to her?

9. Do you think that Chester started a relationship with Desiree just to get back at Carmen?

10. Carmen had a history of helping her friends out of one mess after another. Should have drawn the line the night Desiree begged her to rescue her from the fight with Chester?